# An Affair with a Spare

# SHANA GALEN

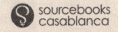

sourcebooks
casablanca

Published by Sourcebooks Casablanca, an imprint of Sourcebooks,
Inc.
P.O. Box 4410, Naperville, Illinois 60567-4410
(630) 961-3900
Fax: (630) 961-2168
sourcebooks.com

Printed and bound in the United States of America.
OPM 10 9 8 7 6 5 4 3 2 1

# One

COLLETTE FORTIER TOOK A SHAKY BREATH AND PASTED a bright smile on her face.

*Do not mention hedgehogs. Do not mention hedgehogs!*

Collette was nervous, and when she was nervous, her English faltered and she often fell back upon the books she'd studied when learning the language. Unfortunately, they had been books on natural history. The volume on hedgehogs, with its charcoal sketches, had been one of her favorites.

This ball had been a nightmare from the moment she'd entered. Not only was she squished in the ballroom like a folding fan, but there was also no escape from the harsh sound of English voices. Due to the steady rain outside, the hosts had closed the doors and windows. Collette felt more trapped than usual.

"He's coming this way!" Lady Ravensgate hissed, elbowing her in the side. Collette had to restrain herself from elbowing her chaperone right back. Since Lieutenant Colonel Draven was indeed headed their way, Collette held herself in check. She needed an introduction. After almost a month of insinuating herself into the inner sphere of Britain's Foreign Office, she was finally closing in on the men who would have knowledge of the codes she needed.

Lady Ravensgate fluttered her fan wildly as the former soldier approached and then let go so the fan fell directly into the Lieutenant Colonel's path. Lady Ravensgate gasped in a bad imitation of horror as Draven bent to retrieve the fan, as any gentleman would.

"I believe you dropped this." He rose and presented the fan to Lady Ravensgate. He was a robust man, still in the prime of his life, with auburn hair and sharp blue eyes. He gave the ladies an easy smile before turning away.

"Lieutenant Colonel Draven, is it not?" Lady Ravensgate asked. The soldier raised his brows politely, his gaze traveling from Lady Ravensgate to Collette. Collette felt her cheeks heat and hated herself for it. She had always been shy and averse to attention, and no matter the steps she took to overcome her bashfulness, she could not rid herself of it completely. Especially not around men she found even remotely attractive.

Draven might have been twenty years her senior, but no one would deny he was a handsome and virile man.

"It is," Draven answered. "And you are…?"

"Lady Ravensgate. We met at the theater last Season. You called on Mrs. Fullerton in her box where I was a guest."

"Of course." He bowed graciously, though Collette could tell he had no recollection of meeting her chaperone. "How good to see you again, Mrs…er…"

"Lady Ravensgate." She gestured to Collette. "And

this is my cousin Collette Fournay. She is here visiting me from France."

Collette curtsied, making certain not to bend over too far lest she fall out of the green-and-gold-striped silk dress Lady Ravensgate had convinced her to wear. It was one of several Lady Ravensgate had given her. She'd bought them inexpensively from a modiste who had made them for a woman who could then not afford the bill. Whoever the woman was, she had been less endowed in the bosom and hips than Collette.

"Mademoiselle Fournay." Draven bowed to her. "And how are you liking London?" he asked in perfect French.

"I am enjoying it immensely," she answered in English. She wanted people to forget she was French as much as possible and that meant always speaking in English, though the effort gave her an awful headache some evenings. "The dancers look to be having such a wonderful time." The comment was not subtle, nor did she intend it to be.

"You have not had much opportunity to dance tonight, have you?" Lady Ravensgate said sympathetically.

Collette shook her head, eyeing Draven. He knew he was cornered. He took a fortifying breath. "May I have the honor of the next dance, mademoiselle?"

Collette put a hand to her heart, pretending to be shocked. "Oh, but, sir, you needn't feel obligated."

"Nonsense. It would be my pleasure."

She gave a curtsy, and he bowed. "Excuse me."

He would return to collect her at the beginning of the next set. That would allow her a few minutes to think of a strategy.

"Do not mention the codes," Lady Ravensgate said in a hushed voice, though Collette had not asked for advice. "Lead him to the topic, but you should not give any indication you know anything about them."

"Of course." She had danced with dozens of men and initiated dozens of conversations she hoped would lead to the information she needed. Lady Ravensgate's tutelage had been wholly ineffective thus far. She always told Collette not to mention the codes. Her only other piece of advice seemed to be—

"And do not mention your father."

Collette nodded stiffly. That was the other. As though she needed to be told not to mention a known French assassin to a member of Britain's Foreign Office. What might have been more helpful were suggestions for encouraging the man to speak of his service during the recent war with Napoleon. Few of the men she had danced with had wanted to discuss the war or their experiences in it. The few she had managed to pry war stories from did not know anything about how the British had cracked the French secret code. And they seemed to know even less about the code the British used to encrypt their own messages.

But she had learned enough to believe that Draven ranked high enough that he would have access to the codes Britain used to encrypt their missives. It had taken a month, but she would finally speak with the man who had what she needed.

She watched the dancers on the floor turn and walk, link arms and turn again. The ladies' dresses belled as they moved, their gloved wrists sparkling in the light of the chandeliers. They laughed, a tinkling, carefree sound that carried over the strains of violin and cello. Not so long ago, Collette had danced just as blithely. Paris in the time of Napoleon had been the center of French society, and her father had been invited to every fete, every soiree.

He hadn't attended many—after all, he made people nervous—but when he was required to attend, he brought Collette as his escort. She couldn't have known that, a few years later, she would be doing those same dances in an effort to save his life.

The dance ended and Collette admired the fair-skinned English beauties as they promenaded past her. She had olive-toned skin and dark hair, her figure too curvaceous for the current fashions. Then Draven was before her, hand extended. With a quick look at Lady Ravensgate—that snake in the grass—Collette took his hand and allowed herself to be led to the center of the dance floor. The orchestra began to play a quadrille, and she curtsied to the other dancers in their square. She and Draven danced first, passing the couple opposite as they made their way from one side of the square to the other and back again.

Finally, she and Draven stood while the waiting couples danced, and she knew this was her chance. Before she could speak, Draven nodded to her. "How do you like the dance?"

She'd been unprepared for the question, and the only English response she could think of was *Hedgehog mating rituals are prolonged affairs in which the male and female circle one another.* In truth, the dance did seem like a mating ritual of sorts, but unless she wanted to shock the man, she had to find another comparison.

More importantly, she did not have much time to steer the conversation in the direction she needed. She had not answered yet, and he looked at her curiously. Collette cleared her throat.

"The dance does not remind me of hedgehogs."

His eyes widened.

*Merde! Imbécile!*

"Oh, that is not right," she said quickly. "Sometimes my words are not correct. I meant…what is the word… soldiers? Yes? The dancers remind me of soldiers as they fight in battle."

She blew out a breath. Draven was looking at her as though she were mad, and she did not blame him.

"You fought in the war, no?"

"I did, yes."

"I lived in the countryside with my parents, far from any battles."

"That is most fortunate." His gaze returned to the dancers.

"Did you lead soldiers into battle?" she asked. Most men puffed right up at the opportunity to discuss their own bravery.

"At times. But much of my work was done far from the battle lines."

Just her luck—a modest man.

She knew it was dangerous to press further. A Frenchwoman in England should know better than to bring up the recent war between the two countries, but her father's freedom was at stake. She could not give up yet.

"And what sort of work did you do behind the lines? I imagine you wrote letters and intercepted missives. Oh, but, sir, were you a spy?" Her voice sounded breathless, and it was not an affectation. She was breathless with nerves.

Draven flicked her a glance. "Nothing so exciting, mademoiselle. In fact, were I to tell you of my experiences, you would probably fall asleep. Ah, it is our turn again." They circled each other, and then she met with him only briefly as they came together, separated, and parted again, performing the various forms.

When he led her from the dance floor, escorting her back to Lady Ravensgate, she tried once again to engage him in conversation, but he deftly turned the topic back to the rainy weather they'd had. Lady Ravensgate must have seen the defeat on Collette's face because as soon as they reached her, she began to chatter. "Lieutenant Colonel, do tell me your opinion on Caroline Lamb's book. Is *Glenarvon* too scandalous for my dear cousin?"

Draven bowed stiffly. "I could not say, my lady, as I have not read it. If you will permit me, I see someone I must speak with." And even before he'd been given leave, he was gone.

"I take it things did not go well," Lady Ravensgate muttered.

"No."

The lady sighed in disgust, and not for the first time, Collette wondered whose side her "cousin" was on. She'd claimed to be an old friend of her father's, but might she be more of a friend to Louis XVIII and the Bourbons who had imprisoned Collette's father?

"Poor, poor Monsieur Fortier," Lady Ravensgate said.

Collette turned to her, cheeks burning. "Do not bemoan him yet, madam. I *will* free my father. Mark my words. I will free him, even if it's the last thing I do."

She knew better than anyone that love demanded sacrifice.

⚜

Rafe Alexander Frederick Beaumont, youngest of the eight offspring of the Earl and Countess of Haddington, had often been called Rafe the Forgotten in his youth. He'd had such an easygoing, cheerful personality that he was easy to forget. He didn't cry to be fed, didn't fuss at naptime, and was content to be carried around until almost eighteen months of age when he finally took his first steps.

Once, the family went to a park for a picnic, and Rafe, having fallen asleep in the coach on the ride, was forgotten in the carriage for almost two hours. When the frantic nanny returned, she found the toddler happily babbling to himself and playing with his toes. When Rafe was three, he had gone with his older brothers and sisters on a walk at the family's country estate. It wasn't until bedtime, when the nanny came to tuck all the children in for the night, that the family realized Rafe was not in bed. He'd been found in the stables sleeping with a new litter of puppies.

In fact, no one could recall Rafe ever crying or fussing. Except once. And no one wanted to mention the day the countess had run off, leaving four-year-old Rafe alone and bereft.

By the time Rafe was nine, and quite capable

of making himself so charming that he could have gotten away with murder (although Rafe was far too civilized to resort to murder), his new stepmother had pointed out to the earl that Rafe did not have a tutor. Apparently, the earl had forgotten to engage a tutor for his youngest. When the first tutor arrived, he pronounced Rafe's reading skills abysmal, his knowledge of history and geography nonexistent, and his mathematical ability laughable.

More tutors followed, each less successful than the last. The earl's hope was that his youngest son might enter the clergy, but by Rafe's fifteenth birthday, it was clear he did not have the temperament for the church. While Rafe's knowledge of theology lacked, his knowledge of the fairer sex was abundant. Too abundant. Girls and women pursued him relentlessly, and no wonder, as he'd inherited the height of his grandfather, a tall, regal man; the violet eyes of his great-aunt, who had often been called the most beautiful woman in England and was an unacknowledged mistress of George II; and the thick, dark, curling hair of his mother, of whom it was said her hair was her only beauty.

Rafe had been born a beautiful child and matured into an arresting male specimen. While academics were never his forte, men and women alike appreciated his wit, his style, and his loyalty. He was no coward and no rake. In fact, it was said Rafe Beaumont had never seduced a woman.

He'd never had to.

Women vied for a position by his side and fought for a place in his bed. Rafe's one flaw, if he had one, was his inability to deny the fairer sex practically anything. In his youth, he might have found himself in bed with a woman whom he'd had no intention of sleeping with only because he thought it bad form to reject her. Eventually, Rafe joined the army, not the navy as two of his brothers had done, primarily for the respite it offered. His time in service did not make it easier for him to rebuff a woman, but he did learn evasive maneuvers. Those maneuvers served him well after he joined Lieutenant Colonel Draven's suicide troop, and his unwritten assignment had been to charm information out of the wives and daughters of Napoleon's generals and advisers.

Back in London, Rafe was busy once again charming his way in and out of bedchambers. One of only twelve survivors from Draven's troop of thirty and an acknowledged war hero, Rafe had little to do but enjoy himself. His father gave him a generous allowance, which Rafe rarely dipped into, as charming war heroes who were also style icons were invited to dine nearly every night, given clothing by all the best tailors, and invited to every event held in London and the surrounding counties.

But even Rafe, who never questioned his good fortune, was not certain what to do about the overwhelming good fortune he'd been blessed with at his friend Lord Phineas's ball. Rafe, bored now that the Season was over, had talked his good friend into hosting the ball for those of their friends and acquaintances staying in London. Too many of Rafe's female acquaintances had attended, and he found himself struggling to (1) keep the ladies separated and therefore from killing one another, and (2) lavish his attentions on all of them equally.

Thus, he found himself hiding in the cloakroom of the assembly hall, hoping one of his gentleman friends might happen by so he could inquire as to whether the coast was clear.

"Oh, Mr. Beaumont?" a feminine voice called in a singsong voice. In the cloakroom, Rafe pushed far back into the damp, heavy cloaks that smelled of cedar and wool.

"Where are you, Mr. Beaumont?"

Rafe tried to place the woman's voice. He thought she might be the wife of Lord Chesterton. She was young, far too young for Chesterton, who was his father's contemporary. Rafe might think Chesterton a fool for marrying a woman young enough to be his daughter, but that didn't mean he wanted to cuckold the man.

"There you are!" she said, just as the light from a candle illuminated the cloakroom.

Rafe squinted and held up a hand, even as he realized the small, crowded room offered no opportunity for escape.

"You found me," he said, giving her a forced smile. "Now it is your turn to hide. I shall count to one hundred."

"Oh, no!" She moved closer, her skirts brushing against his legs. "I found you, and I want to claim my prize."

"Your prize?" he asked in mock surprise. He knew exactly what she wanted for a prize. "What might that be? A waltz at midnight? A kiss on the hand?" He moved closer to her, forcing her backward.

She bumped against the wall of the room, and he put a hand out to brace himself while he gazed down at her.

"I'd like a kiss," she said breathlessly as she looked up at him. "But somewhere far more interesting than my hand."

"More interesting, you say?" He leaned close to her, tracing his free hand along her jaw and down the length of her neck. "Close your eyes, then, and I will kiss you." His fingers traced the swell of her breasts, and with a quick intake of breath, she closed her eyes. Rafe blew out the candle, plunging them both into darkness. He leaned forward, brushed his lips across her cheek, and then bolted.

As he slipped into the servants' stairway, he heard her call after him. "Rafe! Play fair."

"Never," he murmured and climbed the steps with deliberate motions. Perhaps he could use the servants' corridors to find another staircase that would lead him out of the hall. He reached a landing, turned a corner, and Lady Willowridge smiled down at him, the plume in her turban shaking with her excitement.

"Looking for someone?" she asked in her smoky voice.

Rafe took her hand and kissed it. "You, my lady. Always you."

She was the last person he wanted to see. She was a widow and had claws as sharp as any tiger. Once she sank her nails into him, she would not let go.

When he lifted his hand, she yanked him toward her. She was uncommonly strong for a woman, he thought as he attempted not to stomp on her slippered feet. She wrapped her arms around his neck, and tilting her head back so he could feel the diamonds in her coiffure against his hands, she offered her mouth.

Rafe rolled his eyes. He could simply kiss her, but he'd been in this position before, and she'd tasted like tobacco and stale coffee. Why not give her a little thrill and give himself a reprieve?

Rafe slid his arms along hers, lifted her hands over his head, and spun her around. She gave a little squeak when he pressed her against the wall, pushing his own body against hers and leaning down to whisper in her ear, "Do you want to play a little game, my lady?"

She tried to nod, but her cheek was plastered to the wall. "Oh, yes," she said, her breath coming fast.

"Do you feel my hand here?" He touched the small of her back.

"Mmm-hmm."

"Close your eyes and imagine where I will touch you next." His hand slid over her buttocks.

She closed her eyes.

Rafe stepped back. "No peeking."

And he took the rest of the stairs two at a time and burst into the servants' corridor. A footman carrying a tray of wineglasses raised his brows, but Rafe wasted no time on explanations. "Where is the exit?"

"To the ballroom, sir?"

"Dear God, man. No!" Rafe looked over his shoulder to make sure Lady Willowridge had not come for him yet. "To the street. Preferably a back alley."

"You just came from that exit, sir."

"There must be another."

"No, sir."

"Rafe Beaumont!" He heard Lady Willowridge's footfalls on the staircase. Panicked, he grabbed the servant's coat.

"Ballroom! Quickly!"

"Through there."

Rafe pushed on the panel and stumbled into the assembly rooms, where an orchestra was playing a waltz. Men and women twirled under the lights of the crystal chandeliers while the tinkling of laughter and champagne glasses accompanied the music.

A girl seated against the wall next to the panel gasped. "Mr. Beaumont!"

Rafe looked at the wallflower and then at the door he'd come through. It would not be long before Lady Willowridge deduced where he had gone.

"Dance?" he asked the wallflower.

She blushed prettily, then gave him her hand. He led her onto the floor and proceeded to turn her about in time to the music. After a minute or two, Rafe let out a sigh of relief. Why had he not thought of dancing with wallflowers before? They were unmarried and therefore relatively safe, not to mention he enjoyed dancing. He could dance all night. He could dance with every wallflower in atten—

Rafe's eyes widened and he met the wallflower's gaze directly. "Miss…uh?"

"Vincent," she answered sweetly. "Miss Caroline Vincent."

"Miss Vincent, your hand has apparently wandered to my…er, backside."

She smiled prettily. "I know. It is wonderfully round and firm."

Christ, he was doomed. If her father did not kill him, one of the ladies he'd abandoned—he spotted both Lady Willowridge and Lady Chesterton scowling at him—would. Rafe danced toward Phineas, catching his eye and giving him a pleading look. Phineas merely glared back at him, his expression clear: *You wanted this ball.*

What had he been thinking?

Miss Vincent squeezed his arse, and he nearly yelped.

"Would you prefer to find somewhere more private?" she asked, fluttering her lashes.

Rafe was always surprised at how many women actually fluttered their lashes and thought they looked appealing. To him, it always looked as if they had something stuck in their eyes.

"No," he answered.

Dear God, would this waltz never end?

Just then, he spotted Lieutenant Colonel Draven. Draven never came to these sorts of affairs. He'd probably come tonight because three members of his troop were in attendance. He spotted Rafe and gave a grudging nod of understanding when he spotted Rafe's predicament. Rafe gave his former commanding officer a look of entreaty as he turned Miss Vincent one last time and separated from her as the music ended. He bowed, prepared to promenade her about the room. He might take bets on who would kill him first—her furious father, the irritated Lady Willowridge, the abandoned Lady Chesterton, or the icy Mrs. Howe. He'd forgotten that he'd left her in the supper room.

"Excuse me, miss. I do not mean to interrupt,

but I must claim Mr. Beaumont for just a moment." Draven put a hand on Rafe's shoulder and pulled him away from Miss Vincent. Draven didn't wait for her response. His word was an order and always had been.

Draven led Rafe away, and Rafe tried to walk as though he had not a care in the world instead of running for his life. Draven steered Rafe through the assembly rooms, past numerous ladies who would have stopped him if Draven hadn't looked so formidable. The lieutenant colonel led Rafe down the stairs, past a row of liveried footman, out the door, and into a waiting hackney.

Once they were under way, Rafe leaned his head against the back of the seat. "That was too close."

Across from him, Draven shook his head. "Lieutenant Beaumont—"

"Shh!" Rafe sat straight. "Don't start bandying about titles. Do you want someone to hear?"

Draven stared at him. "*Mr.* Beaumont, I can see your popularity has been something of a…mixed blessing. Why do you not simply tell the ladies you are not interested?"

"I try," Rafe said, settling back again. "But it always comes out all wrong. Not to mention, females tend to water when I reject them, and I hate to see a woman put a finger in the eye."

"You don't mind if a woman cries, as long as you don't witness it."

Rafe frowned. "I hadn't thought of it that way. Do you think I've left a trail of weeping women?"

Draven barked out a laugh. "No. I think most women know what you are."

Rafe straightened. "And what is that?"

"A man who flees even from the word 'matrimony.'"

"Not true. I attended Mostyn's wedding."

"And I seem to recall a greenish tint about your gills the entire time." He held up a hand to stay Rafe's protest. "But I didn't come to discuss marriage. I have an assignment for you."

A sensation much like a mild bolt of lightning flashed through Rafe. "For me?"

"Yes."

Rafe could not believe his good fortune. Finally! His chance. "But the war is over."

"There are still dangerous people about, and the Foreign Office asked if I knew anyone who could take this assignment."

"And you thought of me?" Rafe cleared his throat. "I mean to say, of course I came to mind directly."

"Yes."

"Is it dangerous?"

"Yes."

Rafe blinked. He hadn't been expecting Draven to answer in the affirmative. Neil had rarely given him dangerous assignments during the war. Although Rafe had argued once or twice that slipping in and out of the bedchamber of one of Napoleon's men, persuading his wife or mistress to reveal secrets, and slipping back out again without being caught was not without peril, it was not quite the same thing as running across a field while cannonballs exploded around you.

"Good." Rafe clapped his hands together. "I have been wanting something to do besides chasing after women and attending social outings. What is it you need me to do?"

Draven smiled. "Attend social events and chase after a woman."

Rafe sighed and sat back again. "And if I refuse to accept the assignment?"

"I don't recall asking for your acceptance."

"You're no longer my commanding officer."

Draven crossed his arms over his chest. "Would you like me to change that?"

"No." Rafe knew as well as anyone Draven had connections in the highest spheres. One word to the Regent and Rafe might be back in uniform patrolling the Canadian frontier. "Tell me about my new assignment."

Draven sat back. "Her name is Collette Fortier."

"Fortier? Why does that name sound familiar?"

"Because her father was one of Napoleon's most successful assassins."

"And? If I remember correctly, Fortier is dead."

"Yes." The hackney slowed and Draven peered out the window. "I want you to find out more about his daughter."

"How am I to do that?"

"We believe Collette Fortier is in London. We further believe she may be calling herself Collette Fournay and claiming to be a cousin of Lady Ravensgate."

"Suspected French sympathizer and dear friend of Marie Antoinette's daughter."

"You are acquainted with Lady Ravensgate?"

"Not personally, but I've heard rumors. Is Lady Ravensgate taking Mademoiselle Fortier out in public?"

"I danced with the woman in question not a quarter hour ago, a woman Lady Ravensgate introduced as her cousin, a Miss Fournay. Your mission is to ascertain whether Miss Fournay is, in actuality, Collette Fortier, and if it is she, what she is doing in London. If she's spying—and I think from my encounter this evening that there is a very good chance of that—discover what information she hopes to unearth and determine what she knows already."

"And then?"

"And then you kill her."

# *Two*

*He* WAS HERE.

She hadn't been able to help looking for him the moment she entered the drawing room. She would have chastised herself, but she did not think there was a woman alive who would not stare at Mr. Beaumont. He was simply the most stunning man she had ever seen. Not even the opulent room with its moldings and medallions, its porcelain and purfled vases could detract from the beauty of Beaumont.

"Miss Fournay."

Collette dragged her eyes away from Beaumont and smiled at her hostess for the evening, Mrs. Saxenby. "How kind of you to come to our little salon."

Collette curtsied. "Thank you for extending the invitation to include me."

"You will not be disappointed," Lady Ravensgate announced. "My dear cousin is quite enchanting, although I fear she may not be able to add much to the conversation tonight." Lady Ravensgate gave Collette a meaningful look. "She is a cousin from France and does not know much about English politics."

"Oh, that is quite all right," Mrs. Saxenby declared. "We cannot all hold the floor. Someone must act as the audience."

Collette smiled. She was quite content to act as the audience. She had always been somewhat shy and averse to attention, and these traits were valuable considering one of the best ways to gather information was to sit back and listen. Tonight, she hoped to find out more about Lieutenant Colonel Draven. Since the ball where they'd danced, she had not seen or heard any news about Draven. But Draven's secretary in the Foreign Office, a Mr. Palmer, was supposed to frequent Mrs. Saxenby's salons.

In the three months since she'd landed on the coast of England, in the dark of night and in secret, Collette had made her way to London and sought out Lady Ravensgate, a wealthy widow. She'd been told the widow had been friends with her father, and Lady Ravensgate had certainly treated her like a long-lost daughter. Collette even remembered her father mentioning the late Lord Ravensgate as a man who would help them if they ever needed to escape Napoleon's France. But so many people had dual loyalties that Collette had learned not to trust. And if the Ravensgates were so loyal, why had her father not fled when the Bourbons had retaken the throne? He must have known, under the king, he would suffer and be imprisoned for his work for the upstart Bonaparte. Had her father thought the Bourbons would forgive all, or did her father not trust Lady Ravensgate as he had her husband?

She wished she could ask him, but he was imprisoned

in Paris, and the only way to free him was to bargain with the royalists. That was why she needed the British codes.

"Won't you have a seat?" Mrs. Saxenby led Collette and Lady Ravensgate to a couch off to the side of the main grouping. In the center of the room, several men in crisp evening dress stood discussing a poem Collette had not read. Collette looked down, pretending to study her reticule's drawstring while she listened. These few moments before the formal discussion began were the best time to glean information, if there was any here to be gleaned, which she rather doubted. Once the program commenced, most of the conversation would stick to that topic.

It was the ideal time for a spy in London. The Season was at an end and most of the key political figures were in the country. But Britain's security was always at risk, and men like Draven and others at the Foreign Office were still in London.

Collette fingered her drawstring, listened to the voices around her, not hearing anything of substance, and then lifted her head and scanned the room. Her gaze landed on Mr. Beaumont. But then she'd been looking for him, hadn't she?

As usual, he was surrounded by a wall of women. No fewer than five vied for his attention tonight, and he seemed to entertain them effortlessly. The ladies tittered every few moments. If only she had a reason to believe Beaumont would say something of interest, she might join those women. But Lady Ravensgate had instructed her to pay close attention to William Thorpe, a writer and political satirist, and it just so happened that Thorpe was in conversation with James Palmer, Draven's secretary. Neither man was half as attractive as Mr. Beaumont, but Collette brought her attention back to them nonetheless. Palmer had a snooty attitude and round spectacles he liked to remove and polish as he spoke. Thorpe was thin and looked hungry as he listened to Palmer discuss poetry.

"Would you like some wine or lemon water, dear cousin?" Lady Ravensgate asked solicitously.

"Wine, thank you," Collette replied. Her sponsor rose and made her way around the room on the pretense of fetching refreshments for herself and her cousin. In reality, she was listening and collecting as much useful information as she could. But why? Did she have her own agenda or could Collette believe all her efforts were in sacrifice to her father?

Palmer and Thorpe continued to discuss the poem, and Collette found her gaze once again straying to Mr. Beaumont. What was the matter with her? She needn't pay him any attention. His presence here didn't signify. She'd had a fleeting moment of worry after he'd been at the last two events she'd attended, but Lady Ravensgate had dismissed her concern. Beaumont was a gallant who went wherever pretty women might be. His intellect, if he had any, was focused on persuading women to join him in bed. He was a former soldier and a war hero, but since returning from the war, his life had been given over to debauchery.

"Not someone you should associate with, my dear," Lady Ravensgate had warned. Collette detested Lady Ravensgate's insistence on calling her *cousin* and *dear* even when the two of them were in private.

"But do you not think it odd that he is at the same events we have attended?"

"No. With so few social events in London this time of year, everyone is at the same events." Lady Ravensgate had narrowed her eyes. "Don't tell me *you're* half in love with him too?"

"No!" Collette had answered far too quickly.

"Good. Because he isn't chasing after *you*. Women pursue him, not the other way around. And I've yet to see him with the same woman on his arm twice."

Collette's face flushed hot now as she remembered Lady Ravensgate's words. Of course, a man like Beaumont wouldn't be interested in her.

Except he was looking at her.

Collette's cheeks heated, and she lowered her gaze. She should have been paying attention to Palmer and Thorpe, not staring at Mr. Beaumont like some moonstruck girl of sixteen.

"Well, between you and me, Draven hasn't relaxed his guard just because the Bourbons are back on the throne in France. In fact, certain communications we intercepted seem to imply…" He turned away from Collette and lowered his voice.

Collette almost swore in frustration. She'd been attending the theater, salons, garden parties, and every other social outing Lady Ravensgate could arrange, and this was the first time she'd heard anything directly referencing coded messages, even if these were not the codes she needed. If the English were intercepting coded French messages, they had to have the ciphers in order to read them. But what did the French communications say? And what would the English response be? It would be a good time to attack, as France's government and political system were in tatters at present. The French would only know the British response if she could somehow obtain the ciphers England used to code its own messages.

Those ciphers would decode the letter her father had entrusted to her as well.

She attempted to calm herself. She had to move closer and find a way to participate in the discussion. She had to determine if Draven himself coded missives to operatives. If so, he was in possession of the British ciphers she needed. She lifted her reticule and began to rise, only to look up and find a tall figure standing over her.

"Miss Fournay?" Mrs. Saxenby stood before her as well, but off to the side. The figure in front of her blocked her path to Palmer and Thorpe.

"May I introduce a dear friend to you? Miss Fournay, this is Mr. Beaumont."

Collette blinked up at Mrs. Saxenby and then gaped at Mr. Beaumont. She was generally shy around men, especially handsome men, but one look at Mr. Beaumont and she was speechless. She had glimpsed him across the room dozens of times, but nothing could have prepared her for the sheer masculine beauty of the man standing in front of her. His polished boots rose to his knees, which were encased in tight breeches of ebony. His waistcoat was snowy white with silver thread crawling over it like regal vines. His black coat showcased a slim waist and broad shoulders, while his snowy-white cravat highlighted the days' worth of stubble on his chin. He obviously hadn't bothered to shave for the evening, and she might have wondered if he'd even brushed his hair. The chestnut-and-mahogany waves curled about his ears and fell rakishly over his forehead.

His splendor rendered her spellbound, and she was struck mute by his eyes. They were a shade of blue that could not be called anything but violet, and they were striking, especially fringed as they were with thick, dark lashes. Collette could have stared at those eyes forever. She desperately wanted to paint them—to see if she could mix just the right paints and match the color perfectly.

Beaumont bowed, and Collette stared at the top of his head before he lifted it and met her gaze at eye level. He gave her a dashing smile, his eyes crinkling slightly and his lips curving in a most seductive manner. He looked at her as though he knew exactly what she was thinking. As though he knew precisely the sort of effect he had on her.

"Miss Fournay?" The sound of a woman's voice came from somewhere nearby, though Collette could not have dragged her eyes away to locate the source if her life had depended on it. She could not look away from the handsome man smiling at her.

"I believe it is customary for you to give me your hand at this point," Beaumont said, his smile never faltering.

Collette heard his words, but she didn't exactly comprehend them. He had the loveliest baritone voice, not too high and not too low. Exactly perfect.

"Miss Fournay," Beaumont said.

She blinked and raised her brows at the use of the name she'd almost come to believe was actually hers.

"Give me your hand," he said.

She held out her gloved hand. He took it and raised it to his lips, kissing the back with a lingering slowness that sent shivers up her spine. And when he should have released her hand and stepped back, he held on to it when he straightened. His gaze never left hers.

"Well, then, I suppose my duty is done," Mrs. Saxenby said, sounding somewhat miffed. "Excuse me." And with the silk of her skirts rustling, she walked away, ostensibly to tend to her other guests. Collette could not have said because she was physically incapable of dragging her gaze away from Mr. Beaumont. She should have taken her hand back as well, but she would have as soon dipped it in hot tar than removed it from Beaumont's gentle hold. Though they both wore gloves, she imagined she could feel the heat from his skin seeping into her own, and just the idea of his bare flesh touching hers made her face flush hotter. She feared her cheeks were red as apples.

Collette had no idea how long the two of them stood there, gazing at each other, hands clasped together. It felt like hours to her and yet like no time at all when he finally released her hand. And then she didn't quite know what to do with it. She left her hand hanging in midair because it hardly felt like hers any longer.

"Is this seat taken?" he asked, indicating the couch cushion beside her.

It was. Lady Ravensgate would return and expect to sit there. But Collette shook her head.

"May I sit beside you?"

She nodded, wishing she could somehow force her lips to move or her voice to return.

"You have not been in Town long, have you?" Beaumont asked. He didn't seem to require an answer because he went on speaking without waiting for one. "No, I would have noticed you before if you had been here during the Season."

Collette could not have imagined why. There was nothing special about her—she was shy, average in height and looks, and no one of consequence.

"Mrs. Saxenby tells me you are from France. Lovely country. I spent considerable time there during the war."

The war. Her father. Collette snapped out of her trance and hastily looked about the room. Palmer and Thorpe were still standing in the middle of the room, but she had no idea what they were discussing. Had they moved on, or were they still conversing about the intercepted communications?

"I've been wanting to meet you since I first noticed you," Beaumont was saying. His voice carried over those of Palmer's and Thorpe's, and she couldn't hear what the men were saying. She wanted to move closer, but there was no way to excuse herself and do so without drawing attention. Indeed, when she scanned the chamber, she noted that practically every female eye in the drawing room was on her. Even Lady Ravensgate watched her, her expression inscrutable.

"And I think you have been wanting to meet me."

Collette frowned and glanced back at Beaumont. She hadn't been wanting to meet him. She'd admired him on occasion—oh, very well, on every occasion—but she hadn't sought an introduction and had no desire to meet him. He was a distraction, and she could not afford distractions.

"Now is your chance," he said. "What would you like to know about me? Or perhaps you'd rather take a turn about the room on my arm?"

Collette's eyes widened. Was the man serious? Did he really think she had been doing nothing but waiting for the chance to hear all about him or serve as decoration for his side? Oh, she did not have time for this sort of conceit.

But she must say *something*. Even if only a few words to dismiss him. She opened her mouth to say *Pray, excuse me.* Instead, she said, "Hedgehogs show promiscuous mating behaviors."

Beaumont's brows rose, his slumberous violet eyes becoming more alert. "Did you say hedgehogs?"

Collette felt her hot cheeks burst into flames. "Yes. *Erinaceus europaeus.*" Oh, why would she not shut up? Her mouth seemed to move of its own accord. "The sows and boars do not form pair bonds."

Beaumont's lips twitched as though he held back a smile. He had very nice lips. The lower lip was full while the upper lip boasted a decadent indent she would have liked to lick. "What else do you know about the mating rituals of hedgehogs?" he asked.

*Rien. Rien du tout!* But her foolish mouth did not obey. "Both sexes may have several partners during the mating season." She would explode. She would burst into a shower of sparks and explode.

"Ah, so very much like the *ton* during the social Season," he said. "But I wonder—"

No! She could not allow this to go on.

"Excuse me," she said, bounding to her feet before she began to spout off about scent marking. She stumbled forward, feeling almost drunk and desperate to be anywhere but in the presence of Beaumont. Engaging Palmer and Thorpe was but a dream at this point. In her current state, she did not trust herself. It was almost a worse fate to find herself beside Lady Ravensgate at the refreshment table. But at least she was away from Beaumont. She pressed her hands to her cheeks, which felt warm, even through her gloves.

"I thought I told you he was not someone with whom you should associate," Lady Ravensgate said, holding her wineglass close to her mouth so her lips could not be read.

"I did not wish to associate with him," Collette answered, her back to the room so she did not have to cover her lips, only speak softly. How she wished for something cool to relieve the heat coursing through her body. "*He* asked Mrs. Saxenby for an introduction."

Lady Ravensgate's thin brows rose high on her forehead, all but disappearing. "Really? That is most curious."

"It is most inconvenient. I had hoped to move closer to Palmer and Thorpe. I thought I'd overhead something of interest."

"No time now. Mrs. Saxenby is signaling to begin the discussion."

Collette sighed. The last thing she wanted was to have to listen to men drone on about an irrelevant piece of literature. Her father was sitting in a cell at this very moment, and she was stuck in a drawing room hundreds of miles away, helpless to save him.

She angled her body so she might appear interested in Mrs. Saxenby's announcement and, in the process, had a view of the couch she'd been occupying.

It was empty.

She searched the room for Mr. Beaumont.

He was nowhere to be found.

Disappointment surged through her, and wasn't that the biggest annoyance of the evening?

"What do you mean you have nothing to report?" Draven asked that evening at the club that bore his name. Draven had found Rafe in the dining room and signaled to him for privacy. Rafe had gone reluctantly. He was not ready to see Draven yet. But he'd joined the lieutenant colonel in a room on the top floor of the club that no one used. From the looks of it, Porter, the Master of the House, stored linens and paintings here.

"Exactly what I said," Rafe answered. "This assignment is…taking longer than I imagined."

"Then perhaps you should do more than simply imagine."

Rafe bit back the saucy retort on his lips out of respect for Draven. "Yes, sir."

Draven paced, his wild, red hair jutting in several different directions. "What have you found out so far? Has she revealed anything to you?"

Rafe rubbed his temple. He'd had a headache all week. That was what came of being forced to converse about poetry and politics for hours on end. "She hasn't exactly spoken to me, sir." Unless one counted a litany of facts on hedgehogs. Rafe still wasn't certain what to make of that exchange.

Draven stopped midstride. "I asked you to find out who she is working for and what she knows. That means you have to do more than take her to bed."

Rafe clenched his jaw. "Yes, sir."

"What do you have to say for yourself, Lieutenant?"

Rafe didn't have a whole hell of a lot to say. He only wished the problem was too much time in bed and not enough teasing information from her. "I'll do better, sir."

Draven threw his hands up and paced away. "You will try harder. Is that what I'm to tell the Foreign Office? My man will try harder? What exactly is the problem? Is she that tight-lipped?"

Draven had no idea. And Rafe wasn't about to tell him that he'd only managed to get a few sentences out of the chit. And most of those made little sense. He knew his progress wasn't acceptable. He knew his commander expected more. But Rafe didn't bloody well know what to do. He'd never met a woman like her.

Draven sat, attempting to appear patient. "If you don't tell me the problem, I can't help you."

"There's no problem, sir. I will have more to report soon." And he would. This was his chance. He would not fail.

"Report now. I want details."

Hell's teeth, but the whole situation was humiliating. Rafe had never needed help with women before.

"That's an order, Lieutenant."

Rafe blew out a long breath. "I haven't bedded her,

sir." That was a detail. Perhaps it would be enough for Draven.

Draven shrugged. "Fine. That's not part of it anyway."

Rafe nodded, staring at his hands. He didn't like what he had to say next. "I may not be able to…er, bed her, sir."

Draven's eyes narrowed. "You find her that repulsive? I saw nothing wrong with her."

"It's not that. It's simply that she doesn't appear interested in me, sir."

"Are you saying I should get another man? Because I have already tapped you for this."

"I'm not saying that at all." Rafe blew out a breath and folded his hands together as though in prayer. "I mean, I've lost—" His voice caught in his throat. "I've lost my…charm." That wasn't exactly the word he wanted. But it was the easiest way to describe the effect he had on women. Or the effect he had on all women but Miss Fournay. "But I swear I will find it again. There must be a way to reach her…"

Draven said nothing for so long that Rafe finally looked up at him. Draven stared at him, brows furrowed together. "I am no judge of these sorts of things, but you don't look any different to me. You're still as"—he cleared his throat—"handsome as you always were. Christ, I never thought I'd be saying that to one of my men."

"Thank you, sir, but my"—he swallowed—"allure is more than looks."

Draven stabbed his hands on his hips. "What? Am I to list all of your accomplishments? All the reasons the woman should fall, if not in love, in lust with you?"

"Please don't. I'm merely saying that whatever my accomplishments might be and however pleasing my looks to other women, they do not seem to appeal to Miss Fournay."

"Beaumont, are you telling me the woman is not interested in you?"

Rafe didn't answer.

"Are you saying she rejected your advances?"

Rafe winced. "Not exactly."

"Then what's the problem?" Draven bellowed, losing his patience.

Rafe had lost his about three days ago. "I wish I knew, sir. She stares at me, blushes when I look at her, and is all but speechless and flustered when I speak to her. And yet she doesn't try to catch my attention. She never even asked for an introduction! Finally, tonight I approached her and the woman all but swooned when I held her hand, but then she excused herself and walked away. She's not like any other woman I have ever known." Rafe gave Draven a bewildered look, hoping the man could understand the situation because Rafe sure as hell couldn't. "But I will try another tactic. Perhaps it's my approach…"

Draven stood, walked across the room, and then began to laugh. At first Rafe thought perhaps he hadn't heard correctly, but no. Draven's shoulders were shaking and the sounds he made sounded unmistakably like laughter. "You find this amusing, sir?"

"God help me, but I do," Draven answered, laughter in his voice. He turned, and Rafe was annoyed to see tears all but streamed down his cheeks. "It's about time you experienced what the rest of us mortals do."

Rafe didn't bother arguing that he too was mortal. "And what is that, sir?"

"Rejection by the female of the species." Draven began to guffaw again, and Rafe had the urge to punch him.

"I am pleased you find all of this so very amusing. I'm certain you and the Foreign Office will have a good laugh."

Draven sobered. "No, we will not. The Foreign Office won't be told of this. You will complete this assignment, Lieutenant. You will just have to work a little harder."

Rafe did not like the sound of that. "This is a woman, not a profession."

"See, there's the problem." Draven pointed at him. "You will have to approach this woman differently. You must woo her, seduce her, court her."

Rafe balked. "Sir, I have never done anything of the sort, and I do not intend to do so now." *Court* a woman? What was next? Marriage? Rafe felt perspiration break out along his forehead.

"This isn't a suggestion, Lieutenant. This is an order. You will find a way to bring yourself into the young lady's confidence. The safety and sovereignty of your country depend upon it."

Rafe closed his eyes. When Draven put matters in that light, how could he argue? "Yes, sir."

"Very good. What is your plan?" Draven sat and placed his arms on the table, locking his hands together.

"My plan? Right." Rafe had come in order to form a plan. "Now that we have been introduced, I suppose

I will try and speak to her again or perhaps dance with her, although there are precious few balls scheduled."

"You must find a way to speak with her alone. That will be difficult with the horde of females who follow you to and fro."

"What do you suggest?" And so it had come to this. He, *Rafe Beaumont*, was asking for advice on a woman.

"Call on her."

"Call on..." Rafe felt his throat close. "Call...with a calling card?"

Draven nodded.

"During the hours she is at home?"

"If you would like to be admitted, yes."

"But everyone will think I am courting her."

"Exactly. Bring her flowers or a poem you've composed. That will make matters very clear."

"A...a poem?"

Draven burst into laughter. "I was jesting about the poem, but the look on your face. Priceless."

Rafe scowled. He was half-tempted to board a ship for the Continent to escape this mission. But he was weary of traveling. He'd seen enough of the Continent to last him a lifetime.

"If you need more advice, ask Lord Phineas. He knows what to do. Or Lord Jasper. He could tell you."

Rafe did not believe for a moment Jasper, the man they all called the Bounty Hunter, knew anything about social calls.

"And don't look so glum." Draven stood. "There are worse assignments than wooing a woman." He crossed the room and opened the door.

"Then why don't you do it?" Rafe called after him.

"Too old and too ugly," Draven called back.

"Old and ugly," Rafe muttered. "You're far too clever to agree to this." But Draven wasn't the only one who was clever. Rafe wasn't one of the Survivors without reason.

# Three

COLLETTE STARED AT THE LETTER IN HER HAND. SHE'D stared at it many times before. Her father had pressed it into her hand just before he'd been taken away. "This will clear my name," he'd said. Collette did not understand what he could have meant. He was Bonaparte's assassin. How could he be cleared of that? Unless the letter proved that he'd had no choice but to work for Bonaparte? That might help his cause.

Unfortunately, she could not determine the hidden meaning of the letter. It was written in English, but it seemed to describe an idyllic countryside. It had to be in code. And she needed the cipher to decode it.

She had considered it might be a mask letter. She tried cutting out various templates—a bird, a cross, a fleur-de-lis—in order to see if the secret message might be contained in one of these "masks." But nothing had become clearer. She might have had the wrong template or the code might be completely different.

"Have you made any progress?" Lady Ravensgate asked, lowering her embroidery. She'd been making a chair cover with a rustic scene of trees and a waterfall.

"No." Collette wiped at her eyes, which burned with fatigue. "Nothing. Much like my efforts here in England."

To her surprise, tears sprang to her eyes. She withdrew a handkerchief and pressed it to her eyes.

The sound of rustling silk and the fragrance of roses warned her Lady Ravensgate was beside her. Collette did not trust her, but she preferred Lady Ravensgate not suspect as much. Collette did not object when the lady put her hand on her shoulder. "You must give it time, dear. You will find the information we need."

Collette looked up. "Will I?" She pretended to be hopeful, but she wanted to see Lady Ravensgate's expression. *The information we need.* Why did the lady need the codes?

"Of course you will. But you must do all you can."

"I *am* doing all I can."

"Are you? The night before last, at Mrs. Saxenby's salon, was a perfect opportunity to glean information. But you came away with only vague notions of what Thorpe and Palmer might have been discussing."

So the lady thought to chastise her for her lack of progress. Could this be considered more confirmation that Lady Ravensgate and the men who held her father were working together? While her hostess might pretend compassion, Collette did not put it past the woman to use sympathy to manipulate her. "I was interrupted."

"You cannot allow yourself to be distracted by handsome men, even those as charming as Mr. Beaumont."

And there was the crux of her problem. She had to balance the social requirements of her position with the gathering of intelligence. Not for the first time,

Collette wished she'd had more experience in society. Her own upbringing had been one of few luxuries, and when she'd moved from the country to Paris with her father, she'd been intimidated by the elegant men and women of Napoleon's circle. She had little experience with society and even less with men.

A tap at the door announced a footman. "Excuse me, my lady. You have a caller."

"Oh, good." If Lady Ravensgate was surprised she did not show it. They did not often have callers, but the viscountess had some friends and they did come on occasion. "Who is it?"

"A Mr. Beaumont." The footman extended his silver tray where a single white card lay in the center.

Collette, who had risen to excuse herself so her hostess and her friends might talk, sat back down. Hard.

Lady Ravensgate raised her brows and gave Collette a sidelong look. "Did you know about this?"

Collette shook her head. That seemed all she was capable of. She could hardly believe Beaumont was inside the house, only a few feet away. She looked down at her dress, a pretty yellow muslin that she wore because it fit, but which made her look like a schoolgirl again. Why had she chosen to wear this today? Why not the white muslin? And why had she not suffered through the headache and had her maid pin her hair up? Instead, she'd chosen the comfort of a long tail down her back.

"Show him in, Evans," Lady Ravensgate said, replacing the card on the tray. When he'd gone, she patted the seat beside her. Collette walked on leaden legs to take a seat. "Isn't this interesting?" Lady

Ravensgate said. "I wonder if Mr. Beaumont might be of some use after all."

"How?" Collette asked, but her question remained unanswered as Mr. Beaumont swept into the room and bowed deeply. Then he rose and—Collette did not know what to term his next act except to say that he struck a pose. He made a dashing figure in his fawn breeches, dark-green waistcoat, and brown coat. His silver-tipped walking stick and the tall hat under his arm completed the picture of a fashionable gentleman.

"Mr. Beaumont," Lady Ravensgate began. "What a lovely surprise."

"It is, isn't it?" Beaumont indicated the chair opposite the two ladies. "May I?"

"Please. Would you care for tea?"

"I never refuse refreshment," Beaumont answered, his gaze on Collette. She could feel her skin prickling with awareness wherever his gaze roamed. Her cheeks heated as he studied her face. "And how are you, Miss Fournay?" he asked. "Is that your embroidery?" He indicated the hoop Lady Ravensgate had set aside.

Collette began to shake her head, but Lady Ravensgate put a hand on her arm. "Yes. She is quite accomplished, is she not, Mr. Beaumont?"

"I daresay she is. And I do so appreciate all the various accomplishments of ladies."

Collette wondered if his words had a risqué implication, but his face betrayed nothing. Lady Ravensgate rang for the tea tray and then launched into the usual chatter expected during a call. The weather, Mr. Beaumont's family, and the forthcoming entertainments in Town were discussed. Collette listened silently, unable to think of a single word to say. At times, Lady Ravensgate peered at her, and Collette knew she should try and speak. She would even open her mouth, but then Beaumont would look at her, and she would forget what she wanted to say.

He was so handsome he made her head spin. And unfortunately, he knew he was handsome and charming. Even as she was annoyed and disgusted by his conceit, she was still charmed by his rakish smiles and elegant manners.

Finally, the quarter hour drew to a close, but just as Collette anticipated Mr. Beaumont taking his leave, the housekeeper knocked on the door. "I'm ever so sorry to interrupt, my lady. I need to speak with you immediately."

Lady Ravensgate looked from Beaumont to Collette. She could not possibly leave the two of them alone. Now was Beaumont's moment to take his leave. A gentleman would understand the necessity. But Beaumont merely lifted his teacup and took a sip.

"Do excuse me," Lady Ravensgate said. "I shall return in a moment."

Collette gave her a pleading look, but Lady Ravensgate ignored it and followed the housekeeper out of the room.

"So now it is just the two of us," Beaumont said. "How cozy."

Collette swallowed, then lifted her own teacup and took a sip.

"You are quite refreshing," Beaumont said as the silence dragged on. "I thought women who did not prattle on for hours were only a myth."

Collette's eyes widened at the insult to her sex. "And I thought men who babbled nonsense were a fable." She spoke without thinking, keeping her gaze above his head, where she would not be distracted. Too late, she wished she could take her words back.

But to her surprise, Beaumont chuckled. "Oh, I see."

Collette frowned. "See what?"

"You are that sort."

Her face heated, but this time, it was not with embarrassment but anger. "What sort is that, monsieur?"

"The sort who says little, giving her words even more power to pierce one's soul with their sharpness."

Collette narrowed her eyes. She had forgotten to be awed by his attractiveness and looked at him directly. "And have I pierced your soul, monsieur?"

"Of course. Why do you think I am here?" He rose, saving her the awkwardness of answering. Strolling casually around the room, he picked up one item after another. A small porcelain figurine. A vase. A snuffbox. "I never thought I would say this, but I do wish you would speak more often. I like the sound of your voice. Your English is very good, but you have just the right— what is the word? Ah…*soupçon* of a French accent. Perhaps you might tell me more about hedgehogs."

It would be a cold day in hell before she mentioned hedgehogs again. "I am not so able to control my accent when I am angry," she retorted.

He lowered the vase he'd been examining. "Do I make you angry?"

Collette knew better than to answer.

"How is it your English is so good?" he asked her in flawless French.

"How is your French so perfect?" she retorted.

"I spent a good part of the war in France," he said unapologetically. "What a disappointment that we never met when I was there. You lived in Paris or the countryside?"

Collette watched as he crossed the room, her mind turning over the comment he'd made about the war in France. Lady Ravensgate had said he was a war hero. Might he have had some contact with the codes she sought? But she had to avoid any discussion of her life in France before. Although it was extremely unlikely most Englishmen would know anything about her father or have heard of him, she could not take the chance that she might say something that would give away her relationship to him.

But she would have to risk it. "Who did you serve under in the war?" Collette asked. "Perhaps we were in the same town."

"Lieutenant Colonel Draven. And if I was in the same town as you, you would not have known it."

Collette's blood chilled, and she went absolutely still. How had she not known Beaumont served under Draven? Why hadn't Lady Ravensgate told her? Had she not known? And then Collette suddenly forgot all her suspicions concerning Lady Ravensgate because Mr. Beaumont had neared the desk she'd been using to decode her letter, and in her surprise at his arrival, she had neglected to conceal both the letter and her improvised templates.

"Have you been working at your correspondence this morning?" he asked as he neared the desk.

"Yes," she said hastily. Then, "No!" Oh, she had

to do something to distract him. Something to move him away from the desk. Short of jumping up and blocking him, she was at a loss. And then her knee knocked the tea tray and she acted impulsively. She caught the table holding the tray with her foot and knocked the leg over, sending the pot of tea, the dishes, and the cakes and sandwiches tumbling to the floor in a huge clatter. Collette might have jumped if she hadn't been expecting the cacophony. Instead, she watched Beaumont's reaction. The noise did draw his attention, but he hesitated before moving to help her. Was it her imagination or had Beaumont wanted to get a better look at the contents of the desk and only gave up because, as a gentleman, he was honor bound to assist her?

"Are you hurt, Miss Fournay?" he asked, coming closer.

She fell to her knees and righted the tray and the table. "Nothing but my pride, sir. I cannot think how this happened."

"Do not concern yourself. I will have it all set to rights in a moment." He knelt across from her.

"You mustn't. I shall call a footman." And then the footman could alert the maids and see Beaumont out.

"Not necessary," Beaumont said, already at work. "I have it all in hand."

But Collette had reached for the small bell that had toppled off the tray, which Lady Ravensgate used to call the servants to this room, as it had not been outfitted with a bellpull. Beaumont's hand caught hers. Collette inhaled sharply at the touch of his skin on hers. In addition to her carelessness at leaving her correspondence out, she had also forgotten to don her gloves. Beaumont had taken his off to take tea, and now they touched skin to skin.

He pulled her hand away from the bell, holding it lightly but firmly. "You needn't trouble the servants." His warm hand engulfed hers, and when she tried to draw hers away, he didn't release her. "Would it be scandalous of me to remark on how soft your skin is?" he asked, voice low and seductive. "I'm not certain I've ever felt skin like yours."

Collette hardly knew the rules of English society, but she did know that whatever the etiquette might be, the feeling she had with her hand in his was most improper. She had the urge to link her fingers with his and to hold on to him more tightly. He had such a strong, sure grip, and she was so weary of floundering.

Instead, she looked him directly in the eyes. Those lovely, lovely violet eyes. "Release me, monsieur." *During courting rituals the hedgehog sow continually rejects the boar, turning to give him her flank.*

"Ah, the French again," he said, still not releasing her. "Does that mean you are angry? Or perhaps you feel another emotion?"

Desire. That was what he had to mean, what he must have been referring to. Was she that transparent? No matter. What she felt and what she did were two very separate matters. She might find Beaumont handsome and arousing, but Lord help her if she ever dared act on those feelings. Very deliberately, she pulled her hand back and rose to her feet. "Thank you for your call today, Mr. Beaumont," she said pleasantly. Inside, she shook with a churning of emotions she could not begin to name.

"No, thank *you*, Miss Fournay." He made an elegant bow. "Our time together has been most enjoyable. May I claim your hand for the supper dance at Lord Montjoy's ball next week?"

*Hedgehog courting continues with the boar circling the sow.*

Collette shook her head, at a loss as to what was expected of her in this situation. To her knowledge, Lady Ravensgate had not been given nor accepted an invitation to a ball by Lord Montjoy. Collette did not even know the name, which probably meant he was not a friend of Draven's and therefore could not give her any useful information.

"Surely you will attend. It will be one of the last events before the few members of the *ton* still in London finally retreat to their country houses. Those of us without country houses will have to find other amusements."

The door opened and Collette blew out a relieved breath. Lady Ravensgate entered and briskly took center stage. "I do apologize for having been so long detained. May I call the butler to show you out, Mr. Beaumont?" Without waiting for his response, she rang the bell.

"Thank you," he said, appearing unruffled by the blatant attempt to be rid of him. He smiled at Collette. As usual, his smile had the effect of leaving her breathless. "And I look forward to our dance at Lord Montjoy's ball."

"What is this?" Lady Ravensgate asked. "Lord Montjoy?"

"Don't tell me you won't attend." Beaumont tapped

his chest where his heart—if he had one—would have been. "Miss Fournay has promised me the supper dance."

She had done no such thing, but before she could protest, Lady Ravensgate interrupted. "I regret we have not received an invitation to Lord Montjoy's ball. My dear cousin was probably not aware of that fact when she accepted your request." She gave Collette a speaking glance.

"I see." Beaumont looked thoughtful. "I will remedy that situation directly. Leave everything to me, my lady." He bowed again just as Evans opened the door. Beaumont glided out as though he had only been waiting for the butler to arrive. A moment later, Collette heard the front door open and then all was silent. She looked at Lady Ravensgate.

"I did not accept his offer. I would have refused, but then you entered and—"

Lady Ravensgate held up a hand. "I find Mr. Beaumont's visit quite curious."

Collette had found it curious as well, but she thought it rather rude of her sponsor to point out the obvious fact that she was not beautiful or witty enough to attract a man like Mr. Beaumont.

Lady Ravensgate continued, pacing about the room, stepping over the scattered pieces of the fallen tea tray in the process. "Either he is quite taken with you, or he has an ulterior motive."

Collette glanced at the desk and the decoded letter she had left out. Could Beaumont have been trying to peek at her private correspondence or was he merely making polite conversation? It was not as though she had kept up her side of the dialogue.

"I don't mean to imply that you are not eminently desirable, my dear." Lady Ravensgate smiled a little too brightly.

Collette narrowed her eyes. "But it might be wise to consider the possibility that Mr. Beaumont is a threat. After all, he was part of Draven's troop in the war against Napoleon."

Lady Ravensgate's chin jerked. So she'd known. Why had she kept the information to herself?

"If he did hope to glean information by coming here, he gathered none today," Collette said tightly. "I managed to keep him from perusing the desk. From now on, I shall make certain to take all of my correspondence to my bedchamber."

"That is very wise of you, my dear, but not necessary." Collette had not been allowed paper or pen in her private chamber, and Lady Ravensgate did not seem inclined to make any exceptions. "In the meantime, we shall keep our eye on Mr. Beaumont. If we are fortunate, we will not see him again."

"On the contrary, I hope very much we do see him again. He could prove useful."

"Only if you do not allow him to seduce every last secret out of you," Lady Ravensgate bit out.

Ah, so that was why the lady had not mentioned Beaumont's connection to Draven. She worried Collette would succumb to his charms. "He will not seduce me."

Lady Ravensgate snorted. "We shall see."

Collette looked down at the hand Beaumont had held. It still tingled from his touch. What had he meant when he said he would remedy the situation with Montjoy? And why could she not stop imagining what it would be like to dance with him?

❧

A family dinner at the Earl of Haddington's town house was no small, intimate affair. Rafe had stepped into the fray little more than a quarter hour ago and his coat was already sticky from little fingers and his ears ringing from children's shrieks. Hell's teeth but his siblings were a fertile lot.

The monthly dinners were a staple from March until late fall, when the earl and countess retired to the country for several months. The earl's property was not large and he did not have many tenants to oversee. The land was quite rich in minerals, and the income from those provided Haddington with a comfortable lifestyle and the ability to ensure his children were also well taken care of.

Tonight, six of the eight children attended the dinner. John, Viscount Beaumont and the earl's heir, always attended. His wife and their five children were also present. George, Rafe's second eldest brother, and his wife and brood were also present. They only had three children, but his wife looked to be expecting again, although a formal announcement had not been made. Rafe's two other brothers were in the navy and presumably away at sea. But his three sisters more than made up for Harold's and Cyril's absences. Rosamund, Helen, and Mary had ten children between them. Mary was the closest in age to Rafe, only three years his senior, and her children were the youngest and loudest. Rafe could also admit—if only to himself—that three-year-old James and eighteen-month-old Sophia were adorable. Sophia had the prettiest dimpled smile, which she bestowed quite liberally. James had the same violet eyes as his uncle, and he babbled about horses nonstop. Rafe hardly even minded when the lad smeared an unidentified substance on his lapel.

"Admit it," his stepmother said as she made the rounds in the drawing room, while the brood waited to be called to dinner.

"Admit what, madam?" he asked, still nodding to James who prattled on.

"You love children."

"I do," he agreed. "I love to send them home with their parents, preferably far, far away."

She thumped him lightly on the head, an action that caused Sophia to giggle.

"Ouch!" she scolded. "No, no, no!"

"That's right," Lady Haddington said. "No hitting. Ouch!"

"And what was that for?" Rafe asked.

"Because I don't believe a word you say, dear boy. I think, deep down, you want children of your own." She scooped up her youngest grandchild and kissed her cheeks, making the little girl shriek with laughter. Rafe winced.

"Yes, why wouldn't I want to surround myself with squealing children rather than beautiful actresses or a talented opera singer?"

His mother sighed. "One day, you will have to settle down and marry."

Rafe looked shocked. "Why?" He gestured to the overflowing drawing room. "Surely the family line is secure without my assistance. Presumably that is why there was no objection when I joined the army to fight against Napoleon. You could afford to lose a son or two with the heir and spare safely at home."

"We would never wish to lose you, dear boy," his stepmother said. "Then we would have no one to read about in the gossip section of the papers."

"Speaking of which," his sister Mary said, leaning over to intrude in their conversation. "I read you are smitten with a young Frenchwoman in Town."

Rafe wished that if his sister was determined to stick her nose into his business—something she had been doing since he was born—that she would at least keep the information to herself. Either that or blackmail him with it as she had when they were children. "Well, you know the papers are full of lies," Rafe said easily. "*I* smitten with a Frenchwoman? What rubbish."

"Is it?" his stepmother asked. "Whatever gave the papers that idea, Mary?"

"Apparently, Rafe begged an introduction to the lady at a salon a few days ago."

His stepmother's brows rose.

"And then he called on her at home."

His stepmother's brows reached new heights.

"With flowers!"

"Aha!" Rafe pointed at Mary. "Lies, I tell you. There were no flowers. None."

"But you called on her," Mary accused. "Why would you do that if you were not interested in her? Romantically interested."

Rosamund and Helen, always with an ear tuned for gossip, moved closer.

"What is this?" Helen asked. "Rafe is in love?"

"Do not be ridiculous," Rafe said, standing and depositing his nephew in Mary's lap.

"Then why did you call on her?" Mary asked.

Helen, Rosamund, Mary, and even John peered at him, waiting for an answer.

"Because…" But what was he to say? He couldn't exactly admit he was gathering intelligence on her for the Foreign Office. Even if that revelation would not endanger his mission, his family would never believe it. He hadn't told them his role in Draven's troop. How did one tell one's parents the other men called him the Seducer because he charmed wives and daughters out of information? How did one tell one's brothers that he rarely even saw battle and did not even need to carry a weapon? While his friends fought for their lives, Rafe fought to divest a lady of her corset. Of course, his role was necessary. The intelligence he'd gathered had saved all of their lives time and time again. But it always annoyed him that he usually had to sit out the dangerous aspects of the missions.

And while Rafe hadn't lied to his family, he hadn't exactly been forthcoming with the truth. And he'd substantially embellished the few stories he had where he had been involved in actual fighting.

"Because?" Mary prompted.

Rafe gritted his teeth. "Because…I thought we had a prior acquaintance. I thought we had met when I was in France."

"I thought you were too busy thrashing the French to meet gentlewomen and form acquaintances," John said, arching a brow. Rafe wanted to hit his eldest brother. As the heir, John had grown up with a smug sense of entitlement and a hearty dose of arrogance.

Rafe gave his brother a serene smile. "I don't expect you to know this, as you have never defended the country, but we did occasionally encounter men and women sympathetic to our cause. Kind families who offered us shelter or a meal." This was true enough.

"Thank God for their generous hearts," his stepmother said.

The door to the drawing room opened, and Rafe had never been so relieved to see his father's butler. "Dinner is served," the man announced.

Everyone began to gather up children and spouses. Lady Haddington spoke quietly to Rafe. "Will you call on Miss Fournay again, dear boy?"

"I might," he said cautiously.

"Good. If you do, make sure to bring flowers." And she thumped him lightly on the head again. "You should know better," she muttered as she walked away, taking her husband's arm and leading the family into the dining room.

# Four

"ARE YOU CERTAIN THIS IS A GOOD IDEA?" COLLETTE asked Lady Ravensgate for what must have been the third time that evening. They were in the lady's carriage on their way to Lord Montjoy's ball. An invitation had arrived just the day before, much to Lady Ravensgate's surprise and pleasure.

She'd fluttered it in front of Collette. "This is Mr. Beaumont's doing, I presume."

Collette had agreed, but she had not agreed they should accept the invitation. There was a dinner party that same evening, and Collette had it on good authority Draven would be there. But Lady Ravensgate had wanted to attend this more prestigious affair. She'd ignored Collette's objections, just as she did now in the carriage, and accepted the invitation to the ball.

"It is an excellent idea. I have been discussing Mr. Beaumont with some of my most particular friends." By the phrase *most particular friends*, she meant the others she knew who gathered information for France and the restored king. During their exile, the Bourbons had spent quite some time in England, and

Lady Ravensgate had become well acquainted with the daughter of Louis XVI and Marie Antoinette. To Collette's knowledge, her sponsor maintained a faithful correspondence with Marie-Thérèse, who was married to her cousin, the heir to the French throne, the duc d'Angoulême.

"And what do your particular friends have to say about Mr. Beaumont?" Collette attempted to keep the resentment from her voice when she mentioned the royalists. She had never had a reason to hate the Bourbons or the monarchy before they were overthrown. She had disliked Napoleon immensely because he had forced her father to do unspeakable acts. But now that the royalists held her father captive, she despised them as well. And though she made every effort to hide her feelings, she loathed Lady Ravensgate for her association with them.

"No one is entirely certain what his role under Lieutenant Colonel Draven might have been. But there is no doubt he was part of the troop and that the troop was assigned the most dangerous, most impossible missions of the war. Only twelve of the original thirty men came back, and that in itself was a miracle. The Survivors are considered heroes. Mr. Beaumont is not to be underestimated."

What a font of information Lady Ravensgate had become. "You think his association with Lieutenant Colonel Draven might be useful?"

"It is possible. And that, my dear, is exactly the kind of connection you need in order to help your father. Poor man. Have you heard from him lately?"

Lady Ravensgate certainly knew the answer to

that question. Collette received no letters. All were addressed to Lady Ravensgate, who passed the correspondence to Collette after she read it herself. "No," Collette answered.

"I am certain you will hear from him soon." She patted Collette's hand. Collette stiffly drew her hand away. She detested her sponsor's pretense that she cared a whit about Pierre Fortier's life. For her, this was a game to entertain herself, a wealthy widow whose children had grown and no longer needed her. Collette did not know if Lady Ravensgate bore her father any ill will—after all, he had killed many nobles—but neither did she believe Lady Ravensgate wished her father well. To her, and to those who held him captive, Fortier was simply a means to an end.

"In the meantime, you should enjoy yourself tonight." Lady Ravensgate sounded bright and cheery, as though Collette could possibly wish to attend a ball when her father was suffering across the Channel. "And do not forget to save the supper dance for Mr. Beaumont. If he follows protocol and sits with you at dinner, you may be able to discover what he knows about the Foreign Office. Men do so love to brag about their perceived importance."

"And what if he is working for the Foreign Office, and he is gathering information on me?"

"Then you smile and dance and flirt and give the man nothing. On this point, you must be vigilant."

Collette nodded. Lady Ravensgate suddenly seemed far more confident in Collette's ability to rebuff Beaumont's advances. She was naturally somewhat reserved, even shy. She had never enjoyed these sorts

of social affairs, and she was not very good at talking
with people she did not know well. She had not
needed to be very skilled until now because she had
mainly been listening to other people talk and drawing out information. But if this ball was anything like
the last she'd attended, it would be full of important
people. It would be more difficult to listen in on conversations with the orchestra playing and men asking
her to dance.

Or not asking her to dance.

As a wallflower, she might overhear interesting
information, but she would probably hear more if
she were able to move about freely and question men
with ties to the Foreign Office. Once the dancing
began, that would be difficult. As a young, unmarried
woman, she was expected to be dancing or waiting to
be asked to dance.

Finally, the carriage arrived at Montjoy's town
house. It had taken far longer than Collette had
expected, but then she had not anticipated so many
carriages all traveling to the same place. When the stifling air in the carriage gave way to fresh air, Collette
was loath to follow Lady Ravensgate into the town
house and the crush of guests.

But she kept her thoughts on her father and did as
she was expected.

The town house was as lovely on the inside as the
outer facade promised. Marble floors, crystal chandeliers, and expensive furnishings were everywhere
she looked. Collette had known wealthy families
in France, mostly the inner circle of Napoleon.
Those men and women had money and power but

not nearly as much taste. And it was generally new wealth. What antiques they possessed had been stolen from the ousted *ancien régime*. But Collette had been a baby during the revolution and had never seen the homes of the French nobility. She wondered if those homes had been as rich and opulent as Lord Montjoy's. If so, she could hardly blame the starving French people for revolting.

Once she and Lady Ravensgate were inside, Collette stayed close to her sponsor, smiling at the men and women she spoke to and listening—always listening—for any information that might be useful in securing the codes and thus her father's release. And as much as she wanted to forget him, she could not keep from looking over her shoulder or around the room in search of Lord Beaumont. But as the hours dragged on and still she did not see him, she began to worry that he would not attend.

Lady Ravensgate seemed to share her fears. "I do hope Mr. Beaumont will arrive in time for the supper dance."

Collette smiled and tried to appear unconcerned. But inside she was torn. On the one hand, she would be glad not to battle her attraction to him tonight, especially in the close physical quarters a dance would mandate. On the other hand, if he gave her some piece of information that might help her father, then she could not afford to miss an opportunity to spend time with him.

As the evening progressed, Collette accepted several invitations to dance from various men. They were all quite polite, but they were not men who might give her the information she needed. Nor did she particularly enjoy dancing with them. She found the conversations difficult and awkward, and blushed continually. And then as the supper dance approached, men attempted to engage her for that dance. Collette had to decline, saying she had already reserved it. When pressed, she had to admit Mr. Beaumont had asked her to dance. She could not have anticipated the excitement that information caused. It seemed the news had spread through the ballroom in mere moments.

"Why is everyone looking at me?" Collette asked Lady Ravensgate as she sipped champagne after a dance.

"Oh, do not be silly!" Lady Ravensgate said, waving a hand. "No one is looking at you."

Collette inclined her head toward a group of ladies staring at her just a few feet away. "They are." She pointed to a mixed group—the ladies glaring and the men peering at her with interest. "And they are."

"I am certain you are imagining it," Lady Ravensgate said.

"Could it have something to do with my dance with Mr. Beaumont?"

"I very much doubt anyone at the ball is interested in that."

"Lady Ravensgate!" A woman with dark hair and pretty blue eyes approached them. She wore a green silk gown with emeralds at her throat and ears.

"Why, Lady Birtwistle. How are you?"

"Very good." She turned and smiled at Collette. Collette would have sworn she had never met the woman before, but there was something familiar in the way she smiled and in her face. "I came to meet your friend. It seems everyone at the ball is talking about her."

Collette gave Lady Ravensgate a meaningful look. Lady Ravensgate went on as though the interest in Collette was to be expected.

"Oh, this darling creature is my cousin Collette Fournay. She is from the French side of the family and visiting London for a few weeks. So sweet of her mama to send her. You know I am all alone now, and it has been so pleasant to have company. Collette, this is Lady Birtwistle. She came out with my middle daughter, and the two have always been good friends."

"Yes, we have. In fact, I plan to go to the country after Eugenie is delivered of her baby."

Collette raised her brows, not having known that one of Lady Ravensgate's daughters was expecting a child soon.

"She will appreciate that, I am certain." Lady Ravensgate made a point of looking about the room. "And where is your dear brother this evening? He rarely misses an opportunity to sip champagne and flirt."

Lady Birtwistle grinned. "I thought perhaps you might have the answer. After all, I hear he has engaged Miss Fournay for the supper dance."

Collette's eyes widened. Lady Birtwistle must have been Mr. Beaumont's sister. No wonder her smile and her face had looked familiar. Her features were similar to her brother's, though they were softened in Lady Birtwistle's face.

"He has indeed." Lady Ravensgate nodded at Collette.

"Did he?" Lady Birtwistle was still studying Collette,

her gaze so intent Collette could feel her cheeks warming. "I had heard as much and was eager to meet the young lady who has claimed my brother's attention."

"I would not put it that way, my lady," Collette said, forcing her voice to an audible level. "It is only one dance."

Lady Birtwistle looked unconvinced. "Then he didn't call on you at home last week?"

Collette looked down, uncertain what response to make. "He did. I am certain he is simply making me feel welcome."

"My brother does not care about making people feel welcome. And to my knowledge he has never reserved a dance with an unmarried lady or called on one. You must be very special indeed." She tilted her head as though inspecting Collette. "And now that I meet you, I do see the appeal. That shade of yellow is lovely on you. I cannot wear yellow, I'm afraid."

"She has the perfect coloring for it," Lady Ravensgate agreed, and both women stared at Collette's yellow silk gown, trimmed with cream lace. It was a simple gown and not overly embellished, or so Collette had thought until she put it on. Then she realized how cunning the modiste had been with the cut of the dress. It dipped quite low in the back, so low she could almost not wear her stays, and daringly low in the front, although a border of lace rimmed the bodice for modesty. Collette, already self-conscious of her large bosom, had shoved the dress aside and had not worn it to any of the events she'd attended. But Lady Ravensgate had pulled it out tonight and would not hear any objections to Collette's wearing it.

"You look quite lovely," Lady Birtwistle told Collette. "My brother has impeccable taste. I knew you would be a beauty."

Collette had never thought of herself as a beauty. Her lips were a bit too pronounced, her shape curvier than the current fashion of willowy women, and her hair and eyes were an unremarkable shade of brown. "You are too kind," Collette said. Far too kind, considering the supper dance was about to begin and Mr. Beaumont was nowhere in sight. Why had she come tonight? Why had she not stayed home? Everyone would see what a fool she was. She'd come to the ball to dance with Beaumont, and he hadn't even bothered to make an appearance.

All around her, men claimed their partners and led them to the dance floor for the last dance, a waltz, before supper. Lady Ravensgate continued speaking with Lady Birtwistle, but Collette could not hear them. Her ears were ringing and her eyes stinging. Her gaze locked on the floor in front of her slippers. She should not care whether Beaumont made a fool of her. She was not here to impress London Society. She was here for her father and he was all that mattered.

Through the blur of unshed tears, she spotted a pair of men's shoes stop before her. They were attached to muscled legs in white breeches.

She knew those legs.

She looked up quickly and into the face of Mr. Beaumont. His eyebrows lowered and his smile turned to an expression of concern when he saw her face, but his hand remained outstretched. Collette looked at his hand, then at Lady Ravensgate, who gave her a nod. Pasting on a smile, Collette took his hand and allowed him to lead her to the center of the dance floor.

Now her ears rang for an entirely different reason. She hated to be the center of attention. Not only would everyone be staring at her because she danced with Beaumont, but they'd also be watching her because she was in the center of the room. The orchestra began playing, and Collette took a deep breath. Beaumont put his arm at her waist and pulled her closer, then moved in time to the music. Collette glanced up at his face, but that only made her more nervous. How could anyone be so beautiful, so flawless? And why did such a creature want to dance with her?

"Are you well?" he asked, as he moved her across the dance floor. Not only was the man handsome, but he could dance. She'd never been a confident dancer, and she'd felt awkward and tentative all evening as she'd danced. But with Beaumont, she didn't even have to think about her next step. She seemed to know where he would lead her, even before he did so. And he made the more complicated steps feel easy and enjoyable.

"Yes," she whispered. "I am quite well."

He leaned close to hear her words, and she caught the scent of spices, something musky and dark. "You looked as if you were close to tears before. You did not think I would come for you?"

She looked down, staring at the place where her white glove lay in stark contrast to his dark coat. "The dance was to begin, and I had not seen you at the ball."

"I was merely waiting for the right moment to claim your hand. A man would be a fool to miss the opportunity to dance with you."

"I think you have that backward, monsieur. You are the accomplished dancer."

He gave her a nod. "I will tell my stepmother all of the money she threw at my dancing masters was well spent."

Collette glanced at his face again, trying to ascertain whether he was serious. "I think you already know you are an excellent dancer."

"It's easy to dance well with a beautiful woman in my arms."

Her face heated again, and she could have cursed her body for blushing at her every small discomfort.

"I have embarrassed you?" he asked.

"I am not used to so much attention," she answered, her voice low, which forced him to lean close again. She had to stop whispering. Every time he leaned close, her belly fluttered, and she felt even more light-headed. She had the urge to turn her head and bury her face in his neck, inhaling his scent. He smelled so wonderful.

"And you do not care for attention?"

She smiled. "Not as much as you, monsieur."

"Oh, very few people crave attention as much as I do, but I did not mean to make you uncomfortable. Your cheeks are red as cherries."

How Collette wished she had something cold to press against her heated face. She searched for something to say to cover her awkwardness. "It is the exertion of the dance," she said. "Did you know that the lengthy courtship rituals of the *Erinaceus europaeus* are considered a means for the sow to determine which boar is the most fit to serve as a mate?"

Beaumont flashed her a smile that made her heart tumble and roll.

"Are we speaking of hedgehogs again? I believe that is my new favorite topic of conversation."

Collette was mortified. "I would rather not speak of hedgehogs. But when I am nervous, I sometimes say things before I can think."

"Such as?"

She shook her head.

"Tell me," he drawled. "How does a male hedgehog know when a female hedgehog is attracted to him?"

She shook her head again. She would not answer this question. He danced them into the center of the ballroom, so the light from the chandelier shone directly on her. There was no denying every single eye in the ballroom was on her.

"Does the female hedgehog wink at the male or flutter a fan?"

"No. Sh-she—"

He raised a dark brow.

"The boar may be attracted to scent cues produced from females in estrus."

"Scent cues from...?" He gave her an innocent look, but she imagined he looked as innocent as Lucifer fallen from heaven. "Her lips? Her skin? Her—"

"The music is so loud, my throat is quite hoarse," Collette said. The only way to avoid this topic was to pretend she could not speak.

"Fortunately, I can remedy the problem and give us a chance to speak privately."

She did not like the look on his face. "The waltz will be over soon," she objected.

"Not soon enough. Now, just follow my lead."

Collette's heart thudded in her chest. Now what did the man plan to do? She could not allow him to make more of a spectacle of the two of them. "But, monsieur—"

Too late. With exaggerated movements, Beaumont twisted to the side and grimaced in pain. "My ankle!" he cried. Keeping one hand in hers, he bent and touched his ankle with the other. "I fear I have sprained it," he said loudly.

Collette felt her mouth drop open, but when she bent to examine his ankle, she caught him staring at her.

He winked.

The scoundrel! His ankle was perfectly fine. But if this was his plan to remove her from the center of attention, he had not thought it through. This little play was only earning them *more* attention.

"Are you hurt badly?" a lady who had been dancing near them asked.

"Do you need assistance?" her partner inquired.

"No, no." Beaumont waved a hand. "I think a few moments' rest is just the thing. Miss Fournay, may I escort you to the terrace? The fresh air will do us both good."

"O-of course," she said. Her face was so hot she could have touched a wick to it and lit a candle. But Beaumont was playing his part for all he was worth.

He draped an arm over her shoulder and hobbled beside her. Collette was forced to put an arm around his waist to maintain her balance. The other guests made way for them as Beaumont steered her toward the terrace doors. He bent his head, as though in pain, and his warm breath fell on the bare patch of skin between her neck and shoulder.

"You needn't make such a show," she said, speaking without moving her lips.

"Oh, but I like making a show. Even more, I like having your arm about me. I don't know why I didn't think of this sooner."

Collette held her tongue until they finally reached the terrace. She pushed the door open and led him outside, where she released him as though he were the handle of a hot pan. If his ankle had really been injured, he would have stumbled. But he caught himself easily and leaned negligently on the stone balustrade. Collette walked to the other end, only a short distance away. This was no country house, but a London town house and the terrace was only five or six feet across. But even if she could not distance herself from Beaumont, she was grateful for the cool air on her face. She lifted her face to catch the breeze and closed her eyes as it washed over her.

"I take it you did not appreciate my little piece of theater."

She flicked a glance at him. "Truthfully, monsieur, I would have preferred to simply finish the dance and exit the floor unobtrusively."

"You are very good at being unobtrusive."

She froze, her arms on the balustrade going quite

stiff. She chose her next words carefully. "It must appear so to you. You are very good at creating a spectacle."

He laughed. "Yes, I suppose I am."

Collette let out a sigh of relief. She was reading too much into his words. He did not suspect her. He was a flirt and hungry for attention. He didn't mean anything more than what he said.

"And how are you enjoying your stay in London, Miss Fournay?"

Collette bit her lip. Now she would be forced to make conversation with him, a skill for which she had amply shown she had no talent. But it would not last long. Dinner would be served soon, and they would have to go in. "London is…" What should she say? It was not nearly as beautiful as Paris, but she did not want to invite speculation about any time she might have spent in Paris.

"London is rainy. I think it must have rained every day since I have been here."

"And it never rains in Paris?"

"Of course it rains in Paris, but…" She trailed off. She had given away more than she'd planned. "I mean to say, but I have not spent much time in Paris and cannot adequately compare the two."

"There is no comparison," Beaumont said casually. "Paris is architecturally stunning and eminently more sophisticated than London. A simple stroll down Bond Street will tell you it pales in comparison with the Champs-Élysées."

"I have not strolled on the Champs-Élysées in years," she said. "I am surprised you have had the opportunity."

He smiled. "I can be unobtrusive too."

She had seen the truth of that tonight, when he'd seemed to come out of the woodwork to claim their dance.

"If you did not live in Paris, where did you live?"

This was a common topic of conversation, and she launched into her well-rehearsed answer. She'd lived in the countryside with her parents, who had been devastated when her brother died in the Battle of Waterloo. Now that their period of mourning was over, her parents had thought it might be beneficial for her, their young daughter, to travel to London and see her cousin and attend social events. Her mother and father were still far too distressed to interact socially and they did not want their daughter to suffer.

As she spoke, she'd stared out at the small garden behind the town house. Very little bloomed at this time of year, a few roses could be seen in the light filtering from the ballroom. But when she finished speaking, she looked back at Beaumont and almost jumped to see him standing right beside her. She hadn't even heard him move.

"That's a lovely story," he said, his gaze on her face. Collette felt it heat again at the intensity of his look. She wondered if she would ever become used to having such an attractive man so close to her.

"It's all true," she said, and immediately regretted the words. They sounded too much like a protest when one had not been required.

"I don't doubt it. I too was in the war, though I didn't fight at Waterloo. Tell me, was your brother army or cavalry?"

Collette opened her lips, but she had not encountered that question before. Moreover, she had not been schooled in the answer. It had never occurred to her or to the men holding her father that any Englishman would care about the particular placement of a French soldier.

Beaumont noticed her hesitation. "Don't you know?"

"Yes, but…" Should she choose one? Then what if he asked more questions like the brigade number or the commander? "You must excuse me, sir. It is difficult for me to discuss." He was not the only one with acting skills.

"No, you must excuse me. I should never have brought it up." He lifted her hand from the balustrade, forcing her to angle toward him. "Forgive me?" he said, kissing the back of her hand.

"Of course."

His took a step forward, forcing her back if she wanted to keep any space between them, and her shoulders touched the wall of the terrace. "It must be hard to lose a sibling."

She nodded. He was so close. Even in the darkness, she could see his violet eyes. He still held her hand, and his other hand rested lightly on the balustrade beside her hip. "I have seven. You are welcome to borrow any of mine. You met my youngest sister?"

She nodded again, trying to focus on his words, not the feel of his hand holding hers or the closeness of his body or how soft his lips looked, how inviting.

"Did she tell you all of my secrets?"

Collette shook her head. Her voice had deserted her, and she feared if she attempted to speak, he would lean close to her and she would catch his scent and lose all control over her baser urges.

"I suppose I shall have to leave that to my brothers. I have four, and we live to humiliate each other. Two of my brothers are in the navy. Officers and proud of it. They want nothing but to serve the king. And your brother? Did he support Napoleon?"

She nodded, all but transfixed by his good looks and his melodious voice, then realized what he'd asked. "I mean, no."

"He did not support Napoleon?"

"I—" What was the correct answer? She did not want to be seen as a supporter of the dictator who had been England's enemy. "No, he was conscripted."

"I see. And did your father work for Napoleon against his will too?"

"He—" Collette drew in a sharp breath. "My father did not work for Napoleon, monsieur. He was a farmer."

"Did you mention that before?"

"I thought I did."

"I must have been confused." He leaned close and she felt his warm breath on her cheek. "I will confess... May I confess something to you?"

Collette didn't know what to reply. She wasn't certain she could have spoken if she'd tried.

"When I look at you, my brain goes to mush. My thoughts are all muddled. Do you know how that feels?" His body pressed against hers, a warm, solid weight that terrified and excited her at the same time. "All I can think about when I am this close to you is my mouth on yours." He reached out and touched a finger to her lips. He'd removed his gloves at some point, and the feel of his bare skin sent a zing of pleasure through her. "My hands on your skin." He caressed her lips with his finger. "My body pressed to yours."

Collette could not breathe. Her lungs burned and her heart beat painfully in her chest. As though she watched from far away, she stood immobile while Beaumont trailed his finger from her lips to her chin, catching it lightly between thumb and forefinger. Then he lowered his mouth to hers, brushing over her in a slow, tantalizing whisper of a kiss. Collette drew in a sharp breath, and Beaumont moved to the corner of her mouth. "I make you nervous, don't I, mademoiselle?" He spoke in French now, though she barely realized it. "You are afraid I will kiss you, *really* kiss you. And you are also afraid I will not."

Collette wanted to move her mouth to meet his and give in to him—his velvet voice, his teasing mouth, his intoxicating scent. But she could not afford to indulge in flirtations, especially not with men she could not trust. Her father's life depended on her, and she would not gain any useful information on the terrace with Mr. Beaumont.

Collette closed her eyes and summoned all her strength. "I am afraid if you kiss me, you will receive a nasty surprise, monsieur."

His lips paused in their exploration as he undoubtedly felt the pressure of her knee between his legs.

"Step back, or I will make certain amorous activities are the last thing on your mind for the next few days."

Slowly, very slowly, Beaumont moved back. As

soon as he was out of range of her knee, she lowered it and let out an audible breath.

"You might simply have said you had a headache."

"I don't have a headache," she said, keeping her voice steady. "I am not attracted to you."

The fact that she was able to spew such a blatant lie and keep a straight face was testament to how determined she was to free her father. The fact that she could resist Beaumont at all was proof of how dedicated she was to stealing those codes.

"I see." He gave her a puzzled look. "You will forgive me if I'm at a loss. This has never happened to me before."

She narrowed her eyes. "What do you mean?" Now that he was not standing so close and not looking quite so confident, she could almost speak to him as though he were a mortal man.

He shifted awkwardly and raked a hand through his hair. All of which served to make him seem even less like a god and more like a human.

"I mean, no woman has ever refused me before."

"Never?"

"No." He shoved his hands in his pockets.

"Not a single woman?"

"Not until now." He looked increasingly uncomfortable and his voice was quiet and hesitant. Collette had the urge to apologize and to confess that she actually did find him incredibly attractive. But that was lunacy. She could not confess such a thing, even if such an admission would not beg for more information.

Collette moved toward the terrace doors. "I take

no pleasure in rejecting you, sir. Thank you for the dance." She pulled at the latch on the doors.

"I must escort you into supper."

"That's not necessary," she said. "I can find my own way and sit with Lady Ravensgate."

"But—"

She held up a hand. "Please. I think it would be best if you and I do not speak again. Ever."

And she swept into the ballroom, feeling very much as she had when she'd been a child and had her favorite toy taken away.

# Five

RAFE DIDN'T WAIT FOR PORTER, THE MASTER OF THE House at the Draven Club, to answer the door. He merely shoved it open and barreled into the wood-paneled vestibule, noting that candles in the large chandelier lit the room. Then Porter appeared, making his way down the winding staircase. He moved quickly for a man with only one leg, but Rafe signaled to him. "No hurry, Porter. I let myself in."

He shrugged off his greatcoat and tossed it on the suit of armor on one side of the vestibule. There was a perfectly good coatrack beside the door, but Rafe always hung his greatcoat on the suit of armor. Porter had ceased bothering to remove it. Rafe saluted the shield opposite the door. It bore eighteen fleur-de-lis, symbolizing the eighteen men of Draven's troop who had died fighting for England.

"The billiards room, Mr. Beaumont?" Porter asked.

"Not tonight." Rafe wouldn't have been able to pot the ball if the damn thing was directly in front of the pocket. The French chit had muddled his mind. He'd made two wrong turns on his way from Montjoy's ball to the Draven Club, and before tonight, Rafe would have sworn he could find the Draven Club in his sleep. "I want the dining room. And I want brandy." He gave Porter a meaningful glance. "A lot of brandy, Porter."

"Yes, sir."

Rafe started up the staircase, the royal-blue runner familiar and somewhat calming.

Porter followed. "Is anything the matter, sir?"

"Why should anything be the matter?"

"You don't normally drink to excess, sir."

"Oh, that." Rafe reached the top of the staircase and turned toward the dining room. "There is no normal anymore, Porter. Up is down and black is white and front is back. Hasn't anyone told you?"

"No, sir. I regret to say no one has informed me of this change." He opened the doors to the dining room. Rafe paused in the doorway and looked down at the silver-haired man.

"Well, then I suppose the duty falls to me. Porter, it grieves me to tell you that the world as we know it no longer exists. And this new world will require much more brandy."

"Yes, sir."

Rafe entered the dining room, spotted his friends Neil and Jasper at one of the round tables, and made his way toward another table. He sat alone and lowered his head onto the freshly starched white linen tablecloth. The benefit of burying his face in the linen was it eradicated the lingering scent of Miss Fournay—or was it Fortier?—from his nose. He'd spent far too much time the past week trying to determine what scent clung to her before realizing it was the crisp scent of juniper in bloom.

Rafe attempted to ignore the rumble of voices at the other table. No doubt Neil, who was formerly the leader of Draven's men, and Jasper, probably the troop's best hunter turned bounty hunter, would try to engage Rafe at some point. Rafe intended to ignore them. If he'd wanted conversation, he would have gone home. There was always some woman loitering there, hoping to catch him and convince him to take her to bed. Rafe didn't want company—female or male—tonight.

After what seemed like at least a fortnight, he heard Porter's distinctive steps and then two quiet thumps on the table alerted him that a decanter of brandy and a snifter had been placed before him. The splash of liquid was music to his ears.

"You have my unending gratitude, Porter," Rafe mumbled from the cushion of his arms.

"Thank you, sir."

Rafe lifted his head to sip the brandy and stared into the faces of Neil and Jasper. The men had moved noiselessly across the room and taken seats at Rafe's table. Rafe groaned, sipped the brandy, and put his head down again. "Go away."

"Something bothering you, Beaumont?" Neil asked.

Rafe didn't answer.

"He looks in high dudgeon to me," Jasper drawled.

"I'm happy as a lark. Now go away."

"So the brandy is celebratory?"

Rafe looked up. "If I say yes, will you go away?"

"No." Neil poured two fingers of brandy for himself and Jasper. Damn Porter for bringing them snifters as well. "We'll celebrate with you."

Jasper Grantham sipped his brandy. He had dark-blond hair and a ragged scar across one cheek. Rafe was used to the scar, but Jasper usually wore a mask to hide it when he was in public. Neil Wraxall, on the other hand, was dark of hair. He had the coloring of his Italian mother and clear blue eyes that always saw too much.

"What are we celebrating?" Wraxall asked.

"Don't you have a wife and about two dozen children waiting for you at home?"

Neil shook his head. "I trust Mrs. Wraxall has everything well in hand." Which was the most ridiculous statement Wraxall had ever made because his wife was a walking beacon for trouble. And Rafe should know because he'd once had to babysit a dozen orphans while Neil sorted out some sort of trouble she'd caused. And that was before she'd burned down an orphanage.

"And how are things with you, Beaumont?"

"No rum dell on your arm tonight?"

"If by *dell* you mean woman, Grantham, then the answer is no."

Neil and Jasper exchanged looks. Rafe could all but read the silent conversation. Finally, Neil spoke, his voice incredulous. "This isn't about a woman, is it?"

"A plague on the whole species," Rafe said.

Jasper sat back and crossed his arms, his expression smug. Neil looked perplexed but intrigued. He leaned forward, like an eager student. "Did you compromise someone's virginal daughter?"

"Ha!" Rafe drank again. "Nothing so simple."

"You agreed to marry one of them. Again," Jasper guessed.

"Hell's teeth. I told you never to remind me of that…incident."

"Was there another fight? Your hair looks more disheveled than usual." This from Neil.

"It is fashionably tousled, and no. No women were fighting over me."

"Did two of them proposition you again and you had to spend all night being pleasured by them?"

Rafe rolled his eyes. "No."

"Tell us about that time anyway." Jasper drank again. "I can't remember all of the details."

"Stubble it," Rafe said. "This problem pales in comparison to those."

"Is this problem a brunette?" Neil asked.

"With large…" Jasper made curving motions in front of his chest.

Rafe opened his mouth and closed it again. For the first time, he realized Miss Fournay was exactly the sort of woman he preferred—beautiful, dark haired, and with ample charms. He'd been so focused on her as a mission, he hadn't looked at her as a woman. Not that he hadn't felt an attraction to her. When he'd been about to kiss her on the terrace, not everything he said had been pretty words designed to seduce her. He had been imagining his body pressed to hers and his mouth on hers. What man wouldn't imagine it? Her plump lips and the straining of her bodice tonight were enough to give any man ideas.

Jasper and Neil exchanged a look. Neil mimed the hammering of a nail.

"What's the problem?" Jasper asked. "Can't decide whether to roger her on her back or against a wall?"

"The problem is she's a mission," Rafe said. He had no compunction about revealing this here. The Draven Club was entirely safe. The men could talk about anything here and it would never leave the confines of the building. "Draven himself asked me to tease information from her. She's suspected of being in league with the French."

"That sounds simple enough for you," Neil said. "I gave you a score of assignments like that when we were at war."

"Yes, but…" Rafe sipped his brandy again, then poured more. "But something is wrong with this woman."

Jasper raised his brows. "Wrong how?"

"She rejected my advances."

Silence hung in the air for a long, long moment, and then Neil and Jasper burst out laughing. Jasper all but fell out of his chair.

"Bloody hell." Rafe gathered his brandy and stood. He should have known better than to confide in those two.

"Wait, wait, wait!" Neil said, grabbing Rafe's arm and wresting the brandy away. "I apologize. This is very serious."

And then he and Jasper started laughing all over again.

"You think it's so amusing? I'll tell Draven to assign one or both of you. See how you do."

"I won't live through one night. My wife would murder me."

Jasper gestured to his cheek. "I'd scare her away."

"You couldn't do any worse than I am."

Neil grabbed Rafe's arm again. "Sit down. It can't be all that bad."

"She tried to knee me in the groin."

Both men flinched. "So she has some spirit," Neil said.

"I wouldn't have known it until now. She barely spoke before. I could have sworn the chit was tongue-tied every time she looked at me. But she had plenty to say at the ball tonight. And all of it about hedgehogs."

"Is that a new cant phrase? I don't know it," Jasper said.

"Perhaps she is presenting you with a challenge," Neil said. "You're not used to that. She wants to be chased."

Rafe shook his head. "I know that game, and this is not it."

"Then have you considered she really does have something to hide?"

"Why do you say that?" Rafe asked Jasper.

Jasper shrugged. "That's the opinion of the Foreign Office. Maybe she fears you'll pull the plug and all her secrets will spill out."

Rafe rested his hand on his chin, tapping his fingers on his lip. "She does seem skittish. I called on her last week, and I could have sworn she intentionally tipped over the tea tray."

"You were too close to something she did not want to tell you?" Neil speculated.

"Or something she did not want me to see." Rafe thought about the desk in Lady Ravensgate's drawing room. It had been covered with an assortment of letters and papers. What if one of those had been from her French contacts? Something that might tie her to Fortier? But why would her father ask her to spy? He'd been an ally of Napoleon and now the Bourbons were back on the throne. Or what if the royalists had killed Fortier and threatened to kill her too if she did not work for them? But that made no sense. She could easily run away. Lady Ravensgate was not keeping that close a watch on her.

Rafe sipped the brandy again. "Say she does have something to hide. There were plenty of women on the Continent who had secrets to hide. I managed to persuade them."

"Married women." Neil pointed at him. "This one isn't married. She might have limited experience with men."

"Then my task should be simple."

"Not necessarily," Jasper said. "Your methods of seduction are not exactly subtle. You might scare her."

"*You* are schooling me in methods of seduction?"

Jasper grinned. "Best day ever."

"You need to take another approach," Neil said. "If she fights seduction, come at her another way."

Rafe swallowed his brandy and slammed the snifter down. "Hell's teeth, but I don't know another way! You called me the Seducer for a reason."

"Try gaining her trust. Become her friend."

Christ. The last thing Rafe wanted was to become friends with a woman. But, as he'd told Porter, up was down today and perhaps the last thing he wanted was the thing he needed.

Or…perhaps he should approach her as though the world truly were upside down.

"Look at the way his eyes lit up," Jasper said in a mock whisper. "He has an idea."

"Who would you say is my opposite?" Rafe asked.

"I don't know." Neil looked at Jasper. "You mean one of the troop? Guy was quite shy. He stammered every time he tried to talk to a woman."

Rafe felt a twinge of pain remembering Guy. He'd died in an ambush during one of their suicide missions. "And I talk to women easily. I talk…"

"Ewan," Neil said at the same time Jasper said, "The Protector."

"Of course. I should stop trying to figure out how to seduce this woman. It doesn't work. If everything I do is wrong, everything Ewan does must be right."

"I wouldn't go that far," Neil interrupted.

Rafe ignored him. "I should ask myself, what would Ewan do? Better yet. I'll ask the man himself." He rose and started for the door.

"Good luck wheedling a half dozen syllables from him," Jasper said.

Rafe looked over his shoulder. "Good point." But at least none of those syllables would be about hedgehogs.

If Ewan wouldn't talk, he'd just have to make the man show him.

❧

"That's her," Rafe said, pointing across the park to where Lady Ravensgate and Miss Fournay strolled. Miss Fournay certainly did not look like a spy in her apple-green walking dress and matching spencer and parasol. She was beautiful—much more so in the bright daylight than the yellow gloom of candlelight. The sunny day brought out the pink of her cheeks and the glints of gold in her hair. "The one on the green," Rafe said, since Ewan hadn't made any indication he knew who Rafe meant.

Ewan nodded. Rafe waited. And waited. In a moment, he would have to rise from the bench and follow her, as she and Lady Ravensgate were moving out of sight. "Do you have anything to say?" Rafe prodded.

"You dragged me away from the studio for this?" Ewan and Draven were joint owners of a boxing studio. As it had opened recently, it had nothing like the reputation of Gentleman Jackson's, but Rafe had no doubt Ewan would win the hearts and minds of the pugilism enthusiasts in no time. For his part, Rafe could think of other pursuits far more enjoyable than taking a swing at another man in a ring. But Ewan Mostyn, otherwise known as the Protector, was big and brawny, with platinum-blond hair and a square jaw. If ever a man had been born to smash skulls, it was Ewan.

"I should think you would thank me for taking you out into the fresh air and sunshine. It's a fine day, and that's a rare thing."

Ewan continued to glare at him.

"I will have you back to knocking men's brain boxes loose in no time. I simply want your opinion."

Lady Ravensgate and Miss Fournay had paused to speak with an older woman, the wife of a Cabinet member, if Rafe was not mistaken. The exchange looked innocent enough, but who knew what state secrets Miss Fournay might be stealing?

"Why?" Ewan asked.

"I thought I explained all this, old boy."

"Explain again."

Rafe sighed. "As I told you, the world is upside down."

"This time, make sense."

Rafe scowled at him, which had absolutely no effect on Ewan. "I can't make sense because the world makes no sense."

"You are giving me a headache."

"No, that's from all the skull smashing. And since your brain is probably scrambled, let me be brief. Up is down, right is left, and if I can't change the world, I'll trick it. Which means, obviously, I must become you."

"Obviously."

"And so you must tell me what you would do in... well, in your place."

"I do not have to be you?"

"No. Why would you be me?"

"Thank God."

"Ewan, pay attention. There is the chit. What would you do right now?"

"Go back to the studio." He started to move away, but Rafe grabbed his large arm and pulled him back. Rather, Ewan allowed Rafe to pull him back.

"What would you do about Miss Fournay?"

"Nothing. I'm married."

"Yes, but what if you were me?"

"I'd probably kill myself."

Rafe was about to pull his hair out when he caught the quick smile on Ewan's lips. The man was toying with him. One could never tell with Ewan. He was so stone-faced. No doubt he was enjoying frustrating Rafe. Rafe tamped his annoyance down. "Fine. Don't help me."

Ewan tipped his hat and started to walk away, back toward the corner where they had exited the hackney.

"I'll have Draven order you to attend the next soiree with me."

Ewan stopped.

"Or perhaps my next engagement is the opera. I know how you enjoy the opera."

Ewan walked back. "Do it and I will squeeze the air from your throat and crush it with one hand."

"Tell me how to approach her. Nothing I have done has worked."

Ewan stared at Miss Fournay across the green park. His pale-blue eyes were so intense, Rafe wondered that the lady did not turn and look back. "I asked you to help me, not scare her away."

"She looks lonely."

Rafe's brows shot up. "Does she?" He glanced at her again. She smiled often enough, but Ewan was right. The smile did not meet her eyes.

"She's in a foreign country surrounded by strangers. She needs a friend, a confidant."

"Yes! That's what I have been trying to do. Become her confidant."

"No, you have been trying to get under her skirts and wondering why she doesn't respond. You have to give her something to receive something in return."

"Say again?"

"It's like fighting."

"No, it's not."

Ewan ignored him. "When you and an opponent are equally matched, let him land a punch."

"No, thank you. I prefer my face free of bruises."

"Let him land several blows. Then, when he's feeling confident, when he thinks he has you beaten, you pummel the hell out of him."

Rafe stared at Ewan a long time. Ewan started moving away again. "You can thank me later."

"Not likely!" Rafe called after him.

He let out a sigh and began to follow, quite slowly, the progress of Miss Fournay and her chaperone. *Give her something. Let the opponent land a punch.* "Then pummel the hell out of him," he muttered.

Was *pummel* a metaphor?

Was he *really* trying to read something into Ewan's words?

Not that he had any better ideas.

Miss Fournay was lonely. Rafe would give her something without asking for anything in return. He'd give her friendship. He'd take her around London, call on her, and…and whatever else friends did. Then when she trusted him, when she counted him as her friend, he'd take advantage of that trust and pry the information he needed out of her.

Rafe frowned. And some men accused *him* of being manipulative. Ewan's methods were cold indeed. But with his country at risk, Rafe couldn't afford scruples.

"Mr. Beaumont?"

Rafe looked up. He'd been so lost in thought that he'd practically run into Miss Fournay and her chaperone. Lady Ravensgate looked at him quizzically, while her charge pretended he did not exist. "Lady

Ravensgate." He bowed. "Miss Fournay. What a pleasure to encounter you both here."

Miss Fournay snorted and looked away. She was decidedly *un*friendly.

"The pleasure is all ours," Lady Ravensgate said. "How is your ankle? Should you really be walking on it?"

"My ankle?" He glanced at Lady Ravensgate, then Miss Fournay, in confusion.

Miss Fournay rolled her eyes. "You sprained it at Lord Montjoy's ball, monsieur. You had to leave early."

"Yes. I did. I sprained it." He lifted one foot as though his weight on it pained him.

"It was the other ankle, monsieur."

Miss Fournay had a smug look on her face. Rafe wanted it gone. "Imagine that. They both feel as good as new."

"I wish I could say the same." Lady Ravensgate moved toward a bench and sat, arranging her skirts carefully. "I tire easily these days."

"Shall I sit with you and keep you company?" Rafe asked.

"No, no. You two young people continue to stroll. I will wait here for you."

"But I can't leave you!" Miss Fournay protested.

"Oh, I am tired, not dying. Go ahead."

Miss Fournay opened her mouth, obviously struggling to think of another excuse to avoid his presence. Rafe didn't give her the opportunity. He offered his arm, and she had little choice but to take it. "I will bring her back shortly, my lady. I promise she will have no better friend than me."

When they had walked a little distance, Rafe commenting on the trees and the sky and the weather, they finally paused near a small pond, where ducks swam. The pond was somewhat sheltered from view by the low-hanging branches of trees, and Miss Fournay snatched her arm away immediately.

"I meant what I said, you know," he told her.

"About the summer breeze or the oak trees?"

"About being your friend. I'd like to be your friend."

She glared at him, her dark eyes wide and full of fire. "My English may not be as good as yours, monsieur, but even I know *friend* is what men often use to refer to their paramours."

"Actually, the term is usually *special friend*, and that is not what I had in mind at all."

"I am not that naive."

"Good. Then you will understand that there are times when men and women might simply be friends."

She crossed her arms over her ample chest. "And why would you want to be my friend? Have you no friends of your own?"

He had plenty of friends of his own, but his popularity was not the issue. "I don't have any women friends, and Montjoy's ball showed to me that a woman friend, like you, might prove valuable."

"How so?"

"If I am walking in the park with you or dancing with you or speaking with you, I am safe from other women."

"Safe?"

"Yes, safe. You think I enjoy constant pursuit?"

"Yes."

"Well, you're wrong," he said, surprised at his honesty. "I grow tired of it, and since you're the first woman who is not related to me who seems completely immune to my good looks, my unparalleled charms, my witty conversation—"

"Your mammoth arrogance."

He grinned. "I thought you and I might be friends. You could help me stave off the female population, and I can help you."

"There is only one problem, monsieur. I do not need your help."

"Yes, you do. You must be terribly lonely with only that old bat to keep you company."

"Not at all," she protested, rather unconvincingly.

"You have been in London a month? Two?"

"Just about."

"Have you seen the Tower? The British Museum? Vauxhall Gardens? The Thames?"

She didn't reply, and her silence spoke for itself.

"Or have you only seen the inside of stuffy drawing rooms and assembly halls? Why not let me, acting as your friend, show you all of London? There's Bond Street, Covent Garden, ices at Gunter's—"

"I couldn't possibly agree to any of that. I must have a chaperone, and Lady Ravensgate has not the strength for a full schedule in the morning and another in the evening."

"Then bring a maid, or if Lady Ravensgate feels up to it, she may attend. What say you to a play tonight at Drury Lane? I believe they are performing a new comedy."

She shook her head, but not before he saw a flicker

of interest in her eyes. Her arms had dropped as well. Hell's teeth, but Ewan was a genius. It had only been a few moments of this friendship nonsense, and she was already lowering her guard.

"I couldn't possibly accept."

"You have plans tonight?" He knew she did not. He had paid one of Lady Ravensgate's servants to provide him with their schedule.

"It is Lady Ravensgate's decision."

Rafe did not miss how she answered without giving him an answer to his question about her plans. She was cunning. He held out his arm again. "Then we shall ask her. No, I shall invite both of you."

"You have that many seats?"

"I am the son of an earl. I have a box at my disposal."

On the way back to her chaperone, Rafe couldn't help but steal one, or two, more-than-friendly looks in Miss Fournay's direction. She wore a bonnet that hid her face when she looked straight ahead, but he could still see the graceful column of her neck before it dipped under the spencer she wore. And he had better not linger too long on the rise of her breasts beneath the spencer. This friendship scheme was just the thing, but he would ruin it all if he didn't keep himself in check. He'd never before worried about his attraction to a woman who was part of a mission. If he was attracted to her, it made his job easier. Now, his attraction could present a problem, especially as he was more attracted to her than he'd have liked to admit. Rafe wouldn't have thought he could have much interest in a woman of so little experience, even if she was physically the type he preferred. But there was something thrilling in the knowledge that he might be the first to kiss her, the first to touch her, the first to take her…not that he would do any of that. He was only her friend.

Still, it was annoying that, now that he had what amounted to state approval to seduce a virginal miss, he had decided not to. And this just when he, who had never had any interest in untried females, had discovered what other men found so alluring about them. But virgin or not, Miss Fournay would have attracted him. And like the old saying went, now that he couldn't have her, the more he wanted her.

# Six

COLLETTE'S HANDS SHOOK SO MUCH SHE HID THEM IN the folds of her cape and hoped Mr. Beaumont had not noticed. The hackney was dark, but he had a keen eye. And his gaze always seemed to be on her. Though he had been polite and reserved, she'd seen the appreciation warm his eyes when he first saw her tonight. He didn't need to say he thought she looked beautiful. He hadn't said it, as was befitting their new status as friends, but she'd seen it in his face and heard it in the reverent tone of his voice.

She had been told she was beautiful before—not often but on occasion. And yet she'd never felt as beautiful as she did under Beaumont's silent appreciation. She wore a dark-green dress of silk with spangles on the hem that shimmered when she walked. Unlike the yellow dress, the cut of this one was a bit more modest, but she still felt she showed too much cleavage. Beaumont's gaze had not slipped to her chest, so perhaps she was simply self-conscious. Lady Ravensgate had enthusiastically agreed to the night at the theater and agreed to join the two of them.

Collette had told her sponsor that Mr. Beaumont was simply acting as a friend, but Lady Ravensgate still gave her knowing smirks whenever Beaumont wasn't looking. Collette did not care. Beaumont knew Draven, and if he became her friend, she would be able to ask him about Draven and perhaps gain access to the man.

"Ah, here we are," Mr. Beaumont said.

Collette peered out at the brightly lit entryway filled with distinguished-looking men and glittering women exiting gleaming carriages. Columns lined the portico where coaches paused to deliver their occupants. She supposed the lower classes must attend the theater as well, but perhaps they had a separate entrance. As Beaumont led her inside, Lady Ravensgate having waved off his offer of an arm, Collette craned her neck to admire the architecture before being guided up the stairs and to the boxes. "Which play are we seeing?" she asked.

"It is called *The Disguise*. I cannot remember the playwright's name, but this production is new. He's relatively new. I saw his debut last year, and I chuckled for days. You should enjoy it."

"Then you attend the theater often?"

"When I have the chance." He nodded at a group of ladies they passed, and Collette did not fail to notice that two of the four stared longingly after him while the other two shot daggers at him. None of them attempted to waylay him, however. "And you? Do you go to the theater often?"

"Of course. Paris is known for its theater." Too late, she realized she had said the wrong thing, but before she could cover her error, he gestured to the curtain before them.

"This is my family's box." He held the curtain open for her, and as soon as she entered, she gasped in a breath. The light was incredible. It was so bright that she almost thought it daytime.

"Ah, I see they finished the installation of the gas lighting," Beaumont said.

Collette might have admired the colors and the well-lit faces of the other attendees longer, but a tall, handsome man rose and stood before her.

"Rafe. Your sister said you would be joining us." He bowed formally. In the chair beside him, Collette recognized Lady Birtwistle. The man standing must have been her husband. And he'd called Beaumont *Rafe.* So that was his given name. It felt like intimate knowledge.

"Lord and Lady Birtwistle, may I present Lady Ravensgate and her cousin Miss Fournay."

"Oh, we've met already," Lady Birtwistle said. "I am so glad you could join us."

Lord Birtwistle bowed again. "A pleasure as always Lady Ravensgate, and it is lovely to meet you, Miss Fournay. Please do take a seat."

He gestured to a seat beside his wife, but when she moved to take it, Beaumont stepped before her and angled it so Lady Ravensgate might sit. That left one unoccupied seat in the front row and four behind. Collette moved to take the empty seat beside Lady Ravensgate, but Beaumont pulled out a chair behind the older woman.

"You aren't so cruel as to leave me all alone back here, are you?"

Collette hesitated. Lady Ravensgate looked from Collette to the chair to Beaumont. "You had better be on your best behavior, Mr. Beaumont."

"If you look over your shoulder, you will see my halo, my lady." He gave that charming smile of his and, after Collette took her chair, sat in the one beside it. She made a point of pretending to study the theater and peer at the crowd, but mentally she was attempting to think of an explanation for why she would have attended the theater in Paris so often when she had told Beaumont she'd lived in the country. It was the first real mistake she had made while in London, and she cursed herself for becoming too comfortable around him and lowering her guard.

"The theater burned down seven or eight years ago," Beaumont told her. "This building is relatively new."

"The gas lighting is amazing."

"I agree. They've extended it to the stage. I believe it is the first theater in England to be gaslit throughout."

"But isn't gas lighting dangerous?"

"I fear candles and open fire are more dangerous. The theater has burned down three times already, and the owners are hoping the gas lighting will mean there won't be a fourth time. I wish we had a better box, but my father never attends the theater. He only keeps the box for the sake of appearances." He went on, telling her about some of the more memorable productions he had attended, and Collette found herself listening and laughing at his descriptions of actors and mishaps during the plays or operas. When the play began and he turned his attention to the stage, she missed their conversation.

And she also blew out a relieved breath. Apparently, he hadn't noticed her slip of the tongue. She was grateful for that. She was also grateful that it seemed he was sincere when he'd said he wanted to be her friend. He had made no attempt to flirt with her and, except for a few appreciative glances, had treated her as though she were his sister. In fact, he and his sister had exchanged a few comments, and he spoke to her very much in the same manner he spoke to Collette.

She shouldn't have felt disappointed that he had so easily transitioned from a man who had seemed desperately attracted to her to a platonic friend, but that was what she had wanted, was it not?

She turned her attention to the play and enjoyed it for the first quarter hour. Then her sense of unease began to grow. The title of the play was apt, as every character in the play wore a disguise of some sort or another. For some of them, like the pretty young woman in love with a young man whose family owned a print shop, the disguise was physical. She dressed as an errand boy who stood about on the shop's stoop all day so she could be close to the man she loved. He, of course, never noticed her. He was in love with an older woman who was also an artist. Except the artist was not a woman at all, but a man who dressed as a woman because he thought it made his art more interesting if people thought it was the work of a woman.

And then there was the shop owner, whose disguise was more of a mask. He had owned the shop for twenty years, and he had hated every day of it. He didn't care for art or prints. He longed to work in the soil, to farm or garden, to do something with his hands, something that was useful. But he pretended with each of his customers and the artists whose work he purchased.

The play reminded Collette very much of her own circumstances. Indeed, at one point, the similarities must have struck Lady Ravensgate as well because she turned to look back at Collette, who sat stiffly in her seat. She was very much a woman pretending to be someone she was not. And the frequent slips the characters made, slips in behavior or speech that revealed who they really were, made her remember her own misstep earlier tonight.

But if Rafe Beaumont had any idea she was not who she appeared, any idea that the play unnerved her, he did not show it. He paid rapt attention, leaning over to murmur comments once in a while, laughing uproariously at the characters' mistakes, and generally seemed to enjoy himself immensely. He was perfectly charming and perfectly behaved, and she could hardly believe he was the same man who had all but trapped her on the terrace at Montjoy's ball.

Finally, it was time for intermission, and Lady Ravensgate and Lady Birtwistle excused themselves to speak with friends in nearby boxes. Collette made to follow, but Beaumont stayed her. "Please, I beg you, do not abandon me."

She glanced at Lord Birtwistle. "I am hardly abandoning you, sir."

"Oh, he won't be any use. I need you to help me fend off the masses."

"Don't you think you are exaggerating?"

He looked at Birtwistle. "Am I exaggerating?"

Birtwistle shook his head, opera glasses on his eyes as he scanned the crowd. "Not at all. A flock of them will arrive at any moment."

"Miss Fournay, are you coming?" Lady Ravensgate asked. Beaumont gave her another of his pleading looks.

"I will stay behind with the gentlemen if that is agreeable to you, my lady."

"Suit yourself."

Now was her chance. She had to ask him about Draven while she had him alone. "My cousin tells me you served under Lieutenant Colonel Draven," Collette said. "I met him at a ball."

"Did you?" Beaumont leaned close. "He's not nearly as handsome as I."

"No, but he was very entertaining. Unfortunately, he was pulled away because he said he had business with the—what was it now? The International Office?"

"The Foreign Office," he corrected her.

"That's right! What sort of—"

She was interrupted when three women squealed and crashed into the box, screeching with pleasure and cornering Beaumont. Collette was physically shouldered out of the way, and she ended up plopping down beside Lord Birtwistle so as not to be trampled.

"Is it always like this?" she asked.

He lowered his glasses, glanced at the women, then raised them again. "Yes. I used to hate the fellow, but now I feel rather sorry for him."

She did not feel sorry for him. In fact, she felt distinctly annoyed. These women had barged into the Haddington box at precisely the wrong moment. She might have gained the knowledge she sought and been certain Draven had the codes. Then she would have to find a way to sneak into his office or home and steal them. But she could not take such a risk without being sure. These trollops had ruined her careful planning. "Why does he not simply tell them to go away?" she said, bristling.

"He tries," Birtwistle said, looking at her. "They don't listen. Rafe tells his sister you are different. You are immune, so you don't understand how it is."

"Immune?"

"To his charms. Other women seem incapable of summoning the will not to fall at his feet."

Collette frowned at this statement. She was not immune to his charms. She was very attracted to him and more than tempted to throw herself at his feet too. But she had too much to lose to give in to such behavior. And though she knew once the play began these women would leave, and Rafe Beaumont would be hers again, she resented having to share him. She might be using him, but he was using her as well. He'd told her he wanted her to keep his adoring followers at bay.

"Excuse me," she told Lord Birtwistle. She rose and tapped the closest woman on the shoulder. "I'm sorry, you will have to leave. This is a private box and you do not have permission to be here."

"And who are you?" the woman asked, pointing her sharp nose in the air.

"A friend of the family and the only lady currently in this box with a ticket to sit here."

The woman sniffed and made a show of stomping

out. Collette tapped the next woman on the shoulder and repeated the exchange. By the time she actually reached Beaumont, she had lost most of her tactfulness. Instead, she simply said, "This is a private box. Leave."

The two women flanking Beaumont glared at her, then looked with large, pleading eyes at Beaumont. "You don't want us to leave, do you, Rafe?" asked a blond with her large breasts pressed against him.

"Of course he doesn't," said a brunette who was one of the most beautiful women Collette had ever seen, though her hard eyes ruined the effect somewhat.

"Er…" Beaumont began.

"He does," Collette answered for him. "Tell them to go, Mr. Beaumont."

"Go?" Beaumont spoke the words as though they were a question.

"You will speak with them at another time," she prompted.

"Yes. Another time," he repeated.

The women both huffed out breaths. The blond whispered something in his ear that made his brows rise, and then the two women left, their hips swaying. Collette followed them, closing the box's curtain and motioning to an usher just outside. "Sir, please make sure no one but Lady Ravensgate and Lady Birtwistle are able to enter for the rest of the evening."

When he was in place, she returned to the box and took a seat. She could breathe again and the box was no longer stuffy and cramped.

"That's much better," Birtwistle said, voicing her thoughts. "A man can think again. Excuse me, won't you? I need a moment."

He strolled out of the box, leaving Collette alone with Beaumont. She doubted Lady Ravensgate would have approved.

"He smokes," Beaumont said, looking after his brother-in-law. "Surprised he made it this long without stepping away." Then he looked directly at her. "Who are you and where have you hidden Miss Fournay?"

Collette felt her cheeks heat. "I am right here."

"Do not pretend that sort of behavior is typical for you. And here I thought you were a wilting wallflower."

"I am!" she protested. She touched her cheeks. "You see that I am blushing."

"But the way you emptied this box, the way you talked to those women?"

"I forget to be shy when I see someone being taken advantage of—an orphan or a widow. I assure you that now that I think of what I just did, I am mortified. I shall probably faint in a moment." Indeed, her head felt rather light and the theater seemed to spin.

"None of that," Beaumont said. "And no hedgehogs either. I shall forgive you comparing me to an orphan or a widow because you did the one thing I have been trying to do for years—tell all those women to go away."

"I don't understand why you don't just tell them."

He made a face. "Because although the attention can be annoying, it is also rather hard to forego. What man doesn't enjoy a half-dozen ladies hanging on his every word?"

"And whispering in his ear. What did the blond woman say to you?"

He grinned at her. "I'd tell you, but then I'd have to marry you."

She flushed again, this time her cheeks flaming hot. "That scandalous?"

"She isn't subtle." He gave Collette a quick perusal. "Not like you. I never thought I would like women who were subtle, but I find I actually like it very much."

She gave him a warning look, and he smiled and held up a hand. "In a friend. I like it in a friend. And you, Miss Fournay, have proven yourself a very good friend tonight. Thank you."

She ducked her head to hide her red face and heard Lady Ravensgate say, "Why are you thanking my cousin, Mr. Beaumont?"

"Because she is amazing, of course," he answered.

"Really?" Lady Birtwistle commented, her voice teasing. "Wait until I tell Lady Haddington."

Beaumont scowled at her words. "We are only friends," he said. "And I must say, she has proven herself an excellent friend tonight. The intermission is at an end."

At the last minute, Lord Birtwistle entered and took his seat, and then Collette was lost in the story again. It still felt awkward every time one of the characters' disguises came off, but when she'd glanced at Beaumont, he wasn't watching her. At least she did not catch his eyes on her, but she felt his gaze more often than she would have considered coincidence. And why shouldn't he take an interest in her? She'd proven, even to herself, that she too wore a disguise. She simply hoped Beaumont didn't try to peel it off.

❧

By the time Rafe arrived back at his flat in St. James's Square, it was well after midnight. He'd escorted Lady Ravensgate and Miss Fournay home and then directed the jarvey to drive him home. As the Season was over and much of the gentry at their country houses, the streets were relatively empty. The hardworking people of London were fast asleep, resting before beginning their work later that day. But though it took only a half hour to reach his flat, it was long enough for his mind to echo every minute he'd spent with Miss Fournay. It seemed every time he saw her, she was more beautiful. Her dress tonight, though modest, sparkled and shimmered so that it constantly drew his eye to her lush shape. She was not willowy and slim, as was the current fashion. She was curvy and round and delectable. And though he'd been attracted to her all evening, he'd been practically aroused when she'd found her backbone and ordered the women out of the box. If Birtwistle hadn't been there, Rafe might have shoved Miss Fournay up against the wall and plundered that ripe mouth.

But Rafe had restrained his impulses and maintained the illusion of friendship. He rather liked the idea of having a woman as a friend. Any woman not pursuing him, not wanting something from him, was to be welcomed. He only wished it were not Miss Fournay who had to be the token female friend. She was the first woman who'd captured his interest in a very long time.

The hackney stopped before his building, and he jumped out and paid the driver. As the driver drove away, Rafe spotted a gleaming black carriage waiting just at the corner. A footman hopped down from the box and bowed before Rafe. "Sir, Mrs. Monroe would speak with you."

"Of course." Rafe followed the footman to the carriage. He'd recognized it, of course. Kitty Monroe was a close friend of his, a young widow whose husband had left her quite wealthy. At one time, she and Rafe had been very close. He hadn't seen her except in passing since returning from the war. After his experiences on the Continent, he hadn't been interested in seeing any of his former paramours. He wasn't the same man who had left for war, but he wasn't yet certain who he was now.

The footman opened the door and Rafe climbed in. He kissed Kitty's hand and sat across from her as the door clicked shut, leaving them alone in the cozy glow of candlelight. "Shall I have John Coachman drive us?" Kitty asked. She was an American who Theodore Monroe had met when doing business in the former colonies, and though Rafe generally found American accents jarring, he didn't mind hers. Her voice was soft and low, very seductive.

"If you like," Rafe said.

"But you'd rather not." She looked at him closely. "You're tired tonight. I've come at a bad time."

"Kitty, I'm always happy to see you." And he was. He'd enjoyed her company in bed and out.

"But you are wondering why I am here and hoping I don't want to renew our former relationship."

She'd always been good at reading him. "I am surprised to see you, not unhappy."

"You haven't seen me because you haven't sought

me out. I thought perhaps there was someone else. Someone serious," she qualified, since there was almost always a woman on his arm. "But my sources told me otherwise. I see now that's not the case. Who is she?"

"I have no idea whom you might be referring to. You know I am rarely ever serious, especially not about women."

"I do know, yes. You don't really believe in love, do you?"

He made a noise of dismissal. "Do you?"

"Of course! I loved my husband." She leaned across the space between them. "I loved you."

"I don't believe it."

"Because if you had believed it, you would have run from me like a skittish horse."

"Skittish? I resent that comparison!"

She laughed. "Oh, Rafe. Who hurt you, darling?"

He put a hand to his heart in mock pain. "You hurt me with your equine comparisons."

She laughed. "It is good to see you. And it is very good to see the tables have turned."

He frowned. "What tables? And who turned them?"

"Whoever it is who has hold of your heart has turned them. You are the one in love."

"I am no such thing."

She arched a brow.

"I was with a woman tonight, but we are merely friends."

"You? Friends with a woman?"

"That's right. I've changed."

"I won't argue. The war did change you, but this is a stretch, even for you."

He couldn't tell her about the mission, nor did he want to. Why couldn't he be friends with a woman? Despite the rumors, he was actually rather discerning about who he took to bed. "It's true."

"I see. If you are only friends, then perhaps my appearance is not unwelcome. I brought wine. Shall we go inside and open it?"

He was tempted. Sorely tempted. Kitty was beautiful and familiar. He could spend the night with her and nothing would be required of him in the morning. Not to mention it had been some time since he'd had a woman in bed, and the unwelcome attraction to Miss Fournay had left him aroused but unsatisfied.

"Oh dear," Kitty said. "It is worse than I thought."

"I apologize for hesitating. It's just that—"

She held up her hand. "Do not give me excuses. I have heard them all and used several myself. And in any case, I know the real reason. I am not her."

"That has nothing to do with it." But a bell dinged somewhere in his head. Kitty had always understood him. Sometimes better than he understood himself. And he didn't particularly like it because he was not in love with Miss Fournay and he did not want her in his bed.

Wait. He did want her in his bed, but since that was not to be, he could satisfy his needs with another woman.

"No?" she asked.

"No. Come on, then. Let's go to bed."

But to his annoyance, she shook her head. "I don't think so. Even if that had not been the clumsiest proposition I have ever received, I would say no."

"A moment ago *you* propositioned *me*."

"A moment ago I thought you might still want to bed me, but I won't be your substitute for the evening."

"You could never be anyone's substitute."

"Thank you. I prefer to keep it that way." She lifted the bottle of wine from the seat beside her and handed it to him. "Take it. I think you need it more than I."

Rafe left the wine and stomped up the stairs to his flat. He let himself in and slammed the door behind him. He'd given his valet the rest of the night off, and the maid only worked during the day, so he was all alone. Alone with his annoyance and frustration. He scanned the room, looking for something he might smash.

"And I worried you wouldn't be alone."

Rafe spun around, his hands in fists, ready to defend. The man in the black silk half mask merely smiled. "I thought you were a lover, not a fighter."

"Hell's teeth, Jasper," Rafe said between clenched teeth. "What the bloody hell are you doing here?"

"Waiting for you."

"How did you get inside?"

"Your valet took pity on me before he left for the night. The women waiting outside your door were quite adamant you asked them to wait for you. Inside. On the bed. In the buff." He'd dropped the cant he used so often and which was required in his work. Rafe was relieved. He was too tired to wade through the rookery slang tonight.

Rafe spun back around, toward the door to his bedchamber. "Pye didn't let them in, did he?"

"No. Although why that should make you happy, I will never understand."

Rafe turned back to him. "You must have been waiting for hours."

Jasper shrugged as though the point was insignificant. It probably was. He was a patient man and a respected bounty hunter. When Bow Street couldn't find their man—or woman—Lord Jasper was the man they called on. "Draven sent me."

"Does this have anything to do with my mission?"

"Everything."

"Sit down, then."

Jasper was like a brother to him, so Rafe did not even mind that he settled himself in Rafe's favorite chair or that he'd obviously been sitting there for some time as the half glass of Rafe's best port beside the chair would indicate. "Port?" Jasper asked.

"Help yourself," Rafe drawled.

He lit a second lamp, bringing more light to the room, and took the less comfortable seat across from Jasper. Rafe had spent some time choosing the furnishings in this room and the others, just as he did with his clothing. The tables and chairs were heavy wood, suited to the long, rectangular room. Upholstered in greens, blues, and deep reds, they gave the room a quiet, masculine feel. The shelves of books took up one wall and more bound volumes had been stacked on the side tables. Jasper had been here before, of course, as had Neil and Ewan and several of the others from Draven's troop. When they'd marveled at his library, Rafe had passed it off as necessary in the pursuit of women. Ladies liked men who could quote poems and sonnets.

But truthfully, Rafe's love of reading had come when he'd been young. He'd so often been forgotten that he'd learned to amuse himself with a book, usually one with quite a few pictures. After his parents had remembered he needed an education, like the rest of his siblings, his reading skills had improved and he'd been able to read longer volumes and even those without drawings. Now he often read to fall asleep. It was a trick he'd learned when he'd returned home from the war and tended to dream of battles. If he read before sleep, he dreamed of that book.

"Did Draven send you to scold me for my lack of progress?"

"No. He sent me to help you. After all, the chit is unlikely to reveal that her given name is Collette Fortier."

"So she is the daughter of Napoleon's assassin."

"It would seem so. Letters I nabbed indicate her father awaits news of her travels."

Rafe rubbed his jaw, rough with stubble after the long day. "Her father wrote to her?"

"No. They're from someone who writes of her father and addressed to *ma chère amie*."

"A friend. That is innocuous enough."

"If it smells like a dead rat, look for the corpse."

"That's a disgusting phrase." Rafe shook his head. "Fortier is not an uncommon name. Perhaps it is a coincidence."

"Then why does she use a sham one?"

Rafe sat back and blew out a breath. Jasper was not combative, but he had a rebuttal for every point. *And why shouldn't he?* Rafe thought. Rafe might pretend to play devil's advocate, but he wanted to defend Collette Fortier. He didn't want her to be the enemy.

"She may not be a spy," Jasper said, "but if I were the Foreign Office, I would be suspicious."

"I've watched her for weeks, Jas," Rafe said, sitting up. "I don't see any evidence of spying."

"Maybe you're too close to see it."

Rafe took a moment to consider. "No. If anything, I'm not close enough."

Jasper sipped the port. "You? Not close enough?"

"We're becoming friends, but I don't have time to wait for her to confide in me. I need to gain her trust."

"That's easy enough."

Rafe sent his friend a scowl. "This isn't a rogue in Seven Dials. I can't press a ha'penny into her hand and buy her loyalty."

"You couldn't buy any rogue worth his salt for a ha'penny either, not unless you paid it regular."

"Then what do you suggest?"

"Save her. Then she'll owe you."

Rafe sat very still for a long moment. If his plan had been to give her something for nothing, his friendship, this was the perfect extension. Now, he'd save her life. If she were thus indebted to him, she couldn't possibly refuse to answer a few personal questions when he put them to her.

"I can see your brain box working. Don't hurt yourself."

"Stubble it. No, wait. How do I save her? She's not the sort who takes many chances. And if I have to wait for her to jump into the Thames or wander into a dark alley where thieves beset her, it might be years."

"I'll arrange it."

"Is that one of your many talents?"

Jasper gave him a half smile. "When do you see her next?"

"The day after tomorrow, or rather, the day after today since it's already tomorrow."

"Right." He pulled a notebook and pencil from his coat. "Give me all the details."

"Now? It's almost two in the morning."

"Just like old times, isn't it?"

"Yes, but during the war, we always said if we ever made it back, we'd never again take sleeping in a bed for granted."

"And as I recall, you were about the only one of us who had the luxury of sleeping in a bed."

"That was work."

"No, Beaumont. *This* is work." He lifted his pencil and looked at Rafe. "Start talking."

# Seven

COLLETTE WAS LOOKING FORWARD TO SEEING RAFE Beaumont far more than was wise. But she'd had such a wonderful time at the opera and it had been so refreshing to have an actual conversation with someone. Lady Ravensgate only lectured her, and when Collette was required to make conversation at the various functions she attended, it was always about the weather or the scandal of the day. The night before, she'd had to attend a dinner party where the hostess had assured Lady Ravensgate the assistant to the assistant secretary for the Foreign Office would dine. But the man had not made an appearance, and Collette had to listen to the men drone on about foxhunting, which, privately, she thought rather barbaric. Why anyone would want to discuss hounds tearing little foxes apart at the dinner table was beyond her.

And so it was no surprise that she eagerly anticipated her visit to the British Museum today. Lady Ravensgate looked less than pleased and rather weary after the late night out. She was of the opinion the British Museum had little of interest and held nothing that would benefit Collette. She'd been increasingly impatient with Collette's lack of progress. But Collette would not be thwarted. She still believed Beaumont might be useful, and she had all but demanded Lady Ravensgate accompany them.

He arrived exactly on time, rapping the knocker three times. Since Collette was already in the foyer, she might have opened the door herself. Instead, she had to wait for Evans to make his slow, steady way to the door and creak it open.

"Yes?" the butler said, as though he didn't know who was at the door and why.

Collette supposed Beaumont said something in return, but she couldn't hear over the pounding of her heart. They were friends. That was all. She had to remember that. She needed a friend, and that was all Rafe Beaumont could ever be. And then he was walking through the door, and she had to remind herself to breathe. He wore a charcoal-gray coat, gray trousers, and a waistcoat of burgundy. His hat sat rakishly on his head, his dark hair curling around the brim. His high collar brushed his freshly shaven jaw, the white emphasizing its strength. He was dangerously handsome, and Collette began to fear she had made an awful mistake agreeing to go on an outing with him.

She might have turned and run at that moment if her feet were obeying her brain. As it was, Beaumont stepped inside, removed his hat, and bowed. "Miss Fournay. A pleasure as always." He raised his violet eyes to hers and she caught the glitter of mischief, as though they shared a secret that amused them both.

"Mr. Beaumont." She gave a quick curtsy, relieved

her voice had not deserted her. "Lady Ravensgate will be down in just a—"

"Here I am." Lady Ravensgate swept down the stairs, her gaze moving up and down Beaumont. "Don't you look dashing!"

"I do try," Beaumont said, then offered her his arm. She took it, and Collette followed, happy to be given a moment to catch her breath and settle her racing heart. In the hackney, the three talked of trivialities—the weather, the museum's collection, the upcoming social events. The museum tour was equally pleasant. Beaumont was the perfect tour guide. He knew just enough about each piece to add something of interest, but not so much that he became obnoxious. The only problem was that Beaumont proved so interesting and entertaining she found it difficult to find an opening to discuss Draven. She was still searching for the right moment to mention the lieutenant colonel when Beaumont gestured behind them. "I fear Lady Ravensgate is becoming overly tired."

They had finished their examination of the natural history collection, but Collette had barely had time to study the Rosetta Stone before Beaumont came to stand by her side. She glanced a few yards away, where the lady sat on a bench, near one of the classical sculptures donated by Townley. Lady Ravensgate did look weary. Her face was pale and her lips tight.

"Shall I see the both of you home?"

Collette wanted to say no. She hadn't yet seen the Parthenon statues, and she was not tired in the least. But she could not stay with Beaumont unchaperoned. And it was very perceptive—and kind—of him to notice Lady Ravensgate was weary. Undoubtedly, he too could have stayed at the museum longer.

"Thank you," Collette said simply, accepting his offer. "I fear I did not even notice how tired she looked."

"My stepmother has that same look in her eyes when she has exhausted herself on an outing," he said. "She won't admit it, though, so I always claim I am exhausted."

Collette raised a brow. "Does she believe you?"

"No, but she's an intelligent woman and pretends to believe me. I think I shall try the same tact with Lady Ravensgate. If you will excuse me."

Collette watched as he approached the lady and made a show of false fatigue. Lady Ravensgate looked skeptical, much as she imagined Beaumont's stepmother did, but she eventually inclined her head and agreed to leave. Strange to think of Beaumont as a son. She'd met his sister twice now, and he obviously had more siblings and a father, but she could not picture him as a child. Had he always been so elegant and charming? Had he been born with those looks that made women forget propriety? And what of his mother? He only talked of his stepmother. Was it his stepmother who had taught him to take care of his elders and to offer friendship to friendless foreigners feeling lonely in the city?

Once again he took Lady Ravensgate's arm and led her through the museum and to the exit. Collette walked beside them, making last remarks on all that they had seen, including the enormous giraffes that presided over the entryway. When they stepped outside, they saw the sun had made an uncharacteristic appearance, and she squinted in the sudden brightness. "It is difficult to believe there are such large creatures in the world," Collette said as Beaumont led them toward a line of hackneys. He raised his hand to signal one.

"I am certainly glad we don't have such creatures in England," Lady Ravensgate said. "They might eat half of us for breakfast and the other half of the population for lunch."

"I believe they are herbivores, my lady," Beaumont said, steering them around a group of passersby and toward the waiting hackney.

"That sounds even more terrifying!"

Collette smiled, looking down to hide the expression. When she looked back up, a scream lodged in her throat. The three of them had been forced very near the street because of the people passing them on their way to the museum. And on the street, headed straight for them, was a large cart, the sort used to move heavy items, and it careened toward them at breakneck pace. It seemed something had spooked the team pulling it because the horses were wild eyed and out of control. The driver half stood, whip in hand, hollering at the top of his lungs, but the horses paid no attention. They headed straight for the walkway. Straight for Collette, who had been walking on Beaumont's other side, closest to the street.

She barely had a moment to react, and her reaction was quite ridiculous. She stopped, crouched, and covered her head. She knew the defensive posture was ridiculous, but she couldn't seem to summon the will to run, which would have been smarter, although probably just as useless. Collette closed her eyes and said a prayer, waiting for the bone-jarring impact of the carriage on her person.

Instead, she felt strong arms lift her by the waist and drag her away. Then she was falling, something heavy falling beside her.

When she opened her eyes, she realized she must have been killed. The most beautiful man was looking down at her, his violet eyes only inches from hers. And he spoke, but she couldn't hear him over the high-pitched ringing in her ears. The sunlight lit him from behind. He looked over his shoulder and more people gathered, blocking out the light.

People. Not angels.

This was not heaven but London, and the angel had been Rafe Beaumont.

She tried to speak, but her lungs burned and she could not find her voice.

"Just lie still, Miss Fournay," Beaumont said. She could hear him, hear everything around her, the sound returning slowly like each piece of an orchestra added one after another.

"You've had quite a scare," he said.

She nodded, still unable to speak. Then she remembered Lady Ravensgate and looked about frantically for the woman. Though Collette did not particularly like her sponsor, she needed the woman to stay in contact with the royalists who had her father.

"She is fine," Beaumont said, seeming to read her thoughts. "I shoved her aside and then went back for you. I think she may have hurt her ankle. A woman and a man who claims to be a physician are with her. Are you hurt anywhere?"

She didn't know. She couldn't feel her body.

"Just stay still, then. I will take you home and see to everything. If you'll excuse me for one moment."

"No!" She grabbed his hand, holding on tightly so he could not move away. Her voice sounded strained, as though she had pushed it through a tight opening. "Stay with me."

"I won't leave you, sweetheart." He touched her cheek with one gloved hand. "But I must see to Lady Ravensgate. I promise I will be right back."

Collette knew she should release his hand, but she could not seem to manage to uncurl her fingers.

"I won't leave you," he said. "I won't ever leave you. Do you believe me?"

She did. His eyes, his beautiful eyes, were so sincere. Though it terrified her, she let him go. As soon as he moved away, feeling seemed to come back to her body. Everything hurt. Her back, her arms, her head. She had fallen hard, and though she didn't think anything was broken, every bit of her felt battered and bruised. She closed her eyes against the sting of tears. She could hear the people around her whispering and murmuring about her. How she wanted to move away, to have her privacy back. The whispers and the crowds looking at her reminded her too much of Paris. But then the crowds had not murmured with sympathy. They'd whispered out of fear.

She felt a cool hand on her cheek and opened her eyes again. Beaumont was there, his bare hand on her skin. "Can you stand, sweetheart?"

"Yes," she whispered. She tried to rise, to make her body do as she commanded, but when she lifted her head, the world spun. "Give me a moment," she said, putting her fingers to her temple.

"Don't move," Beaumont said. "I have you."

Collette tried to protest when he lifted her into his arms. She did not need to be carried, especially not in front of the prying eyes, but there was no point in arguing. He was already carrying her and doing so with very little effort. He seemed to behave as though she weighed nothing, carrying her as one might carry an infant.

And there was another reason she did not object. She liked being in his arms. The scent of him—spices and musk—tickled her nose. She leaned her head against his strong shoulder and breathed him in. His arms tightened around her, strong arms, powerful arms that cradled her against a muscled chest. For all his appearances, this was not a man given to idleness. She wondered if he would look like the men the Greeks had sculpted. If his legs would be as shapely, his torso as defined, his buttocks as round. And then because the very thought of him naked made her blush, she closed her eyes again.

He carried her into the hackney. When the door closed and Beaumont called out the direction, she opened her eyes again. He hadn't set her down, and she found herself on his lap, her arms around his neck. Across from them, the seat was empty.

"Lady Ravensgate!"

"I sent her with the physician and his wife. They had a private carriage, and I thought she would be more comfortable."

"I see. That was thoughtful of you." Except that it

left the two of them alone. And he was still holding her, his arms around her in a way not permitted before marriage. "But we have no chaperone."

He quirked a brow. "Do you think I will suddenly turn into a beast and ravish you? I thought we were friends."

"You're right." He still thought of her as a friend. Holding her meant nothing to him. But what she felt in his arms was decidedly more than friendship. "I think you should put me down."

"If you like. Are you feeling steadier?"

She nodded and he slid her off his lap and onto the seat beside him. But he did not move across the conveyance to take the seat opposite. Instead, he stayed beside her, his body warm and strong.

"Are you concerned about your reputation?" he asked. "There really did not seem another way to escort you home. Lady Ravensgate was laid across one seat and the physician and his wife took the other."

"I suppose it is fine. No one could be compromised in one short carriage ride."

He gave her a slow smile but didn't speak. Still, she understood his meaning well enough. A short carriage ride was plenty of time to compromise a woman. Wonderful. The last thing she needed was to be ruined and shunned from any remaining social events where she might learn information that would save her father. "I don't care if I am whispered about," she said. And she didn't. At this point, all she cared about was rescuing her father. "I am just grateful to be away from all of the people staring at me."

"You are shy?" he asked.

"I don't like to be stared at. I've had enough of that for one lifetime."

"When were you stared at before?"

"In Paris, whenever my father and I would go out, people would stare at us from windows and shops. But when we'd turn to meet their gazes, they would look away."

"Why is that?" he asked almost casually.

"Because my father…" She trailed off. She was hurt and emotional. But she could not slip now and reveal who her father really was, even if it was unlikely a man such as Beaumont would know of him.

"It's not important," she said quickly. "That is over."

"And I promise you this day will be but a bad memory soon enough. And I swear if there is any talk of you being ruined, I will challenge the liar to a duel."

Collette had thought the typical response was to marry the ruined woman, but she could not see Rafe Beaumont as a husband. "What if the gossip originates from a woman?"

He shrugged. "Then I will let her shoot me. It's the only chivalrous thing to do."

She couldn't help but giggle. Collette looked out the window and there was Lady Ravensgate's town house. The physician's carriage was already in front of it. Beaumont helped her out of the hackney, paid the driver, and took her arm on the walk. The more she moved around, the better she felt. Nothing was broken or even strained, but she surmised she'd be a little stiff in the morning. Evans opened the door before they reached it and pointed to the stairs. "They've taken her ladyship to her bedchamber."

"Shall I go up and see her?"

"The physician is with her, Miss Fournay. It might be better to wait until he gives instructions."

"And his wife?" Collette asked.

"She is assisting the gentleman."

Collette looked at Beaumont. "Shall we wait in the parlor?"

She could have kissed him. Now would have been the perfect time for him to slip away, but he kept his promise. He did not leave her alone.

"Evans, will you send the tea tray? Miss Fournay has had quite a scare and could use a bit of fortification, I think."

"Yes, sir." The butler departed, and Collette sank into a chair. Hysteria churned within her. She had almost died, almost been killed today. Beaumont had saved her life. If he had acted even one second slower, she would have been dead. But she couldn't think of that. She couldn't allow what-ifs to enter her mind or she'd dissolve into a crying fit right here and now.

"You look a bit shaky, Miss Fournay," Beaumont said. "I say we add brandy to the tea. Does Lady Ravensgate keep any in here?"

"As far as I know, she has none in the house at all. She drinks only wine and then only claret."

"That is a travesty. Claret won't keep you from falling apart." He sat beside her on the couch. "How are you holding up?"

"I'm fine." But the hand she lifted to smooth her hair back shook.

He caught it and held it firmly, linking her icy fingers with his warm ones. She was suddenly very, very cold. "Stay with me, Miss Fournay," he said. "Take deep breaths."

She nodded, her throat too choked for her to be able to speak.

"Are you certain there's no brandy?"

She nodded again.

He shrugged. "Then I suppose there's nothing else for it. I'll have to kiss you."

The look she gave him was half fear, half longing. He had been teasing, for the most part, but he could admit that if he hadn't seen the fear, he might have taken her mouth right then. He certainly wanted to kiss her enough. He'd wanted to kiss her since he'd first stepped into Lady Ravensgate's residence and Miss Fournay had been standing there in her proper white dress and stiff straw hat tied under her chin with prim blue ribbons.

Now, he held up both hands as though he meant no harm. "I was not serious. As your friend, I admit to worrying about you. You are so pale and shaky." And he had only himself to blame for that. What the devil had he been thinking? Why had he agreed to Jasper's scheme? Even knowing the driver of the cart had been paid to miss the lady, Rafe's heart had jumped into his throat when he saw it bearing down on her. He'd saved her, as they'd planned, but if anything had gone wrong, she might have been seriously injured or killed.

Lady Ravensgate was fine. He'd shoved her out of the way, and she'd fallen on a soft patch of grass. Rafe was sorry she'd twisted her ankle, but if the Foreign

Office had the right of it, the woman was a traitor and deserved far worse.

That meant Miss Fournay—rather, Fortier—was a traitor too. Rafe wasn't quite so resigned to her inevitable fate.

"I only need a few minutes to gather my wits," she said. "The tea will help."

Brandy would have helped more, but he'd have to make do without it. He'd also have to make do without taking her into his arms. He had a mission, an assignment, and he could not afford to fail. His replacement might not be so civilized.

"I daresay it will. I could use some myself. I've seen carriage strikes from time to time, but the cart seemed to come straight for us."

"What happened to the driver?"

"The bastard, forgive me, didn't even stop. If I ever find him, he'll be sorry. He must have been drunk or…" He paused, as though something had just occurred to him. "There isn't any reason to think the man was heading for you, is there? There's no one who would want you dead?"

Her face paled further, and Rafe had to keep his expression from changing to reflect the rush of disappointment he felt inside followed by the surge of fear for her. The woman had something to hide, something worth killing for, and Rafe wished to God that, for once, the Foreign Office and Draven had been wrong.

"Did I say something to upset you?" he asked.

"No." She smoothed her hair back. Her hat had long since fallen from her head and dangled by the ribbons about her neck. Her hands shook violently as she reached for the ribbon to release the hat. But the silky blue trimming had knotted, and her hands were shaking too badly to grasp it, much less untangle it.

"Allow me," he said. Before she could object, he took the flimsy ties in his hands and began to work on the knot. He could feel her trembling. Her body quaking under his hands. Her pulse beat against his knuckles, which lightly brushed her throat. Her skin was soft and warm, lush and ripe beneath the starched muslin of her dress. But he could not afford to think of that.

"The majority of snorting during hedgehog courtship originates from the sow."

Rafe paused in his efforts. She must have been anxious if she was referring to hedgehogs again. "And the male? He is silent?"

She nodded. "For the most part, the boar does not snort, although there have been reports of boars snorting."

"I can well imagine." He freed one of the knots. "Can you think of any reason someone would want to kill you?" he asked casually, starting on the next knot in the ribbons.

"No!" But the answer was too hasty, too vehement to be believed.

"Good." He loosened the other knot and lifted the hat away, placing it on the table beside the couch they occupied. "I wouldn't want you to be in any danger."

She bit her lip, looked at him, then looked away.

*Come on*, he thought. *Tell me. Trust me.*

"I can't think of a single reason," she finally answered,

firmly though not convincingly. "It was an accident, nothing more."

Evans entered with the tea tray, and Rafe served, noting she had to set her cup on the table since it shook so much. "Do try and drink," he told her.

"I think I might feel better if I lie down."

That was his dismissal. Rafe didn't like it, but he didn't have much choice. He took his leave and walked straight to his club.

After greeting Porter, Rafe ascertained that Phineas and Stratford were playing billiards while Neil was alone in the reading room. Since Jasper was not at the club and Rafe had no idea how to find the man, he headed to the reading room to join Neil. He needed to think and might have gone to one of the empty chambers, but he didn't particularly enjoy being alone.

He entered the small chamber, which was paneled in dark wood with high-backed chairs flanking a crackling fire. He sat in a chair beside Neil, who briefly glanced up at him from some papers. Rafe didn't bother to engage his friend in conversation. He stared into the fire and tried to scheme, a skill he lacked for the most part.

Finally, Neil lowered the paper. "I can hear you thinking. Stop before you hurt yourself."

"Don't you have a dozen orphans to harass?"

"Yes, but they aren't as much fun to goad as you. In any case, Lady Juliana took them to the park today. Something about taking advantage of the sun or some such nonsense, and as I had business to attend to, I could not accompany her."

"Business?"

"That's right, and if you ever tell her any differently, I will shave your head and your eyebrows. Ewan will hold you down while I do it."

The thought of himself bald made Rafe shiver. "Your secret is safe with me." He went back to staring into the fire. Neil lifted his paper again. Rafe sighed and tapped his fingers on his chair. Finally, Neil tossed the paper down.

"Out with it."

"I didn't say—"

"Just say it already. I don't have much time left, and the sooner I am rid of you, the sooner peace and quiet is restored."

"Do you remember the French soldier we followed in Portugal? The courier?"

"Unfortunately." It had been unfortunate for the courier as he'd ended up dead. But such was war.

"We followed him for half a day, and then when he made camp and fell asleep, Aidan relieved him of his courier's bag."

"We wanted to see the dispatches he carried."

"It was cold and rainy," Beaumont said.

"I recall because you complained without ceasing. Jasper was this close to *accidentally* shooting you in the foot so you'd really have something to complain about."

"Very amusing."

Neil's face didn't change expression, and Rafe wondered if perhaps he wasn't kidding. "In any case," he continued, "the weather distracted me somewhat. Seems like Aidan returned the bag, and we sent the courier on his way, waited for him, and then…" He drew a finger across his neck. "Why didn't we just kill him after we'd stolen the contents of his satchel?"

"Who is this *we*?"

"Fine. Why didn't *you* three kill him after you rifled his satchel?"

"Because then he wouldn't have been able to deliver the false documents."

Rafe nodded. "I remember something about that. You took the real papers he'd been carrying and replaced them with false ones."

"Exactly. We carried the real ones, orders from Jourdan himself, back to Draven and Wellington."

Rafe remembered gathering intelligence about Jourdan, who had been one of Napoleon's most trusted and skilled military advisers. "And the false ones gave incorrect orders to the French."

"They were to rendezvous with the core of the army, but we sent them in the other direction. A small thing, but by the time their general realized his mistake, he was too late to be of any service in the intervening battle. And that's how wars are won."

Rafe smiled and rose. Perhaps he was not so lacking in the ability to scheme after all.

"Now what are you doing?" Neil asked.

Rafe looked back over his shoulder. He had risen and was already halfway across the room. "I have a war to win."

"This is a first."

"Let's hope it's the last."

# *Eight*

COLLETTE WAS PANICKING. SHE'D BEEN TO EVERY salon, musicale, and fete Lady Ravensgate could wheedle invitations to, and still she had not been able to ascertain whether Draven had the codes and, if so, where they were kept. Although Lady Ravensgate's ankle was still swollen, Collette had dragged the lady to this garden party today because it was her last hope. Draven had been invited and the hostess had intimated he would attend. But she hadn't seen him yet, which meant the garden party was turning out to be as useless as the other social events she'd attended. The upper classes were ensconced at their country houses this time of year, and the clerks and assistants who might have known juicy tidbits were not invited to the same events as Lady Ravensgate. The only gossip Collette collected concerned the newest hairstyles and speculation about waistlines lowering next Season.

She wanted to cry and scream and rage at God at the injustice of it all. Instead, she pasted a serene expression on her face and pretended to admire the flowers and shrubs artfully arranged in the garden of the Mayfair mansion. It was often difficult to distinguish which were the more colorful—the blooms or the ladies' dresses. The women strolled in their colorful muslins, twirling delicate parasols and fluttering painted fans. They were like chattering birds who made much noise and all of it signifying nothing.

Collette stayed as long as she could tolerate the scene, then angled herself away from the ladies and the refreshments. When she'd wandered far enough from the main party so as not to be noticed, she slipped behind a section of shrubbery and closed her eyes, squeezing back tears. Then, taking a shaky breath, she dabbed at her eyes with her handkerchief. She could not cry. She would not give anyone the satisfaction of seeing poor Miss Fournay weeping. It was bad enough she had a reputation for being painfully shy, a necessary thing and easy enough because she was naturally reticent, but she did not relish these Brits cooing over her and pitying her.

"I had hoped you would have the color back in your cheeks the next time I saw you" came a familiar voice. Collette opened her eyes, knowing she would see Rafe Beaumont. She was not disappointed, and he looked as handsome as ever in riding boots, tight breeches, and a close-fitting coat. He doffed his hat, revealing hair tousled and curling slightly beneath. His jaw had been freshly shaven again, and she found she missed the habitual stubble he wore. His eyes were the same mesmerizing shade of violet.

"I am feeling much better," she said. "I just needed a moment. It has been a long day."

"It has been a long week," he said. "I called on you, but you weren't at home."

"I had shopping to do."

He gave her a look that said he knew she was lying. Knew she had been avoiding him.

"You were too occupied to reply to my notes?"

"You must forgive me for that," she said. "I have never been a very good correspondent."

"I see. I feared our friendship was at an end. Are we still friends, Miss Fournay?"

She didn't know how to answer. After that day at the museum, she'd needed to distance herself from him. Her already-confusing feelings for him had grown stronger. He had saved her life, after all. How was she not to feel grateful? And if gratitude had been all she'd felt, she would not have worried so much. But she was even more attracted to him than she had been. When he'd teased her about kissing her, she had wanted to say yes. She had practically begged him to do it.

He was a weakness, and she couldn't afford a weakness right now. There were other ways to discover information about Draven. There had to be.

"Of course we are friends," she said with a smile.

"I am glad to hear it. May I escort you back to the party?"

"Thank you." She took his proffered arm.

"How is Lady Ravensgate? Has she recovered from her fall?" He led her past the shrubs and strolled slowly past the late-season flowers.

"Quite well, yes. She still favors that ankle and must elevate it, but it is growing stronger every day. You will see she is seated on a longue with her foot on a pillow. I fear she rather enjoys the attention and pretending she is a queen on her throne."

He chuckled. "And how are you? Fully recovered?"

"I was not injured."

"Yes, but you suffered a terrible scare…" His words trailed off as a servant in gold livery approached, carrying a silver salver. Instead of cups of tea or glasses of lemonade, the tray held a white envelope. "What is this?" Beaumont asked.

"Miss Fournay?" the footman asked.

"Yes," she answered, her heart beginning to thud painfully in her chest. "What is it? Has Lady Ravensgate taken ill?"

"No, miss. This letter arrived for you. The boy who brought it said it was urgent."

She took it off the tray, her gaze touching on Lady Ravensgate near the refreshment table, still reclining on her longue.

"Thank you," she said, transferring her attention to the envelope. Then she looked at Beaumont, who appeared only mildly interested.

"My throat is parched. Would you like lemonade?" he asked.

"I…" She looked down at the note again.

He understood immediately. "You want to read your letter. Of course, you do. Shall I show you somewhere you won't be disturbed? There's a small gazebo just through those hedges. Shall I take you?"

"Please." As usual, she was grateful to him. He led her through an opening in the hedges and along a worn path toward a small stone gazebo. The structure was covered with vines, some of them flowering, and inside were two stone benches. He led her into the center, seated her on a bench, and stepped away.

"I'll wait over there for you," he said. "That way you will have privacy."

"You needn't wait. I can find my way back."

Horror crossed his face. "I would never leave a lady unaccompanied in the wilderness. I'll be just over there should you need me."

He strolled away and made a show of turning his back to her and studying a small tree. This was hardly wilderness, but Collette was glad he had not left her alone. It was late afternoon and the party would end shortly. Already the air had grown cooler and the sun was low in the sky, the last rays filtering through persistent clouds.

She opened the letter in her hands and read.

At first the words were incomprehensible to her. She had to read them three times before her terrified mind could take it in. The letter was ambiguous and mentioned her friend and an unfortunate change in his condition. But she understood well enough.

Her father. He was ill. He'd become sick while in prison and his condition was steadily worsening. The warden of the prison—he must have been the author—wanted to hear from her as soon as possible. She could only imagine that was because her father needed a nurse or the warden wanted her to send funds for medicine.

Send funds! Ha! The man would probably use them to line his own pockets and leave her father to shiver without so much as a blanket or straw pallet. She needed to free her father from the prison. She knew the men who could do it. They had promised her they would release him if she gave them the codes.

Her hands shook, rattling the paper violently. She had nothing.

Her father would die in prison, and she would be all alone in the world.

She rose quickly, stumbled over the hem of her dress, and barely caught herself. She had to go, had to do something, had to find those codes! Even if it meant breaking into the Foreign Office tonight. She stumbled out of the gazebo, and Mr. Beaumont turned to face her, the smile on his face fading. "What is the matter?"

"Nothing," she answered hastily. Even she knew she was unconvincing.

"Something has happened. You look as pale as a sheet." He caught her arm, and she was grateful for the feel of his warm hand on her. She shivered with cold. "Was it something in the letter?" Beaumont asked. "Please, sit down." He led her back to the gazebo. "You look unsteady, and if I catch you when you swoon, it will give the other ladies ideas. I simply can't go through another month of having women fall over every time they see me."

She didn't know if his words had been intended to distract her, to add levity to what he must see was a distressing moment, but she couldn't help but give him a wobbly smile when she pictured hordes of women swooning whenever he walked by, in the hopes he might catch them.

"You have a hard life, Mr. Beaumont."

He seated her on the cold stone bench. "Some days I wonder how I manage to crawl out of bed." He winked. "Of course, it's not usually my own bed."

"You're terrible."

"I am. Tell me, what has you so shaken?"

She crumpled the letter in her hand. "I cannot."

"If you can't say it, give it to me. I'll read it and—"

"No!" She clutched the letter close to her chest. "You cannot read it. You cannot help me."

He sat down beside her, his thigh brushing hers. His violet eyes met hers. "You would be surprised what I can do." The way he looked at her, the way he sounded…she almost believed him. She wanted to believe him. She couldn't do this alone anymore. She didn't even know how to proceed. Lady Ravensgate was not her friend. She worked with the enemy. Perhaps they had threatened her or perhaps she was sympathetic to the Bourbon cause. Whatever the reason, Collette could not trust her with this. She strongly suspected Lady Ravensgate had orders to slit her throat if Collette failed in her mission.

"Let me help you," Beaumont said.

Collette's hand loosened on the letter.

"Have I given you any reason not to trust me?"

"You fought in the war against Napoleon."

"That's right. And I was decorated too. A hero." He shrugged, his expression sheepish, as though he did not like to admit he had ever done anything selfless. "Whatever this is, it pales in comparison with the missions I was given and successfully completed."

A tiny spark of hope flared in her. Could he really help her? Could she risk her life and her father's by placing them in his hands? "But your loyalties." He was a soldier, the son of an earl, and had served under Draven. Who was to say he wouldn't take what he learned straight to the king and the government?

"My loyalties are to England," Beaumont said carefully. "But I don't see the world in black and white. I would never betray a friend."

Collette looked at the letter in her hand and then at Beaumont. She didn't have to confide in him, and she didn't have to trust him. It was a risk either way. Her father would die in a Bourbon prison or she would be hanged by the British government. But maybe, just maybe, if she confessed to Beaumont, she and her father would live.

She put her hand in his, then pulled it away, leaving the letter on his palm. He stared at her, then opened the letter and read. He looked up at her, then read again. "Does this say what I think it says?"

"That I am the daughter of Napoleon's notorious assassin Fortier?"

"Yes. And does the prison warden's request for money for this sick friend of yours and your presence here mean what I think it means?"

"That I am in England spying? Is that what you believe it implies?"

"More or less."

"Then yes."

He took a breath and looked into the distance, where the dying light cut through the foliage, making strange but wonderful patterns on the grass. "This puts us in a precarious position."

"Us?"

"If I'm to help you, yes. Us."

She clutched his hands, her heart suddenly a thousand pounds lighter. "Then you will help me? You won't turn me in?"

"I'll help you."

She narrowed her eyes. She knew that pause, knew a condition was coming. "If?"

"If you tell me everything."

Now it was her turn to pause. If she told him everything, she would doom herself if he decided to turn on her. But what other choice did she have? She had to trust him. She had to believe he truly was a hero.

"It started during the revolution," she said. "Or so I'm told. I was too young to remember or to know what was happening."

Beaumont lifted a finger and placed it delicately over her lips. She blinked at him in surprise. "Not here. Not now. Your...guardian will be looking for you, and there are too many people nearby who might overhear."

"Then when?" she whispered.

"I'll come for you tonight."

"How? Lady Ravensgate won't let us be alone together."

"What time does she retire?"

"If we are at home, she goes to her bedchamber at ten or eleven."

"Then wait for me in the garden at midnight."

"How shall I manage to sneak out to the garden without being seen?"

He grinned at her. "You're a spy, Mademoiselle Fortier. Figure it out."

❧

Rafe had spent many hours waiting for rendezvous with women. At one point, years ago, he'd added up all of the hours he could remember, and it had amounted to several days. So it came as a surprise to him that his gut clenched and his throat was dry while he waited for Collette Fortier. This should have been rote and tedious. Instead, he felt like a giddy lad of sixteen.

This wasn't about bedsport. He knew that. This was a mission. This was the sovereignty of his country. This was his plan coming to fruition. He had lured Fortier's daughter without touching her, kissing her, or whispering nonsense into her ear. He wouldn't need do any of that tonight.

But he wanted to.

He'd have her all alone, and God help him, he wanted to touch her and kiss her and whisper words that would make her blush. He wanted to do things to her that would make her cheeks pink with mortification and pleasure. After the war, he'd been so weary of seduction. He'd come home and never wanted to see another woman again.

That wasn't quite true. He didn't mind seeing them. He just didn't want the effort of interacting with them for any length of time. Rafe found that women always tended to want more than he could give, and when he considered giving more, he worried what would happen when the woman grew tired of him. Then his chest would tighten and his stomach roiled. He'd end the relationship before the woman could leave him.

Rafe had begun to doubt whether he would ever meet any woman who managed to secure his notice for more than an evening.

But he'd been wrong. Collette Fortier had caught it

and kept it. She might have caught it with her beauty alone—the lush body, the pretty blushes, the tantalizing smiles. But she'd kept his attention because, unlike other women, she presented a challenge. She didn't flutter her lashes. She didn't compliment him. He sometimes wondered if she even found him attractive. She was clever enough to pass through society without ever causing even so much as a whisper that she was a French spy. And she was skilled enough to manage Lady Ravensgate, the men she spied for, and, apparently, him. And now she'd put her trust in him, and that was the most seductive quality of all.

As he watched, the servants' door to the garden opened, and a figure in a dark cape emerged. The hood of the cape was up, and Rafe did not immediately step out of his hiding place in the shadows of a large tree. He wanted to be certain before he moved. The figure looked this way and that and then hissed out a few words. "Mr. Beaumont?"

He stepped forward, letting her see him before he stepped back again. Making barely a sound, she crossed the distance between them and joined him behind the tree.

"I was afraid you would not come." Her voice was breathless, leading him to wonder what she might sound like in the throes of passion.

"As you see, your fears were unfounded. You must come with me."

"What?" She tensed. They were standing so close he could feel her body go rigid.

"We can't talk here. It's cold and I don't relish standing outside all night. I'll take you home with me."

"I can't go home with you!"

He chuckled. "Still worried about your reputation? I would have thought that was the furthest thing from your mind tonight. I promise not to ravish you. I may, however, give you a glass of wine and fruit and cheese. I'll wager you didn't manage to eat anything tonight."

Her silence spoke for itself.

"There will be a fire. And privacy. I've dismissed my staff. We'll be all alone."

"That doesn't reassure me."

"It shouldn't, but I give you my word I will not take advantage of you."

She let out a sigh of relief.

"Unless you want me to."

"I won't."

Oh, didn't she know it was dangerous to give him a challenge?

He led her to the hackney he'd paid to wait at the corner a block away and climbed into the carriage behind her. She'd raised her hood again, and Rafe had donned a hat and kept his face down. If someone had been watching them, they might have been able to deduce their identities, but no one passing by would know who they were.

They sat in silence during the short ride to St. James's Square, and then Rafe knocked on the roof and the jarvey pulled to the side of the street. Rafe paid him and took her arm, leading her into his building, up the stairs, and into his flat. He'd asked his valet to stay until midnight, sweeping away any women who might stalk him, and he was pleased to find the building quiet and his path to the flat uninterrupted. Inside, all was as he'd ordered. The fire roared in the hearth. In the front room, grapes and cheese had been set on a platter with a bottle of wine beside them. The atmosphere was cozy and quiet, just as he'd wanted it.

He locked the door behind her, then held out a hand for her cape. "Oh. You needn't—"

He waved his fingers impatiently. He was not about to allow her to wear her cape all evening. Finally, she untied the ribbons and slid it from her shoulders. Beneath, she wore a deep-red dress with a tightly fitted bodice and sleeves. No wonder she'd wanted to keep the cape on. Rafe had to swallow at the sight of all the creamy flesh on display. But he forced himself to hang her cape on the rack and to remove his own greatcoat and do the same. His eyes, disobedient as they were, attempted to stray back to the half-moons of her plump breasts, but he resisted. It took damn near all the willpower he possessed to resist, but he did it. He'd faced more difficult assignments.

"I know this is a ball gown," she said. "It's the darkest color I have and doesn't have any ornamentation that would catch the light. I didn't want anyone to see me."

"Wise choice." He led her to the couch beside the tray of food and poured her a glass of wine. Ordinarily he would have wondered at such a plain ball gown, but not when he saw it on her. She didn't need any ornamentation. Her body was ornament enough to attract the eye.

After handing her the wine, he poured himself a glass, then sat in the chair beside her. He plucked a green grape from the tray and slid it between his teeth. He watched as her eyes widened slightly. "Isn't this more civilized than the back of the garden?"

"Yes." She sipped her wine, downing half of it before she realized and lowered it from her lips. Red lips, like the gown. But he couldn't focus on those right now. He had to remember his purpose.

"We're here so I can help you," he said. "But I can't help you if you don't confide in me."

"And you'll forgive me if I want some assurances before I confide at all."

Now this was an interesting twist. She'd obviously been thinking since the garden party this afternoon. She wanted assurances. He liked the way her shoulders straightened, the way she lifted her chin. It reminded him of that strong woman he'd seen in his box at Drury Lane.

"Of course. Name them."

"What I tell you tonight remains between the two of us. You must swear to tell no one."

He sipped his wine. It was sweet and cold and tingled on the tongue. "You know I can't promise that. But"—he held up a hand—"I will promise that I will only reveal our discussions if I feel I have no other option. For example, if the sovereignty of the country is at stake or if a man's or woman's life is in jeopardy."

She sipped her wine again, the line between her eyes deepening.

"That's the best I can give you on that account. What other assurances do you want?"

"That you won't use this information against me."

"Against you? I said I was here to help." But then

he caught the flush on her face and understood what she was not saying. "Oh, I see. You think I might blackmail you. I might force you to sleep with me so I will keep my silence."

"I didn't say that."

Rafe plucked the empty glass from her fingers. "Collette— May I call you Collette?"

"I suppose there's no point in remaining formal."

"Collette, I can promise you that if I wanted you in my bed, I would not need to blackmail you to get you there. You'd go quite willingly."

Now her flush deepened. Rafe gave her a few minutes to recover while he refilled her glass and selected fruit and cheese for her. "You had better eat something or this wine will go straight to your head."

She took the plate he offered, ate a grape, and then sipped her wine. "This is excellent wine."

He smiled. "It's French."

❧

She took another sip, hoping the wine would slake her thirst. Her throat was so dry and her tongue felt too big for her mouth. He sat across from her, in his well-appointed flat with its plush carpets and soft furnishings and a blazing fire. The room would have been perfectly comfortable if Beaumont hadn't been occupying it. Nothing about him made her comfortable. He seemed to fit among the lushness of this flat and among the glittering *ton*. She didn't belong in his world, and she would have to confess exactly how little she belonged in another moment.

He was a patient man. He didn't rush her. He

merely sipped his wine and watched her. He didn't gulp the crisp liquid down. He savored it. He savored the grapes as well, placing one between his lips and drawing it slowly into his mouth. Collette could not decide if he was effortlessly seductive or if he was trying to make her blush, trying to steer her thoughts to…places she could not allow herself to go.

Finally, she took a breath. She'd held off long enough. She would tell him of her dilemma because she had no other choice and because she needed help. She was fully aware she might be making the biggest mistake of her life. If that was the case, then she would make it boldly and suffer the consequences.

"As I said before, it began during the revolution. I was born in the midst of that bloody time, just as the Reign of Terror gripped the country. My father had been a blacksmith. I know that word conjures images of sweaty men with bare, dirty arms, but my father created masterpieces for the upper classes. When the revolution came, he was suspect because of his close ties with the *ancien régime*. Fortunately, or perhaps not so fortunately, Robespierre liked my father's work. He hired him to create beautiful pieces for the revolutionary government.

"I remember some of those pieces. I remember watching him create them and marveling at how talented my papa was. He was strong and kind, and I knew he loved us. Some weeks, he worked so long and so hard I would not see him for days. And when he finally emerged from the forge, he would bring me some beautiful creation, a butterfly or a metal flower. He was a good man, a loving man."

Beaumont had set down his glass, his violet eyes focused on her, but she could see he struggled to hold back questions.

"And you are wondering how a blacksmith became an assassin for Napoleon."

That was how everyone saw her father. No one knew him like she did—the loving father who told her stories and who listened to her as though she were the most interesting person in the world. He'd sat up with her when she was ill. He'd played games with her when she was lonely. He'd taught her to read and climb trees and spot the constellations. There was not a better father in all the world.

Rafe sat back. "I am prepared to let you tell the story as you like. But I spent years on the Continent, and much of that time was in France, even in Paris. I know who your father is and what he did."

She nodded, then sipped her wine again. "You're not wrong about him. I am not here to argue that he was not an assassin, but I want you to understand my father was not only an assassin. He was a man, a husband, and a father. He loved us and he would have done anything for us." Her voice broke as she said it because she wished she could have one of those days back again. Just one. One last chance to bask in the love of her mother and the pride of her father.

"And then Robespierre went to the guillotine. Again, I was too young to remember any of that, but the loss of Robespierre was devastating for our family. My father no longer had a benefactor, and because he was once again associated with the enemy of the people, our family was under suspicion again.

My father still had loyal customers, but his business dwindled to a mere trickle. I often went to bed hungry, and I suspect if I was hungry, my mother and father ate nothing."

Collette closed her eyes, remembering the gnawing in her belly as she'd lain in her small bed, the soft blankets tucked securely around her. She hadn't really been scared, hadn't understood that hunger meant poverty and poverty could mean death, until death came for her mother.

"My mother became ill," she said, keeping her voice steady and unemotional. "I don't know what was wrong with her. No one ever told me, but the medicines she needed were very expensive. My aunt came to stay with us, to care for me and my mother, and I remember hearing her berate my father for failing to provide for his family. The next day, my father left early in the morning and did not return until late. I saw him across the breakfast table the next morning, and at first, I was so giddy at the sight of bread and porridge that I did not notice." She paused so long Beaumont leaned forward.

"Notice what?"

"The change in him." She swallowed the lump in her throat. "The emptiness in his eyes and the haunted look on his face. Later, I would think of that morning and know that the night before was when he'd sold his soul to the devil. I don't know any details, and my father would never speak of it, but he was a large man, a strong man. He went to those in power and asked for a job, any job. I suspect they had him do away with their political enemies."

"Everyone says he was one of the best," Beaumont said softly. "You must know that."

She lifted her wineglass and watched the light filter through the golden liquid. "No one ever said it to my face, but I heard whispers. My mother and aunt sheltered me from much of it, but when my mother died, there was no one to protect me. My father kept me safe, of course. He fed me and provided shelter for me. In fact, we moved to a better house in Paris. We left the forge behind and moved into a fancy flat, much like this one. My father often worked at night, and I was alone much of the time. I didn't have any friends. Everyone was afraid of me—not me, of course, but my father. Even then, I didn't fully understand. I knew my father had a position in the new government, the one under Napoleon Bonaparte. I knew he was an important man and he did not talk about his work. But then I met Marcel."

Beaumont's eyebrows lifted. "Marcel? I don't like him already."

She smiled. "I did. I liked him too much. Remember, I was all alone. I was desperately lonely. What little education I had I'd gathered from books and my mother's teaching. But now that my father had funds, he hired me a tutor to teach me the classics as well as music and drawing. Marcel was quiet and shy, like me. I don't think he took the position with the intention of seducing me, and I don't think I can even argue that I was seduced. But I was young and he was young, and my lessons gradually turned into something less innocent."

Beaumont nodded, and though she hadn't expected to see censure in his eyes, it still relieved her to find it absent. She had made a mistake and knew that it was one that could never be put right. She'd been ruined, not publicly, but ruined nonetheless. She was not the sort of woman any man would ever want for a wife. The most she could hope for was to be some man's mistress, and she had too much pride in herself to settle for that life.

"Your father found out," Beaumont said.

"Of course, but not before Marcel told me what he knew of my father. He said half of Paris didn't consider Fortier real. He was known for his stealth. He could be silent as a ghost and he could slit a man's throat cleanly with a flick of his arm. That was his preferred method of killing, but he would not argue if Napoleon wanted a man strangled or shot. My father always got his man. Always."

"He did have that reputation," Beaumont said, placing his empty wineglass on the table. "We all made sure to steer clear of him when we were in Paris."

"I didn't believe Marcel at first. The way he described my father was not the way I knew him. He was always gentle and kind to me and to my mother. I never saw him raise a hand in violence to anyone. He rarely even raised his voice. But when I confronted my father, he didn't argue." She wiped the moisture from her eyes. "He said, 'So now you know.' And he apologized." She rose and paced the room. "But he didn't need to apologize to me, Mr. Beaumont. Because I knew why he'd done it. He'd done what he had to for the money to save my mother. And then when she was gone, he was in too deep." She stopped before the fire and stared into the dancing flames.

"And what has any of this to do with why you are here now and with the letter? Your father died in the war."

But she simply stared at him and then very slowly shook her head. "No, my father is alive."

# Nine

RAFE'S BLOOD CHILLED. COLLETTE MIGHT HAVE described Fortier in sweet, glowing terms, but the man was a monster. He'd killed dozens, and he'd done his work coldly and expertly. Was the assassin in London? The very thought made Rafe want to peer over his shoulder. Instead, he clamped his hands on the wooden arms of the chair he occupied and took a breath.

He had to question her. He had to find out how everything fit together, how Fortier was involved. The note he'd sent her had been vague enough. He had deduced she had someone to report to and something to lose if she failed. But her reaction had been akin to panic. He thought he might have to send more notes before she confided in him, but whatever she stood to lose terrified her.

And he didn't like seeing her terrified. He didn't like knowing he was the one who'd caused it. "I need more wine." He rose and crossed to the bottle, collecting her glass on the way. "So do you." He poured them both a healthy measure of wine and set the empty bottle down. Returning to his chair, he placed her glass beside her, then sat and drank deeply from his own.

"You are upset," she said.

"Rather more afraid for my life, but I'll set that aside for the moment. Where is your father now?" *Not London. Please, not London.*

"Imprisoned in Paris. He was arrested under orders of the new king."

Rafe let out a breath. "Then he can't kill me tonight."

"He wouldn't kill you anyway. I told you, he is not a violent man. He only killed because it was his job. He didn't take any pleasure in it. He did what was required of him because he didn't have a choice. I even have a letter from your own Foreign Office that says as much—if I could only read it." She waved a hand to dismiss this last statement. "It's not as if an assassin can simply retire and walk away. He knows too much. Napoleon would never have let him live."

"We didn't think Napoleon had let him live. The reports I saw stated that his body had been recovered and he was dead."

"A ruse. One my father and I concocted. Before Bonaparte was sent to Elba, we knew his regime was falling. We orchestrated my father's death and left Paris. We hid in the country, becoming the Fournay family. Although my father had never farmed before, he bought a small plot of land and a cottage and made an effort. So when I told you my father was a farmer, I didn't lie."

Rafe stared at her. "No, you simply left out some important details."

She raised a shoulder, not disputing the statement.

"Then Bonaparte escaped Elba and came back. But my father and I stayed in hiding. Bonaparte had many enemies when he returned. My father could have made a fortune, but he had finally escaped that life and we wanted to live quietly and safely."

"But now you are in London, not living either quietly or safely."

"The Bourbons have been restored to the throne, and though the king seems to want forgiveness and peace, not all of his supporters feel the same. Courtiers who suffered with him while he was in exile, those who watched their ancestral lands stripped from them, who saw their husbands or wives dragged from their beds to be hung from lampposts or sacrificed to Madame Guillotine want blood. And they want power back."

"Secrets are power." No one knew that as well as he did. He had been in the business of collecting secrets throughout the war.

"Yes. They had my father arrested, and when I pled for his release, they sent me here to collect secrets."

"How did they find your father?"

She sighed. "One would think after the turmoil of the revolution that the people would have learned something, but that's not the case. Neighbors still turn on neighbors, and one of ours had grown suspicious and reported us. One of the courtiers who came to investigate remembered seeing my father at Versailles all those years ago. They took him prisoner."

"And they sent you here to spy because he might be recognized, but you are virtually unknown."

"And the warden of the prison has written to say my father is ill. He will die if he's left in that prison.

That's why I need your help. I don't have the information they want. Will you help me?"

"Just one question." Rafe raised a finger, interrupting her. "What happened to our friend Marcel? Did your father…" He drew a finger across his neck.

"When my father discovered the relationship, he discharged Marcel without a reference. As far as I know, Marcel is still alive. He's probably married by now with children. I told you, my father didn't kill for pleasure. You worry about your own throat?"

"We are alone in my flat. I didn't want your father to learn of it and formulate the wrong idea."

"And what is the wrong idea?" she asked.

"That I brought you here to seduce you."

One of her brows lifted. "So the fire, the fruit, the wine—none of that was calculated to seduce me?" She set her wine down and moved closer to him.

"I am your friend. Nothing more."

"And as a friend, will you help me?"

This was the opening he'd been looking for. This was why he'd sent the false note and—if not lured her here—orchestrated this meeting. He'd weaseled his way into her confidence and he would take advantage of that position. Not that he felt smug about it. But he had done worse in service to his country.

"I'll help you." He raised a hand to stave off any exclamation from her. "But I cannot betray my country. What is it the royalists want?"

She glanced down. "Codes," she murmured. "They want the codes to be able to decipher British secret messages."

Rafe shook his head. "You know I cannot give those to you, even if I had access."

She looked up at him. "Your former commanding officer, Lieutenant Colonel Draven, has access."

"And he's a man I would never betray."

She slumped. "Then my father is doomed."

"We will have to think of another way to help you and your father."

"I don't know another way! I have a coded letter in English, which I believe states that my father was forced to work for Napoleon. If I could get my hands on the British codes, I could decipher the message. But even that knowledge would not be enough to exonerate him completely. It might sway the French king toward leniency, but there is no guarantee. I have to hand over those codes to ensure my father's freedom. If I can't steal those codes, I may never see my father again."

Rafe could not feel sympathy for the brutal assassin, but he did feel it for the woman who loved him. But even sympathy would not sway him to deceive Draven or play traitor to his country. "I will think of something. Give me a day. Meet me tomorrow night, and we'll discuss the plan."

"Will you bring me here again?" she asked.

"Not if you object. I don't enjoy standing about in cold gardens in the middle of the night, but it won't be the worst hardship I've had to endure."

She glanced about his flat, her eyes lingering on paintings and a few of the pieces he'd collected—vases, lamps, and other accoutrement. "It's dangerous coming here," she said.

"Because you think I will try to take you to bed?"

"Because I think you won't."

Rafe stared at her. Women did this sometimes. As well as he understood them, at times, they still managed to say something that flummoxed him. "I'm at sea here," he finally admitted. "We are friends, nothing more."

"Correct."

"And when I proposed something more, you were not interested."

"I was interested. I simply did not think becoming your lover a good idea."

"And now it is?"

"Oh, definitely not."

He gave her a long look. "My ship is sinking."

"That's why you're dangerous. Because you make me want what I cannot have."

"Oh, you can have me," he said, rather too quickly. "What I mean is—"

She laughed. "I thought you didn't want me anymore."

Where the devil had she acquired that notion? She was the only woman he *did* want. "How could I not want you? That has never changed. If you want to change your position on the matter…"

"No. I meant only to say you tempt me. Coming here tempts me."

"Good. I like to know I'm not the only one tempted."

She rose, and he did the same. She twined her fingers, looking nervously about.

"What would we do were we hedgehogs, Miss Fortier?"

Her eyes widened. "I don't—"

"Would you approach me? Would I approach you?"

"The, uh, boar pursues the sow, attempting to mount her."

"I see. And what does the sow do?"

"She will persistently reject his advances. A high percentage of observed hedgehog courtships do not result in cop-cop—"

"Copulation?"

She nodded.

"I do wonder what tempts a hedgehog." Before she could answer, he moved closer and placed a finger lightly over her lips. "That was a rhetorical question."

"I wonder what tempts you," she said shyly. "Do I tempt you now?"

Washed in the golden firelight, she was lovelier than words. And Rafe knew a lot of words to describe women. With her glossy hair piled on her head and her cheeks tinged pink by the wine and the flickering fire, she looked young but regal. He dared not allow his gaze to dip lower than her chin. "Immeasurably," he murmured. She stepped closer, and he took her hand. It felt warm and soft in his, and he lifted it to his lips and kissed her knuckles. Then, turning it over, he placed a lingering kiss on her palm. Her dark eyes turned even darker when his mouth skated up her flesh to brush against the skin at the inside of her wrist. She must have dabbed scent here because, above the clean smell of her skin, he also detected the fragrance of juniper.

His mouth explored her sensitive flesh until he found her pulse, which fluttered rapidly. She might have pulled her hand away at any time. He held it with the lightest touch, but when he slid his lips higher to the tender skin at the inside of her elbow, she trembled. Rafe's gaze never left hers when he flicked his tongue out and tasted her flesh.

She inhaled sharply. "You are very good at this, aren't you?" she whispered.

"If my imaginings count, I've had extensive experience touching you."

"Did you ever imagine kissing my lips?"

He grinned. "Once. Or twice."

Her free hand wrapped around his neck, sliding into his hair. He straightened and she pulled him close. When he released her hand to wrap his arms around her, she linked her arms about his neck and looked up at him. Rafe had never wanted to kiss a woman so badly. And he'd never feared doing so before. The last time he'd tried to kiss her, she had pushed him away. What if he kissed her now and frightened her? What if the kiss ruined the friendship, and she wouldn't see him any longer? Draven would kill him, but even worse, Rafe would lose Collette.

"Kiss me," she said when he hesitated.

"Are you certain this is a good idea? I don't generally kiss my friends."

"Surely you can make an exception for me."

"Surely." He bent closer, then pulled back again. "But should I? This might change everything, and I do value our friendship."

"As do I." She pressed closer to him, and the air caught in his lungs when her breasts pushed against his chest.

"Then we stay friends," he said, voice choked.

"Friends who have shared a kiss."

"Yes." He brushed his lips over hers, then jerked back again. "That's actually a new category of friend-ship for me. Should we discuss its parameters before we go on?"

She sighed, sounding suspiciously frustrated. "No. Just kiss me, Rafe." But she didn't wait for him to comply. Instead, she rose on tiptoe and took his mouth with hers. Her lips were soft and gentle but insistent. He couldn't have refrained from kissing her back if he'd wanted. Kissing her was as necessary in that moment as breathing. And when her mouth became more insistent, he met her demands, kissing her deeper, holding her tighter, teasing her with his mouth until he felt her tremble.

He trembled as well. He'd never reacted this way to kissing a woman before. He'd always enjoyed kissing women—some more than others—but he'd never been so moved, never felt as though he needed a woman like he needed Collette.

"I think this is enough for now," he said, pulling back.

She blinked up at him, her brown eyes almost black. "Really?"

He ran his thumb across the satin of her cheek, marveling at the silky flesh. "I think it's for the best."

"And I thought it best if we continue."

That was a rather appealing idea as well. Who the devil cared about restraint and all the rest of that rot? She was in his arms and he wanted her and she wanted him…and if he took her, he might just ruin everything. Because he was not who she thought he was. At least, he hadn't been entirely truthful with her about his intentions and reasons for becoming her friend. And there was the small detail that he'd created the crisis he now offered to guide her through. Added to those damning facts, he had already decided he would do all he could to protect her from any sort of punishment, but his determination was no guarantee of success. He might just be the one who was responsible for her father's death and her imprisonment and possible execution.

One of those reasons alone was reason enough to resist further complicating their relationship by taking her to bed.

Cursing Draven and the French government and his own surprising reaction to her, Rafe stepped back and held her at arm's length. "It's late and you've had a scare today. I'll see you home."

She nodded. "You're right. I should go home before I'm missed."

With a nod, he reluctantly released her and strode to the rack where he'd hung her cloak. She allowed him to drop it over her shoulders, but before she drew the hood up, she said, "Perhaps we can continue where we left off tomorrow."

Rafe closed his eyes. This mission had just become the most difficult of his career.

⟡

Collette went through the day in a haze. When Lady Ravensgate asked about her inattention or her new habit of staring at the walls or at nothing in particular,

Collette told her ladyship she had not slept well. That was not far from the truth. She'd barely slept at all. Rafe Beaumont had seen her safely back to the town house and behaved as the perfect gentleman throughout. But when she was finally in her bed, she hadn't been able to sleep. She hadn't been able to stop thinking about the way he'd kissed her.

No one had ever kissed her that way before. She had been kissed by but a handful of men and boys in her little over two decades of life. The problem was that even if she had kissed a hundred men, Collette didn't think she would have experienced the same rush of pleasure she'd felt last night when Rafe had kissed her back. The kiss had been arousing when he allowed it. Just putting her arms around him, feeling his body against her, his scent engulfing her, had been arousing. But when she'd put her mouth on his, she'd thought she might moan with pleasure. He had the perfect lips and he held her with just the right amount of tenderness and possession.

And then he had kissed her back. Slowly at first. The man had patience. He did not attack as other men did, did not thrust his tongue into her mouth as soon as he'd pried her lips apart. He brushed and slid and teased and nipped until she clung to him. And when she opened her mouth, willingly and with a sense of desperation, he took his time stoking her desire before filling her and tangling his tongue satisfyingly with hers.

The kiss had been everything and more than she could ever have imagined kissing a man like Rafe Beaumont would be. She'd thought her knees would give out, wanted them to fail her so he might sweep her up and carry her to the bedroom. Because if Rafe Beaumont could kiss that well, what else could he do well?

And then he'd turned into a gentleman. Not that he'd never shown signs of being one before. Even when he'd backed her into a corner at Montjoy's ball, she hadn't really been afraid he would do anything she didn't want. The problem was that she did want him to do all the things she could think of—and others she hadn't even considered. And the other problem was he was right to halt their kiss. He was right to stop when he had. She needed his help with her father, and she was scared and uncertain and vulnerable.

But she wasn't scared and uncertain or particularly vulnerable in the light of the day after. She knew she didn't owe him her body for offering his assistance, and she knew she wanted him regardless of the situation with her father. She'd wanted him from the first moment she'd seen him. That had been pure physical lust. Now it was more than that. It was lust combined with respect and genuine affection for the man. He made her laugh. He made her happy when she was with him. He made her quiver when she was in his arms.

If she and Lady Ravensgate had had some event that evening, Collette might have been distracted from her salacious thoughts. An event where she might gather political information would have been even more welcome. But they'd had no invitations for that night and no engagements, which meant after dinner, Collette had nothing to do but pretend to read and think about later that evening when she would be alone with Beaumont in his cozy flat.

She'd retired early, but instead of sleeping for a few hours, she'd spent the time in her room brushing her hair and trying to find the most attractive style. In the end, she'd left it down and dressed in her yellow muslin, which made her feel like a schoolgirl, but which she could don without help and was reasonably modest. Beaumont either wanted her or not. She would not be one of the women she constantly spotted around him, women who tried far too hard to gain his attention with low-cut bodices and caught hems that revealed ankles.

The cloak was voluminous enough to hide the lighter color of her dress when she sneaked out into the garden just before midnight, and though she was early, she found Beaumont waiting. As soon as she saw him—stepping out from behind a tree to make himself visible to her—she practically ran to him. She'd wanted him to sweep her into his arms, but instead, he caught her hand and kissed it. "Shall we talk out here tonight?" he asked.

Disappointment stabbed through her. "I had hoped we would return to your flat."

His violet eyes were unreadable, and then he nodded and led her out of the garden and to the waiting hackney. Once on their way, when they could not be overheard above the clatter of the horses' hooves, he said, "I have a plan."

"Tell me."

"It's rather daring and risky, but if it works, it will solve most of your problems."

*Daring* and *risky* were not her favorite words. She would have preferred *infallible* and *safe*, but she supposed she'd left words like that behind when she'd left France.

"Tell me."

"I will. When we reach my flat and after you have a glass of wine. I fear we will both require fortification."

Her heart thudded painfully in her chest all the way to St. James's Square. And then when they were alone in his flat, she waited impatiently while he hung her cloak. She'd thought he might offer her wine, but he stopped and stared at her.

"What is it?" she asked, having forgotten all about her earlier attempts to look alluring. Now that she did remember, she wished she hadn't worn the yellow muslin. It wouldn't help to look sixteen.

"I've never seen you with your hair down," he said. "It's beautiful."

"It's brown," she commented, but her belly had done a slow roll at the compliment. The color of her hair might be ordinary, but she knew it was quite lovely when loose. It was glossy and thick, with perfect waves that would have curled if it had been shorter. As it was, it reached to the middle of her back, a manageable length since she often had to style it herself.

"I like brown," he said. "Very much. Wine?" He crossed the room and lifted a bottle of red wine from a side table. "I thought we might try a wine from Burgundy tonight."

"And how did you acquire that?"

He spread his hands. "I have my methods." He poured them both wine, then sipped his slowly. Collette couldn't manage more than a taste of hers. Her stomach felt as knotted as a ball of yarn rescued from a kitten.

"You mentioned a plan."

"I did." He set the glass of wine on the table and paced away, then back again. "I thought long and hard about this, and I believe the only way to save your father is to have him brought here."

She shook her head. She had planned to take her father to America. That was the only safe place for them. But freeing her father from France was one step. "How? He is under lock and key in France. Even if I did go to France, how would I get to him?"

"You misunderstand. *You* won't bring him here."

She lifted a brow. "*You* will?"

He laughed. "No! Absolutely not. As exciting and daring as the prospect of sailing to France and rescuing your father sounds, I'm afraid I would almost certainly fail. No one ever gave me the exciting missions, and this probably isn't the time to start."

"Then what are you proposing?"

"I am proposing the men who imprisoned Fortier bring him here. How did you plan to communicate with them? If you had the codes and wanted to let them know, how would you do so, short of returning to Paris?"

She hesitated, staring at the wine in her glass.

"If you don't trust me, this will never work," Rafe said. "I might as well take you back."

"You're right." She looked up from the glass. "I suppose I would ask Lady Ravensgate for her help."

"What does she have to do with any of this?"

"She is able to contact the royalists."

"Then she is not a distant relative of yours?"

"Not at all. I was told she and my father were friends, but I don't believe it. She has ties to the Bourbon family, and if she sympathizes with them, she likely blames my father, in part, for the rise of Napoleon."

"Then she is more of a jailor than an ally. She'll kill you if you become a liability. Is she a spy as well?"

Collette looked back at the wine. It was one thing to tell her secrets but quite another to divulge someone else's.

Rafe didn't push her. "Then you write a note to the royalists holding your father and tell them you have the codes. But, you write, you don't dare send these codes. Too dangerous. You will only hand them over in person, and after the exchange, you want to go immediately into hiding with your father."

Collette stared at him. "But I don't have the codes."

"That's not the point. Once the men have brought your father, once he is on British soil, we'll be able to spirit you both away."

"Who is we?"

He lifted his wine and sipped again. "I have powerful friends, and if I ask, they will help. No questions."

Collette considered the proposal. "And then you never have to betray Draven or steal the codes." It was as bad as she had feared. *Daring* and *risky* were understatements. So much could go wrong. And yet she knew Beaumont was correct when he said the only way to save her father was to bring him here and then escape. Who was to say that even if she obtained the codes her father would be freed? As long as the royalists could squeeze information out of her, they would. Her father might never be free. She would never be free.

Unless she took her freedom into her own hands.

The plan was dangerous, but that didn't mean it wouldn't work. She sipped her own wine and walked away from him to peer out the window at the street below. Carriages clattered by as did men in hats and greatcoats on their way to gambling hells or other male amusements. The question in her mind was not whether the plan would work. She believed it could. But could she trust Rafe Beaumont? How did she know he was an ally?

And what reason did she have not to trust him? Yes, he'd been a soldier in the war against the French, but all of that was over. There was no indication he had any involvement with the government or the army now. And he'd been her friend. He'd been there in the garden when she needed him. He'd saved her from the runaway cart outside the museum. He'd treated her with kindness and was helping her here tonight instead of out on the street like the men she saw passing by.

And then there was one other issue. She *wanted* to trust him. She already liked him far too much. She was attracted to him. She felt more than mere friendship for him. She wanted to believe he could help her. She wanted to be more than his friend.

Collette turned from the window. "Why should the royalists believe I have the codes? I've been here months and haven't managed to even come close to these codes. If I suddenly tell them I have the codes in hand, I don't think they'll believe me."

"I thought of that."

"Did you?"

"Of course. One always has to give an adversary a taste of the prize, to whet her—or his—appetite, so to speak."

"And how should I whet the royalists' appetite?"

He moved closer, pulled the curtains closed behind her, and leaned close. "You'll tell them three words."

"Three?" she whispered, her voice deserting her at his closeness.

"One." He held up a finger. "Two." Another finger. "Three."

"What are they?"

His lips brushed her ear as though he would whisper the words of a lover. "Rafe Beaumont's lover."

She closed her eyes, her head spinning. How had he managed to make three words so utterly arousing? Her whole body had grown warm. "And you think they know who you are?"

He drew back slightly. "They can easily find out. And when they do, they will know not only did I serve under Draven, but also that he trusts me implicitly. As my lover, you could get close to the codes."

"The royalists will know this?"

"Count on it."

She stared at him for a long moment, looking into his eyes and searching for any sign of deceit. She saw nothing. Nothing but those lovely violet eyes in a too handsome face.

"Shall I drive you back to Lady Ravensgate's town house?"

"I…" Yes. She should tell him yes. Now that she

had agreed to the plan, she should go back and write the note. But she didn't want to go back to her cold, empty bed. Not yet. And unless she was wrong about the way Beaumont was looking at her, he didn't particularly want her to go either.

"You?" he prompted. He wouldn't make this easy for her. She'd have to say it.

"I don't want you to take me back. Not yet."

"Would you like to finish your wine first?"

She shook her head. "I don't want the wine. It's very good," she added quickly, knowing he had probably opened the bottle just for her. "But I would rather have you."

His mouth curved in a slow, seductive smile. "I thought you would never say it."

Her cheeks were so hot that she feared she would probably burst into fire now that she had said it. "You didn't give me much choice." She drank a gulp of wine.

"Only because I didn't think you wanted me."

"Me not want you?" She gestured at him. "Have you looked in a mirror?"

"Have you?" He took her glass before she could take another gulp and set it down with his. He held her hand lightly, his fingers around her wrist. "Do you know you are the first woman who has ever refused me?"

"That must have made you incredibly arrogant. Perhaps I should keep refusing you."

"No!" He brought her hand to his lips and kissed it. "Because you are also the first woman I have ever wanted. Really wanted."

"I don't believe you."

He quirked a brow. "Do you think I have many female friends? I have precisely one. You. Because if I couldn't have you in bed, at least I could have your friendship."

"Perhaps you can have both."

"I'll take both." He wrapped an arm around her waist and pulled her close. "I haven't ceased thinking about the kiss we shared last night."

"Neither have I."

"This one will be better."

"I don't see——"

But his mouth was already on hers, claiming her lips in tender nips and grazes. He explored her lips with his own, with his tongue, with his teeth, until she could take no more. She wanted more. Wanted his tongue inside, dueling with hers. "More," she breathed, yanking on his shirt to bring him closer. Opening her mouth, she darted her tongue out and slid it across his mouth. The hand on her back tightened, and he let out a groan.

His own tongue mimicked hers, then entered her mouth, exploring and tantalizing. He pulled back. "Was that what you wanted?"

"More," she said.

His eyes darkened at the invitation. He kissed her again, and then she was swept off the floor and into his arms. Without pausing in the kiss, he carried her to his bedchamber. At least she assumed it was a bedchamber. It was dark, lit only by a low fire in the hearth. Gently, he set her on a bed and stripped off his coat.

"Servants?" she asked.

"Gone for the night," he answered, taking a tinder-box from the table, striking the flint into the char cloth in the bottom, and lighting a sulfur-tipped splint. With that, he lit a lamp on the table, then crossed the room to light another. When he turned back, he pulled the tail of his shirt from his trousers. "I want to see you."

"You first," she countered, having no idea where such words had come from. She had not planned to say them, had never thought of herself as the sort of woman who would demand anything from a man, much less that he undress before her. But something about Rafe Beaumont made her brave. He wasn't just any man. He was her friend. He was her ally.

For a moment, he looked as surprised as she was at her words, but then he licked his lips. "I suppose that's fair." He backed up and sat in a chair where a dressing robe hung. Ignoring it, he brushed it aside and toed off his boots. When his footwear was gone and he stood before her with bare feet, he unfastened his cuffs. Collette rose on her knees to watch. It seemed strange to see him so vulnerable, without shoes or the formality of a coat. But when he loosened the cravat at his neck, she did not think it strange at all that her heart thudded at the sight of his neck and the skin under the open V of his shirt. And then he tugged the shirt over his head and dropped it on the chair.

He had a magnificent chest. She had been pressed against it enough times to know it would be hard and sculpted, but this was like something a master would have chiseled. The broad shoulders tapered to a slim waist and firm abdomen. Just below was the hard bulge of his erection. If she had doubted he wanted her, if she had felt as though she weren't pretty enough or exciting enough, the sight of his desire erased all doubts. He wanted her, and she wanted him just as badly.

"The rest," she said, her mouth dry.

He reached for the placket of his trousers, unfastened it, and slid the material over his hips, down muscled thighs, and into a pool on the floor. Without any sense of embarrassment, he retrieved the trousers, crossed to the chair, and laid them over the top. Collette let out a slow breath. The back view was as impressive as the front. Seeming to know the effect he had on her, he crossed back to the bed. "Your turn."

# Ten

HER EYES WIDENED, MAKING THEM APPEAR MORE BLACK than deep brown. They were already dark with desire. Rafe hadn't realized he would enjoy undressing for a woman so much, but Collette's gasps and audible swallows just encouraged him. And now that he was naked, he wanted her to disrobe.

Fingers trembling, she reached for the pins holding her bodice. She couldn't quite free the one she'd taken hold of, and she looked down, a lock of her hair falling over her shoulder. He wanted to wrap his hands in that hair and tug it back so he could kiss her neck. He wanted to spread it over his pillow as he bent over her.

Finally, she freed the pin but dropped it on the blue coverlet of the bed. Rafe lifted it before it could be lost and cause one or both of them injury in a few minutes. "Will you allow me?" he asked.

"To undress me?"

He nodded.

"I can do it."

He took her hand in his, kissed the pads on her

fingers. "I'd rather neither of us ends up as a pin cushion. Besides, you might like my efforts."

"Very well," she said, her voice catching.

He had undressed many women, more than he cared to remember, and it was a simple matter, but he took his time with her. He liked the anticipation as he revealed each little swath of flesh. He liked the way her bodice sagged with the removal of a pin and the way they clinked when piled on top of one another. Then there were ties and laces and all of the complicated fastenings underpinning a lady's clothing. Finally, he removed the pretty, little muslin dress and petticoats, and she stood in chemise and stays.

"Turn around."

When she turned, he forced himself to draw a deep breath. He'd needed her to face away from him. She was absolutely glorious. With her breasts barely contained by the stays and the half-moons of creamy flesh within reach, he might have bypassed undressing her at all. He wanted that flesh in his hands and in his mouth.

And he wanted this to last more than three minutes. And so he would force himself to slow down and take his time. He took hold of her laces and began to loosen them, then slid the stays over her hips. "Untie your chemise," he whispered in her ear. Brushing her hair aside and over the opposite shoulder, he rested his chin on her shoulder as he watched her tug at the tie holding the drawstring chemise closed.

And then that too fell to the floor, leaving her in stockings and slippers. He rather liked her wearing that and only that. "That's better," he murmured. He trailed his lips over her shoulder and along the back of her neck. Gooseflesh appeared where his lips touched, and she shivered. His hands had been at his sides, but now he brushed them over her shoulders and along her arms, then back up again and down her back. In the firelight, her skin was the color of a blushing rose. Her back was long and straight, her hips a lush curve after what seemed like a tiny waist.

And her bottom.

It was full and heart-shaped. He ran a hand over it, loving the way the skin was as silky soft as the rest of her. "You really are perfect, aren't you?" he said, pressing a kiss to her neck, just behind her ear. She inhaled sharply. He dragged his lips across the back of her neck and, lifting her hair from her shoulder, kissed her behind her other ear.

"I'm really not," she said.

Rafe drew back. He wasn't used to women arguing with him when he complimented them. Of course, most of the time, those compliments had been part of an act, the opening volley of a seduction that, if successful, would yield useful information for Draven's troop. Rafe didn't have to give meaningless compliments tonight, and he hadn't. Slowly, he turned Collette to face him. Keeping his eyes on hers, he cupped the sides of her face gently. "To me, you're perfect."

Her cheeks turned pinker than they already were. For some reason, the admiration embarrassed her.

"You mean, other than the fact that I'm a spy."

He shrugged. "A small detail that only makes you that much more interesting." His fingers traced the bones of her cheeks and trailed across her lips, then down her pointed chin and across her long, graceful neck.

"You're the perfect one, Rafe," she said, putting her arms around him. He felt the hard tips of her nipples brushing against his chest.

"That might be the first time you've used my name. I like how it sounds on your tongue."

He brought his mouth to hers, kissing her, and she sighed and kissed him back, pressing her body against his. His hands refused to take things slowly, and he couldn't stop touching her everywhere. Her sighs and moans told him exactly where to linger and where to return, and when his hand slid between her thighs and cupped her, she murmured, "Rafe. Yes."

She couldn't have said anything more arousing. He lowered her to the bed, bracing himself on his elbows to keep his weight from crushing her. She wrapped one leg around his waist, but, though it was torture to wait, he refrained from accepting the invitation. Instead, he ran his lips over every inch of her, stopping to worship at her breasts, which were firm and heavy in his hands. She was damp where his hand had cupped her, but he wanted her unquestionably ready. He dragged his mouth down past her navel, around her hips, over her thighs, then parted her thighs. He was about to taste her when her legs tensed, and she levered herself on her elbows. "What are you doing?"

He raised a brow. "I was about to kiss you."

"*There?*"

He almost smiled. He should have realized she'd probably never done this before. A few quick trysts with a tutor had not taught her everything. "Yes." Using his finger, he traced the sensitive flesh. "Here.

And here." He slid over the small nub hidden between her folds. "And here."

Her eyes closed for a moment, then opened very slowly.

"If you don't like it, I'll stop."

"If I do like it?" she asked, voice husky with need.

"Then say my name." He spread her legs again and kissed a path from her inner thigh to her sex. She jerked at the first touch of his mouth there, and he paused.

Then he heard her murmur. "Rafe."

She tasted sweet, her flesh quivering, and her body responding to every flick of his tongue or caress of his lips. "Rafe," she said again and again. And when he flicked the small bud that he knew would give her the most pleasure, his name became all but a chant until she fell back on the bed and seemed to lose all power of speech. Rafe could have done this all night. She was glorious on the cusp of ecstasy, her body rising and falling with her rapid breaths, her cheeks pink, her hair a tangle of waves spread over his bed. Her legs were long and all but wrapped around him. He was tempted to start all over again so he could draw her pleasure out further, but he needed to see her climax. He wanted to watch as the coil of pleasure unwound through her body.

"Rafe," she said again, her voice a plea.

He spread her further, teasing and suckling until her hips pistoned beneath his hands. She cried out when she came, the words unintelligible, though he liked to think he heard his name. And then all he could do was stare at her because she was so amazingly beautiful. He wanted to do it all again, do it even better, but his cock had other ideas. Normally he could ignore his own needs, but tonight his cock throbbed to be inside her.

Of course, that was a risk. He'd protect her at the crucial moment, but there was always a chance of pregnancy. "Collette." He looked down at her and lifted a lock of hair from her forehead. Her eyes opened slowly, the color of midnight and just as brilliant. "I want to be inside you. I'll do my best to protect you, but if you don't want the risk, I understand."

"Yes," she murmured, lifting her arms to wrap around him. "I want you. All of you."

"You can say no," he managed as his willpower began to desert him.

"I'm saying yes. Rafe, yes."

He positioned himself between her legs and kissed her long and slow as he entered her. She was tight and wet and hot. And thank God she was not a virgin because he could barely restrain himself as it was.

He had the unexpected urge to thrust mindlessly until he found release, and the impulse shocked him. No one had ever made him lose control like this. Her hands scraped down his back and gripped his buttocks. He'd held back slightly, but he couldn't resist that invitation and sheathed himself completely. Her head fell back on a moan and he gritted his jaw to hold on to what little power he still had over himself. Taking her arms, he slid them up and pinned her wrists to the bed with his hands. With her arms over her head, her breasts thrust out, and he took his time teasing her distended nipples, suckling them until she was grinding her hips against his.

She wanted him to move faster and harder, but he kept up a slow, deep penetration that from the tightening of her muscles around him would bring her to a deliberate, powerful climax. She'd kept her eyes closed, her lashes fluttering with each of his thrusts, but as he began to move a little faster, she opened her eyes and her gaze fixed on his. The intimacy of that moment was like nothing he'd ever experienced before. He felt a zing of connection and all but heard the click of a lock inside him open. He wanted to look away, wanted to break the hold she had on him. Her eyes seemed to look right into him, into the part of him he'd never let anyone see—the part that wasn't a charming gentleman, but a boy who desperately wanted to be loved.

And then there was the shot of guilt because he wasn't the hero she thought him to be. He'd manipulated her into telling him her secrets, and though he hadn't seduced her into his bed, he was fully aware that, if she knew about his mission, she wouldn't be here with him. They were enemies, but he was the only one who knew it.

Her eyes drew him in, trusting and honest. And then, because he couldn't take it any longer, he shifted position, turning her onto her belly and lifting her hips so he could enter her. "Collette?" he asked, waiting for her permission. He ran a hand over her bottom, then kissed the pale flesh and eased a hand over her slick, swollen sex. She wriggled her bottom and he slid his cock over the flesh he'd teased with his hand. She gasped.

"Rafe." She looked over her shoulder at him, her

eyes glittering with excitement. When he entered her again, he took his time as much for himself as for her. She moved with him, her hands digging into the coverlet as her pleasure mounted. When he felt her body tighten, he reached around and opened her folds. Finding the slippery nub, he circled it slowly until she bucked and her muscles clenched around him tightly.

And that was when he lost control. His hips moved on their own, his body taking what it wanted, with hard, deep thrusts. He had enough mental capacity left to pull out before he spilled his seed inside her. Instead, he spilled it harmlessly onto the coverlet.

His valet would have something to say about that. At the moment, Rafe didn't care. He pulled Collette into his arms and onto the other side of the bed, holding her for a long moment until he could catch his breath and perhaps understand what the hell had just happened.

❧

Collette felt Rafe's arms come around her, pulling her against him so their bodies were pressed together, her back to his chest. Her body still sung, weak and limp from the things he had done to her. She hadn't known lovemaking could be like that. She hadn't known she could feel like that. Yes, she'd enjoyed it before, but Rafe was… She didn't even have the words.

Perhaps that was because the experience had been more than physical. Yes, his skills there were probably unrivaled. Even inexperienced as she was, she knew he was a man with tremendous patience and sensitivity. He knew when to hold back, when to move faster, when and where to touch her. He'd been so focused on her, so attuned to her every breath, that when he withdrew, she couldn't help but notice. Something had happened when their gazes had locked that had… What was the word? Unsettled him?

No, she hadn't minded the way he'd flipped her over or the way he'd taken her from behind. But she'd had the smallest flicker of doubt niggle her brain. And for the first time, she'd wondered if he didn't have something to hide.

He kissed her shoulder, the stubble on his cheek tickling her. "Why did we wait so long to do that?"

"Because we were friends," she reminded him.

"I'm still your friend." He kissed her ear. "And as such, I should take you home. It's almost two."

She only had about three hours before Lady Ravensgate's servants would be up and her absence noticed. But she couldn't stand to leave the warmth of his arms yet. She'd felt so alone the past few months. For once, it was comforting to feel as though she didn't have to carry the entire weight of the Napoleonic army on her shoulders. And, of course, it helped that the shoulders bearing some of it were muscled and strong.

"Let me regain my strength," she murmured. He didn't object, merely gave his acquiescence with another lazy kiss on her shoulder. She closed her eyes, warmth tingling through her as he ran a hand through her hair, down her back, then fondled her breast. His movements were languid and easy, but they roused her nonetheless. When her nipple hardened against his palm, she felt his sex respond in kind against her buttocks.

"You like that," he murmured in her ear, rolling the pebbled point between his fingers and squeezing gently. She gasped out a breath. And then his hand repeated the gesture on her other breast and she felt an answering tug of need in her belly. His hand slid down, his fingers brushing over her sex. She heard herself moan with pleasure, but she couldn't seem to find the energy to be mortified at what she was allowing. Again.

His finger stroked over that little nub that made her whole body purr, and then he skated lower and slipped inside her. A second finger joined the first, while the heel of his hand pressed against that nub. Her hips moved with the seductive rhythm he played, and she felt him grow harder against her skin. "Lie still." His voice was a rumble through the haze of pleasure engulfing her. "You don't have to do anything."

But she didn't want to lie still. She felt as though she'd spent her whole life lying still and allowing others to dictate her life. Now she would take what she wanted, and she wanted him. She grasped his wrist with her hand, and he paused. "You don't want this."

Still holding his wrist, she turned and pushed it onto the bed. "I do, but I want more. Let me show you." At some point, she had lost her slippers. She straddled him and watched as his throat worked. His eyes skimmed down her body, and he licked his lips. She knew he wanted her, knew he desired her. She took the evidence of that with one hand and stroked its length. Rafe closed his eyes and his legs tensed beneath her. She suddenly understood why he seemed to enjoy giving her pleasure so much. It was heady to see the power she had to stoke his desire.

She rose and positioned herself above his erection. He opened his eyes and she could see he fought to stop himself from wresting control back. The hand she held clenched and opened. "Please," he murmured.

She took him inside her, moving her hips until she found a rhythm she liked. He watched her and moved with her, complemented her. She linked her fingers with his on the bed, leaning over him as their bodies came together again and again. This time, though he might have taken her breast into his mouth or used his strength to shift positions, he didn't look away from her. "You're close," he said.

She didn't know how he knew. She could barely answer. Her body demanded release, but it eluded her. "Yes."

"Stop waiting for it," he said. "Take it."

She shook her head, not knowing what he meant. "Touch me," she all but begged, releasing his hands and leaning back. If he simply touched her, she knew she would come apart.

"Oh, no. It will be better if you take it. Claim it."

"I can't!"

"You can. Christ, you're beautiful." His eyes raked over her again. "I want to watch you come."

Her hips moved faster, her body using his to reach higher. But just as she felt insecurity or modesty, he gave her another compliment, another encouragement. She knew he was close as well. His hands gripped hers more tightly, and his voice had become a husky rumble. Her own words had deserted her and she moaned as she slid over his hard length one last time. And then the whole world seemed to go black as everything inside her unraveled. She cried out, and either he broke their grip or she did, because he pressed his hand against her sex and then the world went white hot as her climax climbed higher. She bucked and took until the pleasure ebbed, and then he slid out from under her and she heard his gasp of pleasure as he spent himself into the coverlet.

She hadn't expected that. She hadn't expected that even at her most vulnerable, even at the moment when she had clearly been using him, he would protect her. Her heart lurched and the lump in her throat made it difficult to breathe. She lay back on the bed, and when he turned to look down at her, she *was* rendered completely breathless. His violet eyes looked sleepy and seductive, his mouth was fuller from their kisses, and his hair was wild about his face. And, of course, he was still completely and magnificently naked.

"Keep looking at me like that, sweetheart, and you will never make it home tonight."

"I can't quite believe I'm here with you."

He sat beside her and brushed the hair back from her forehead. "I feel exactly the same. How did we get so lucky?"

She smiled up at him and he bent to kiss her, then stopped himself. "If we begin this again, I'm afraid you have no hope of returning to Lady Ravensgate's undetected. As much as I want you to stay, I really must take you home."

She nodded. The look of regret on his face was real. He did want her to stay as much as she wanted to stay.

"Do you need help dressing?" he asked.

"No." She'd had to dress herself earlier that night

and had chosen clothing she could manage on her own. They both rose and he pulled his trousers on, then padded to the door.

"I'll bring us some wine and cheese. I haven't even fed you."

"There's no need," she said as she pulled the chemise over her head. But he waved away her protests and was gone. Alone, she smiled to herself. She should have been telling herself not to fall in love with him. She knew she wasn't the first woman he'd brought to his bed or probably even the first he'd wanted to stay the night. But was she wrong to believe that, when he said the words to her, he'd meant them?

She had been in his arms, and what they had shared was more than just physical. Something had happened between them, and she'd known he'd felt it too, even if he'd shied away from it. Dare she allow herself to think of what might be? What her life could be like once her father was safe again, once the nightmare of the last few months of her life was over. Could she and Rafe be together? Would he want to marry her?

Was she leaping far, far ahead?

The last was probably true enough. And she had better finish dressing.

She struggled into her stays and her petticoats, then began the laborious process of pinning her dress together. She had almost finished when she could have sworn she heard voices. She paused and listened. Yes, she definitely heard voices. Hadn't Rafe said he didn't have any servants living in the flat? Who could he be speaking to?

Suddenly the voices lowered as though hushed, and

Collette told herself she was probably hearing things. Or there was a perfectly good explanation for a visitor at almost three in the morning.

Her fingers trembled as she tried and failed to secure the last pin of her bodice. Her skin suddenly felt cold and the blood pounded loudly in her temples. She had no reason not to trust Rafe. None. But the hair on the back of her arms prickled.

Still in stocking feet, she moved silently across the thick rug in Rafe's bedchamber and to the door. The bedchamber opened into a small sitting room with a desk and a comfortable chair that had a stack of books beside it. Rafe Beaumont apparently liked to read. A quick glance at the titles told her all the volumes were fiction. She saw *Emma* and *Waverley* as well as poetry by Byron on the stack. Nothing that might edify the mind, as her father would have said in his mock-scolding voice. She smiled remembering his words and knowing that she and Rafe had similar tastes in literature.

She almost turned back to the bedchamber to slide on her slippers and return some order to her hair, but she heard the voices again. This time she was sure of it—Rafe's voice and that of another man's. Silently, she padded to the door of the sitting room, which had been left open but a crack. She inserted her fingers in the crack and eased it open farther. She had no wish to be seen by anyone and completely compromised. Collette Fortier's reputation didn't matter. As the daughter of an assassin, no one paid much heed to whether or not she was a virgin. Her character was already irreparably damaged. But Collette Fournay couldn't be caught in Rafe Beaumont's flat. She couldn't afford for the *ton* to realize they had spent even a few minutes unchaperoned, much less hours.

"You have to go," Rafe was saying. She knew his voice at least, low and melodic with just a hint of playfulness. Though he sounded less than playful at the moment.

"I see." The other man's voice hinted that he knew exactly why Rafe was sending him away. Collette could imagine Rafe often had female companionship, and the fact that she was the female here only made her feel cheap and tawdry. "I'll come back in an hour."

She couldn't hear Rafe's response, and she widened the crack. Rafe and another man were in the drawing room. Rafe had set the wine and a plate with cheese on a table near the door she had opened and presumably left it there to answer the door. If the man he was speaking to had called on him at three in the morning, the two must be good friends. And the way Rafe was speaking to the other man and attempting to guide him by the shoulder spoke of familiarity.

She couldn't really see the other man. He was tall, slightly taller than Rafe, and thinner. She thought she saw dark-blond hair.

Rafe glanced back at the door and she pulled it closed silently, her breath catching in her throat at the near miss.

"Step outside with me," he said, his voice low. She heard the outer door open. Collette thought about returning to her toilette. Not ten minutes ago, she had been in bed with Rafe, trusting him with both her body and her heart. Nothing had changed in a few minutes. Why shouldn't she trust Rafe now? Why did her skin feel prickly and her heart beat faster? Her fingers tightened on the door handle before she cracked it enough to squeeze out, then ran across the drawing room to press her ear to the outer door. The men must have been standing on the other side.

"—after speaking to Neil. Your idea to send her a false note was brilliant. Much better than throwing her in front of the cart."

"I'm not entirely inept," Rafe said.

The blood thudding in Collette's temples thudded harder, and she had to clench the door to keep standing. She didn't understand the other man's words. She didn't *want* to understand.

"Did she believe it? Did you find out everything from the little spy you needed? If not, we had another idea." The visitor's voice lowered even further.

She couldn't make out his words or Rafe's low response. Not that she cared. Her mind had put it together, despite her heart's refusal to believe.

Tonight, last night, probably every moment she'd known Rafe Beaumont had been a lie. He'd known she was a spy, and he'd seduced her to find out what she knew.

No, that wasn't quite true. He hadn't had to seduce her. She'd practically thrown herself at him.

Collette backed away from the door, but she didn't hurry to return to the bedchamber. Her legs felt as though they were stuck in heavy mud, and she could barely manage to lift them to trudge through it. The latch on the door lifted, but Collette did not move. The door opened, and the visitor saw her first. She gasped reflexively. His face was horrible, disfigured. She couldn't see very clearly, but the quick glimpse she had gave her the impression of skin too smooth and too pink stretched tight over the bones of what might have once been a handsome visage.

Both Rafe and the other man looked at her. She looked from the scarred man to Rafe and saw his expression turn from horror to guilt to resignation.

It was the look of guilt that made her snap. She didn't care if all of London saw her. She looked at Rafe, only at Rafe, and refused to acknowledge the sting behind her eyes. "You must think I am the most foolish woman that ever lived."

He shook his head.

"You must think me pathetic. How did you manage not to laugh at my complete gullibility?"

"Collette, I can explain—"

The scarred man looked from her to Rafe. "I should…" He didn't finish his sentence. He pulled a mask over his face and then looked back to give her a last perusal. "Sorry we had to meet like this, Miss Fortier."

"I'm not," she said, voice steely. "Meeting you has been most enlightening. Not that I know your name, of course."

"I'll speak with you later." Rafe closed the door and turned to her. Collette considered taking a large drink from the wine nearby, or perhaps lifting the bottle and hurling it at Rafe. Instead, she leaned back against the wall, her legs too shaky to be trusted.

Rafe came toward her, arms outstretched. "I know what you're thinking."

"Do you?" She arched a brow. "I very much doubt that." She glanced at the bottle again.

"Throwing that at me won't solve anything."

Perhaps he did know what she was thinking. She put a hand to her belly, which had clenched tightly and painfully, and tried to slow her rapid breathing. "What will solve things, Rafe? Tell me, because I promise you I am anxious to hear, what will make all of this better?" She'd slipped into French, something she became aware of when he answered her in the same language, his speech fluid and his accent almost that of a native's.

"You have to trust me, Collette. I know that seems ridiculous—"

"You're right. *Absolument*! I don't trust you. I can never trust you!"

"What you heard"—he was still walking toward her, slowly but steadily—"isn't the whole story. You have the wrong impression."

That statement was like a slap in the face. It cleared her head immediately. "Stop." She held her hand out to keep him at bay. To his credit, he did stop, not attempting to come any closer. "I have the wrong impression, do I? So you did not know from the first time we met that I was Collette Fortier, daughter of the notorious French assassin?"

"I didn't know conclusively."

"Weak, Monsieur Beaumont. An argument, but a weak one. What about this supposition—you became my friend in hopes of gathering damaging information about my father from me."

He didn't speak.

"And then when I didn't reveal anything, you

devised other strategies to…shall we say, persuade me to confide in you? A near-death brush with a cart outside the museum?"

He closed his eyes, his face looking pained. And still she could not stop the back of her mind from noting how beautiful he was standing there, sans shirt, his golden chest the epitome of strength and vigor, his perfect face and the hair her own hands had tousled just a few minutes before.

"And when all of that did not succeed, you—tell me if I have this right because I am a bit confused here—you wrote the note from my father's jailer." The note had been vague, she could see that now. The words had been generic, but enough for her to draw the conclusions Rafe had wanted. She gave a little laugh at her own naïveté. "And I believed it all. I fell right into your trap and told you everything. All you had to do was give me empty promises. And then what must have been your crowning glory, I went to bed with you. Not only did I betray my father, but I handed you my body to use as well."

He flinched. "Collette, it wasn't like that. You know it wasn't like that."

"I don't know anything at all. I don't even know who you are or who you work for."

He raked a hand through his hair, his gaze downcast as though he at least had enough dignity to seem ashamed.

"I don't expect you to tell me. And even if you wanted to, I don't have time to hear it. It may not matter what I do at this point, but I'd rather not alert Lady Ravensgate to the fact that I've been telling her enemies all of my secrets."

"I'll take you home."

"No. I cannot stand to see you for another moment. I'll take a hackney, and you may secure that for me while I find my slippers."

He didn't argue. She watched as he went to the door and threw his greatcoat over his bare chest. Then he stepped outside.

Her legs wobbled, but she refused to fall apart. She knuckled the tears away and squared her shoulders. She didn't care that she had just signed her own death warrant. She regretted that she'd failed her father.

# Eleven

"HELL'S TEETH! CHRIST! BLOODY DAMN HELL!" RAFE said to the empty flat after he'd seen Collette safely into a hackney. He hadn't wanted her to go alone, but he'd paid the jarvey extra and threatened to come for the man and beat him to a bloody pulp if any harm came to the lady or she did not make it home without so much as losing a hair on her head. He understood why she didn't want to see him. He understood that she hated him and would probably hate him for the rest of her life.

But she would have to put up with him a little longer because he wasn't about to leave her to her own devices. At some point, this mission had become less about rooting out a spy as a service to the Foreign Office and more about saving Collette. He might not like her father, but Rafe was damn well prepared to do exactly as he'd said and bring the man to England. Draven wouldn't like it, but Draven be damned. This was about more than who knew what, when, and where. This was about an innocent woman used as a pawn by two governments who couldn't care less whether she lived or died.

Rafe cared. And Rafe would not abandon her.

No matter how much she hated him.

He heard a quiet tapping on the door and whirled. His first thought was Collette had come back. She'd forgiven him and come to tell him. His second thought was that he was a complete nodcock. She hadn't forgiven him, and she would never forgive him. Which meant something must have happened and she needed help. Rafe threw the door open, practically ripping it from the hinges.

Jasper stood on the other side, the black mask he wore over the upper part of his face making him look rather menacing.

Rafe narrowed his eyes.

"I see from your expression it ended as badly as I feared."

"It's my own fault. I shouldn't have risked speaking with you, even outside. I thought she was dressing and hadn't heard your arrival. We've ruined weeks of work."

"You call that work?" He gestured to Rafe's bare chest. Rafe closed the door on him, but Jasper managed to wedge a boot in the opening. "Let me in."

He hadn't come to apologize. Rafe knew Jasper well enough not to expect anything of that sort. But Jasper might just be useful, and his aid would serve as apology. Rafe pulled the door back and stood aside. Jasper strolled in, but was it Rafe's imagination or did the man look a trifle unsteady on his feet?

"Why did you come back?" Rafe bolted the door behind Jasper.

Jasper slid into one of Rafe's chairs and propped

his boots on another. "I thought I'd make certain you were still in one piece."

Rafe shoved Jasper's muddy boots off the silk upholstery. "I didn't know you cared."

Jasper looked around. "Do you have anything to drink?"

"By the looks of you, you've had enough. Go home." But Jasper didn't rise. Rafe lifted his brows. "Unless there was something else you wanted."

Jasper seemed to consider, then he took a breath and held it, looking like a man diving into a deep pool. "You have nieces and nephews, don't you?"

Rafe peered at his friend. Where was the Jasper he knew? That man had never asked a single personal question of Rafe. "I have them by the buckets. Why?"

"So you have experience with babies."

What the devil was this about? "I don't know that *experience* is the correct word, but I've been around my fair share and then some." He paused. "You haven't just found out you're a father, have you?"

"No," he said emphatically. "But my brother, the heir, just became a father. He asked me to be the godfather."

"You?"

"I tried to tell him no."

Rafe waved a hand. "Of course you are the right man to ask. You're the uncle of the… Was it a boy or a girl?"

"Yes," Jasper said.

"You don't even know?" Rafe sat, his anger over the fiasco with Collette cooling slightly. No one had ever come to him about advice not related to a female before. And he'd never seen Jasper so flustered.

"Listen, I'm godfather to at least six or maybe seven. You hold them at the christening and say whatever you're told to say."

Jasper nodded. "Sure you don't have anything to drink?"

"Jas, you spend half your life in the rookeries. A half hour in a church is a walk in the park."

"What if I drop it?"

"The baby?"

"What if I break it?"

"Treat it like a pistol and you'll be fine. If that's all, I'd like to discuss—"

"I can't wear my mask into a church."

So this was the crux of the matter. If he attended the christening, he'd have no protection. Everyone would see the damage the fire had wrought on his face.

"I don't care about the people attending and my brother has seen my face already."

"So?"

Jasper stood, paced, and turned on Rafe. "Don't you understand? I'm worried about the baby! What if I scare it? What if it cries when it sees me?" He lowered his voice. "What if I scar it for life?"

"You really don't know anything about babies, do you?"

"Why the bloody hell do you think I'm here?"

"Listen, Jas, babies don't care about what you look like. They can't even see that well. If it cries—and really, we should determine the sex and quit calling the baby 'it'—it will be because the baby wants its mother. Just speak softly and kind of rock it." Rafe illustrated with a pillow. "Like this."

"Babies like that?" Jasper sank into the chair again, propping his boots up.

Rafe pushed the boots off. "They like being jiggled. A little."

"What else?"

"Soft voices, high voices, singsong, cooing."

"Cooing? I draw the line at cooing."

"If that baby starts to cry, you'll coo."

Jasper blew out a breath. "I owe you. Do you want me to talk to Draven?"

Rafe realized they were discussing Collette again and Jasper's botching of Rafe's mission. "I'm not five. I can take responsibility for my own missions." He paused. "But I do have a job for you."

"Of course you do." Jasper looked resigned. "Between Ewan, Neil, and you asking me to traipse all over Town for you, it's a wonder I track a single rogue."

"I wouldn't need your help if you hadn't scuttled my entire mission."

Jasper raised a hand. "Don't blame all this on me."

"Fine. If you hadn't helped me scuttle the mission."

"Better." Jasper leaned back. "What do you need me to do?"

☙

Nine hours later, Rafe knocked on Lady Ravensgate's door. Her butler answered and gave Rafe and the flowers he held a snooty appraisal. "Her ladyship is not at home."

Rafe knew her ladyship wasn't at home. He'd been skulking in the shadows in the square across the street watching her town house. About twenty minutes ago, she'd left. Collette had not gone with her. He'd then gathered the flowers he'd bought this morning from one of the ubiquitous girls who sold them and put his plan into motion.

"I came to see Miss Fournay," Rafe said.

The butler's frown drew down farther. "Miss Fournay is not at home."

"No?" Rafe slid an arm around the butler. "I'll wait for her, then."

"I don't think—"

But Rafe was already insinuating himself into the foyer. He'd known dozens of butlers in his time, and he knew exactly how to handle them. Some men thought threatening butlers was the most effective way to deal with them. But that only worked temporarily because usually the butler's fear of losing his position was stronger than his fear of bodily injury. Rafe knew a butler's true weakness—a nip from the bottle.

"What's your name again, old chap?" Rafe elbowed the door closed, keeping his arm companionably around the butler's shoulders.

"Evans, sir."

"Evans. Good, strong name. Evans, you know what they say, don't you?"

"No, sir." He had been lifting his shoulders in an impression of an aboriginal dance in a futile effort to remove Rafe's arm. Now the man took the arm and pushed it back toward its owner.

"When the cat's away, the mice will play," Rafe said in a conspiratorial tone. "Why don't we tuck down to your quarters and have a nip of whatever you've set aside for after dinner?"

"I couldn't do that, sir."

"I won't tell." Rafe slung his arm about Evans's shoulders again and backed him toward a pedestal. The pedestal supported a lovely vase—Ming, if Rafe was not mistaken. It was a shame, but there were casualties in any war. "And if I know you, Evans, you have set aside some of the very best"—he looked at Evans closely—"port? No, sherry."

Evans blinked.

"I do love a good sherry. Just a taste, Evans, and her ladyship will never even know I was here."

Except that he steered Evans right into the pedestal, making it rock back and forth. Evans gasped and reached out to catch the vase. Rafe had to admire the servant. He caught the vase and managed to look graceful doing so. But a quick elbow to the pedestal ensured it would fall and the clatter was more than enough to wake the dead.

"Oops!" Rafe said, his eyes focused on the steps leading to the upper floors. As he'd expected, there was a thunder of feet as servants came running to investigate. He spotted a maid and another maid and what must have been the housekeeper and then... Yes, there she was—Collette.

Her eyes widened when she saw him and not with pleasure. More like horror. It wasn't an expression he was used to seeing on a woman, but he supposed he deserved it. Rafe held up the hand not clutching the flowers, taking control of the situation. "No need to worry. Just a small accident. The Ming is perfectly safe." He glanced at the butler. "You might set that down, Evans. Your hands are shaking."

"What are you doing here, Mr. Beaumont?" Collette asked. Her voice held rather more ice than he would have liked.

"I've come to see you, Miss *Fournay*." He deliberately stressed her false surname. "I brought flowers." He held them aloft like a knight might wield a sword.

She crossed her arms over her chest—her quite spectacular chest, if memory served—and arched a brow. "You may give them to Mrs. Terris. She will see they are put in water."

Rafe shoved the flowers at the housekeeper who had stepped forward, then he took the steps two at a time until he reached Collette. "A moment of your time, Miss Fournay."

"I'm afraid I am terribly busy at the moment, Mr. Beaumont."

"I see." He made a show of consternation. "Then I suppose I will have to say what I came to say here. In front of everyone."

"A better idea would be for you to return—"

He took her hand, holding fast when she tried to snatch it away. Then he sank to one knee. For an instant, his head spun and his chest tightened, but he shoved his discomfort away. "Miss Fournay, you must allow me to tell you—"

The maids gasped and Evans said, "Mr. Beaumont!"

"Come into the drawing room." Collette practically pulled him to his feet. "Let's speak in private."

Rafe stood. Strangely enough, his knees were a bit wobbly. He followed Collette into the drawing room, knowing by the end of the day, half of London would be talking about his proposal to Miss Fournay.

The things he did for his country.

Collette closed the drawing room door and rounded on him. "What are you about, sir? Haven't you done enough without coming here and causing a scene?"

"That's just the problem," Rafe said, drawing her away from the door, where he expected half a dozen servants had their ears pressed to the wood. "I haven't done nearly enough."

"If by that you mean you haven't had me arrested, then I'm certain you can accomplish that without humiliating me with a proposal for marriage."

"I wasn't attempting to humiliate you."

"No. You would never do any such thing, would you? You would never befriend or seduce a woman with the intention of betraying her. I know what you are, Mr. Beaumont." She glared at him, her pretty eyes filled with anger and hurt. "I asked my maid about you and the troop you served with. They called you the Seducer."

Rafe drew in a breath. It was true. That had been his sobriquet. He'd been the one charged with teasing out information from lonely women left behind while their husbands were on the front. He'd never been ashamed of his work. It wasn't the sort of thing one boasted about to one's mother, but he had done his duty and the intelligence he'd gathered had saved lives. But last night had not been a mission, and the fact that she dismissed all they'd shared as a mission galled him. "They did call me the Seducer," he said, voice cool. "But I didn't seduce you."

She stepped back as though she'd been struck. "No, you didn't. I suppose you didn't have to."

He took her shoulders. "I didn't want to. Last night was not about a mission." Or not wholly about a mission.

"What lies! The only reason you ever took any interest in me was because you were ordered to apprehend my father."

He didn't actually apprehend assassins—or anyone else for that matter—but now was not the time to point out that distinction. "That's not true. I was your friend, Collette. I *am* your friend, and I am here to help you."

"I don't need your *help*." She spat the last word.

"Oh, but you do. And if you don't want it, then think of your father. The letter I sent you and the concern you felt might have been false, but how long until the concern is real? You aren't a very good spy."

"I am an excellent spy!" she retorted.

"Then perhaps my countrymen are simply too careful with their words. My point is that the longer you take to acquire the codes, the longer your father rots in prison and the more likely you are caught and hung. Or done away with by the very people who are supposed to be your friends."

Her eyes filled with tears, but to her credit, she didn't allow a single one to fall.

"Let me help you."

"Why should I trust you?"

"You trusted me last night." He let the words hang in the air between them, let the memory of her body sliding over his form in both their minds. "You trusted me enough to let go—"

"Do not remind me," she hissed. Her cheeks turned as pink as foxglove.

"Trust me to bring your father here to England."

"And what happens then? Do I have the privilege of watching him hanged?"

"I cannot make you promises, but I can assure you I will do all I can to see you are both safe. We already have a plan, Collette. It's a good plan. We put it into action."

She stared at him, her small teeth worrying her bottom lip. Rafe knew she would give in. The royalists had her backed into a corner. She had no one else and no other options. But Rafe also knew it might take time for her to realize she had no other choices. And that was time he didn't have to spare. "If we hesitate, we might be too late." Too late for her father or too late for him. The Foreign Office wouldn't be put off forever.

"What do I do?" she asked.

Rafe pulled her close, even more determined that this part of their conversation not be overheard. She didn't argue, but she held herself stiffly. He felt a pang of regret, especially when he caught the scent of juniper, of what might have been. But he had no one but himself to blame. He'd taken her to bed and asked for her trust when he had no right to ask anything of her. He hadn't given her his trust or shared any confidences. He never did share such things with women. He didn't like to get too close. He didn't want to trust a woman—trust anyone, for that matter—and then be let down. The irony that he was asking exactly what he himself was not willing to give was not lost on Rafe.

"How would you have delivered the codes to

your royalist contacts? How do they know how to contact you?"

She gave him a sidelong look, her eyes wary. "The few times they have contacted me they did so through Lady Ravensgate," she said carefully.

"And Lady Ravensgate delivers any communication? Personally?"

"Yes."

"Does she ever take you? Do you know who she deals with?"

"No. She's too careful for that."

And wasn't that a pity because it would have saved them time and effort if Collette had been able to reveal who her contact in London might be. It would also give Rafe something to use to hold Draven. That was exactly the sort of information the Foreign Office needed.

Instead, Rafe would have to use Jasper's talents. Not that he minded. Jasper was firmly in Rafe's debt.

"Can you give Lady Ravensgate a note today? I will have her followed, and once we know her contact, we can go to him or her directly."

She nodded. "I wondered how we would get around the fact that Lady Ravensgate reads all my correspondence. If I wrote to the royalists that they must bring my father to England, she would never agree to deliver the letter."

"Then write something benign today, some fluff you might have gathered at the garden party, and send that."

"She won't be pleased to come home and have to go out again."

"Will she delay?"

She shrugged delicately. "It's possible. She may read the note and decide delivery can wait another day."

"Then we give her two days. Meet me tomorrow night in the garden. Midnight."

"No. I don't want to see you again."

Rafe gave her a long look, so long he expected her to blush and look away. She blushed, the color high on her cheeks, but she didn't look away. "No doubt you would be pleased never to lay eyes on me again, and if you are fortunate, one day, you will have that privilege. But that day has not yet come. You're stuck with me for a little longer."

She glared at him. "I hate you."

"Tomorrow night. In the garden." With that he kissed her hand, which she snatched away, and bowed before he strode out the door.

❧

Collette dreaded the two days that followed. She'd obeyed Beaumont's orders. What other choice did she have? As she'd anticipated, Lady Ravensgate had read her letter and deemed it not important enough for immediate delivery. And when she'd gone out to deliver it the next day, Collette had watched her carriage as it sped down the street and turned the corner. Had Beaumont followed? She hadn't caught sight of him.

Collette supposed he might have asked someone else to follow Lady Ravensgate. That would have been safer, as the lady would surely recognize Rafe. Not to mention he tended to draw attention wherever he went. She could do nothing but wait and hope all went as they'd planned. And when Lady Ravensgate returned, Collette struggled to pretend she had not just set a plan in motion that would most certainly end with Lady Ravensgate, and quite possibly herself, on trial for treason. Collette attempted to read and sew and even draw, although her drawing skills left much to be desired.

"Are you feeling well, Collette?" Lady Ravensgate asked.

"No!" Collette answered, seizing on the opportunity to escape. "I have a slight headache." No need to worry Lady Ravensgate. "I think I shall lie down."

"Of course, my dear. Shall I check on you later?"

"Thank you." Collette made her way to her bedchamber. Later, when Lady Ravensgate looked in on her, she would tell the lady she felt better but a little tired and ask not to be disturbed. Then she would need only wait until midnight to meet Beaumont. Once in her chamber, Collette closed the door and leaned against it. Although she'd wanted to escape Lady Ravensgate, she hadn't feigned the headache. Lately, whenever she thought of Beaumont, her head started to throb.

She moved toward the bed, then froze when the curtains rustled. She had left them open, hadn't she? One of the maids might have closed them, but that didn't explain why they moved. Or the man who stepped out from behind them.

"Don't scream," Beaumont said.

Collette covered her mouth and only a small squeak emerged.

"You're earlier than I thought."

"What are you doing here?" she hissed. He looked even more handsome than she'd remembered. Had he always had a dimple in his right cheek? Why hadn't she noticed it before?

"I need to talk to you."

"Midnight. In the garden. Remember?"

He waved a hand, dismissing her. "I can't wait that long."

"Lady Ravensgate might come in at any moment. I don't have a key to my room. I can't lock it."

"If she comes in, I'll hide. The curtains work well enough or I can squeeze behind that chair." He looked around and nodded at the bed. "There's always the mattress. I'll lie under it and you lay on top."

Collette narrowed her eyes. "You seem to have some experience in this area."

"Hidden talents." He shrugged. "I had Lady Ravensgate followed. She met with a man in a bookstore. My information is that he lives above the store. We'll return tonight, and you will give him the letter demanding your father come to London for the delivery of the codes."

Collette stared at him. "*I* am to give him the letter? In the middle of the night?"

"I can't do it," Rafe said. "He'll know who you are, and you tell him Lady Ravensgate has taken ill and sent you in her place."

"And what will you do?"

"I'll take you there and wait for you below. We don't have time for a discussion. You need to write the letter. Have you paper, pen, and ink?"

She shook her head. "She doesn't allow me use of any except in the parlor."

Beaumont blew out a disgusted breath. "Must I do everything?" But apparently he was prepared for that eventuality because he pulled out parchment, an ink pot, and a quill from his greatcoat. Collette studied the garment.

"What else do you have in there?"

He gave her a quick grin. "Wouldn't you like to know."

Her heart gave a painful kick and a simmering heat began to build low in her belly. How could she still feel attracted to him when he'd lied to her? Betrayed her? She hated him even more than she might have because he'd made her love him. She didn't—she *wouldn't*—care for him any longer. Snatching the paper out of his hand, she took a bound book and placed the paper on top of it. Then she indicated the nightstand, and Beaumont set the ink pot and quill there. She didn't have a desk in the room, so the book would have to do. She sat on the bed, placed the book with the paper before her, and dipped the quill in the ink. She wrote, *Dear Sirs.*

"What do I say?" she asked, looking up. Beaumont was right beside her, looking over her shoulder. He was so close that she jerked and splattered several drops of ink on the paper.

"Do I make you nervous?"

"No." She blew on the ink to dry it. "I would finish this before Lady Ravensgate finds you and ruins everything."

"She won't find me. As to the wording, you tell

them you have the item they requested. You tell them you have made a special friend of a Lieutenant Colonel Draven. That's all. As I said before, just whet the appetite." His voice was close, low and velvety by her ear. "Tease them. Make them want more."

His voice made Collette shiver. She could all but feel his hands skating over her flesh. Gritting her teeth, Collette gave him a sharp look. Rafe merely raised his eyebrows in what she knew had to be feigned innocence. "Are you certain I should give them Draven's name?"

"Yes, but after you state your terms. You will only give them the codes in person. And after you do so, they must allow you and your father to go into hiding." He pointed to the paper. "Put it in your own words. There must be no question that this too comes from you."

The ink on her quill had dried and she reached to dip the nib into the pot again, but her body went rigid when she heard Lady Ravensgate's voice addressing one of the servants. "She's coming!" Collette hissed. Oh, why hadn't she told the lady she wanted to be left alone? Now she would be found not only with a man in her room, but also paper, pen, and ink.

"Lie down," Beaumont ordered.

"Rafe, this is no time—"

"Lie. Down."

She obeyed and managed not to yelp when he lifted her skirts and shoved the book and paper beneath them. Then he whisked away the ink pot and quill and disappeared behind the curtains. There was no question he'd done this sort of thing before. He was too practiced.

"Miss Fournay?" Lady Ravensgate tapped on the door.

Collette glanced at the curtains. They still swayed from Beaumont's rapid retreat.

"Collette?" Another tap on the door.

*Stop swaying! Be still!*

"May I come in, dear?"

*Dear. Dear?* As though the woman actually cared for her. The door opened, and Collette closed her eyes and hardly dared breathe. She prayed the curtains had stopped swaying and didn't draw Lady Ravensgate's attention. She heard the woman's slippers on the carpet and then felt her standing nearby and looking down at her. Slowly, as though just waking, Collette opened her eyes.

"How are you feeling?" Lady Ravensgate asked.

"A little better. I must have dozed off."

"Poor dear. Shall I fluff your pillows?"

"No! I mean, no thank you." The last thing she wanted was Lady Ravensgate fussing with any of the bedclothes or asking her to sit up or move in anyway. The paper wedged between her knees would rustle and that would be the end of everything. "I think I will just go back to sleep." She closed her eyes again, hoping the lady would take her cue and depart. Collette heard no sound for a long moment and then the lady's slippers shushed on the carpet again. Cracking her eyelids, Collette saw she was straightening a pile of books that had been knocked over when Beaumont had put the ink on the nightstand. That accomplished, the lady moved around the rest of the room. It was small and Collette did not have much, so the room was neat. Fortunately, the prevailing wisdom was that cool air and sunlight were to be avoided if one was ill, so Lady Ravensgate had no reason to open the windows or the curtains. But the longer she tarried, the more nervous Collette became.

Finally, Lady Ravensgate went to the door. "I will have a maid bring some supper a little later."

"Thank you," Collette said, not opening her eyes. "Just sleep for now."

Collette nodded and pretended to fall more deeply asleep. Then the door closed. Collette did not dare move for fear the lady would return to impart some forgotten words of wisdom. Finally, she heard the curtains swish and Rafe moved across the room. "Easy enough," he said.

Collette wanted to strike him. She hadn't stopped shaking. When he reached the bed, he began to lift her skirts, presumably to retrieve the book and paper, but she swatted his hands away. "Don't touch me." She had to whisper it because the servants might have been outside her door, but she managed to slap his hand hard enough that he frowned at her and shook it. "Let me have the ink and quill. I want to finish this before someone else interrupts."

He produced the items again, and she hastily scrawled the note. She waved the paper, waiting for the ink to dry. "Midnight in the garden. Do not come in my bedchamber again."

"That's the first time a woman has ever said that to me."

"I hope it's not the last. All I want is to help my father and go far away from you."

"Again, that's not a sentiment I usually hear from—"

She shoved the paper at him. "Take it. I'll see you at midnight."

He bowed. "I look forward to it." And then he pushed the curtains aside, opened the window, and slid out. She didn't know how he managed to make it to the ground. Perhaps there was a tree he used or he'd found a trellis to climb? She didn't care. She would have rather he'd fallen and smashed into a thousand pieces. Her head rather hoped he would.

Finally, she rushed to the window, but there was no sight of Rafe Beaumont. He'd made it away, apparently unscathed. Her heart, curse it, rejoiced.

# Twelve

RAFE DIDN'T LIKE THIS PART OF THE PLAN. HE DIDN'T like leading Collette to danger, even if the danger was minimal and he'd be right there all the time. But there was nothing for it. As Jasper had reiterated, she must be the one to give the intermediary the letter. Rafe would have to allow her out of his sight, but not for long. It had been hard enough not seeing her the past two days, but now that she was here, walking beside him along an alley that would take them to Bond Street, it would be even harder to allow her to take the risk—as small as it was.

"How much farther?" she asked, her voice muffled inside the cloak she wore. He'd insisted she pull the hood over her head. Any number of dangerous men were out on the streets at night, and they didn't need a reason to accost someone they encountered. Better to stay in the shadows and keep one's head down.

"Not far. It would have been faster to take a hackney or the main streets, but I don't want to be seen."

"You still have the letter I penned?"

"Yes." He'd held on to it even after they'd met in

the garden. He wasn't sure why he hadn't just given it to her when she'd first asked for it. Perhaps he wanted to make sure it wasn't lost or perhaps he felt he needed to give her a reason to stay beside him.

"What if the bookseller doesn't believe the letter?"

"It's not for him to believe or not believe. He just delivers the letters." Rafe had thought about how this was possible and determined the man must have dealt in books from all over the world. He either traveled back and forth to France or had the letter sent along with orders to French merchants for volumes in demand in England. The answer would be known soon enough. Once the Foreign Office knew about the man, he'd be taken into custody and all his secrets revealed.

The alley forked into two streets, and Rafe took Collette's arm, leading her toward the left. As soon as she understood the direction he wanted her to go, she yanked her arm away. "I can walk on my own, thank you."

She was colder than the Frost Fair of '14. He couldn't really blame her, and it surprised him that he minded so very much. Once he'd taken a woman to bed, Rafe had usually felt as though the chase was over. That didn't mean he ignored her or spurned her. He wasn't a scoundrel. But he didn't often have the urge to have her again.

And he never lost sleep wishing she had stayed the night. Women never stayed the night. In fact, he preferred to go to a woman so he could be the one who left and not face the awkwardness of having to, in essence, ask her to leave. But when Rafe had finally shoved Jasper out the door and lay down to sleep, he hadn't been able to. Her scent had lingered on his pillow and his sheets, the faint fragrance of juniper mixed with the scent that was Collette. Every time he'd breathed, he'd remembered flashes of the night they'd spent together. He'd relived the thrill of kissing her and running his hands over her soft skin and silky curves. When those thoughts had driven him all but mad, he'd retreated to the drawing room to sleep on the couch, but when he'd closed his eyes, he'd imagined her naked. He'd imagined the feel of her sex closing around him as he'd thrust into her.

Finally, he'd given up on sleep and chosen a book to read. But he hadn't even finished a page. He couldn't stop smiling as he remembered things she'd said and done the past few weeks. He had enjoyed their time at the theater and the museum. He'd enjoyed dancing with her and walking with her. And yes, he'd enjoyed taking her to bed. If all went as planned, she would be out of his life forever before long. And Rafe was torn between wanting things to go as planned so she would be safe and wanting everything to go wrong so he could keep her with him longer.

He had those same divided feelings tonight. He wanted everything to go as planned, but if the letter was lost or the bookseller not at home, or if something else went wrong, then he would be able to meet her again and soon. He would have another chance to make amends for having to lie to her.

Then all of those thoughts faded as he heard the echo of footsteps fall in behind them. At first Rafe thought he had imagined them. A glance at Collette showed her face, though somewhat hidden in shadow, didn't appear concerned. Feeling his gaze on her, she glanced at him, her brows arched in question. The footsteps grew closer, and he saw the moment she heard them as well. Her eyes widened and she twisted to look over her shoulder. Rafe caught her arm as they walked and leaned close so only she could hear. "Follow me and don't look back."

"I will," she murmured. Then he thought he heard something that sounded like *Contrary to Aristotle's claims, hedgehogs adopt a rear-mounting position during copulation.* She must have been nervous.

Rafe quickly scanned their location. They'd emerged from the alley, but they were still away from the main roads, where carriages and people might spot them. If they had been able to walk another few blocks, they would have reached Bond Street. As it was, the deserted gardens at the back of rows of terraced housing lay on one side and mews lay on the other. Rafe might not have been a skilled fighter like Ewan or a veteran soldier like Neil, but he knew when the odds were against him.

He often bemoaned the fact that he was never included in any of the exciting missions. He was always the one to stay back or rendezvous with the others when all was clear. But now that danger was right behind him, Rafe didn't feel nearly as confident. What if he couldn't protect Collette? What if Draven's men had been right and all he was good for was bedsport?

Rafe pushed the idea away. He could play the role of hero. He'd been waiting for his chance, and now he had it.

The footsteps grew closer, and Rafe could either turn and face their pursuers or run. There was no shame in running—Draven's men had done it when necessary—but there was no glory in it either. Rafe grasped Collette's hand and spun around. Two men were quickly approaching. One was older with stringy gray hair that hung long over his collar and framed his thin, leathery face. The other was a good deal younger. His dark hair was held by a piece of cord into a queue and the brim of his hat was pulled low over his forehead. He slapped a wooden stick about the length and thickness of a walking stick in his hand.

"Can I be of some assistance, gentlemen?" Rafe asked, giving his most charming smile. It worked best on women, but men were not immune.

The men halted—that was a good sign—and gave each other amused looks. "'E thinks we're gentlemen." That from the younger man.

"I am a gentleman," said the older man. This caused both men to erupt into a round of chuckles.

Rafe laughed too, edging himself in front of Collette as he did so.

"You're a rum duke," the younger man said. "Give us yer coin and the moll, and ye go on yer way."

"That hardly seems a fair trade."

"We can split your skull and then take yer coin and yer moll," said the older man.

Rafe scratched his chin. "I don't like that option either. How about this? You turn around and walk the other way, and I won't shoot both of you with my pistol."

The two thugs looked at each other, then back at

Rafe. He was a good card player. He could bluff his way through most any game, but as the seconds crept by, Rafe began to think these two might just have been better at this game than he.

"You don't have a barking iron." The younger man crossed his arms over his chest.

"So sure, are you?" Rafe drawled. He did have a pistol. He might not have had it with him, but he owned one. At least he had owned one at some point in time.

"Let's see it," demanded the older man.

"You want to see it?" Rafe reached beneath his coat. Apparently, he wasn't as good at bluffing as he'd thought. "How's this?" he bellowed, flinging the ink pot still pocketed in his coat at the two men. The stopper popped off and ink sprayed in an arc over both men. They held up their hands and yelped. Glory be damned. Rafe took advantage of the distraction and ran, pulling Collette along with him.

"This way!" he called, heading for Bond Street. The busier the street, the better.

She stumbled, gathered her skirts in her hand, and was right on his heels.

"Faster!" Rafe called, dragging her around a corner.

"They're right behind us," she warned.

"Hell's teeth!" Would his luck ever change? Shoving Collette behind him, he motioned for her to keep running. Then he crept closer to the corner and as the first man—the younger one—came around it, Rafe stuck out his foot. The man never even saw the obstacle, and he flew forward, landing with a thud on the ground. The older man was wise enough to avoid his friend's mistake. He plowed into Rafe, sending them both sprawling. Rafe hit the hard ground, and his first thought was for his greatcoat. He'd paid a fortune for it. He didn't have a second thought because the older man's fist slammed into his cheek.

It would have been his nose, but Rafe had turned his head at the last second. Blinding pain exploded in his head followed by a sprinkle of stars.

"Get her!" the older man screamed as he straddled Rafe and held him down.

Rafe shook the stars off and smashed his fist into his assailant's jaw. He heard a satisfying pop, and the man fell sideways. From the pain in his hand, Rafe wasn't certain if the sound was his own hand breaking or the impact of fist on face, but he didn't waste time finding out. He shoved the man off and staggered to his feet. The earth tilted like a ship in a storm at sea, and Rafe fell against the wall of the building he'd rounded. He heard the *thunk* of boots as the younger man pursued Collette, and Rafe shuffled after him. *This is no time to fall over,* he chided himself. *Stand up and save her.*

"Rafe!"

He recognized Collette's voice and kicked up his pace, weaving as he ran but staying on his feet. The dizziness was passing, and he was able to make out Collette just ahead. The younger thug had hold of her arm, and she was kicking and scratching wildly. The thug reached for her other arm and pushed her against the wall. She struggled, pushed away, and he knocked her back. Another hard shove like that and he'd bash her senseless.

"Rafe!"

Rafe jumped, knocking the man back and away

from Collette. He kicked out, but the man caught his boot and pushed, sending Rafe sprawling. From the ground, Rafe blinked. That move seemed to always work when Ewan used it. The assailant reached for Collette again, but she was quick. She ducked under his arm, circling him and causing him to turn to follow her. Rafe took advantage of the man's inattention, leaped (very well, crawled) to his feet, and jumped on the man's back.

It wasn't the most elegant fighting move he'd ever seen, but when the man slid to his knees, Rafe judged it one of the more successful. He wrapped his arms around the man's neck and squeezed until the man clawed at him. Fortunately, the greatcoat was made of thick wool and his efforts were largely ineffective. When the man slumped, gasping for breath, Rafe stood and, panting, held out a hand to Collette. "Mademoiselle." He wiped the back of his hand across his mouth and his glove came away bloody. "Shall we?"

Her eyes widened when she caught sight of his face, but she took his arm without hesitation. "Thank you, sir." And the two of them strolled away.

⁂

Rafe walked confidently enough, but Collette couldn't stop darting glances at him. She'd never seen him look less than perfect. Now his hair was disheveled, his cheek red and swollen, and his lip bled. His coat was torn and dirty, and his eyes glittered with anger. He looked dangerous.

Each time she looked at him, her heart pounded so

hard in her chest that she caught her breath. She wanted him. She wanted to push him against the wall of one of the shops right here on Bond Street and kiss him until neither of them could breathe. His gaze met hers, held, and then she was off her feet and being carried into the doorway of what smelled like a bakery. Under the shelter of the doorway's canopy, Rafe pinned her to the wall and bent his head to hers. "Are you hurt?" His voice was husky and low, almost breathless.

"No," she managed. "But your cheek…" She lifted a hand to touch the swollen skin, but he caught her. Slowly, he pressed her hand back against the building, just above her head.

"I thought… I didn't think…"

She understood what he couldn't find words to say because she felt the same way. He had almost lost her. She had very nearly lost him. "You won't be rid of me that easily."

"I won't be rid of you at all."

She looked up at him to ask what he meant, but his mouth closed over hers, hot and demanding. She lost any thought of anything other than kissing him back. Their tongues tangled and dueled, and his hard body pressed against her soft one. When he would have gentled the kiss and possibly drawn back, she lifted her free hand and fisted it in his hair, pulling his lips back to hers.

"Oy! You there!" The man's voice slowly penetrated the haze of arousal. "None of that here or I'll have you arrested, I will!"

Collette loosened her grip on his hair, and Rafe looked up. He let out a disbelieving breath. "It's the

Watch. Why don't you go chase a real criminal!" he yelled back.

"Wot was that?"

"Now you've done it," Collette muttered as the Watch, a man three stone overweight and at least fifty years old, lumbered toward them. "Come on!" She tugged at Rafe's coat, but he hesitated. She could tell he was spoiling for a fight. She'd seen this sort of reaction before. Emotion ran high—fear, anger, pain—and a man needed somewhere to put it. Based on her behavior just now, she was not immune to that impulse either. But they didn't need any trouble from the Watch. She grasped Rafe's hand and tugged.

"We'll be on our way," she called to the approaching watchman. "Which way to the bookstore?"

"This way." Rafe quickened his step, and when they were far enough away that the Watch would have been forced to run, he gave up the chase. "Useless coward," Rafe grumbled.

"Do you still have the letter?" she asked. He felt in his battered coat and then nodded.

"I have it. And this is the shop."

She paused and stared at the small shop with a black sign displaying the drawing of a book and the words *W. Morgan, Bookseller*. The shop was dark, of course, but in the window a selection of bound volumes was on display behind the thick glass.

"The entrance to the living quarters are around back," Rafe said. She followed him past another few shops and then down an alley and around the back of the businesses. After their interactions with the thugs, she didn't particularly want to stand around.

"Shall we go up and knock on the door?" She indicated a wooden staircase leading to the first floor.

"You go. I'll wait here."

"You want me to go alone?"

"No, but there's no other way. It's better if he doesn't see me. If we make him nervous, he's likely to flee the city, and then we've lost our only means of contacting your father's captors. If he asks, tell him you took a hackney and gave the driver a ha'penny to come back in a quarter hour."

She swallowed and nodded. He was right, of course. She would have to go alone. And he'd be waiting for her here. He wouldn't leave without her. Rafe pulled the letter from his coat and put it in her hands. With a nod, he stood back, under the steps so he couldn't be seen from above. Collette lifted her skirts and started up the stairway. At the top, she knocked lightly on the worn wood. She didn't see any light or hear any sound coming from inside, so she assumed W. Morgan was sleeping.

She counted to ten and then knocked again, this time louder. The sound seemed to echo across the dark buildings, and she peeked over her shoulder to see if she'd roused anyone. Then the sound of a lock being turned made her jump, and she swung back around. The door opened a sliver.

"What do you want?" asked a papery voice.

Collette lowered her gaze to settle it on one blue eye looking out at her and a gnarled hand holding the door wide enough for that eye to see her.

"I have business," she whispered, not wanting to say too much before they were in private. "May I come in?"

"What sort of business?" the old man asked.

"The sort Lady Ravensgate comes to you about."

The eye peering at her blinked. The door opened wider and the man moved aside. Collette squeezed through and was all but shoved out of the way as the man hurried to bolt it again. Now that she was inside the room, she could see, by the light of a single lamp illuminating the room, that the man was thin, small, and garbed in a burgundy dressing gown that had once been rather lovely and elegant but now was thin and shabby. He was short, not quite her height, and he had white hair and wrinkled yellow skin. "Where is Lady Ravensgate?" he asked in a hushed voice.

Collette had rehearsed her answer and responded without hesitation. "She ate something that has upset her stomach. We've called for the doctor."

"You fear poison?" the old man said, coming to exactly the conclusion she'd wanted.

She paused, allowing the thought to seep in. "She sent me in her stead. The information in this letter"—now she held it up to the light—"is too valuable to delay in sending. I am—"

He waved a hand. "I know who you are."

Did he also know where her father was? Did he know the men holding her father? Surely he was too old and frail to make the crossing and deliver the letters. But he undoubtedly knew something of their contents.

"Then you will send the letter right away?" She offered him the letter, but he didn't take it.

"Who else knows you are here?" he asked.

"No one but Lady Ravensgate. She did not wish to tell me where to go, but we had no other choice."

"And you say she has been poisoned?"

She hadn't said that at all, only implied it. "It might have been a bad piece of fish. The doctor has been summoned."

"How did you come to be at my door, all alone, in the middle of the night? I didn't hear her ladyship's carriage."

"I took a hackney and asked the driver to stop a little ways from the shop. I gave him a ha'penny to come back in a quarter of an hour. My time is almost up. Will you deliver the letter?"

"And if I won't?"

She hadn't expected this response. She had wanted this exchange to go quickly. The sooner she could be away from this dark flat and this man of questionable loyalties, the better. She straightened, determined not to show any fear. Only her courage would save her. "Then Lady Ravensgate and I will find someone who will."

The old man's face didn't change. "Do you really think you can save him?"

She could only assume the old man meant her father. "That's not your concern." She moved toward the door. "If you'll excuse me."

"What makes you think he isn't dead already?"

She paused. "What makes you think he is?"

The old man met her gaze with pity in his eyes. "A man like that, better to let him die."

"You don't know what you're talking about!"

"I know that soon it will be your head in the noose. Run while you still can."

Collette did run. She flung open the door and scrambled down the steps as fast as her legs would take her.

When she reached the bottom, she didn't stop running. Her only thought was to put distance between herself and the bookseller. All she had wanted was a quiet life for her father and herself. All she had wanted was peace.

But she'd never have peace. Collette had begun to think she'd never see her father again. And what then? She'd be alone in the world, without family or friends. She had nothing. Even the clothes on her back did not belong to her. If Beaumont's plan didn't work, what would she do and where would she go?

Strong arms caught her about the waist and she struggled for freedom until she heard the familiar voice. "Collette, it's me."

She ceased fighting but kept her head averted, not wanting him to see the tears in her eyes. She'd forgotten he waited for her below. She'd only wanted to get away.

"What happened?"

She shook her head, her throat too choked for words.

"Did he hurt you? Touch you?"

"No, nothing like that."

His arms tensed and then he released her. "We can't stay here without attracting attention. You can tell me more later." Hand on the small of her back, he guided her around a corner.

And they both stumbled into a girl carrying a bundle of flowers. The girl let out a screech and all the flowers scattered. Roses, lilies, daisies, and tulips rained down and littered the hard-packed earth.

"Oh, I'm terribly sorry," Collette said, bending to collect a bunch of daisies.

"Who do you think you are?" the flower girl hollered, her Cockney accent so thick Collette could barely understand her. She was a small thing, skinny and scrawny and the size of a twelve-year-old. But she had the voice of a fishwife. "Look wot you done. All me flowers—ruined!"

"They are not ruined, miss," Rafe said, his voice low and civil. He swept several roses into his hand. "We'll help you collect them and you can be on your way."

Unfortunately, one of the roses he held out as proof against hardship had a bent stem and the bud flopped over. The flower girl wailed even louder.

"I'm done for! How could you do this to me? I ain't done nothing to you."

Candles flickered in windows above them, and a few people leaned out and yelled down for them to cease the noise and clear off.

Collette exchanged a look with Rafe. The last thing they needed was the neighbors' attention or for the Watch to intervene.

"Look, miss, there's no need for all this racket," Rafe said. "I'll pay you."

Like a wind-up doll, the flower girl stuck out her hand. Rafe reached into his coat and then placed a coin in her hand. She looked down. "A shilling? That's it? I could have made a pound selling all them flowers."

Rafe straightened. "Now, see here. Not only is that patent exaggeration, but our collision was an honest mistake. A shilling is more than fair."

"Watch!" the flower girl cried. "Watchman!"

Collette grabbed Rafe's arm and squeezed. The Watch would likely not take the flower girl's side, but

that didn't matter. How would she explain her presence here to the Watch? What if they took her home?
What would she tell Lady Ravensgate?

"Hush!" Rafe commanded. "If you bring the
Watch here, I'll tell him you're harassing me." He was
not dressed as finely as usual tonight, but his stylish
greatcoat, shiny boots, and the froth of white linen at
his neck proclaimed him a nobleman. Although, with
his disheveled hair and the bruise on his cheek, he
looked a bit less reputable than usual.

"Did you hear that?" the flower girl screamed to
the buildings around them. Collette hunched her
shoulders. "He threatened me. Watchman!"

Rafe took Collette's hand. "There's only one thing
to do," he said.

"What's that?"

"Run!" Rafe yanked her with him, and though
Collette's legs felt as though they couldn't possibly
manage another step, she kept pace with him. Behind
them, the flower girl screamed as though being
murdered.

"What now?" Collette panted as the girl's screams
grew farther away.

"I wish we had run toward Oxford Street. We
might have hailed a hackney or ducked into a tavern."

"You there!" a new voice called out with authority.

Collette did not bother to look. She knew it was
a watchman, possibly the same one they had encountered earlier. She could not be caught out with Rafe.
Lady Ravensgate would surely hear of it, and if the
lady couldn't take Collette into public to spy any
longer, she'd be of no use. She had to get back to the

town house and play her part for a little while longer, to give her father's captors time to cross the Channel.

That was *if* W. Morgan actually sent the letter.

"Halt! Halt in the name of the king!"

Rafe ran faster.

"Where are we going?" she managed between pants.

"Brook Street," he said.

"Brook Street? What's on Brook Street?"

"Residences and you know what that means."

"No."

"Horses."

Wonderful. She would end the night as a horse thief. Between the flower girl, the king's men, and Rafe Beaumont's schemes, this night was turning into the longest of her life.

# Thirteen

BUT RAFE HAD NO INTENTION OF STEALING A HORSE. The thought had never entered his mind. Instead, he turned onto Brook Street, then arrowed back into the mews behind the houses, where the carriage hacks were stabled when the residents of Brook Street were in Town.

Fortunately, the Season was over and many were not in Town. Some of the mews would be empty. When he and Collette had outrun the watchman—never a doubt in Rafe's mind they would—he pressed himself against a lamppost and caught his breath. Hand to her rapidly rising chest, she did the same.

"How do we know which are empty?" she asked after he'd told her his plan.

It was a good question. "If the family is in Town, the horse will be exercised daily and the grooms will be in and out. The empty mews will likely not have stray pieces of straw outside and will probably be padlocked."

"Won't they all be locked?"

"Not from the outside. The grooms sleep in the mews with the horses. He wouldn't be locked in."

"Let's go then, before one of our friends catches up."

"Agreed."

They passed the first set of mews, Rafe waving her on because he wanted to put as much distance as he could between their pursuers and their hiding spot. Finally, toward the end of the lane, he spotted a door with a large padlock. The dirt that made up the path in front of the doorway looked relatively undisturbed. "This one," Rafe said. Collette moved closer, watching his back as he examined the padlock. It was sturdy and fastened tight.

"Can you pick the lock?" she asked.

He glanced up at her. "What do you think I am? A criminal?"

She raised her brows in accusation.

Rafe cleared his throat. "I may have acquired a few skills here and there." He withdrew a pick about the length of his finger from the inside pocket of his coat.

"Your lock-picking tools?"

Rafe shrugged. "One never knows when they will be useful."

She gaped at him in disbelief, and he rather liked that she hadn't expected this of him. She'd find he had more than one hidden talent. He bent low and, mostly by feel and sound, sprang the padlock. Unfortunately, the doors didn't squeak open as he'd expected.

"Hell's teeth! It's barred from the inside." Leave it to him to pick the one mews where the owners took extra precautions.

"Then there must be another entrance."

"Undoubtedly, but we don't have time to search for it. We'll have to find another way in." He looked up and spotted windows above the door where the horse and carriage would be brought out. Tack might be kept in a loft above as well as cots for the grooms. The windows had heavy material fastened over them from the inside, but he could kick through it—if he could reach them.

"There," he said, pointing to one of the windows.

Collette looked up. "How will we get inside?"

He studied the buildings again. These buildings were brick, and between this building and the next, an uneven brick pillar had been erected. The design repeated itself down the length of the row. The pillars served to differentiate the various buildings as well as provide additional support to the structures. "I'll climb up, hop in the window, then climb down and open the door for you."

She looked at him skeptically. "And if someone sees me while you're inside?"

"Pray they don't." He tested the pillar beside him and placed one foot on the first brick sticking out.

"Rafe!"

"Stand in the shadows"—he pulled himself up and felt for another foothold—"and hope for the best."

"I hate you," she muttered.

"Then this might be your lucky night." The bricks were old and some had crumbled, which accounted for their unevenness. "If I step wrong, I'll probably fall and crack my head open."

She made a sound he couldn't quite distinguish as pleased or uncaring, and he pulled himself up again. She was angry with him. He could hardly blame her, but the thugs and the watchman hadn't been his fault. And they were out here tonight to save her father.

Well, he didn't care a damn for her father, but somewhere between Draven's order to gather information on her and taking her to his bed, he'd come to care for her. He couldn't leave her to whatever fate Lady Ravensgate and her compatriots had in mind. Rafe might not know exactly who they were, but he knew what they were. No matter what information she gave them, they would never have let her or her father go free.

The window was within reach, and he pulled himself up and lodged a foot on the ridge that made up the door of the mews. He'd been in and out of his share of windows and was relatively confident here. The canvas covering the window was tacked down tightly, but Rafe managed to punch a section away and slide his shoulders through. It was a tight fit, but he squeezed in, then pulled the rest of the material away. He'd put it back once Collette was inside. He didn't want a passerby to notice something amiss.

The room was dark and smelled strongly of horses and dust. His nose itched from the tiny particles of straw he'd stirred up. He scanned the darkness, waiting for his eyes to adjust. First, he discerned the shapes of saddles and bridles and tools to repair a carriage. He looked the other way and saw cots and a small table, where the grooms might polish the leather of the tack or mend broken pieces. Beside the table was a long trunk and beside that a ladder down to the first floor.

Or at least there should have been.

Rafe leaned down and felt for the ladder, but it

was not there. Damn! He couldn't get down to lift the bar on the door without a ladder. The drop was too far. Rafe looked at the trunk again. He crossed to it, opened the top and lifted out riding whips and strips of leather that might be used for reins. Below that, he found exactly what he was looking for. The rope could be used to lead the horse out of the mews for exercise or grooming when the animal wasn't needed to pull the conveyance. Rafe went back to the window and threw the rope down, tying the other end of it to a hook in the wall.

"New plan," he hissed. Collette looked up at him. The rope only reached her shoulders. She might grasp it while he pulled her up, but if she let go, she'd fall. Certain injury and possible death would follow. She needed to have some purchase of her own. "Hold the end of the rope and use the pillar to climb higher. Once you've a solid hold, I'll pull you up," he called down, keeping his voice low. "If your hands slip, grasp the bricks."

She stared at him, the light too poor for him to see the expression on her face. "I am in skirts," she said finally.

"I'll pull you up quickly."

"Is there no other way? Why not unbar the door?"

"No time to argue. Hurry."

She muttered something in French and then she put her hand on the pillar, lifted her skirt, and tried to place her foot. Slowly, she began to climb. Rafe alternated between watching her and the end of the street. The Watch would eventually make his way down here. Rafe could only hope he'd gone to find a partner so as not to be walking the streets alone. She climbed higher, level with the rope, and Rafe nodded approval. "Good. Grasp the rope tightly, and I'll pull."

"I'm doing fine, thank you." She was. Perhaps she hadn't lied about growing up on a farm. She looked as though she'd climbed before. In fact, even in skirts she seemed more adept at the task than he. Finally, she reached the top of the pillar, but her skirts were too cumbersome to allow her to reach a leg over and balance on the thin ledge above the door. Instead, she wrapped the rope around her hands, then gave him a nod. "Pull me up."

He'd been holding the rope all this time, but once her full weight was on it, he had to dig his heels in and tug her up slowly and steadily. When he spotted her head at the window, he paused. "Grasp the casement. I'll take your hands."

"You won't let go of the rope?"

He had to loosen his hold on it if he hoped to move to the window and take her hands. "Let me know when you have the window."

The rope jerked and the tension eased, then returned. Finally, it eased again. "I have it."

He could see her fingers curled over the casement. Dropping the rope, he crossed to the window and caught hold of her wrists. He pulled her in slowly, taking her waist when he had her halfway inside. It was then he heard men talking in low voices. Rafe didn't know if it was the Watch or the thugs or another banshee flower girl, but he did not want Collette's legs sticking out when they passed this way.

With a jerk, he pulled her inside the window. Her

legs never touched the floor, and her fall was broken as she fell hard on top of him.

"What are you—"

He put a hand over her mouth. "Shh!"

She slid off him, sitting on the floor beside where he lay. Rafe barely dared breathe as he listened. When the sound of the men's voices grew louder, she gripped his hand and squeezed.

"You check that side. I'll check this one."

"The Watch," she whispered.

He nodded. Rafe wished he'd had time to replace the burlap over the window, but he didn't want to risk the watchmen spotting any movement. Collette's leg was pressed against his side. Her skirts had ridden up, and he could just make out the skin of her calf and knee. He glanced at her face, but she looked away from him. It would have been too dark to see her expression at any rate. From the way she gripped his hand, he knew she was worried. He gave her a reassuring squeeze and she looked back at him, her long hair falling over her shoulder and brushing his hand. Rafe had the urge to slide a hand behind her neck and bring her mouth to his for a long kiss. She might have hated him, but he still wanted her.

Finally, the men's voices faded and Collette released his hand. Rafe rose to his feet and, keeping low, peered out the bottom of the window. The alley between the rows of mews was empty again. He dragged the burlap back over the window, then shrugged his greatcoat off and hung it there too as an added layer of protection.

Now the room was shrouded in blackness, and he felt his way to the small table and then the trunk. He thought he'd seen a tinderbox inside. He felt around the leather strips until his fingers closed on the box. There would be a lantern, most likely near the doorway. Rafe would probably break his neck trying to climb down the ladder to the first floor in the dark. Instead, he stumbled across the loft toward the hanging tack.

"What are you doing?" Collette whispered.

"Looking for a lantern. I'd rather not sit in the dark for the next few hours."

"Hours! I have to get back."

His foot caught on something hard and square and before he could stop himself, his shin collided with it too. Stifling a curse, Rafe went around the object.

"Rafe!"

"I'll have you back," he said through teeth gritted in pain. "But we cannot go right now. We're far too popular. If we give it a couple hours, the criminals and the Watch will have moved on to other prey." He felt the polished leather of a saddle and reached for the hooks to investigate what else might be hanging on the racks. Finally, he traced the contours of a lantern. Setting it on the floor, he spent about ten minutes trying to use the tinderbox to light a match by feel. When he managed to ignite the lantern, he sat back on his haunches and blew out a breath. Collette was standing a few feet away—the loft was only about four paces long and three wide—her hands twisted together.

"It will be close," she said, and he knew she still worried about returning to Lady Ravensgate's before the servants awoke.

"I'll have you back," he promised again.

"I don't even know if the bookseller will deliver the letter."

"What happened?" Rafe asked. "Did he say he wouldn't deliver it?"

"He threatened as much." She swallowed visibly. "And he taunted me. He told me a man like my father was better dead. He said my neck would soon be in the noose, and I should run."

Rafe crossed to her and took her shoulders. "I won't let that happen."

"I don't believe you."

"I'm not the enemy, Collette."

"You're not my friend."

"I am. I want to help you."

"By turning me in to your friends at the Foreign Office?" She shrugged her shoulders, easing his hands off. "I'm just another woman you seduced for information."

"No."

Hands on her hips, she narrowed her eyes at him. Perhaps he shouldn't have lit the lantern. Then he wouldn't have been able to see her disdain so clearly. "How am I different?" she asked.

Rafe opened his mouth to answer but couldn't think of anything to say that she would believe. Finally, he said the only thing that made any sense to him. "Because you *are* different."

"Different because we're here in England, different because the war is over, or different—"

"Different because I care about you."

She stared at him as though he had grown two heads. He feared he might have. What had possessed him to admit he cared for her? It was an opening for her to scoff at him, and Rafe did not allow himself to be vulnerable.

"You say that to every woman."

"No, I don't."

She tilted her head, giving him a skeptical lift of her brows.

Hell's teeth, but she infuriated him. Here he was saying everything he had vowed he would never say to a woman, and she didn't even believe him. The irony was almost poetic.

"Don't give me any more of your pretty lies. I'll give you this, Rafe Beaumont—you are very good at what you do. You almost made me fall in love with you the other night." She went on, saying something about how his words had been perfect, but he couldn't make sense of anything except that she loved him.

No, she *almost* loved him.

"Collette—"

"And then there was the wine from Burgundy and the—"

"Collette." He took her shoulders again. "What can I do to make you believe me?"

She gave him a level look. "Help my father and me escape."

Rafe closed his eyes and released her. It would have to be the one thing he could not do. He had already decided to help her get away. Draven would not be pleased, but he would look the other way. She was a pawn, nothing more. She didn't know anything and wasn't a threat to England's security.

Her father, on the other hand, had been responsible

for countless deaths, not only of Napoleon's political opponents, but also of British citizens. He couldn't go unpunished. And if Rafe helped him evade capture, it would be akin to treason.

"That's what I thought," she said quietly.

"You ask the impossible."

"Then why even bother taking me back to Lady Ravensgate's tonight? Just turn me in. I want this nightmare over."

"Then you'll never see your father again."

"I'd rather that than to watch him suffer on the scaffold."

He reached for her, but she stepped back. "Don't touch me."

"I won't let your father suffer, and you know I will do all I can to help you go free."

"You'll go against your orders?"

"If I must. The circumstances have changed."

"Nothing has changed."

"Everything has changed." He stepped forward, and when she moved back, her legs brushed the table. She was out of space to escape him. Rafe put his hands on her waist. "For me, everything has changed."

"If this is a ploy to wheedle more information, I have no more to give."

He shook his head, lifted a hand, and brushed it over her cheek. He felt the silk of her skin and his finger tingled. She closed her eyes briefly, then opened them again. They were dark and unreadable.

"It's no ploy. I care about you." He leaned forward and kissed her soft cheek. He couldn't stop himself from inhaling her addictive scent. His body tightened. "I want you." He kissed her other cheek.

"If you think I'll let you bed me in exchange for—"

He put a finger on her lips. "No exchanges. No bargains. No deals."

"No thinking about what happens tomorrow or next week?"

He nodded. The blood thrummed in his ears. His heart raced.

"I'm not as good at that as you seem to be."

"Then allow me to help you." He leaned forward and kissed her. He wanted desperately for her to kiss him back, but he held her loosely, kissed her lightly. If she rejected him, he could retreat to the other side of the room and lick his wounds. It would be a much-needed reminder of why he never allowed himself to care too much about a woman.

He felt her hesitation, knew she was still thinking. He couldn't let her leave him, not without trying to show her how he felt. It was dangerous to open himself up more, but he would hate himself if he didn't at least try. The hand still at her waist slid back and down, cupping her bottom and bringing her tightly against his arousal. "Don't think," he murmured. "Just feel. Let me show you how *I* feel."

A long moment passed, then another. His head swam with desire. The feel of her against him, her sweet flesh in his hands made him hard and focused. Nothing but Collette mattered in this moment. Time seemed to drag on as he stood holding her. And then she put her arms around him and kissed him back. Rafe was all but undone by the sweetness of her kiss.

It was tentative—a fragile thread of trust and hope wrapped around something else he couldn't quite name. He returned the kiss, putting all of the emotions he couldn't name into the act of meeting her lips with his. He would show her she was not wrong to trust him, not wrong to believe in him.

He would show her she was different to him. She'd come closer to his heart than any other woman, and when he kissed her, when he touched her, he tried to show her a piece of his heart.

The kiss deepened and he lifted her onto the table and stepped between her legs. He held her face between his hands, his lips reverently tracing every line of her lovely features. Her hands were not quite so reverent. She pushed his coat back and unfastened the buttons of his waistcoat. Then her hands were tugging his shirt out and sliding under the linen to touch the bare skin beneath. Rafe hissed in a breath and, because he could not focus, moved his lips to her neck, untying her cloak and pushing it off her shoulders. His lips were on the skin of her shoulders and his hands were filled with her breasts, still swathed in yellow muslin. He wanted to feel her warm, naked flesh, but the bodice was too tight to push down. His hand worked between the fabric until his knuckles brushed the swells of her breast, and she moaned quietly.

Then her hand was on the placket of his trousers, tracing the outline of his erection. He freed his hands and stepped back, a sacrifice he thought he deserved some sort of medal for. "Let me pleasure you tonight."

She shook her head. "Let's pleasure each other. If this is the end, I want one more night with you."

She reached for his hips, brought him back between her legs.

"You don't need to do anything."

She gave him an arched look. "And if I *want* to?" Her hand found him again, and this time she opened the placket. "If this gives me pleasure?" She reached in and drew him out, slid her hand up and up and then down, down, down his swollen flesh.

"Who am I to argue?" he said through clenched teeth.

Her hand slid up and then down again, her actions sure but by no means practiced. Rafe had exercised self-control before—not that anyone ever gave him credit for it—and he summoned every last ounce to gather her skirts to her knees and slide his hands over the plump skin of her thighs. She was so warm, so soft, and when he skimmed the apex of her thighs, she was so wet. She did want him as much as he wanted her. Her legs wrapped around him, and he eased her back onto her cloak, raising her skirts as he did so to reveal her pink center. He stroked a finger over her sensitive flesh and watched her shiver. Then he parted her and traced the small nub that gave her pleasure until her head whipped back and forth and her hips bucked. Her legs tightened on him, and he yanked her hips forward, then plunged into her.

Her eyes opened, glittering in the soft light, and filled with pleasure. "Yes," she murmured. "Rafe. Yes."

He couldn't look away from her. Even as the intensity of the connection between them grew, as his body plundered hers, as he gave and she took and then she gave and he took, he could not break the link between them. Somewhere in his mind, a part of him urged him to look away, to turn her over, to concentrate on the feel of his body joining with hers. But his instincts had taken over, and he knew no matter how good it felt to thrust into her—and it felt better than he could ever remember—nothing could match the way she looked at him in that moment.

And when she climaxed, his name on her lips, he held her gaze and allowed himself to come, allowed her to see the pleasure crash over him, to hear her name on his lips, and watch as she took him over the edge to a place he'd come close to but never before reached. She drew him down, kissing him gently, cupping his face, and whispering that everything was all right.

It wasn't all right. He'd revealed too much of himself. He'd let her see into not just his heart but his soul. If she didn't know that she'd seen the truth about his feelings for her, she had to be blind. But then again, what if she had seen the truth and then used it against him?

He knew the thought didn't make sense. Knew he was the one with all the power here, the one who held her life in his hands. And yet, she was caressing his hair and telling him over and over that it was all right.

And then he realized what she meant. He was still inside her. He had spilled his seed inside her.

Hastily, he withdrew and stepped away from her, rearranging his clothing. "I apologize. I wasn't think-ing." That was certainly true enough, but little good an apology did when the damage was done. His friend Neil Wraxall was a bastard, and Rafe had seen the pain his illegitimacy had caused Neil. That was only one reason Rafe had always been careful about his relations with women. Now he might very well have gotten Collette with child.

She sat up and pushed her skirts down. Obviously, the mood was completely broken. He'd gone from experiencing one of the most amazing moments of his life to feeling utter terror and remorse.

"It's fine," she said. She reached for his hand, and Rafe knew he should allow her to take it. He could hold her, perhaps recapture some of the intimacy they'd both felt a few moments ago. But instead, he couldn't seem to move. He couldn't quite believe she hadn't trapped him. It was ridiculous, of course. She hadn't forced his actions, but his mind wasn't thinking rationally. He was like a wild animal after the cage door had slammed shut.

"I might have gotten you with child."

"It's unlikely. Besides, didn't you just tell me not to think about what happens next month or next week?" She smiled.

"This is serious, Collette."

"Oh, well, in that case, you have nothing to worry about. I'm sure I'll be dead in a few weeks. Then you needn't worry about the consequences." She pushed off the table and swept past him.

"I won't let that happen to you." He raked a hand through his hair. "I told you."

"So you will keep me from being prosecuted as a traitor, but God forbid you make any additional commitment to me or your child."

A chill ran through him. "You just said it was unlikely there would be a child."

She shook her head in amazement. "What are you so afraid of? Do you think I want you to father my child? Do you think I'll try to make you marry me?"

Rafe didn't know what she saw in his face, but she took a step back. "That's it, isn't it? You think I'm trying to trap you into marriage."

"No—"

"And how exactly did I force you to lie with me? How did I force you to climax inside me?"

"I didn't say that."

"Oh, you said all that and more, just not in so many words."

"That makes no sense."

"It makes perfect sense!" She slashed her hand angrily through the air. "And for the record, I no more want to be saddled with a womanizing—what is the word you English use?—*dandy* than you want to be trapped in marriage to a French spy!"

"I am not a dandy."

She gaped at him. "That is your rebuttal?"

Rafe was so angry he was practically shaking. "Lower your voice," he ordered.

"Why? Let them find us. Let's end this now." She crossed to the window and opened the burlap. "We're up here! Come and find us!"

Rafe pulled her away and pushed her up against the wall. "Stop this now."

"Why? This will solve your problems."

He took her face in his hands. "You are not a problem."

"You are!" Tears wet her eyes. "I don't want to feel like this. I don't want to care about you. I want this over."

"I don't." He kissed her. He couldn't stop himself.

He knew it was a bad idea. He knew he shouldn't want her, shouldn't take her, shouldn't entwine himself any further with her. But he couldn't make himself stop any of it. Because he had never felt what he'd felt with her, and now he wanted more of it. Rafe could understand why opium addicts took the drug long after it had ruined their health, their finances, and their lives. Rafe *needed* Collette.

But she didn't kiss him back. She pushed him gently away. "I can't do this anymore. I don't know what to feel. I hate you and then I love you and then I hate you all over again."

Rafe's hands clenched into fists. "You love me?"

She pressed her hands against her eyes. "That frightens you. I can see by the look in your face." She scooted away from him, but this time her movements were calm and measured. "I don't understand you, Rafe Beaumont. I don't want to."

"What does that mean?"

"It means stay away from me until we're forced together. I'll have to intercept mail before Lady Ravensgate sees it. When I receive word from France, I'll leave you a message in the Ravensgate town house. We needn't see each other until I go to meet my father."

"That might be weeks."

"Good."

"Yes," Rafe agreed, but for some reason, the thought of not seeing her was the one thought that terrified him most of all.

# *Fourteen*

COLLETTE COULDN'T HAVE SAID HOW SHE MADE IT back to Lady Ravensgate's town house safely. Perhaps waiting a few hours, as Rafe had suggested, had been all it took to make certain the men pursuing them were otherwise engaged. She'd been afraid the servants would catch her sneaking back in, but the house had still been silent when she'd crept in the back door and up the stairs to her room.

That was when the waiting began. And with the waiting came the worrying because she had no way to know whether or not W. Morgan would actually send her letter. What if he sent a letter to Lady Ravensgate asking her about it and inquiring after her health?

And when Collette was not worrying about the bookseller, she worried about the royalists sending a reply to Lady Ravensgate. Collette didn't want to be seen as skulking about the vestibule, waiting for the mail, but she had to skulk about if she had any hope of intercepting it. In addition, she had to do all this skulking while pretending to be dreadfully ill, lest Lady Ravensgate force her to attend soirees and parties so she might spy. Not only did Collette not want to spy, but she also didn't want to chance seeing Beaumont out and about. She didn't trust herself around him. She wasn't certain if she would kill him or embrace him, but either option was to be avoided.

"Whatever has happened to that handsome Mr. Beaumont?" Lady Ravensgate asked one morning at breakfast. Collette was eating rather heartily after feigning stomach troubles the last few days and subsisting on weak broth. But just in case Lady Ravensgate had plans for this evening, Collette had already sneezed several times and pretended to blow her nose in a handkerchief. "I thought the two of you were friends," the lady said, sipping her tea.

"We were—are, I mean." Collette dabbed at her nose, which she'd pinched to redden. "I think he must have gone to the country to be with his family."

"He never goes to the country, or so I am told. Not to mention, I saw him last night at Mrs. Ware's dinner party."

Collette tried to appear uninterested. "Perhaps he has found a new friend," she said.

"He certainly seemed to have found several. He was making quite a show of himself, feeding one young lady from his own plate and fending off another who I am quite certain had her hand on his leg under the table. Mrs. Ware was scandalized."

Collette bit her tongue. Mrs. Ware was probably thrilled at having something interesting occur at her boring function. Collette might have wished it didn't have to do with Beaumont and women. She had no claim on him at all. In fact, she had told him she wanted to be left alone. Then why did she feel a slice of jealousy cut her to the quick? Why did she have the urge to not only murder those two women but Beaumont besides?

"It is too bad you and he are no longer friends," Lady Ravensgate was saying. "He might have been useful."

"I know we both thought so," Collette answered, "but I never heard him talk about anything other than frivolities."

"True enough."

Collette sneezed again, hoping it sounded convincing.

"I suppose you will not be able to attend the theater with me tonight," Lady Ravensgate remarked.

"My stomach is much better." Collette blew her nose with a loud honk.

"Yes, but your respiratory condition has worsened. Shall I call for a doctor?"

"No. I am sure with a little rest, I will be much better." Was that her imagination or had she heard a sound in the vestibule? Could it be a messenger with a letter?

"More rest? You have rested more in the past few days than I have in a lifetime." Her eyes narrowed. "You had better find a way to heal soon, Collette, or you will have more serious concerns."

Collette's gaze locked with Lady Ravensgate's. The threat was very, very real. The royalists wanted those codes, and if Collette could not deliver them, then they would find someone who could. At that point, she would be superfluous and discarded. Permanently.

"I'm afraid I am still so weary. In fact"—Collette rose—"I think I shall go up to my room."

Lady Ravensgate waved a hand in dismissal. Clearly, she was past annoyed with her charge. Collette slipped out of the dining room, but instead of going to the stairs, she paused and scanned the table near the door. Her breath caught when she spotted a silver salver with several letters on it. Evans was nowhere to be seen, but he could reappear at any moment and then he would take the letters in to Lady Ravensgate. This would be Collette's only chance to see if the royalists had sent a message back. She hurried to the table, keeping her steps on the marble silent. Heart pounding in her chest, she flicked through the letters. Invitation, correspondence from one of Lady Ravensgate's friends, a letter from the lady's solicitor, and—Collette gasped. This was it. She knew the writing.

She snatched the letter up just as she heard Evans's step.

"Might I help you, Miss Fournay?" he asked.

Collette froze. She held the letter in her hands, and if she turned or he came closer, he would see that she had it. To buy herself time, Collette bent and began a coughing fit worthy of an actress on Drury Lane. Then she slid the letter into her bodice and stood upright again. "No, thank you, Evans," she said, turning. "I am on my way to my bedchamber. I had better rest."

"Your bedchamber is that way, miss." The butler pointed toward the stairs.

"Of course. Thank you again, Evans." And she hurried away, hoping he would not notice the missing letter on the salver. She rushed to her room, while trying not to look as though she were rushing, and then closed the door. Immediately, she looked for a place to secrete the letter in case Lady Ravensgate should come looking for it. But Collette quickly realized that keeping it close to her bosom was probably the safest place for it after all. She would read it when she heard Lady Ravensgate go out for the day. That would be the only time she could be certain she was safe from her guardian. In the meantime, she would feign sleep.

It was not an easy task. She had rested so much the past few days that she had grown restless. She might lie on the bed, but she could hardly keep her body still.

Especially when she thought about Rafe Beaumont. She didn't know what the letter might contain, but she knew she would have to leave a note for him in the garden tonight. And that would be the first step to seeing him again. Her body burned with the very thought of seeing him, touching him, being touched by him. A day had not passed when she hadn't relived every moment of their time together—every touch, every kiss, every caress.

Something had happened that night in the mews. She'd felt it, and she'd known he felt it too. It had been powerful enough that he lost himself and forgot to pull out at the last moment. Collette touched her belly. What if she was carrying his child? Why did that thought terrify him so much? Why did he want to avoid marriage? Besides the obvious: she was a spy.

He might have married before. He had his pick of women, and yet he never had. Was it because he disliked the idea of fidelity to one woman? If so, she didn't see why that would have been an obstacle. As far as she could see, English society was no different than French—the men had dalliances where and when they wished. The women did the same after the line was assured.

There was something else. Had a woman tried to trap him before? That was a foolish question. Countless women had tried to trap him, but he was an expert at escaping. So why hadn't he tried to escape from her?

And here was where the problem lay. She wanted to believe she was somehow special. He wanted to believe she meant something to him. But she didn't. He'd made that fact very, very clear. She was just another of the many women who had fallen for his charm and handsome face. Only she was fool enough to believe he had fallen back.

Her thoughts were interrupted by a quiet tap on the door, and she thanked God she was lying down and pretending to sleep because Lady Ravensgate did not wait to open the door and peer inside.

"Feeling any better, dear?"

Collette fought to keep her lip from curling in disgust. "A little."

"I have sent for my carriage to take me to Bond Street. Do try and rest. I want you to come out with me tonight."

"I'd like"—Collette pretended to sneeze—"that." She was not going anywhere, except to the garden.

Lady Ravensgate closed the door, and a little while later, Collette heard her go out and the house went quiet. The servants were obviously taking this opportunity to retire to their quarters and rest for a little while or attend to sewing or ironing. Collette withdrew the warm, wrinkled letter from her bodice, sat, and read it.

Then she read it again.

Her fingers trembled as she tucked it back into her bodice. She had to compose herself before she could write a note to Beaumont to hide in the garden tonight. It would not be an easy task. The letter said all she had hoped it would.

Her father was on the way to England.

❧

After more sneezing and blowing of her nose, Collette was able to convince Lady Ravensgate to go out without her. Since the lady had no real affection for Collette, she felt no need to stay home and nurse her. And that meant Collette was once again alone except for the servants. To her surprise and delight, all but Lady Ravensgate's lady's maid and the butler had been given the night off. That meant Collette felt relatively safe sneaking down to the garden at a little after ten, rather than waiting until Lady Ravensgate returned home and the staff retired.

Once in the garden, Collette made for the tree she and Beaumont had met under before. She didn't know if he had been back to look for notes from her, but she had to hope he came to check regularly. She would need him in the next few days. The trees in this part of the garden made it darker, and when Collette paused under the tree she thought was the one she and Beaumont had met under before, she had to wait for her eyes to adjust to the gloom. When they did, she screamed.

His hand came over her mouth to stifle the scream, and he pulled her behind the tree and out of sight. Collette pushed his hand away and stepped back. "What are you doing?" she hissed. "Why are you skulking about?"

Rafe straightened his shoulders. "I never skulk. I was waiting for you."

Collette put her hand to her heart to still the pounding. When she'd caught her breath, the words sank in. "How did you know I would come out tonight?"

"I didn't."

"Then why are you here?"

He opened his mouth, paused, and then cleared his throat. "That's not the point. You are here. What do you have for me?"

She looked down at the small paper in her hands. She'd gone to some trouble to write it as she was not allowed pen or ink or paper in her room. "My father is on his way to England. The royalists believed our story, and they are bringing him here. They'll send word when he lands and tell me when to meet him so I may give them the intelligence."

Rafe leaned against the tree. "When did you receive this information?"

"Today."

"Then we can safely assume your father could already be in England."

Collette could not stop herself from grabbing on to his arm. It seemed the ground she stood on had shifted and she needed support. "Do you really think so?"

"It's possible. If his captors read your letter, replied,

and departed immediately. The reply might have sailed on the same ship as your father."

"Then I shall see him soon."

"I said it was possible, but it's unlikely. I think it more likely your father travels a day or two behind the packet that brought this letter. But there's only one way to be certain." He disentangled his arm from her grip. "Go inside, Collette. I'll contact you when I have more information."

She stared at him. Did he mean to send her back inside to sit and wait for his return? Her father might even now be only a few miles away. Collette didn't care if she ever saw Lady Ravensgate or her town house again if it meant she could see her father tonight. "I would go with you."

He shook his head. "It's not safe. You'll be safe inside."

"I don't care about my safety. Do you think it was safe for me to come to England? Safe for me to spy for France? I'm not concerned about safety. I only want to see my father."

Even in the dimness of the garden, she could see him frown. And perhaps because she had not seen him in several days, she couldn't help but think that even with the frown, he was the most handsome man she had ever seen. "I don't think your father's captors will want to risk traveling by coach. They'll sail into the Thames on a ship with legitimate cargo and take the first opportunity to slip off."

"And go where?"

"I don't know. They probably won't risk any of the inns. Perhaps they have a hiding place in

London, more friends they can trust on this side of the Channel."

"And if you mean to find out this information, I mean to come with you."

He took her by the shoulders, and for a moment Collette half hoped he might kiss her. It was a foolish thought, one she pushed away. There would be no more kissing between them. She had made that mistake twice already, and she would not make it again. "Collette, if you leave Lady Ravensgate's house, she will know something is amiss. She will send word to her contacts."

"And if her contacts are on the way here, it matters not." She didn't want to admit she feared Lady Ravensgate was already planning to dispose of her.

His fingers tightened on her shoulder. "If I could shake sense into you, I would," he muttered. "I must go to the docks to find out if your father has already come ashore. That is no place for a lady."

"I am not a lady. I'm the daughter of an assassin, so you need have no worry for my sensibilities."

He released her with a flourish. "The daughter of an assassin who was sheltered from her father's work."

"But who lived in Paris, where the worst sights might be seen daily. Do you fear I'll see starving children? Prostitutes? Drunken men? I have seen it all."

"Fine, but where we go, I will be fortunate to escape with my life. I can't protect you."

"Then I'll protect myself." She pointed at him when he shook his head. "If you go without me, I'll just have to make my own way there. Either way, I won't stay here another night."

"You are that eager to die?"

She notched her head up.

"Fine. Let's go die together."

∾

Rafe had never met such an obstinate woman. Women always did what he asked. They were *eager* to do his bidding. From the very beginning, Collette Fortier had been difficult. He should have realized back then that she would be too much trouble and passed the assignment to another of Draven's men. And then another man would be here with her. Or she would be in prison. Or worse.

Rafe took her by the arms again, stopping himself when he realized he meant to pull her into an embrace. He cleared his throat. "You had better go inside and take what you need. You won't be coming back here."

"Oh, and while I am inside, you will make your escape."

"You have so little faith in me?"

"I think you may have mistaken ideas of chivalry."

He laughed. "I promise I have very little chivalry. If you don't trust me, I'll go with you. I might be able to help you change into a darker dress, or at least a plainer dress."

She looked as though she might argue, then closed her mouth and gave a stiff nod. He wondered if she knew he didn't want to see her partially unclothed any more than she wanted him to assist her dressing. Rafe was tempted enough by her without seeing her creamy skin bared. "How will I go in without being spotted?"

"The butler and Lady Ravensgate's maid are the only servants here. I believe they are in the servants' quarters. I haven't heard or seen them in hours. Her ladyship isn't expected back for another few hours at the earliest. She's at the theater."

"We'll hurry nonetheless. You lead the way. I'll follow."

She was quick and sure as she made her way through the garden and into the house. As she'd claimed, the house was quiet and no servants were about. They went silently to her room, where she closed the door. The lone candle flickered, and she trimmed the wick before pulling a small valise from under her bed.

Rafe shook his head. "That's too conspicuous. You'll attract every thief for miles. You'd be better with a small satchel you can put over your shoulder and hide under your cloak."

She nodded, then crossed to the nightstand. She pushed it aside, careful not to allow the legs to scrape on the floorboards. Then she pushed on one end of a short board that had been cut so as to meet the wall. The edge bowed slightly but did not pop up. "Can you help?" she asked, looking over her shoulder.

Rafe knelt. She must have hidden something under the floorboard. Something she didn't want Lady Ravensgate to see or confiscate. Rafe grasped the other end of the floorboard and used his fingers to pry it free. Collette reached down into the darkness and felt about, then pulled up a worn, tattered satchel. "I brought this with me from France," she said. "When Lady Ravensgate ordered everything I had brought burned or taken from me—for my own safety—I hid this here."

"What's inside?"

"A dress that will suit our purposes, my official papers, and a few mementos." She pulled the dress free of the satchel and several other items spilled out. He saw the yellowed papers that must have been her identification papers, but he looked past them to the miniature of a young woman. She had the same eyes and forehead as Collette, though her hair was lighter and her expression more serious. He lifted the small painting.

"Your mother?" he asked.

She nodded, taking it back. "This is all I have left of her."

It was more than Rafe had of his own mother. "And you would have left it behind if I had threatened to go immediately?"

"What other choice would I have?" she asked. "My father is everything."

He was beginning to see that. What must it be like to have the sort of love Collette had for her father? Rafe was certainly fond of his father and his siblings, but he did not know if he would go to the lengths Collette had for a single one of them. He couldn't say whether he would have gone to any trouble for anyone in his life, save the men he had fought with in Draven's troop.

And now Collette.

She held up the dress, and it was more than suitable for a trip to the London docks. The color was a rather dull brown and the dress had no embellishments. Wrinkled and stained, he wondered when she had last worn it. She must have read the question in his face because she said, "I wore this on my voyage to

England. When I met Lady Ravensgate, I changed into a better dress. I might as well have left this one on, because I never saw that dress again. I think her ladyship burned it. My father and I didn't have much need for fine clothing in the country, but considering I sewed all my own dresses, I rather resented her burning that one."

"I understand."

She raised a brow. "You? You have never even lifted a needle and thread."

He couldn't argue. "Would you like help unfastening this dress?"

She blew out a breath. "This is not an invitation, Rafe Beaumont."

He held up his hands, his expression all innocence—he hoped. "I understand."

She presented him her back, and he began to unfasten the ties and tapes and laces. She dealt with the pins in the front and soon the garment began to sag, exposing the skin of her shoulders. Rafe looked at the wall above her head.

"You never said how you knew I would be in the garden tonight," she said. Her movements indicated she had stepped out of her skirts and stood in her chemise, petticoat, and stays, but Rafe kept his gaze on the wall. And when that proved a challenge, he turned his back.

"I didn't know. I wait for you every night."

He heard her gasp and, a moment too late, realized what he'd just revealed. "You stand out there every night?"

"Not every night." That was a lie. "At least not all night. Not most nights anyway."

She grabbed his arm and turned him to face her. He looked down at her face, then down farther, and quickly brought his eyes back up. Her full breasts swelled over the tops of the stays. "Are you lying to me? Lady Ravensgate said she saw you at a dinner party."

"I've gone to several events, hoping to see you." *Keep looking at her face,* he reminded himself. "To speak with you in case you had new information," he added.

"I have pretended to be ill."

"I gathered as much when I overheard Lady Ravensgate speaking. And so the last few nights I've waited in the garden for you."

She stared at him, her mouth parting slightly as more questions seemed to form in her mind. He wouldn't allow her to ask them. He didn't quite understand why he stood outside the town house most nights himself. He did not want to try and explain it. "Do you need help with your dress?" He gave her a slow perusal to remind her she was standing half-clothed before him. At least that was the reason he gave himself for the survey. Her cheeks reddened and she grasped the ugly brown dress.

"I can put it on. If you could just help with the laces in the back."

"Of course." She turned and bent to step into the skirt. *Look up. Do not look at her bottom. That rounded, sweet bottom…*

"What was that?" she asked.

"Nothing." His voice sounded strained. "I cleared my throat."

"It sounded like—"

"How old were you when your mother died?" he asked, desperate to change the subject.

She paused and began to don the bodice. "Twelve, almost thirteen." She held laces out to him, and he studied them a moment, then went to work. He had dressed and undressed enough women to understand the workings of most every type of dress.

"A hard age to lose a mother," he said.

"It was, and losing her was made harder by my father's frequent absences. But I had my aunt until she married when I was fifteen."

"It's not quite the same, is it?" He'd had a stepmother.

She glanced back at him, her eyes shrewd. "No, it isn't."

"Ready?" he asked.

She nodded.

"I don't know what trouble we might find, but you have to promise to do as I say."

She nodded.

"And the first rule I make is for you to wear this cloak at all times." He dropped it over her shoulders. "With the hood up. You're too pretty for your own good."

She laughed.

"That is not amusing."

Then she saw his look and her face changed. "You are serious? You think me pretty?"

He waved the question away. "You know you're pretty." But from the look of astonishment on her face, he thought perhaps she didn't. "The second rule is not to ask questions. Put everything you want in the satchel. We are leaving."

"For the docks?"

"Yes, but not directly."

"Then where first?"

He pulled the hood of her cloak up. "No questions."

They left the town house as quietly as they'd entered. Rafe thought Collette might look back one last time as she walked away, but she never even slowed. He could all but hear the questions forming in her mind, but to her credit, she refrained from asking them. Rafe had barred them not because he didn't want her to know what he was doing, but because he didn't like to admit he was a bit out of his element. Fortunately, he knew someone who could help. He'd always said that it wasn't what you knew but who you knew, and knowing Jasper Grantham would serve him well tonight.

But where to find the thief taker? If he was on the trail of a criminal, he might not surface for days. Rafe could only hope business was slow at present. He'd try the Draven Club, and if Jasper wasn't there, then the man's home. As they had to make their way down King Street to the club, Rafe was glad he had told Collette to keep her hood up. At this time of night, all sorts of men were out on the street. The brothels and the gaming hells were open and thriving, and reputable women were not usually to be found in St. James's Square after dark.

Once at the Draven Club, he ushered Collette up the stairs and tapped on the knocker. As though he had been expecting them, Porter opened the door a moment later. The Master of the House inclined his head at them. "Good evening, Mr. Beaumont. Good evening, miss."

"Is Jasper here?" Rafe asked.

"Lord Jasper is in the dining room. Shall I fetch him?"

Rafe looked back at Collette. Women were not allowed inside the club. No exceptions. But Rafe could not leave Collette on the street alone.

"I'd rather speak with him inside. Would it be possible for Miss Fortier to wait in the vestibule?"

Porter's face showed no emotion. "She may be seated just inside the doorway, and I will keep her company. I trust you may find the dining room on your own, sir?"

"Yes." Rafe shouldered Collette and himself inside. Porter indicated a stiff-backed chair, and Collette sat gracefully, rearranging her cloak as she did so. Rafe rushed halfway up the steps and then back down again. "Thank you, Porter. I appreciate this."

"Of course, Mr. Beaumont. Think nothing of it, sir."

"But it isn't nothing, Porter. I know"—he put his arm around Porter's shoulder and drew the man a little away from Collette—"I know my reputation. Miss Fortier isn't like the other women."

Porter looked him straight in the eye. "Yes, sir. She wouldn't be inside right now if I thought she were."

Rafe gave Porter a long look, then bounded back up the stairs. He found the dining room deserted except for Jasper, who sat at a back table with a bowl of soup and a book. When Rafe entered, he lowered his book, revealing his scarred face. Never more than in moments like these did Rafe marvel at the dichotomies inherent in his friend. He was the son of a marquess but lived most of his life in the London rookeries. He wore a mask in public because his face scared women and small children, and yet here he sat, the epitome of elegance, sipping soup and reading a book. Jasper was a man who could fit into any situation, a veritable chameleon.

"What the devil happened to you?" he drawled, setting his book down but keeping a finger between the pages to mark his place.

"I need your help."

Jasper shook his head. "I told you before, I don't want to be involved with your hordes of women."

"You're not amusing. This is a question about a packet from France."

Jasper drew his finger out of the book. "Go on."

"If a ship arrived in London from France, where would they drop anchor to attract the least notice?"

"Ships from France generally arrive at Dover."

"I don't think this one will. The passengers will want to avoid a land journey with its turnpikes and toll gates."

"Are they smugglers?"

"Of a sort."

"Then Wapping. It's far enough away from the center of London that the customs officials are not quite so strict. Plus, it has a history of smuggling and pirates. If this ship wants to avoid notice, I imagine they'll seek out the quay in Wapping. The customs officials there might be easily bribed to overlook one or more passengers who wish to disembark without the proper paperwork."

Rafe closed his eyes. "I don't want to go to Wapping."

"No one wants to go to Wapping. Hire a carriage. It's four miles at least and the highway can be dangerous." Jasper lifted his wine and Rafe expertly plucked it from his hand.

"Where am I to find a carriage at this hour?" He drank Jasper's wine down.

Jasper glared at him. "I would have suggested you ask Porter. But now you've drank my wine, you can go to hell."

Rafe grinned at him. "I'll see you there."

# Fifteen

COLLETTE'S EYES DROOPED. IT WAS ALMOST DAWN BY the time Rafe had negotiated the use of the club's carriage and the conveyance was ready. She'd all but fallen asleep in the chair. In fact, she thought she might have been forgotten except that she heard the lovely older gentleman, Porter, chastising Rafe for keeping her out all night.

"Where is this young lady's home? She should be in bed, sir."

"Your concern is touching, Porter. Are you also worried for my health?"

Porter harrumphed and hobbled away. One of his legs was wooden, but he was so adept at using it, it had taken a little while for Collette to notice.

Finally, Rafe shook her shoulder and, taking her arm, escorted her to the coach. It was black lacquer and shone in the early-morning light. The team of six black horses stamped their feet and looked eager to be away. The coachman wore a high-collared coat with his hat brim pulled low on his forehead. He lifted his hat a fraction of an inch as they approached.

And then Rafe opened the door and helped her inside. He climbed in after her, seating himself across from her and facing the rear. Porter had followed them outdoors, but instead of closing the door to the carriage, he handed Collette a wrapped parcel. Collette looked down at the square of linen, and when she looked up again, Porter slid a thickly wrapped brick beside her feet. "To keep you warm, Miss Fortier," he said. Then he looked at Rafe. "The victuals are for Miss Fortier, not you, sir."

Collette looked down at the package in her hands again. She lifted the linen and revealed a loaf of bread, an apple, and a flagon of wine. "You are very kind, Mr. Porter."

"If I were truly kind, I wouldn't send you off with Mr. Beaumont."

Rafe blew out a breath. "Need I remind you I pay your salary?"

Porter smiled. "That's not my fault, sir." And he closed the door.

"The man is impertinent," Rafe groused as he tapped on the roof to indicate they were ready to depart.

"Oh, anyone can see he cares for you." Collette set the parcel of food on the seat beside her. "He simply knows you too well. You have an awful reputation, Mr. Beaumont."

"If he knew me, he'd know half of that is pure fiction."

"Half is still far worse than the reputations of a dozen such men."

Rafe considered her, the side of his face lit by

sunlight. And then he drew the curtains to shield them from the eyes of the curious they passed. "And what do you believe, Collette?" he asked, his voice rising from the darkness.

"I don't know what to believe," she answered. "Ask me again in a few days."

"Believe me, I will."

The carriage moved at a slow pace, as the streets were crowded. Collette was lulled to sleep by the easy motion of the conveyance, then all but fell off her seat when the coach bounced over something—hopefully not some*one*—in the road.

"You'd better come sit with me," Rafe said, his form still shadowed in the darkness. "You can lean your head on my shoulder, and I'll keep you anchored. Or better yet, I shall sit with you." He waited and when she gave no answer, he said, "May I?"

Collette drew a breath in. It was dangerous to be in close proximity to Rafe Beaumont. Her body tended to betray what she knew was in her best interest. "Very well. But—"

Beaumont paused in the act of rising from his seat.

"But this is not an invitation to kiss me or do anything else of that sort."

"No kissing." He slid beside her, his body solid and warm, and she realized even though her feet had been resting on the brick, she'd been cold. She was about to rest her head on his shoulder, but then he spoke again. "What other things of that sort do you speak of? Can you be specific?"

She let out an annoyed breath. "You know what I mean, Rafe."

"Not at all. For example, would putting my arm around you to keep you from falling be *of that sort*?"

"It depends where you put your arm."

"The shoulders?" He put his arm about her shoulders.

"That is fine."

"Hmm. What about your waist?" His arm slid down her back and wrapped around her waist.

Collette drew a shaky breath. "That is acceptable."

"Are you cold? Your voice is trembling."

"I'm fine."

"Shall I warm you up?" He took the arm not holding her and reached across her to rub his hand up and down her arm. "Better?"

"Yes. Really, I am fine, sir." She said this more forcefully. And then, before she knew what had happened, he had touched his nose to hers. She jerked back, surprised because she had not been able to anticipate his movements in the dark. "What are you doing?"

"Your nose. It's cold."

"It's fine."

"I can't have your nose ice cold. I'll warm it for you." He touched her nose with his again and this time his forehead tapped against hers too. She knew she need only move a fraction to press her lips to his, and his mouth would be warm and inviting and so, so wicked. "I know you are a hedgehog expert, but were you aware that in some northern cultures, this is considered a kiss?"

"What is?" She could hardly breathe. His sweet breath feathered over her chin.

"Rubbing noses. It's like a kiss for them."

"So then you are breaking my rule."

"I've never been very good at following the rules." His mouth brushed hers so lightly she could almost believe she'd imagined it. Heat and longing flared inside her. She could not seem to stop wanting this man. Even when she knew she should not want him. Even when she knew she could not have him.

"Neither have I." Her mouth met his and warmth raced through her. She felt as though she'd been sleeping and now that he kissed her, held her, she was awake and alive again. His mouth slanted over hers, his hands tangling in her hair and cradling her head. He might have pulled her into his lap, but he made no move to do so. Instead, he lowered her to the soft squab and looked down at her, his hair falling over his forehead so she could not see his eyes at all.

"Just let me hold you," he whispered. "I cannot seem to ever hold you close enough."

She closed her eyes and reveled in his scent and the feel of his body pressed against hers.

"This will most likely be our last day together," he said quietly. "If we are right and your father is already in England, you will see him today."

And then what would happen? she wondered. Would Rafe turn them all in to the Foreign Office? Or would he let her go but imprison her father? He must have known that she would never be willingly parted from her father. Where he went, she would go. And if Rafe was the one responsible for her father's death, she would never be able to forgive him.

"And then we will be enemies once more," she said.

"We were always enemies. We just forget. From time to time."

She smiled wryly. "I never wanted this." And she didn't know if she meant her life as a spy or falling in love with him.

"Neither did I. And yet…" He trailed off, sounding thoughtful.

"And yet?" she prompted. For some reason it was easier to speak to him like this, in the dark, when she couldn't see how beautiful he was and he couldn't see her expressions.

"And yet I always knew this was coming. I always knew I'd meet a woman I couldn't dismiss quite so easily."

"Have there been no women in your life you cared for, truly cared for?"

"If I say you are that woman, would you believe me?"

Her cheeks heated, and she was glad he could not see them in the dark. "Ask me—"

"In a few days. I shall add that to the growing list. In that case, I suppose I care for my sisters and my nieces, although the nieces are all too young to be considered women. But I love them all. In my way."

*In my way.* What did that mean? She dared not ask, but she thought she might already know. He had been the perfect man to play the role of seducer in the war. He was a man who did not grow attached, who did not care for women beyond the moment they were together. It didn't seem to her that Rafe Beaumont was capable of love. He felt strongly for a little while and then the passion faded and he moved on. Was he incapable of love or could he simply not allow himself to love?

"And what about your mother?" she asked.

He stiffened. The gesture was so unlike him, so unlike the Rafe who was at ease in every situation, never ruffled, never flustered. "What about her?" Even his voice sounded different—tense and guarded. He sat, breaking the contact between them. Collette levered herself up as well.

"Don't you care for her?"

"I don't know her. She left when I was four. My father remarried a few years later when he learned of her death. My stepmother is a good woman, but by the time she came into our lives, I no longer needed a mother."

Poor man. Everyone needed a mother. "I'm sorry," Collette said simply. "I didn't know about your mother."

He waved a hand, the gesture barely discernable in the dark. "It's not as though she was a very good mother at any rate."

"Why do you say that?"

"My brothers and sisters always called her neglect-ful. On more than one occasion, I was forgotten or left behind. I am the youngest and easy to forget, I suppose."

Collette could not think of a more ridiculous state-ment. He was the most memorable man she had ever known. Women sought his attentions and his favors. Men emulated his way of speaking and his dress.

"When we were all younger, my brothers and sisters blamed me for her leaving."

Collette sat straighter, surprised at this revelation. "How is that possible? You were only a child. A four-year-old cannot be responsible for the actions of an adult."

"She didn't want me."

"I don't believe that."

"I heard it whispered many times. My brothers discussed it when they thought I slept. Servants talked of it when they did not know I could overhear. From the moment she realized she would have another child, she made it clear she thought the pregnancy was a burden. She had seven children already. She did not want another. To make matters worse, she was very sick during her pregnancy. The doctor actually feared for her life because she could not manage to take any sustenance. Food and even water made her ill."

"I have seen such sickness in other women. It usually passes after the first few months."

"Not with my mother. When she finally birthed me, she was so glad to have done with me, she would not even hold me for the first few days."

"Rafe." Collette reached for his hand, but he moved it away. He didn't seem to want her comfort.

"And then there were all the times I was forgotten or left behind. It happened so often they called me Rafe the Forgotten as a sort of joke. But it was not funny when my mother left. She had been with me in the nursery, or so she had said." His voice took on a rather hard quality she was not used to. The tenor of his voice was usually so musical and lilting, but now it sounded like the edge of a blade. "We were in London for the Season, and the rest of the family had gone to a museum or some sort of performance and left me behind because I was too young. My mother had claimed she wanted to stay back with me. She dismissed my nurse and stayed in the nursery with me herself. I was told hours later the family returned and found me with the nurse, crying inconsolably."

"And your mother?"

"No one knew where she had gone, but they deduced she had been gone for hours. The nurse had heard me crying and came to investigate. You see, I never cried as a child."

"All babies cry."

In the darkness, she made out the quick shake of his head. "Not I or not often. Everyone knew something dreadful must have happened to cause me to cry."

"And what of your mother?"

"She had taken a valise, some clothing, her jewelry, and gone. My father had her tracked as far as Italy, where we think she settled for a time. And then a few years later, we received word she had died from a fever that came on quite suddenly."

"You must have been devastated."

He was silent for a long time, the wheels of the carriage on the packed earth below and the muffled snorts and hoofbeats of the horses the only sound she heard.

"I don't remember very much from those early years of my childhood. I don't think most people do, but I remember that day. And I remember why I was crying."

"Why?" Collette asked, her voice little more than a whisper.

"Because my mother had been in the nursery, but she ignored me and all my efforts to engage her in play. She stood at the window and stared out. And then after what seemed to me like many hours, but was probably only three-quarters of an hour or so, she picked up her skirts and walked out. I ran after her. I called her name. Mama! Mama! She caught me at the door and with rough hands pushed me back into the nursery. And then she closed and locked the door. I cried in part because I was afraid to be alone, but mostly I cried because I knew she did not care. I knew she did not love me, and somehow I knew she was leaving me."

Collette sat very still, letting all he had said wash over her. His behavior toward women made more sense to her now. After all, why would he seek any sort of genuine relationship with a woman? The one woman who should have cared for him and loved him left him. And then he'd been blamed for her departure. To make matters worse, women all but threw themselves at him, and these women did not want to know Rafe Beaumont. They only wanted the excitement of having the attentions of a handsome man and a skilled lover.

"Not all women leave," she said quietly.

He made a sound like a snort of laughter. "It doesn't matter. There's always another one." But she heard the brittleness of his voice, and she knew it did matter. And she knew she was but one more woman who would leave him. He'd told her he cared for her and she was different. How much had it cost him to say those words, to admit he felt something more than lust for her? And yet, even when she had pushed him away, even when he knew they would never be able to be together, he was still here. He was beside her, taking her to see her father. Taking her to begin the journey that would separate them.

At least that was what she wanted to believe. She did not want to think that he took her to Wapping now because this was part of his grand plan to capture her father and turn them both in to the British government. But she could not discount that option. There would always be another woman for Rafe Beaumont. The question was whether he cared enough for her not to want another woman.

It was almost midday by the time the coach arrived in Wapping. Rafe had not been here in some time, having no reason to go to the town. There was little here, and what there was had been built up around the river. From the Thames rose one main street lined by taverns and inns frequented by sailors. Rafe supposed there were homes and perhaps better areas of town, but he instructed the coachman to take them to the quays.

Wapping had a marine police force, but Jasper had made it clear any ship from France carrying a wanted man would do its best to avoid not only the customs men, but also the police. The ship would not be docked too close to police headquarters. More likely the captain would want to stay west of the town in order to be able to make a quick escape, if need be. With that in mind, Rafe had the carriage leave him and Collette some distance west of the police. He'd given the coachman a few shillings and told him to see to the horses and himself but to stay close and be prepared to leave at a moment's notice. Before the driver could spur the horses forward, Rafe held up a hand and turned to Collette. "Are you certain you wish to come along? Even in broad daylight, the riverfront is dangerous. You can stay with the coach. I will return when I have located the ship." If it was even here. He dared not hope.

"I am coming with you," she said, and he knew that look of determination in her eyes. Lowering his hand, Rafe stepped away from the coach. It pulled away, and he and Collette were left alone. Rafe gestured to an old set of stone steps leading down to the river, and he and Collette began to walk.

He didn't know why he had told her about his mother. He'd never told anyone about his mother, save one or two of Draven's men and that had been when he'd drank too much wine the night before a mission that was surely suicide. It hadn't seemed awkward to say such things when all of them would most likely be dead in the morning. It hadn't seemed awkward to tell Collette his secrets either. He'd wanted to tell her, wanted her to understand who he was. He was not the man the gossip pages made him out to be—a rake and a seducer of women. He had seduced his share of women, that was true, but they had all wanted to be seduced. And although he had been able to make dozens of women love him, he had not been able to secure the love of his own mother. In fact, he had driven her away. He knew Collette would leave him too. She had to leave or find herself imprisoned in Newgate or worse.

She was with him now, following him closely, and it wasn't long before Rafe wished he had a spyglass or some other sort of mechanism with which to see the ships anchored in the river better. Some were tied to the quays, but most of those were guarded by sailors who did not take kindly to being questioned. This Rafe gathered after he'd had a dagger pulled on him by one sailor with tattoos of naked women decorating his forearms.

Rafe had walked quickly away, pulling Collette with him, but they hadn't gone far before he noted that the stone path they had been following along the water ended in a stone wall that reached above both of their heads. A rocky outcrop jutted into the water, and whoever had built the path along the water had obviously not wanted to go to the effort of cutting through it. Clearly, he and Collette would have to go back to the last set of steps and go up before coming back down again where the path resumed.

She had already come to this realization and turned back. Just as he made to do the same, she clutched his arm. "Rafe."

He frowned at the wall one last time. "I know. Doubling back will cost us time, but there's nothing for it."

"I think we have a bigger problem than losing time."

Unease pooling in his belly, Rafe turned slowly to see the sailor with the tattoos on his forearm had followed them. And he'd brought a few of his friends. About six friends to be exact. They stank of unwashed bodies and rotting fish and their open shirts and stained breeches reminded him more of pirates than men operating a merchant vessel. They were armed with knives and daggers, several of them held a weapon in each hand and a knife between yellowing teeth. Rafe looked at Collette. Too late, he realized her hood had fallen back.

A wall of stone at his back and a wall of men before him. He'd faced worse odds, but never alone. "Hullo, gentlemen," Rafe said, giving them his most charming smile.

The tattooed sailor chuckled with menace. "We ain't no gentlemen. Give us yer purse and we'll let ye pass."

That sounded easy enough. Rafe hadn't much in his purse, a sovereign and some shillings. He took it from his coat and tossed it to the leader. "There you are. Now allow us to pass."

The sailor peered into the small pouch with Rafe's coins, the naked women on his arms moving obscenely as his muscles flexed. "All right, boys." He gestured and the men parted. Rafe didn't much like the idea of walking a gauntlet, but he wasn't in a position to argue.

"Stay close to me," he murmured to Collette. Taking her arm, he pushed her in front of him, reasoning he could better protect her if he could see her. He did not want to risk her being torn away behind his back.

Collette began to walk, but the tattooed man blocked her path. "We said he could pass, not you."

Collette looked back at Rafe helplessly.

"She's with me," Rafe argued. "I gave you my coins. We don't want any trouble."

"But we want the woman," the sailor said. "And we mean to take what we want."

# Sixteen

THE SAILOR WITH THE DRAWINGS ON HIS ARMS AND the small, dark eyes lunged for her, but Collette was quick. She ducked below his arm, swerved to avoid being caught by another man, and darted behind Rafe. Rafe stepped back, edging closer to the wall at their backs. Rafe bent and extracted a dagger from his boot, but the small weapon only elicited loud guffaws from the sailors.

"I use that to pick my teeth!" one called.

"I use it to clean the blood from under my finger-nails," another said.

"Gentlemen," Rafe said, sounding as though he had not a single concern, "I do not want to use this dagger. I don't like to kill and maim, but I will do it if necessary. I suggest you disperse immediately. Go back to the ship you crawled out of and allow this lady and myself to pass."

"Listen to 'im talk!" the tattooed man said. "'E thinks 'e's the bloody king."

"I have met the king," Rafe said quite convincingly. Perhaps it was true. He was a war hero, after all.

"I will be more than willing to share the story, if you allow us to pass."

But the sailors were moving closer and Rafe was slowly backing up. Collette looked behind her. She had less than a foot before she would be trapped against the stone wall. There would be no escape, then. Even if they could manage to scale the wall, the men would grab their legs and pull them back down before they could reach the top.

"We don't want yer stories. We want the woman."

"I 'aven't seen a woman for seven months," one sailor said.

"Then use the coin to buy all the women you want," Rafe said. "There are brothels with willing women all along the street. A sovereign will buy all of you a woman for the night."

"But she won't be as pretty as that one," said the man with the tattoo. "Or as clean. Them whores all 'ave the French disease."

Rafe chanced a quick look back, and he saw the dismay in her eyes before he faced their attackers again. "When I lunge for them," he muttered, his voice low, "you run. If you're caught, fight until I can reach you."

"Yes," Collette said, her voice failing her and sounding like little more than a whisper.

❧

Rafe took a breath and tightened his grip on his dagger. He'd always complained he was never chosen for the exciting missions. Lately, he seemed to be making up for lost time. He shifted his grip on the dagger, readying it, then balanced on the balls of his feet, prepared to spring forward. But before he could attack, a blur of black flew in front of him. And Rafe jumped back as a large, dark-skinned man blocked his path.

What the devil? He'd finally had his chance!

The man's back was to Rafe. He was tall, his shoulders broad, and his hair thick and curly, though neatly brushed. He wore a dark coat and black trousers with polished boots ending at the knee.

And he held a pistol.

The sailors must have recognized him because, as a group, they took a step back. "What do you do here, Brimble?" He nodded to the tattooed man.

"Nothing that concerns you, Gaines."

"Oh, I don't know about that. Everything that happens here concerns me." He glanced back at Rafe and Collette. His skin was the color of walnuts, his nose straight and strong, and his cheekbones high and proud. His dark eyes flicked over Rafe and Collette with interest, then he turned back to the sailors. "I don't like to see women abused. You'd best be on your way."

Brimble lifted his weapon again, but Gaines merely cocked his pistol. It sounded impossibly loud in the tense silence. Brimble stared at Gaines. "Ye'll be sorry, ye will." And then the sailor gathered his men and retreated.

Gaines tucked his pistol under his coat and gestured to Rafe. "We'd better go. They'll come up with a new plan and be back." Without waiting for an answer, Gaines began to walk. Rafe looked at Collette, who stood with her mouth partly open.

"I had the situation under control," Rafe said, knowing he sounded petulant and not caring.

"Good to know I don't have to save you next time. Hurry up," Gaines answered without looking back.

"How do we know you're a friend?" Rafe called.

Gaines continued walking. "You don't."

Rafe hesitated.

"But I can tell you this," Gaines said, still walking. "I know what it is to have my body belong to another. I would never inflict that pain on anyone else. Your lady is safe with me."

"Let's follow him," Collette said. She pushed past Rafe and rushed to catch up with Gaines.

Rafe spread his hands in defeat. Apparently, he had little choice but to trust the man. His long strides quickly brought him to Gaines's side, and Rafe was pleased the man did seem to be leading them to a nearby set of steps. He gestured to them. "There is your escape. Might I give you some advice?" He didn't wait for a response. "Stay away from the ships and the sailors. They'd just as soon slit your throat as watch you pass."

"That will be difficult," Collette said. "We are looking for a ship."

"I see." Gaines started up the steps. "Maybe I can help."

"We don't need your help," Rafe said.

"Yes, we do. You seem a man who knows this town."

Gaines smiled, showing a flash of white teeth. "That I do. You won't find another man in Wapping who knows more about this village than me. But we shouldn't stand about in the open here. Would you like a cup of coffee?" He looked at Collette. "Or tea?"

"Yes, thank you."

"We don't have any blunt to pay for it," Rafe muttered. "You may have saved our lives, but you didn't ask those thieves to return my money."

Gaines shrugged. "Even I cannot work miracles. Perhaps we can work it out in trade." He gestured to Rafe to follow him, and as Collette fell into step beside him, Rafe had little choice. Gaines led them along the main street, past several taverns, to a small shop with a picture of coffee and tobacco on the sign. He pushed the door open and the scent of ground coffee invited Rafe in. There were a half-dozen tables in the front of the building and a shopping area behind, selling coffee and tobacco in bulk.

Gaines led Rafe and Collette to a round table, pulled out Collette's chair for her, then signaled to a waiter. There were two, one white and one black. The short white man came forward. "Yes, sir?"

"Crutchley, my friends would like coffee and—" He glanced at Collette.

"Coffee would be lovely."

"Three cups, then. Are you hungry?"

"No," Rafe said.

"Yes," Collette answered at the same time.

"Then bring us bread and soup," Gaines added.

"Yes, sir. Right away, sir."

"Do you own this shop?" Collette asked.

"I do. This and others. I apologize we have no private room for you to dine in."

"You have nothing to apologize for, sir. We are grateful for your assistance earlier."

"What kind of trade?" Rafe asked. He wanted

to like Gaines. The man seemed genuine enough, but among other things, it irked Rafe how quickly Collette had rushed to follow him.

"Excuse me?" Gaines asked.

"You said we'd trade for the price of the coffee and now you've added a meal. I have nothing to trade."

Gaines's gaze fell to Rafe's waistcoat and his watch fob.

"Oh, no. This watch is worth far more than the price of coffee and soup."

"Is it worth your life? I did save it."

"I did not need saving." Rafe glared at him, then pulled out his watch and set it on the table. "I knew I didn't want to come to Wapping."

"Why *are* you here?" Gaines asked. "The lady mentioned you are searching for a ship."

"I am not a lady," she said. "You may call me Collette." Though giving her Christian name to a man she had just met was far too informal a gesture, Rafe thought it wise to refrain from giving her surname, real or counterfeit.

"Rafe Beaumont." Rafe gave a quick bow out of habit.

Gaines stuck out his hand. "Thomas Gaines." Rafe shook hands. Gaines had removed his gloves when they'd sat down, and his bare hands were rough and callused. The coffee arrived, and for a moment, everyone enjoyed the warmth of the drink.

"Miss Collette, you are searching for a ship?" Gaines asked. "I don't mean to boast, but I know every ship that comes in or out. I do a fair enough trade in coffee and tobacco, but I have a few other investments."

"It would be a French ship," Collette said.

"Ah. I did not think you had a British accent."

"I am French," she admitted. "And what is your accent, sir?"

He smiled. "American."

Her eyes widened. "Were you a—"

She broke off and glanced at Rafe, her cheeks flushing. But Rafe was curious as well. Many noble families employed men and women of African descent as servants, but it was rare for one to own his own shop. Not to mention, this man had obviously earned the respect of even the criminally minded.

"A slave? Yes. I escaped from a plantation in Virginia about ten years ago and hid on a ship bound for England. I came ashore at Wapping. I've been here ever since."

"You've done well for yourself," Rafe said.

"Well enough. I know tobacco from my time in Virginia. I sell the best in the country." He leaned forward. "But you don't want tobacco. You want a French ship."

Collette nodded. "It may not have arrived yet. We don't know the name or the captain or anything about it except it carries an important passenger."

"There are several French ships docked here at present. Do you know its cargo?"

Rafe leaned forward, his head close to Gaines's. "This is a ship that would wish to avoid the notice of customs. The cargo may be entirely legitimate, but they will want to send men ashore without too much notice."

Gaines sat back and rubbed his chin thoughtfully. "A ship did arrive last night. I don't know much about it, but the men I employ at the quays tell me it bears the name *The Amaranthe*. Thank you, Crutchley," Gaines said when the waiter returned with the bread and soup.

"That might very well be it," Rafe said. The soup smelled delicious, and he found himself dipping his spoon in the thick liquid despite his annoyance at having to give his watch for it.

"When you finish eating, I will take you to see it," Gaines said. "We will bring a few of my men to deter those who might wish us ill."

Collette descended the stone steps yet again, although Thomas Gaines had led them to a set of steps a good distance from where they had first gone down. He had two men with him, large men who looked more like pirates than clerks, as Gaines had claimed they were, and a spyglass. This stretch of water was shallow and muddy, and Gaines explained that most ships did not anchor here because the currents were unfavorable and unpredictable. But a lone ship did sit at anchor, bobbing with the current.

"Do you see how the captain of the ship has positioned it?" Gaines asked. "The current will jostle anyone on board, but facing that way means he can make a quick getaway if needed. That is an old trick of pirates and smugglers." He lifted the spyglass and studied the ship, then handed it to Rafe.

Rafe peered through the tool, then handed it to Collette. She frowned as the masts and the bow came more sharply into view. "I don't see anyone on deck."

"Try and approach and they'll appear quick enough," Gaines promised. "Could that be your ship?"

"It could be," Rafe admitted. Collette agreed. *The Amaranthe* was unmistakably French in design. And it was small enough to have made the crossing from France to England relatively quickly.

"Did anyone come on shore from this vessel in the night?" she asked.

Gaines shook his head. "I cannot say for certain, but it put down anchor in the wee hours of the morning. If anyone departed, they would have had to do so in daylight." He lifted the spyglass again. "All of the boats are still on board. That doesn't mean one might not have departed and returned, but I think it unlikely."

"You think they will wait for cover of darkness," Rafe said.

"Wouldn't you?"

Rafe nodded.

"Then if my father is on board, he will come ashore tonight," she said, the twin sensations of nausea and giddiness making her stomach bubble.

"Thank you," Rafe said, holding out a hand to shake Gaines's. "I don't know that we would have found this without you."

Gaines's smile was knowing. It seemed he had his own thoughts on that subject. "I will bring you back later," he said.

Collette raised her brows. She hadn't intended to leave, now that she had the ship in view. If her father was on that ship, she would not leave him.

"That's not necessary," Rafe answered.

"And still you do not trust me. You can't think to

sit here the rest of the day. The wind on the water is cold."

"I don't mind," Collette said.

Gaines looked at Rafe. "As you said, your watch is worth more than a cup of coffee and bowl of soup. I have an inn where you might rest until nightfall."

Rafe glanced at her, then back at Gaines. "That's convenient."

"I'm a businessman."

"How many businesses do you own?"

"Enough. You wonder why I would offer you shelter and an escort back. You think I hope to gain something."

Collette didn't answer, but it was as though he had read her mind.

"I'm merely curious. As I said, I know everything about this town, but I don't know this ship. This is a sad circumstance for a man with as much curiosity as me."

Rafe looked at Collette. His eyes held a question, and she knew the decision was hers to make. She liked Thomas Gaines. She trusted him—as much as she trusted any man she had only known for a couple of hours. But could she trust him with her father's life? And if anything went wrong, wouldn't it be wise to have a powerful man like Gaines on their side?

She nodded. Rafe raised his brows, seeming to ask if she was certain. She nodded again.

"I have a coachman," Rafe began, looking back at Gaines.

"He's welcome, of course," Gaines said. "The inn has a stable and a common room. Shall I reserve you one room or two?"

"One," Rafe said at the same time Collette said, "Two."

Gaines's teeth flashed. "Two rooms with a connecting door, I think." He put his arm around Rafe's shoulder and steered him back toward the main village. "Now, tell me what you do in Town."

Collette was glad to be spared the effort of conversation. She could think of nothing but her father. How had he fared on his crossing? She had not seen him in months. Had his captors treated him well? How would they react when they realized she had come to them and that she did not have the codes she'd promised? She had to hope that in the confusion of coming ashore in the dark, she and Rafe could spirit her father away before his captors even knew what had happened.

And then…

She did not want to think about what would happen next. If she had her way, she would take her father and continue running. Her plan had always been to take her father to America. It seemed to her somewhere far, far away. Somewhere the French and the British could never reach them.

But as Gaines's innkeeper showed them to their rooms, she couldn't help but look at Rafe. She would miss him. She had fallen in love with him, and not a little in love, as she had with Marcel all those years ago. What she felt for Rafe was stronger and deeper. He wasn't the man she had thought the first time she had seen him. Yes, he was handsome—too handsome for his own good—and charming and rakish, but he was also loyal, steadfast, and courageous. No one had ever done as much for her as Rafe Beaumont. No one but her father.

She closed the door to her room and leaned against it, holding the small wooden box the innkeeper had handed her close to her chest. Rafe might care for her, but he would never love her, not like she loved him. His revelations in the carriage had told her more than he probably wanted her to know. He'd been abandoned by a woman, the most important woman in his world, as a child. Was it any wonder that he had turned into the kind of man who, rather than wait for yet another woman to abandon him, left her first? Why not? In his experience, there was always another woman and one was pretty much the same as another.

She wanted to believe she was different. Rafe had said she was different, but how many other women had heard those words from his lips? How many times had he meant them?

She wanted to believe he'd meant those words when he spoke them to her. And perhaps this afternoon, while she bided the long hours until darkness fell, she wanted one last memory with Rafe Beaumont. It would be something sweet she could hold on to during the long years ahead, years that were as shrouded in darkness as the coming night. She would have her father, and he would be enough if she could also have one more memory of Rafe.

She lowered the box and freed the latch. Inside was a key to her room, as she'd expected, but also two steaming towels. She sighed in pleasure at the thought of using them to wipe away the dust of the journey to Wapping from London. Collette stripped off her cloak and went to the washbasin. She poured cold water into it and splashed her face and arms. Then, when gooseflesh had broken out along her skin, she took one of the warm towels and slid it over her face, neck, and arms. The sensation was heavenly, but it made the rest of her feel grimy. She removed her dress and used the other towel over the rest of her body. She even removed her boots and washed each toe. Then, in only her chemise, she stood before the fire and allowed it to dry her damp skin.

It didn't surprise her when she heard the tap on the door adjoining their rooms. She had known he would come to her, but she had thought he would wait longer. She had thought she might change her mind.

She hadn't.

Instead of calling out, she went to the door herself and opened it. Rafe stood in shirtsleeves and trousers, his hair slightly damp at the ends. He'd obviously put his own towels and the water in the washbasin to use. His gaze rested determinedly on her face, though she knew he had taken in the fact that she wore only her chemise. With the curtains of the window in her room drawn and the midday sun streaming in to make rectangular patterns on the carpet, she could imagine her thin chemise did not conceal much.

But his eyes were on hers, his gaze respectful and polite. He would not force himself on her. He didn't expect anything. She could close the door right now, and he would not pound on it or ask anything of her.

"How is your room? Is everything to your liking?"

"Yes. Your watch has provided fine accommodation."

He gave her a wry smile. "Would you like me to send for tea and sandwiches? Are you hungry?"

She shook her head, then stepped back and out of the doorway. "I'm not hungry. Not for sandwiches."

Now his gaze drifted lower. She felt the heat of it on her shoulders, her breasts, her belly, and the V between her legs. She grew damp there as his perusal went on, as he examined what she offered. Slowly, his gaze returned to her face, and she saw what she had hoped she might: hunger. For a moment, she had feared he no longer wanted her. But the look he gave her made it clear he wanted her very much. "What are you hungry for?" His voice was low and rough, and though he must have known the answer, held a note of genuine interest.

"You," she said simply and held a hand out to him. He was in her chamber in an instant, the door to his own slammed shut. He didn't take her hand but swept her off her feet and into his arms. Collette laughed as he carried her to the bed.

"I have been praying you would say that." He kissed her, then set her on the bed, coming down on top of her. "I have been pleading with God, promising all manner of reform and good deeds if I could just kiss you once more."

"You will have to do more than kiss me," she answered with a flirtatious smile.

"Christ, you'll have me building churches to honor my promises."

"Take off your shirt," she said, bunching the hem and lifting it to reveal the flat skin of his belly. She wanted to see all of him today, she wanted him naked in the sunlight, that perfect body of his all hers until dusk crept over them.

He pulled it over his head with none of the seductive finesse she had expected. She'd thought he might undress slowly, as he had that first night. But he did not seem inclined to take his time, and she was in a mood to savor. She pushed him back and off her. He stood at the side of the bed, his expression curious. She rose to her knees and slid her hands over his broad, muscled shoulders. The light was behind him, the window on the wall parallel to the bed, and the sunlight made his skin look golden. She stepped off the bed and circled him, one hand drifting to his waist and holding him in place as she traced his shoulders and back with her lips. That hand dipped lower to feel the bulge of his erection through his trousers, and he let out a small groan.

Her hand drifted away to meet the other on his back. She traced his form down to his slim waist and hips, then over his firm buttocks. The quick sound of his indrawn breath made her smile. "Remove your trousers," she murmured.

She thought he might object. Most men would have bristled at a woman who gave orders, but he obliged her without a word. He'd taken his boots off in his room, so it was an easy matter to strip himself of his last vestments. The trousers dropped, followed by his smallclothes, and he stepped out of the clothing, his back still to her.

Collette had to swallow to relieve the dryness in her throat. Sculpted calves and powerful thighs made a trail to his rounded backside. Two dents marked his lower back, and she started by putting her hands there. He stiffened as she moved down, squeezing that ripe flesh of his buttocks, then sliding her hand between his legs to cup him and then stroke his hard member. He put a hand on the bedpost to brace himself. Tension and strain seemed to hum through him. From the way his fingers had turned white against the dark wood of the bedpost, he must have been desperate to take her, but he allowed her to do as she would. She knelt behind him, pushing his legs wider as she gripped him more securely, then as she moved her hand up and down she pressed her lips to that taut flesh of his behind.

"Christ," he said, his voice a growl. "I'll embarrass myself in a moment if you keep this up."

"You mustn't come," she said, her lips moving against his plump flesh. She'd never used such a word before, but she'd heard men use it. Knew what it meant. "You have to wait for me."

"Then this is just torture," he gritted out as her hand worked him.

"I call it foreplay."

"Semantics," he muttered. "Let me undress you."

She would have refused but for the way he'd said it. *Let me…* Desperation hung in his tone, and she thought he might just want her as much if not more than she did him.

"Very well," she said and moved to face him. If he'd been glorious from behind, he was even more so straight on. His member jutted proudly, looking as hard and unyielding as the firm flesh of his chest. His legs were planted on the floor as though he were a pirate balancing on a tossing ship. The muscles of his legs were defined and straining as he held himself in check. "Undress me," she said.

He moved quicker than she'd expected to take her waist in his hands. She thought he might rip the chemise, but he merely gathered the material in his hands and allowed it to inch up her calves. Then as the fabric in his fists grew, she felt the sun on her knees and her thighs and then cool air on her buttocks. When he'd bared her to the waist, he used both hands to yank the garment over her head. Her flesh prickled with cold and anticipation as he stepped back slightly to take her in.

"I don't know where to begin," he said, voice husky. "I want to taste every inch of you." Her nipples hardened almost painfully, and his smile widened. "You want me to start there." He reached out and took one nipple between thumb and forefinger. Heat pulsed between her legs as he rubbed the distended tip, causing a delicious friction. She arched her back, offering herself to him, but he didn't ravish her as she'd half wanted. Instead, he cupped her breast, his palm brushing that aching nipple. She shifted as the ache between her thighs intensified to match the yearning he stoked in her.

"What are you hungry for?" he asked. "I could look at you all day. I could spend hours learning every single curve and dip and swell and"—his fingers manipulated her tender nipple again, making her gasp with pleasure—"and tip. Is that what you want? Do you want me to tease you until you gasp so that you think you can't breathe, until you beg me to thrust inside you, until you are forced to touch yourself with your slim, long fingers because to refrain would be sheer torment?"

She knew her cheeks flushed at his words, but she also knew he could do every single thing he'd promised. Already the tension between her legs made her squirm and imagine wanton acts.

"Don't tease me," she whispered. "Not this time."

His violet eyes went dark to almost purple. "Shall I take you hard and fast now, only to lay you out afterward in that stream of sunlight and stroke you until you want me inside you again?"

"Yes," she whispered. "Hard and fast."

The hand on her breast slid to her hip and then across her abdomen. She shivered as he brushed over her curls and parted her legs. "You're already wet."

"I want you."

His eyes met hers again. There were questions in his eyes, but he seemed to know now was not the time to ask them. They would come later when they were both sated and drifting in a haze of pleasure. "Bend over."

Even as a thrill of desire shot through her, disappointment curled around her heart. It was better this way, she told herself. Better that they don't allow their eyes to meet, that he didn't look into her soul to see just how very much she cared for him. Better that she didn't look into his and see the regret that he could not feel the same for her. He could give her pleasure, but he couldn't give her his heart.

He already had her heart, and she would take the pleasure. Slowly, she turned, her thighs brushing against the bed. Then she bent, lowering herself until her breasts brushed the coarse fabric of the coverlet.

"Spread your legs." His voice sounded choked, and though she felt incredibly exposed as she was, she spread her legs, opening for him. He didn't move, but she could feel the heat of him behind her. And then the hair of his legs brushed the back of her thighs and she felt his heavy member brush against her sex. He didn't enter her. Instead, he stroked her bottom with his hands, mirroring her actions earlier. Gradually he slid his fingers between her legs, brushing against her hot flesh. He guided his hard shaft into her so very slowly that she could feel her body straining to take him in. Then his hands were on her hips, pulling her back until he had sheathed himself completely, filling her to the point of delirium.

"Yes." She rocked back, taking even more of him, and he growled his approval. They stood still for a long moment, and she could feel him pulse inside her, then his hands moved to explore her breasts and down to her belly and then to the slit of her womanhood. He parted her, revealing her thrumming bud, and he began to circle it.

She made an unintelligible sound as pleasure began to curl through her in little spirals. And as the pleasure built, she rocked back against him. He didn't move, didn't take his own pleasure, just gave to her. She moved faster, sliding up and down his length as her climax approached, and he encouraged her. "Use me. Like that. Christ, Collette. Yes."

And then everything tightened and went white hot, her body seemed to implode on itself. And just as she was about to shatter, he pushed her onto the bed and drove into her. The feeling was indescribable. She rode the waves of her climax as he pounded into her, bringing her higher and higher until she was whimpering and crying and yet begging for more. Her body seemed to spark, and she could have sworn she saw fireworks as he drove into her a last time. And then as the last ounce of pleasure slowly drained away, he drew out and moaned.

# Seventeen

RAFE TOSSED THE USED TOWEL TO THE FLOOR AND braced a hand on the bed beside Collette's hip. Her white skin bore the red imprint of his hand, where he'd held her hips in an effort to keep his need under control.

She was still bent over the bed, her body open to him. He could see the pink, swollen flesh between her legs, and he felt his cock twitch. Her head was turned on the bed and she looked over her shoulder at him, her eyes glassy with pleasure. She seemed to read his mind and lifted her hips again in what was probably an unconscious invitation, but he knew what he wanted next and it was not another quick rogering.

He pulled her up and turned her in his arms, cupping the back of her neck with his hand and kissing her gently. She seemed surprised at the gesture, but she wrapped her arms around him and responded sweetly. Too sweetly. It was impossible for him not to know how she felt. She'd said it with words, but did she know that she said it with her body every time he touched her? Her lips said it now, and her hands as they twined in his hair.

When they parted, he took the other towel and handed it to her. He climbed on the bed, moving to the far side and leaving the side nearest the window for her. When she'd done her ablutions, she crawled beside him. He pulled her into his arms and held her, not speaking, just knowing this would be the last time he would ever hold her like this.

After a little while, her breathing slowed and her body went limp. She dozed, but Rafe watched the sliver of light on the coverlet widen and grow longer until it slid over their legs, then up to their entwined thighs.

If all went as planned, she would see her father tonight. Tonight he would have to make a decision—to allow her and her father to go free, or to turn them in to the Foreign Office. Duty versus honor. If he did his duty to his country and his former commanding officer, he would turn Fortier over to the Foreign Office. He should turn them both in, but that was where honor came in. How could he give Collette over to men who would undoubtedly see her questioned, perhaps tortured, and imprisoned if not hanged? What kind of man would he be to take her body, lie with her in his arms, then betray her trust?

He had told her he would help her to get away. He would stand by his word, even if it meant losing Draven's trust forever. Even if he too might be brought up on charges of treason for aiding spies.

He could go with her...

Rafe's hand, which had been caressing the curve of Collette's hip, paused. What if this was not the last time he held her, kissed her, touched her? What if he could have her every day and every night? But leave his life in London? Leave his friends and his family and his bevy of admirers for a life as a fugitive?

It might be worth it to have Collette at his side if not for one problem: he would never run away like a thief in the night. Rafe had too much respect for Lieutenant Colonel Draven to disappear without a word or an explanation. Duty and honor went hand in hand on that point.

Collette stirred and Rafe moved his hand over her silky skin again, cupping the lush curve of her hip. Under his touch, her skin pebbled with gooseflesh and then her eyes fluttered open. As soon as her gaze focused on him, she smiled. Rafe's chest seemed to constrict, making it difficult for him to breathe. How many women had smiled at him? How many come-hither glances had he received? None had ever affected him like Collette's. None had ever made him feel nervous and tender and randy all at the same time.

"You're still here," she murmured, her voice husky from sleep.

"Still here." He kissed the tip of her nose.

"I didn't think you were the kind of man who stayed after…" She made a motion with her hand to indicate the bed and what they had done in it.

"I'm not. But I keep telling you, you're different." He gathered her closer until her warm body pressed against his. "Don't you believe me?"

"I am trying."

He knew what she was not saying. She could not fully trust him until he was put to the test—tonight. He didn't blame her because he didn't trust himself.

"I like waking up beside you." She kissed him

lightly on the mouth and his blood started to hum as it raced through his veins.

"Do you?" His hand drifted from her hip to her round bottom. "What else do you like?"

"The way you touch me. The way you look at me. The way you kiss me."

He resisted the urge to claim her, instead taking her lips tenderly. He moved down to her jaw, then her cheek, then her temple, her brow, and the bridge of her nose. His mouth moved over her skin in feathery strokes until she was sighing with pleasure. He angled up on an elbow and looked down at her. Rafe didn't think he had ever seen a more beautiful woman than Collette with her moist, red lips and her pink cheeks. He spread her dark hair out on the bed beneath her, then kissed her neck and her clavicle.

She wrapped her arms around him, urging him back to her mouth, but he shook his head. "I want to worship you. I want to kiss every inch of you."

Shoulders, arms, fingers, belly, knees, and toes. By the time the sun streaked over her breasts, he knew every inch of her. And she was panting with need. He understood that need because his own cock throbbed with desire for her. Her nipples had hardened into points, the sun making their pink tips look almost golden. Her legs had opened, giving him a peek at her womanhood. He hadn't kissed her there yet, but now he spread her legs wider and brushed his jaw along her inner thigh.

Collette sighed, her breath hitching as he inched closer to her core. She was pink and petal soft here, her skin glistening with the evidence of her arousal. That little, rosy bud looked swollen with need, and when he scraped his tongue over it, her entire body quivered. Her knees fell open wider as she gave him her trust. Rafe took his time pleasuring her. He'd always been good at pleasuring women and he'd always enjoyed it, but never so much he would forgo his own pleasure. But Rafe could have spent the rest of the day pleasuring Collette and never once thought of himself. After her first climax, she tried to close her legs, but he coaxed them open again, and under his ministrations, she was soon writhing and moaning once again.

And then, quite unexpectedly, she tugged at his hair. He looked up at her, at her dark, shining eyes. "I want *you*. All of you."

He couldn't resist the plea in her voice. He didn't even want to. He covered her body with his, sliding over her and then into her slick, wet sheath. She moaned and her hips rose to take him in until he'd buried himself to the hilt. Her eyes went hazy, her focus drifting as he began to move within her. And then she met his gaze again, and her fingers twined with his so that he pinned her arms to the bed. Rafe was not gentle. He took his pleasure, thrusting deep and hard in a quickening rhythm. He felt her muscles squeeze, and she let out a soft exclamation in French as she climaxed.

He looked into her eyes as she came, felt her body tighten around him, and he had never felt closer to another person than in that moment. His own release was hard on the heels of hers, overlapping it, and he withdrew quickly, but his eyes never left hers as he spilled his seed.

He stared at her, panting, pleasure spiraling through him. He'd never sought intimacy before. He'd wanted encounters designed to give him release, not to feel emotions. But now so many emotions coursed through him that he didn't know how to categorize them much less what to do with them. But as they finally drew apart and he flopped on the bed, chest rising and falling, Rafe's rib cage still felt tight. And he knew the specific area where the constriction was strongest—his heart.

He loved Collette Fortier. He, Rafe Alexander Frederick Beaumont, was in love.

And there was nothing he could do about it.

◈

Collette's empty belly woke her. She opened her eyes to find herself alone in her chamber. Rafe had covered her with the counterpane, but he'd taken his clothing and gone. She sat and peered at the door adjoining their rooms. It was closed.

Lying back with a sigh, Collette closed her eyes against the sting of tears. He had retreated again. She'd thought...but she was a fool to keep hoping he would ever love her. And even if he did love her, they had no future together. She would never sacrifice her father, not even for a man she loved as much as she loved Rafe Beaumont.

The room was dark, but the sky outside was still a pewter gray. Gaines had told them he would fetch them at full dark, which gave her a little time to dress and to think. She washed and pinned her hair and considered her options. She did not know what sort of shape her father would be in, if he would be well enough to travel, but she knew she had to take him far away from England as quickly as she could. If possible, tonight. Wapping was too close to London, too close to the Foreign Office and Lady Ravensgate. She did not want to risk being found and losing her father once again.

She had reasoned it this way. They couldn't return to France. Her father would never be safe as long as the Bourbons were on the throne. He'd perpetrated too many crimes against them. And they could not go anywhere within easy reach of the British. That left one good option: the United States.

Fortunately, she had found the last piece she needed to make her plans reality. She knew just the man to help her book passage to America.

She had just finished dressing, no easy task when attempted by herself, when Rafe tapped on the door and entered. As usual, he looked as though he had spent an hour with a valet. His clothing, though it had been tossed on the floor like hers, was pressed and unwrinkled. His hair was stylishly tousled and his eyes looked at her with his usual mixture of sinful charm. Only his jaw gave any indication he had not dressed for a night at Almack's. Dark stubble gave him a dangerous look.

"I took the liberty of ordering tea and scones. Will you come into my chamber and eat something? We have a long night ahead of us."

She nodded, wondering if he knew exactly how long it would be for her. She did not think she would have time to sleep or do much more than eat a few bites for days, perhaps weeks. Though her belly was tense, she forced herself to drink a little tea and nibble on a scone.

"I have been thinking, and now that I've seen this place, I've formulated a plan."

She nodded. "Go on."

He related the particulars, and though she could see several potential problems, it was better than she might have conceived. She agreed, then set down her uneaten pastry.

"You're not hungry?" he asked. She might have asked him the same since he hadn't touched the food.

"I'm nervous. I haven't seen my father in months."

"You won't wait much longer. Gaines has had time to gain information on the ship and its passengers. If we had guessed wrong or anything he discovered contradicted our theories, he would have let us know before now. If your father is on that ship, we will see him before the night is over."

She took a breath and tried to smile. Collette tried to think of something else to say, but her thoughts spun away before she could grasp one. The silence between them grew, and she was relieved when a tap on the door ended the awkwardness.

Rafe crossed to the door. Gaines stood in the doorway, his brows lifted. "Ready?"

Collette nodded.

"Yes," Rafe said. "But I need to step out to the stable and speak to my coachman. I want the horses and the coach ready for a quick departure."

"Of course. We will wait for you in the private dining room."

Once downstairs, Rafe went his way and Gaines escorted her to a small room lit by a fire. No one dined there now, but beyond the door that opened into the public room, she could hear the rumble of men's voices and the clink of silver.

"I think you have something to say to me," Gaines said softly. "Best to say it now before he returns."

She looked at him, praying she could trust him.

"Am I mistaken?"

"No," she said. "I may need to leave quickly."

"And that is why Mr. Beaumont readies the coach?"

"I may need to leave without him."

Gaines nodded slowly. "And you want help securing passage?"

"I want to go to the United States. I think you are the best man to help me there."

"I know all the captains and their destinations—their *real* destinations," he added. "I can put you on a ship bound for America. There is one that may sail as early as tomorrow evening."

"Nothing sooner?"

"Not out of Wapping. But if it's your companion you fear, trust that I will make certain he does not prevent you from boarding the ship. The sailors will not allow him to take you off."

"I don't have any money. My father may have some—"

Gaines waved his hand. "I can call in a favor."

"You would do that for me?"

"I would never have reached England if several men hadn't done me a good turn. How can I refuse a fellow human in need?"

"Thank you."

"If I may, why is it you want to escape Mr. Beaumont? He does not seem a cruel man."

"He is not, but we…we have different loyalties."

"I see. Then put your faith in me."

"Why must she have faith in you?" Rafe asked as he strolled into the room.

Collette felt her cheeks redden as heat raced to her face. How much had he heard?

"She must have faith I will take you to the ship we saw this afternoon. Are you ready, sir?"

Rafe's eyes met hers, and she looked away.

"Ready," he said, sounding very much like a man to be marched before the executioner.

The night was cool, and Collette pulled her cloak close around her. The Thames stunk less in the evening, as the sun did not beat down on it and fewer ships moved through it to stir up the noxious fumes. And still Collette found herself holding her breath as they made their way along the quay toward the set of steps they had descended earlier. Even from the pathway she could see a couple points of light on *The Amaranthe.* Lanterns had been lit, and that was a good sign. Someone was on the ship. It had looked so deserted this afternoon.

Gaines led them past the set of steps they had descended earlier, and Collette gave him a curious look. "I assumed you would want to observe from the shadows," he said in answer, and led them toward the doorway of an old brick warehouse, leaning from age and neglect. Many of the warehouses butted the quay and overlooked the river. If the Thames rose too high,

Collette imagined they flooded. "You may watch from here and you will not be noticed." He brought the spyglass to his eye and stared at the ship for a long time. Then he lowered it and handed it to Collette. She raised it and peered at the ship.

"They're lowering a jolly boat."

"Is the man you seek aboard?"

She squinted and concentrated, but she simply could not make out any details of the passengers. There were four or five, but the shapes were indistinct in the dark, and it was difficult to be sure.

"I cannot say."

"If he does come ashore, it will most likely be along the quay near here. A boat like that can pull alongside a dock and the men can disembark easily. Or they might choose to come in shallow and beach the boat. Be careful if you go down. The stairs are slick at night and the riverside is rocky."

Rafe held out his hand, and she put the spyglass into it. He peered through it. "Wherever they come ashore, we won't reveal ourselves until we know Fortier is with them. And even then, we wait until they're ashore. We don't want them rowing back out and escaping that way."

Collette frowned. "Do you think they will try and escape?" That had been the least of her worries. Her fear was once they realized she did not have the information she'd promised, they would try and hurt her or her father.

"I don't know what they will do." Rafe took a pistol from his greatcoat. "But I am ready for it."

He must have retrieved the pistol from the coach

when he'd gone to see the coachman. She wished its presence made her feel safer, but she couldn't help worry that he might use the pistol to take her father prisoner.

"One shot from that," Gaines said, "and you will have the Thames River Police here. I would not use it unless it's truly necessary."

"Point taken." Rafe dropped the pistol back in his pocket and lifted the spyglass. "They're getting closer."

Collette shrank back into the shadow of the warehouse, touching her hood to make sure she was still concealed.

"I would leave you now," Gaines said. "I don't want any part in this." His brown eyes met Collette's. "But I will be at the inn if you have need of me. I will tell my innkeeper I am to be at your disposal."

"Thank you," Collette said, grateful that he seemed to remember their earlier discussion. She knew he must have been referring to her request that he help her find a ship to take her to the United States.

With a nod and then a bow, Gaines took his leave. When they were alone, Rafe handed the spyglass back to her. "Do you see him?"

She peered through it, scanning the dark water until she found the boat. "It's hard to tell."

"Look at the man seated in the middle. If one of them is a prisoner, it's that man."

Collette studied the man in the middle. He sat in the boat, neither rowing nor directing the other men. His back was hunched and his head down. He wore a dark hat, which shielded his head, and she could not make out the color of the man's hair. "It might be him," she said. "I think his size is about right, but I simply cannot see well enough." But even the prospect of the man in the middle of the boat being her father made her heart pound with anticipation. She found herself praying over and over that she would see her father tonight.

"They're heading for that dock," Rafe said, pointing toward a small dock that jutted out from the riverside. It did not seem to belong to any particular warehouse and wasn't long enough to accommodate a large vessel. But a small boat like this one could pull alongside.

"Should we go down?" Collette asked, no longer needing the spyglass to see the boat's progress, which was only a few yards from the dock.

"Not until we're certain he's with them."

The boat seemed to make excruciatingly slow progress, and then finally, it was within range of the dock. Collette raised the spyglass again and focused on the man seated in the center of the boat. Lamps lit the quay at sporadic intervals, and she could make out the features of the man in the bow of the boat. He had a long, thin nose and high cheekbones. His pewter hair had been brushed back to reveal a high forehead. She didn't know this man, but she couldn't believe he was a sailor. Everything about him, from the way he stood to the tilt of his upturned jaw, spoke of the nobility. The man rowing behind him was bigger and bulkier, but he too wore a coat and neck cloth.

And then the man in the middle looked up. The hood of his cape fell back slightly and Collette saw the glint of white hair. Her belly tightened and her chest sagged. It wasn't him. Her father had dark hair, like she. In the murky lamplight, this man's complexion looked pale and sallow, whereas her father had always had olive skin that made it look as though he spent much time outdoors.

And then he looked up, and Collette gasped.

"What is it?" Rafe was beside her in an instant, his hand on her back. She shook her head, unable to lower the spyglass. Unable to comprehend what she saw.

The prisoner in the middle had looked up. He'd looked directly at her, though he couldn't have seen her. He must have simply looked in her direction. But there was no mistaking what she had seen. He was her father. Only he bore very little resemblance to the healthy, youthful man she'd known. This man had aged years, decades, in only a few months.

Her hand shook and she had to lower the spyglass.

"What is it?" Rafe asked again.

In answer, her eyes filled with tears.

Rafe took the spyglass and peered through it. "His hood has fallen back. Is that him?"

"Yes." Her voice broke on the word. Rafe lowered the spyglass and took her by the arms.

"You have to tell me what's wrong. Is that your father or no?"

"It's him, but he…" She looked at Rafe. "What did they do to him?"

He gathered her in his arms, and she was grateful because she did not know if her legs would hold her. Her father looked so old and frail. She could see the hollows beneath his eyes and cheeks.

"They won't touch him again. I swear it, Collette."

She nodded, closing her eyes and savoring the warmth

of his body as he held her close. Then she found her strength again and straightened. "I want to go to him."

"You should wait here. It's not safe."

She shook her head. "We had a plan, and my father's life depends on how well we execute it. I'm ready, Rafe."

He gave her a dubious look, but whatever he saw in her face must have convinced him. "Come with me, but stay close. The last thing I need is to have to rescue two prisoners."

He moved out of the cover of the warehouse, and she trailed in his shadow. She wanted them to wonder who she was until the moment she revealed herself, so she kept her hood up and stayed out of view. She and Rafe moved silently, and she needed all of her wits about her to concentrate on picking her way down the slick stone steps.

At the bottom of the steps, Rafe put a hand back to hold her in place. The wall of the stairwell and the quay were on their right; to the left of them, the wall had been set back and was more open to the riverside. The dock, however, was to their right. They might prefer another staircase, one they could see upon approach, but that would mean walking along the river for some way. As Gaines had pointed out, the shore was rocky and difficult to traverse, especially with a sick man. Collette knew Rafe believed her father and his captors would choose to approach the stairs, and to her advantage, they would do so almost blind to who waited for them there.

Rafe tugged his pistol from his coat, primed and loaded it. Then he reached into his boot and extracted his dagger. He handed it to her, and she took it grate-fully. She couldn't imagine using it, but she did not want to face these men completely vulnerable. "Do you have a pocket?" he whispered.

She nodded.

"Put it away. We stick with the plan, and the dagger comes out if things don't go as expected." He hugged the wall and motioned for her to do the same. She stood two steps above him, and the instinct to race down the remaining steps and run straight into her father's arms almost overwhelmed her. She wrapped her hands around the fabric of her cloak and willed the men to hurry. How long did it take to climb from a boat and walk to a stairwell?

Finally, she heard the crunch of their boots and the low whisper of one of them. Rafe held a hand up again, staying her even as she leaned forward. He didn't move, and the whole world seemed to stop and stand motion-less. And then Rafe stepped down and out, blocking the men from the stairway. She was still hidden from view, only able to make out the shadow of the man before Rafe.

"Stop right there," Rafe said in French. Hearing him speak her language so unexpectedly gave her a jolt. "You have something I want." He brandished the pistol. Collette could not see the men's reactions, but from the way Rafe strained forward they must have stepped back.

"Monsieur, you must have us mistaken for some-one else" came a voice in answer. Collette would have bet all the money she had it was the man she had seen in the bow of the boat, the one with the sharp features. He spoke French like a nobleman.

"I don't think so." Rafe gestured with the pistol. "Fortier, come forward."

The silence seemed to press like a weight on her ears.

"There is no one by that name among us," answered the same voice she had heard before. "As I said, you have mistaken us. And while you might have a pistol, it is four against one. I suggest you be on your way, monsieur."

"And I suggest you hand Fortier over, else I put a pistol ball in the temple of the spy you've come to see."

Although Collette knew what was coming, she was still startled when he grabbed her arm and pulled her against his chest, wrapping an arm about her throat. He did not point the pistol at her head, but he held it close enough that the threat was real and present.

She could see all of the men, though her hood shadowed her face. The man in the front was indeed the man who had been in the bow, and his features looked even crueler in the yellow lamplight. Behind him was the other man, the one who'd been rowing. He held her father on one side, and on her father's other side must have been the fourth man in the boat. He had been in the back, and she hadn't seen him clearly. She didn't look at him clearly now. She looked only at her father.

Now that she was closer, the changes in him were even more apparent. He stooped, and she could hear his breathing was labored. But his eyes were still sharp, and they were fastened on her with something that looked very much like horror.

"No," he croaked, his voice sounding like the scratch of a pen nib on paper. "No!" he said again.

"Shut up!" the man holding him said.

Collette could hardly drag her gaze from her father back to the leader. When she did, his expression had not changed. He looked impassive. "And who is this?" he gestured to her with a weak flick of his wrist.

"Lower your hood," Rafe said, his voice hard and cold. She could almost believe she really was his captive. She lifted her hands and pushed the hood back.

"No!" her father said, though it sounded more like a groan.

The leader narrowed his small eyes. "And why should I care about this woman?"

"Because she's been spying for you for months, and because I believe she has codes you found so valuable that you crossed the Channel to meet with her. All I want is Fortier."

"No!" Collette had worried she would give all away when she spoke. She was no actress, but the sight of her father standing there was enough to bring real fear into her voice. "No! Let him go. If you give him to this man, I swear I will tell you nothing."

The leader's gaze flicked to her and then back to Rafe. His haughty expression didn't falter. Clearly, he had ways of making her talk. She prayed he would never have the opportunity.

"How do you propose we make the exchange?" the leader asked.

"Send Fortier up the steps. When he reaches the top, I hand her over."

The leader frowned and turned his head slightly toward her father. "I'm not certain he can make it up the stairs on his own. He hasn't been well."

"You bastards." The words came from deep within her. "You did this to him! I kept my end of the bargain—"

"He is an old man, Mademoiselle Fortier. I cannot be responsible for the health of old men."

Her hand itched to grab the dagger and plunge it into his belly. Never before had she wanted to hurt anyone, but now she could have cheerfully killed all three men. And then her gaze met that of her father. His eyes flicked to Rafe and then to her. She stepped closer to Rafe, to try, in some small way, to let her father know he was their ally. At least she hoped he was.

"I can make it," Fortier said. "I'm not so weak I can't climb a set of steps." He never looked away from her as he spoke. And she gave him a subtle nod. *Yes, go far away*, she thought. She wanted him on the quay if Rafe was forced to begin shooting.

"Go then," the leader ordered. "Release him."

The two men released his arms, and for a moment, he seemed to stumble. But he righted himself and squared his shoulders. In that instant, Collette saw the man her father had been. Hope flared in her. And then terror because she saw what he intended the moment before he struck.

# Eighteen

RAFE HADN'T EXPECTED THE ATTACK. HE'D THOUGHT the old man would fall over as soon as he wasn't propped up. The haughty leader of the French contingent must have thought the same because his attention was on Rafe, not on Fortier.

And that was his mistake.

Fortier might have been weak, but he'd also been the best assassin Napoleon had ever employed. And he struck quickly and with deadly force. Fortier knocked the leader to the ground with his shoulder and followed him down, his hands wrapping around the man's neck. Even as Rafe jumped to action, kicking the first man who rushed to his leader's defense, he heard the snap. Rafe knew without looking the leader's neck had been broken. The second man came for Rafe along with the man he'd kicked—who looked decidedly angrier—and Rafe swung his pistol in the closest man's direction. He could get off one shot and even the field, but it would still be two against one. Those weren't his favorite odds, but he'd seen worse. He cocked the pistol and fired, bracing for the blow that would come from the other side as the man he'd not shot plowed into him.

But the blow never came. The smoke from the pistol shot cleared, and Rafe saw the man he'd shot on the ground, hand clutched to his shoulder, where the ball had hit. He swung around and saw the other man lying on the ground, hand to his thigh, where a dagger protruded.

His dagger.

He would have stared at Collette, but there was still one more man to deal with. Rafe took a step toward him, and the man turned and ran. Ha. That was more like it. Where were Neil and Ewan to see this? He'd told them he was better at fisticuffs than they gave him credit for.

Then he turned and saw Fortier had pointed a pistol at the man running away.

Rafe heaved a great sigh. Perhaps when he told this story at the Draven Club later, he would leave the pistol and Fortier out of it.

Then Fortier pointed the pistol at him. Rafe raised his hands. "You should point that pistol elsewhere, old man. I'm the rescue party."

Fortier's hand shook badly, and Rafe doubted he could fire straight. He had to have taken the pistol from the man whose neck he'd snapped, and Rafe was willing to wager it was primed and loaded. He wasn't quite willing to wager his life that Fortier would miss.

"You had a pistol to my daughter's head," Fortier said, voice low and controlled. His hand steadied as he spoke.

Collette moved beside Rafe. "It was a plot, *mon père,*

to fool the men who held you. Mr. Beaumont is our ally." She glanced at him as though to confirm this.

He nodded, and he was never certain whether Fortier would have lowered the pistol or not. Before he could either fire or stand down, he was seized by a coughing fit that had him doubled over. Collette ran to him, her arm going around his shoulders. The pistol clattered to the ground as Fortier covered his mouth with the back of one hand. Rafe scooped the pistol up and put it and his own into his coat. They had to leave before the river police arrived. Surely they would be alerted by the sound of pistol fire.

He moved to Fortier's other side. "Put your arm around me, monsieur. I'll help you up the stairs. We can't stay here."

Fortier shoved him away. "I am fine. Damn damp prison air. Give me another day and I'll be good as new. I'm not so easy to kill." But he took a step and stumbled, and Rafe caught him.

"Monsieur, are you injured?"

He shook his head. "Just need to gather my strength again. Come, help me out of here."

Rafe glanced at Collette. Her dark eyes were large in a face that seemed drained of any color. Slowly, she put her arm around her father's waist, and together, they helped him up the stairs to the quay. "We have to take him to the inn," she said when they reached the top of the stairs. "He needs rest and care."

"I agree, but it's a long walk. We require a carriage."

"There aren't likely to be any hackneys here at this time of night. You'll have to leave us and hail one a few streets over."

Rafe shook his head. "I'd rather not leave you alone."

Fortier made a sound somewhere between a laugh and a wheeze. "My daughter can take care of herself." He gulped in breath. "Give her the pistol. We'll be fine."

Rafe's gaze met hers. She nodded. "I'm an assassin's daughter. I know a few tricks."

"Such as knife throwing?" Rafe quipped, thinking of his dagger, still lodged in the thigh of the man on the riverside.

"To begin with."

Rafe still didn't like it. He didn't want to leave her. He didn't want to admit he half worried she'd be gone when he returned and he'd never see her again. But her father wasn't well enough to travel. They couldn't run from him.

"Fine, but we move you out of sight in case the police arrive before I return." He supported her father again and led him and Collette to a dark doorway of a warehouse. "I'll be back in a quarter hour. Don't move."

She nodded and as he walked away, Rafe had to force himself not to look back.

❧

A few minutes later, two policemen did arrive. The bodies of the men on the riverside drew their attention, and they never even saw Collette and her father huddled in the doorway. Collette held her father to her, much as he had held her when she was a little girl. He was weak and, except for the one moment on the riverside, seemed frail. But she would nurse him back to health at Gaines's inn. A few days of rest and good food and he would be ready to leave for America.

More coughs wracked his body, and he tried to muffle them by covering his mouth with his arm.

"You shouldn't have come for me," he said, his voice paper thin.

"Nonsense, *mon pére*. I would never leave you, not when I could save you."

"Better for you to save yourself, *ma chère*. You have your life ahead of you. I've lived mine."

"You have many more years ahead of you." She clutched him tighter as though the sheer strength of her desire could infuse him with vigor. "You need rest and fresh air."

"I'm unlikely to receive that in a British jail. I'm no safer here than in Paris."

"I have a plan. I'll take you to the United States. We'll be safe there, and I hear there are vast stretches of land. The air is clean. You'll—"

He put his finger on her lips. "Rafe?"

"Mr. Beaumont. He went to fetch the carriage."

"I see." He closed his eyes and leaned his head back against the door. His chest heaved up and down, his breaths labored and shallow. Collette held his hand, her heart pounding with terror. What would she do if she lost him? Where would she go? How was she to go on without him? He was her father. He'd always been by her side, always protected her, always kept her safe. She needed him. She wasn't ready to let him go and to face the world without him.

The clip-clop of horses' hooves alerted her to the approaching hackney, and when she peered around the building, she could just make out the outlines of a conveyance approaching. Fog had come in as the darkness deepened, and while it served to hide her and her father, it also gave the warehouses and the quay an eerie, otherworldly look. For a moment, Collette was tempted to hide in the shadows. The hackney looked too much like what she imagined the Grim Reaper might drive on his nightly rounds.

And then it stopped and Rafe jumped out. She couldn't see his face, but she knew him nonetheless. She'd know that confident manner in which he moved and the easy way he walked even without seeing him clearly.

"Collette." Her name floated by on the fog.

She considered not answering. She had her father here beside her. She couldn't give Rafe the opportunity to take him away.

"Answer him," her father said. She glanced at him sharply. His eyes were still closed, his head still leaning against the door. "You care for him. Your Rafe."

"His loyalty is to England and the Foreign Office, *mon père*. I can't trust him."

"Then give me to him and run. Let the Foreign Office do their worst. It's not as though I don't deserve it."

"No! I would never leave you."

"Collette!" It was Rafe's voice again, and he sounded more urgent.

"Then answer him. I may not know him, but any man who calls after a woman like that feels something for her. He won't betray us."

Collette wished she could be so certain. In any case, she was a fool to think she could stay out in the damp with her father, who was already ill and needed a bed and rest. "Here!" she called quietly. Leaning out from their little alcove, she waved her hand. The indistinct shape moved toward her and finally sharpened into Rafe. "The jarvey is skittish. We have to hurry." He bent and hoisted her father to his feet. Collette had to help because her father seemed to go limp. He groaned when Rafe tried to move him and his head slumped forward.

"Let me get on his other side," she said, trying to move around the small space.

"No time for that. Go on ahead. I'll carry him."

"You'll what?"

Rafe gestured with his arm and she moved ahead, toward the boxlike shape of the hackney and the more sinewy shape of the horse. She looked back and saw Rafe moving, her father cradled in his arms like a limp child. "Are you certain you have him?" she asked. She had not thought Rafe weak—after all, she'd seen him without his shirt and his chest was impressively muscled—but her father was not a small man.

"I have him." The slightest strain tinged Rafe's voice. "He's not as heavy as he looks."

Collette did not want to think what those words might have meant. And then they were at the hackney, and Rafe and her father were inside with her, and she needn't think any longer.

Hours later, when dawn broke, she rose from her father's bedside, wincing at the ache in her back. She'd nursed him all night, urging broth on him, mopping his brow, moving his pillow so his head might be supported and his coughing lessened. But nothing had seemed to help. What had they done to him in prison? A younger man might have withstood the lack of food and light, the foul air and absence of exercise, but her father's health had paid the price. She'd given what little money they had so he might be able to buy bedding and food, but she had been in England longer than she'd wanted. He had run out of funds and been forced to sleep on the floor and subsist on meager crusts of bread and stale water.

He slept, and she hoped his rest would last. Sleep would heal him—peaceful sleep—that and a new start. The ocean breeze would revive him when he was strong enough to travel. She moved to the window and parted the curtains. In the early-morning light, the world looked new. Carriages passed, men and women went about their shopping, dogs snatched at dropped food, birds sang, and, in the distance, the ships' white sails waved on the Thames. Everyone went on about their lives as though the world was not in turmoil, as though everything was the same as it had always been when, for her, nothing would ever be the same again. She had gained her father, but she would lose Rafe. How was it possible her heart should be so full and yet she felt as though her chest were being ripped in two?

She looked at her father. He was so pale, his hair so white, that he seemed part of the pillow. Under his eyes, dark shadows looked like bruises blossoming and his cheekbones were sharp and stark. She was encouraged by his quiet breathing and his lips were no longer blue. At least the broth and rest had begun the healing process.

"Oh, Papa," she murmured. Now that he was asleep, she could allow the tears to fall that had pricked her eyes since she had seen him the night before. She swiped at the moisture on her cheeks and closed her eyes, closing her hand on the drapes to keep her knees from buckling. She had to be strong. For him. All of the sacrifices they had made could not be for nothing. She had to leave London. Her father had wanted more for her than a prison cell. He'd wanted peace and happiness, and perhaps they could find that in the United States.

A quiet tap on the door interrupted her thoughts and she crossed to it quickly. Mr. Gaines stood in the hallway, and not wanting to wake her father, Collette stepped outside and closed the door behind her.

Gaines took in her face. "How is he? Or should I not ask?"

"Better. A little better." She tried to smile and look as though she believed it.

"I spoke to another captain I know, and he has agreed to take you to the United States. He's sailing for a place called Pennsylvania. I haven't been there myself, but I've heard of it. Large cities there, so a person might easily lose herself. Society too, if you have a yearning to see the theater or a museum."

"When does he leave?"

"Tomorrow at the earliest, but if his cargo is not all loaded, then the day after."

"Thank you." Collette swallowed. "I cannot accept. My father isn't well enough to travel. I must stay with him until he improves or…" She trailed off. She did not want to add *or we are put in prison*.

"I understand. Nevertheless, the captain will hold the cabin for you. If circumstances change, you go aboard. In a few months, all of this will be a distant memory."

That was what she wanted. She wanted Rafe's smile, his violet eyes, his soft lips—all of it—to be a distant memory. She wanted to stop hurting, to stop feeling the pressure in her chest and the sting of tears behind her eyes. In the room behind her, she heard her father cough. "I have to go to him."

Gaines nodded. "You let me know if there's anything else you need. More of that medicine I sent? More broth?"

"Yes, thank you." She would take all of the help she could.

Gaines turned to go, and Collette grasped his hand in hers. His was large and dark and the fingers roughly callused. But they were strong hands, good hands, honest hands. He squeezed her hand back. "Thank you, sir," she said. "Thank you for your kindness."

"It's my pleasure, miss."

Her father coughed again and she released Gaines, turning to go back into the room.

❧

Gaines stood outside her door for a long moment, then looked at Rafe's door. "You hear all of that?" he asked.

Rafe pushed his door open. There was no point in pretending he hadn't had it cracked, hadn't been eavesdropping. "Enough."

Gaines crossed his arms over his broad chest. "Seems to me the lady is eager to be rid of you. Will you let her go, or will we have a problem?"

Rafe narrowed his eyes. "If there's a problem, it's mine. And you can mind your own business, Gaines."

Gaines shook his head. "She's in my establishment. That makes her my business."

Rafe didn't have a quick retort ready.

"I may be wrong—never have been before—but I think it's the father you're after." Gaines waited. When Rafe didn't argue, Gaines rocked back on his heels. "The father is no threat to you. He's weak as a kitten. When I was a slave in Georgia and one of ours got to this point, we dug the grave. Of course, she's strong enough to fight for him. He may yet pull through. Either way, she'll be on that ship to Pennsylvania, and if you try to stand in her way—their way—you'll be sorry for it."

Rafe wanted to tell Gaines that he was the one who would be sorry, that he had powerful, even dangerous friends. But he wouldn't ask Ewan or Jasper to bring Collette back to London so the Foreign Office could throw her in prison. She wasn't any threat to king or country, and Rafe wasn't about to stand back and watch as she was hung as an example. The best place for her really was far away—far away from England and from him.

Once the Fortiers were gone, Rafe would return to Draven and report that Fortier was dead and his daughter had disappeared. And what did it matter if he lied as long as Fortier was no longer a threat? Rafe would be reprimanded for losing her, and Draven probably wouldn't give him any more assignments. That was fine with Rafe. He'd go back to his life before Collette. He'd spend his days at the club and his nights surrounded by beautiful women. He could take his pick from the bevy of widows and courtesans, and maybe with a woman on either arm and too much wine, he'd forget Collette's smile, her scent, the sound of her voice.

Rafe looked back at Gaines. "I won't stand in her way."

Gaines studied him. "You look like a man who just lost his life savings at the tables. Do you want some advice?"

"No." Rafe slid back into his room and closed the door. Gaines's foot caught in the opening just before it closed. "Move your foot or lose it." Rafe shoved the door hard. If the pressure pained Gaines, his face didn't show it.

"You could go with her," Gaines said.

"To America?" Rafe laughed. "It's barely civilized."

Gaines shrugged. "You might be surprised."

"Besides, if I went to the Americas, which I have no intention of doing, I'd have to marry her."

Gaines kept his gaze steady.

"I am never marrying. I have two elder brothers and a handful of nephews. I have no need to marry." Nor did he want to marry. Wives were notoriously unreliable. Look at his own mother. She'd left his father without a word. Rafe preferred to be the one leaving, not the other way around.

"Men have committed deeds far more foolish for love," Gaines said quietly.

Rafe felt the words like a punch to the sternum. "Undoubtedly, but I'm not in love."

"No? Then you wouldn't mind if I tried to persuade Miss Fortier to stay. I'm not married, and she's brave, beautiful, and intelligent. I wouldn't want a woman like that to slip through my fingers."

Rafe's hands were around Gaines's neck so fast that he couldn't remember moving. He slammed the man against the wall across from his room and put his face a fraction of an inch from Gaines's. "If you so much as look at her—"

Gaines raised his brows. Behind him, Collette's door opened. Rafe released Gaines immediately and stepped away, straightening his coat.

"What's the matter?" she asked, her gaze darting from one to the other.

"Nothing," Gaines said.

"Why do you ask?" Rafe inquired.

She frowned. "Perhaps because your hands were around his neck." She nodded at Gaines.

"Just a discussion. I'll fetch the medicine for you, miss, and be right back."

"Thank you."

When he was gone, Rafe looked past her and into the bedchamber. "How is he?" He immediately regretted asking.

Her eyes filled with tears. "Not well enough to travel, so if you were hoping to drag him to London so you might collect your reward, you will have to wait."

Rafe took a breath. He deserved that, he supposed. He had been ordered to find out what he could about Fortier. If he brought the assassin in, Rafe would have been praised and rewarded. Perhaps given a knighthood.

And he would have never forgiven himself for losing Collette's affection.

The war was over. Ewan and Neil and Jasper had killed plenty of Frenchmen. Hero or traitor was a point of view, and Rafe couldn't see one side clearly any longer.

"I have no intention of taking him or you anywhere," he said. "I'm not your enemy."

"You'll forgive me if I'm not always certain."

"No, I won't."

Her lips pressed together in annoyance.

"May I come in? Perhaps there's something I can do to help."

"You have experience in sickrooms?"

Rafe thought of the men who hadn't made it back from France and the men of his troop who'd been wounded but didn't die immediately. Then there were the men like Jasper and Nash. Men who had been wounded so badly that he hadn't known if they would survive. "I know something of them." And without waiting for more permission, Rafe pushed past her.

Fortier lay on the bed, a small form under the counterpane. His white hair was almost the same color as the pillow, and his skin was pale and sunken. But Rafe had seen men on the precipice of death more times than he liked to remember, and Fortier still had life in him. As Rafe stood at the foot of the bed, Fortier coughed, raising a handkerchief to his mouth reflexively as he did so.

Collette went to her father's side immediately, dipping a cloth into the basin of water beside the bed, wringing it out, and then placing it on his forehead. Fortier's eyes fluttered, but otherwise, there was little response.

"You see," she said quietly, "he is too weak to travel."

But she would heal him. She was a determined

woman, and she'd decided her father would live. The old man had little to say on the matter. The problem was that she could not wait for him to recover. If she waited, the matter of Fortier's life might be taken out of Rafe's hands.

"I'm sorry," Rafe said. "But you can't afford to wait. You have a day or two at most. Then you are both in danger."

She whipped to look at him. "Don't threaten me. If anyone tries to touch him, I'll kill them."

She'd probably try it too. How many days, how many months had she been dreaming of seeing her father again? And now she had him back, and he was ill and weak. She dipped the cloth in the basin again and wrung it out.

"Let me help you," Rafe offered.

"I think you've helped quite enough," she hissed pressing the cloth to her father's brow.

"Collette," the old man whispered.

"I'm here, *mon père*," she said tenderly. "I'm right here. I won't leave you."

"Good girl." Whatever else he intended to say was lost in a barrage of coughing. Someone tapped on the door just as Collette struggled to help her father sit up so he might be more comfortable. Rafe went to the door, growling when he opened it to see Gaines.

"Go away."

Gaines didn't look any happier to see him. "This is medicine. Give it to her from me. The maid will bring broth."

Rafe looked at the vial, then at the man before him. He held out a hand, and when Gaines dropped the vial into it, Rafe closed the door in his face. Fortier's head was higher on the pillow, and though he struggled to breathe, he had ceased coughing. Rafe crossed to the bed. "Medicine." He handed it to Collette.

"It will help him sleep," she said, her eyes brimming with tears of appreciation.

Rafe was suddenly glad he had answered the door. If she'd looked at Gaines the way she looked at him, Rafe would have had to kill the man.

"Thank you." She took it and opened the stopper. "Can you hold him up while I feed him some from this spoon?"

Rafe swallowed. He couldn't very well say no. He moved to Fortier's other side and propped the man up. He weighed almost nothing, his bones protruding through the thin shirt he wore. The old man's head lolled to the side, and Rafe steadied it as Collette poured the liquid onto the spoon. She pressed the spoon against Fortier's mouth, and when she slipped it inside, Rafe allowed Fortier's head to tilt back slightly so the liquid might go down his throat.

"Drink this, *mon père*," she said as she poured another dose on the spoon. Rafe repeated his actions. Who would have thought he would be sitting on the bed beside Napoleon's most notorious assassin and helping spoon-feed him medicine? Three years ago, he would have killed the man without a second thought.

Three years ago, he didn't know Collette.

"You can lay him down," she murmured. Rafe did so and stepped away again. Collette tucked her father in and mopped his brow. Rafe retreated to the back of the room and tried to stay out of the way. Soon her father's breathing sounded less labored, and his chest rose and fell in a light sleep. Collette continued to hold his hand and mop his brow, but eventually her movements slowed. Rafe knew she must have been exhausted because he was hardly awake on his feet. He barely breathed as she rested her head on the mattress beside her father's arm. After a little while, her breathing grew regular and deep, and he crossed to her, lifted her, and carried her through the door adjoining their rooms. He lay her gently on the bed, pulling the coverlet over her.

She murmured softly, and Rafe sat beside her and pushed the hair back from her forehead. "My papa used to do that," she said quietly, her eyes still closed. "And when I cried because he had to go away"—she swallowed—"to do his work, he would always tell me the same story."

"What was it?" Rafe asked, his fingers threading through her long tresses.

Her eyes fluttered but remained closed. "Once there was a girl whose father was a shepherd. When the sheep had eaten all the grass in the fields near their home, her father would take the sheep to the mountainsides to graze on the sweet, green grass there. Her father would often spend months in the mountains with the sheep, and the little girl missed her father dearly."

"Go on," Rafe said, stroking her gently.

"One day, the little girl's mother, seeing how lonely the child was, gave her daughter a small sack of potatoes to carry to her father, who had been living off what he could forage in the mountains and would appreciate heartier fare. The five potatoes were heavy for the child, but she carried them diligently out the door and to the mountains.

"But then, as she climbed, she became weary. She stopped to rest, and when she set the sack beside her, one potato rolled out and down into a ravine. She had to cross a stream to reach her father, and she lost her footing on a slippery stone, and two more potatoes fell out of the sack. Then she was chased by a ram, and she dropped the potatoes and the ram gobbled them up."

"This girl has the worst luck," Rafe grumbled.

Eyes closed, she smiled. "And so it was by the time she reached her father, she had nothing to offer. Not even the sack. She ran to her father, who took her into his arms, crying happy tears. 'But why are you crying, my child?' he asked. 'Because I lost all the potatoes I brought to you, and now I have nothing to offer.' Her father lifted her face to his and wiped her tears away. 'Daughter, don't you know that you are the greatest gift? Your presence here is worth a thousand potatoes.' The little girl cried, 'But I've missed you so much. I wanted to bring you something to remind you of me.' 'I don't need to be reminded, child. You are always here. In my heart. No matter how long we are separated or how far apart we may be.'

"And to this day, whenever the father and daughter are separated, the little girl, who is not so little anymore, need only look up at the sky and think of her father. She knows, somewhere, her father is looking at the same sky and thinking of her too."

Rafe's heart clenched. "Sleep," he said quietly. "I'll watch over him."

She desperately needed sleep, and as little as Rafe

wanted to stay with Fortier, he couldn't very well leave the man alone. He'd keep watch over the man and wake her if Fortier asked for her.

Rafe sat beside the bed and stared at the assassin. He was a lucky man to have a loving daughter like Collette. When the end came, he wouldn't die alone. Rafe felt his brow. It was warm, and he dipped the rag into the cool water in the basin and bathed the man's face. Rafe wondered how he would die. Would he live to be an old man and die in bed? If he did, he would die alone. No one would mop his brow or sit by his side. Would he lie restless, unable to forgive himself for allowing the only woman who had ever meant anything to him to get away, or would he go peacefully, knowing he'd done what was right for both of them?

Rafe sat beside the assassin for most of the day, and when the medicine wore off, he gave him more. Rafe closed his eyes and rested, drowsing lightly until he heard the old man speak. Rafe sat up, jumping when he noted Fortier's eyes on him. Fortier had dark eyes, like his daughter. They were clear and focused, and his face had a bit more color.

"Who are you?" Fortier asked.

"Rafe Beaumont, monsieur. A friend of your daughter's."

"Her lover?" His tone was an accusation.

Rafe swallowed. He didn't know what he was to Collette anymore. "Yes."

The old man closed his eyes. "If anything should happen to me, take care of her."

Rafe didn't think Collette particularly wanted him

to take care of her, but who was he to deny a father's wish—especially when that father was lethal.

"She won't need me. She has you, but if something should happen, she has my loyalty and my pledge to keep her safe." It was the sort of thing one said to an ill father, but Rafe was surprised to find that his heart lightened when he'd said it. The weight pushing on him seemed to lessen.

Fortier coughed again and then seemed to want to say more, but Rafe had made enough promises to this enemy of England. He rose. "Let me fetch your daughter."

He crossed quickly to his room, stopping short when he spotted Collette on the bed. She'd curled into a ball, her hand under her cheek. She looked so young and so vulnerable. Soon she would be gone. On a ship to America.

How could he let her go? Fortier coughed again, and Rafe knelt and shook Collette gently. Her eyes opened, and she looked about her in confusion.

"Your father," Rafe said. "He's awake and seems a bit better."

She threw the covers off and rushed past him without a word. He didn't move, still kneeling beside his bed. In Collette's chamber, he heard her quiet voice, speaking soothing words. Her father answered, his speech halting but his voice stronger.

Slowly, Rafe rose and closed the door to give them privacy. When he turned back to the bed, he spotted a crumpled sheet of paper. Collette must have had it in her hand or it had fallen out of a pocket. He lifted it, scanning the words. It was written in English but made very little sense. He noted the date was several years earlier. Why would she have kept a letter like this and who could it be—

Rafe inhaled sharply. She'd mentioned a missive in English. A coded missive that would prove her father had been forced to work for Bonaparte. She was right that it would not exonerate him, not in the eyes of the Crown. But perhaps it might be enough for reasonable men to believe the man was not a threat.

Rafe secreted the paper in his coat pocket and then gathered his things. Quickly, he strode out of his room, down the stairs, and out of the inn. When he reached the coach yard, he ordered the carriage made ready. Thirty minutes later, he was on the road to London.

He didn't look back. After all, he'd given his oath to Draven, and he would keep his word.

# Nineteen

"DON'T SPEAK." COLLETTE HELD HER FATHER'S HAND tightly. He squeezed her hand back, his grip weak but stronger. At least she wanted to believe it was stronger.

"I must," her father said. His voice was a hoarse whisper, and she leaned close to hear him.

"You can talk later. We will have lots of time when you are feeling better."

His eyes opened briefly, and he focused on her. She tried to muster a smile, but she felt it wobble. Fortier shook his head. "Listen—" He broke off into a fit of coughs, and Collette clutched his hand tightly. Finally, he gasped in a breath.

"I'm here, *mon père*."

"You're strong." He nodded at her. "Good. You will need to be."

She couldn't stop the tears. They spilled down her cheeks. "You are strong too. And you are good."

"No. I was never…good." His face seemed to cloud as he remembered the past. "But everything I did was for you and your mother. I did it to keep you safe."

"I know, *mon père*. You kept me safe. I'm here,

and I'm safe. We're together again. Just like we were before. When you're well again, I can book us passage on a ship for the United States. We'll start over there. They have lots of country, and no one will know you. We'll be safe."

He gave her a weak smile. "We must go right away."

"No. You're not strong enough."

"I'd rather die free than live in a jail. Make the arrangements."

She didn't want to. She was too frightened to lose him. A voyage like the one to America might kill him. She laid her head on his chest, only slightly relived when she heard his heart beating steadily.

"Look at me, Collette."

She looked up at him. His eyes were open, but the lids drooped. He would sleep again soon.

"Do what I tell you."

"*Mon père*—"

"No arguments. I do this because I love you." His eyes closed.

"I love you too, *mon père*. I love you so much."

"Tell me," he murmured as sleep descended.

She could barely hear him, and she bent her ear close. "Tell you what, *mon père*?"

"The story."

She shook her head, tears stinging her eyes. "You always tell me the story. You'll tell me again when you wake."

He squeezed her hand. "Just this once, you tell me."

"Once there was a girl whose father was a shepherd."

He squeezed her hand again. His eyes were closed, but a small smile flitted across his pale lips.

"All the sheep…they ate the grass so her father took them to the mountainside." She pushed down a sob. "And the little girl missed her father so, so much."

He slipped into sleep, his breath deep.

She needed Gaines. She'd ask Rafe to fetch him. But when she walked into the adjoining room, it was empty. He was gone. And she knew it was for good. He'd taken everything with him. Collette sank onto the bed, her breath hitching. She wrapped her arms about herself to stop the shaking. She'd lost him. She'd known she would. Tears streamed down her face, and with them, the words she'd left unspoken just moments before.

"One day, the little girl took him a sack of potatoes, but she lost them all on the way, and when she reached him, she wept bitterly. 'But why are you crying?' he asked. 'Because I lost all the potatoes I brought to you, and now I have nothing to offer.' He lifted her face to his and wiped her tears away."

Collette swiped at her tears. "To me you are the greatest gift," she whispered. "You will always be in my heart. And even when we are separated"—her voice caught—"even then, I will look up at the sky and know somewhere you are looking at the same sky and thinking of me."

❦

By the time he reached London, the sunlight was fading. Rafe hesitated as he rode through Aldersgate, wondering if he should head for Draven's home or his office. At the last minute, he directed the coachman to drop him at Draven's office. Draven was not married.

He had no reason to go home early. But when he finally made it to the offices, Draven's secretary informed him the lieutenant colonel had already left for the day.

"Has he gone home?" Rafe demanded of the snooty man with the round glasses and upturned nose.

"I couldn't say, sir," the clerk replied in a nasally voice.

"Can't say or won't say?" It was perhaps the least charming thing he might have said, but Rafe couldn't seem to muster his usual amiability. There had been a handful of times in his life when all of his affability had left him. This appeared to be another to add to the short list.

The secretary gave Rafe an annoyed look and wrinkled his nose with distaste. "I really must ask you to leave, sir."

"Oh, of course," Rafe said with a smile that felt more like a knife cutting through the stiffness of his face. "I'll leave." And then in imitation of a move he had seen his friend Ewan make, Rafe stepped forward, wrapped a hand around the clerk's scrawny neck, and slammed the little man against the wall. "Just as soon as you tell me where the hell Benedict Draven can be found."

The secretary's eyes widened. "There's no call for violence."

Rafe had lost all patience, which was even more uncharacteristic than losing his charm. He never lost his patience, not even as a toddler. "Is there a call for breaking your neck? Because right now I think I'd like to break your neck." Rafe heard himself utter the words, but he couldn't quite believe they'd come from him.

What the hell was wrong with him? He was in no hurry to find Draven. Fortier was leaving England. He was no threat. He and Collette would soon be on a ship bound for America. Whether Rafe informed Draven of these facts now or the next day made no difference.

Except Gaines had said the ship would leave tomorrow, and Rafe hadn't told Collette goodbye. He'd told himself it was better that way. He rarely took his leave of women. They made such scenes. Collette wouldn't make a scene, though. No, she would hold her head high and walk away from him without a backward glance. She was strong and brave. She might love him, but she could live without him.

So Rafe could release the secretary. He could return tomorrow and speak with Draven then. Except something continued to nag at him to hurry, hurry, hurry. Rafe needed to find Draven, this minute, and God forbid this…this *clerk* stand in his way.

"Sir!" the secretary gasped out. "I will report this behavior to the lieutenant colonel."

"I'll bloody well report it myself." Rafe shook the secretary, punctuating each word. "Tell. Me. Where. He. Is!"

The clerk blinked rapidly, looking dazed. Rafe felt a bit dazed himself. He had never behaved like this before. Even in the midst of war, he'd maintained his civility and charm. Now, all pretense of gentlemanly behavior had deserted him. He didn't even know himself.

"He…he said something about his club earlier today," the clerk mumbled. "He might—"

Rafe let the man go and turned on his heel, leaving
Draven's office behind. Why the hell had he dismissed
the coach? He didn't have any coin, didn't even have
his pocket watch. How would he pay for a hackney to
take him to St. James's Square? And he couldn't waste
time walking. It might take an hour or more to make his
way there. Rafe reached out a hand and flagged the next
hackney. He climbed in and gave the jarvey the direction
for the Draven Club. He'd worry about the coin later.

Right now he was running out of time.

She didn't know what she would have done without
Gaines. He'd arranged everything, helped her pack,
bought her all the necessities she and her father would
need. She'd stayed with her father, holding his hand.
He'd slept, but his coughing had abated, and she had
begun to hope.

She didn't want to think about Rafe. She felt dizzy
and unsteady when she thought of him. At one point,
she'd decided to lie on the floor beside her father's
bed, hoping that might ease the spinning in her mind.
The maid found her like that a few minutes later. The
rest was something of a blur to Collette, except when
Gaines had come. His dark face and kind eyes filled
her vision and became her anchor. She didn't ask if
Rafe had returned. She knew he was gone for good.
Of course he had left her. She had always known he
would. And when she could feel again, if that day ever
came, she imagined the pain of losing him would be
sharp and sweet and unbearable.

But at this moment, she could rely on the need

to see her father safely out of England to obliterate everything else. At least for a time. And so she held on to Gaines who bade her sip the brandy-laced tea and spoke to her in his deep, musical voice.

Sometime later, Gaines and the maid—the same one who'd answered her summons earlier—had tucked her into bed. Gaines had assured her he had called for a doctor and would stay with her father. Collette had pressed her head into the pillow. This wasn't the bed she'd shared with Rafe or where her father lay. She was in a new room—a dark, quiet room. The brandy had made her tired. Life had made her tired. She wanted to close her eyes and sleep until the crushing numbness of it all passed.

"I can't feel anything," she'd said, looking up at Gaines.

"That is a blessing, miss." He'd taken her hand. "Sleep. Soon you will be on the ship, and then sleep will not come so easily."

But the pain would. She feared the pain she knew lurked at the edges of her awareness. Pain so great she could not see any way around it, and she was not certain she could survive the path through it.

"Sleep." Gaines released her hand and signaled to the maid to turn the lamp down. Collette realized it was dark. Somehow night had fallen, and she hadn't even noted it.

Collette reached for Gaines's hand. "When does the ship sail?"

"Don't you worry about that. Sleep."

Collette sat, pushing the covers off her legs. "I need to be on that ship. We cannot miss it, Mr. Gaines."

"I will take you aboard the ship myself," Gaines promised. "You have time to rest. The captain won't sail until night falls tomorrow."

Collette sank back down onto the pillow. It was too soon and an eternity from now. "You'll come for me."

"I'll escort you to the gangplank myself and have your father brought aboard."

Collette closed her eyes. She knew she wouldn't sleep, but it seemed to be what everyone wanted. Finally, the sounds around her quieted and she heard the door of the room close. Alone, she opened her eyes and stared at the flickering candlelight on the ceiling. Her eyes stung with fatigue and sorrow, but no tears would come. There was only the numbness.

⤳∞⤫

"What do you mean he's not here?" Rafe bellowed when Porter returned from paying the hackney driver. Though the Master of the House had taken Rafe's unceremonious arrival in stride, he looked less than pleased at Rafe's outburst. Rafe could hardly blame him. He didn't know what the hell had gotten into him either.

And all of his bellowing had attracted an audience. A footman carrying a tray lingered on the steps, and above him, Phineas and Stratford stood with their arms crossed and eyebrows raised. The two of them were known for their skills in negotiation and strategy, respectively, and were generally imperturbable. At the moment, they looked somewhat…perturbed.

"I am sorry, sir, but Lieutenant Colonel Draven has not been here tonight or for—"

Rafe cut him off the same way he had Draven's secretary. He wrapped a hand around Porter's neck.

"What the hell are you doing?" Stratford or Phineas bellowed. "Beaumont, release him."

Rafe ignored them. "Tell me where he is."

Porter remained still. "I don't know, sir."

"I know."

Rafe knew that voice. It was Neil. His boots clicked on the wood as he strode into the vestibule. Rafe didn't look away from Porter, didn't release him, but somehow Neil's presence calmed him. Rafe could count on the man who'd been his commanding officer, the man known as the Warrior.

"Stratford, Phineas, Jasper—dismissed."

Rafe hadn't even realized Jasper was here. Stratford and Phineas grumbled, but they retreated up the stairs. Jasper didn't move.

"Jasper, dismissed."

"That's Lord Jasper, and you can go to hell, Neil." Jasper stepped forward, his scarred face coming into Rafe's sight line. "Let him go, Rafe, before I draw your cork."

Rafe's nose itched at the threat. "This has nothing to do with you, Jas."

"It has nothing to do with Porter either," Neil said. "You want Draven? I know where he is."

Rafe released Porter and turned on Neil. Jasper had Rafe by the arms in mere seconds, preventing Rafe from taking a swing at Neil. Rafe fought Jasper's hold but not with any real effort. These men had been instrumental in taking down Napoleon. They could handle Rafe Beaumont. "Where?"

"He's with Ewan, at his pugilist club."

Now Rafe fought Jasper's hold, and Jasper swore. "Are you bloody dicked in the nob, Beaumont?"

"Let me go, or so help me God, Jasper, I'll kill you."

Neil raised one brow. "As much as I would like to see you try and kill Jasper, Porter frowns on cleaning blood from the carpet, even spangled and sequined blood like yours, Rafe."

"Go to hell!"

"Obviously. But before I do, why don't I send for Draven?"

"I'll go get him."

"I don't think so." Neil signaled and Jasper released Rafe. Rafe thought about hitting Neil, but the urge had left him. There was just that insistent drumroll in his head telling him to hurry, hurry, hurry.

"*Lord* Jasper will fetch him."

"The hell I will," Jasper argued.

Neil didn't say a word. He merely held Jasper's gaze. And even though Rafe knew Jasper was feared throughout the underworld as a hunter who could find anyone and who, if threatened, killed with his bare hands, it was Neil who made him shudder in that moment.

"You owe me a drink," Jasper said, pointing a finger at Neil as he strode out the door. "Two drinks."

Neil ignored Jasper and put his arm around Rafe's shoulder. It might have looked like a friendly gesture, but Rafe knew better than to shrug it off or fight the way Neil directed Rafe up the stairs of the Draven Club and into the reading room. "Now tell me what this is about, and hurry up before I lose my patience and smash that pretty face of yours through the window."

By the time Rafe had given Neil the short version of the story, Jasper had returned with Ewan and Draven in tow.

Draven took one look at his men and pointed to the door. "So much for state secrets. Out."

"There's no point. I know everything."

Draven's nostrils flared.

Neil rose. "On second thought, there was something I hoped to discuss with Mostyn here."

Jasper turned to follow Neil. "I'll come along."

The door closed, and they were alone in the reading room. The small wood-paneled room was lined with shelves of books. Small groupings of armchairs were clustered throughout, each with side tables nearby holding lamps. Neil had led Rafe to the chairs nearest the hearth, which crackled. Draven stood before him, hands clasped behind his back, the light from the fire making his red hair appear even redder. "Report," he ordered.

"Fortier is no longer a threat."

A muscle in Draven's jaw clenched. "You saw his cold, lifeless body?"

"He's not a threat," Rafe repeated.

Draven didn't move. "You don't say he's dead."

Rafe withdrew the missive he'd taken from Collette. He prayed it said what Collette had hoped. If not, he would be the one in prison.

"What is that?"

Rafe held the letter out. "It's a coded letter. If I'm correct, it proves Fortier only killed in order to keep his family safe. He had no choice."

Draven snatched the paper from his hands and held

it close to the lamp. He looked up at Rafe. "Can you read this?"

"No. But I thought you might know the code or know where to find it."

"I know it. It's an old one. Give me a moment." Muttering to himself he turned the paper this way and that, his lips moving silently as though he were counting. Then he said, "Get me a paper and pen."

Both were stored in a table near the bookshelves. Rafe fetched them and watched as Draven listed letters and numbers and then went through methodically crossing them out and scratching out a message. Finally, he looked up.

"What does it say?" Rafe asked.

Draven took a clean sheet of paper. "I'll copy the part that relates to Fortier." He wrote and then handed the sheet to Rafe. It read:

> *As to the assassin Fortier, he works under duress. Bonaparte has repeatedly threatened the life of his daughter.*

"May I have this?" Rafe asked. Not waiting for a response, he slid it in his coat.

Draven leaned back. "I assume you learned something else about Fortier."

"He was not dead as we thought. He was held by French royalists, men who wanted to secure the Bourbons on the French throne. Men who had reason to despise Fortier for the crimes he committed against their class. In exchange for keeping him alive, they forced his daughter to spy for them."

"And where is the woman?"

"I'll come to that."

The scowl on Draven's face indicated he did not care for that response.

"You'll want to take Lady Ravensgate into custody," Rafe said, staring at the fire in the hearth rather than Draven. "She is working for the French. There's a bookseller on Bond Street, a W. Morgan, who is also working for them. There may be others."

"*May* be?"

Rafe waved a hand. "With the men you have at your disposal, I'm certain you can gain that information. That's not my specialty."

"Where's the woman?" Draven asked again.

"We devised a plan to lure the royalists to England and to persuade them to bring Fortier with them."

"I see. I do not remember being apprised of this plan."

"I thought it best to keep the plan secret."

"You *thought*? Beaumont, I never asked you to think."

"I'll refrain in the future, sir. Miss Fortier and I intercepted the royalists and Fortier in Wapping. There we…took custody of Fortier."

"And the royalists?"

"Dead or on the way back to France, I imagine."

"Was that more of your thinking, Beaumont? You thought it wouldn't be helpful to take those men into custody?"

"I thought it would be best to keep Fortier and his daughter alive. But soon after we had him in custody, the two of them escaped."

Draven leaned forward. "And do you think for even one moment I believe that? You're protecting them!"

Rafe didn't answer. He stared into the flames. The sound of the logs hissing and popping in the fire and the clock on the mantel ticking seemed to grow louder until finally Draven sat in the chair beside Rafe. Rafe glanced at him.

Draven had his head back, and he stared up at the ceiling. "I would speak to you as a friend, Rafe."

Rafe started. He hadn't realized Draven knew his Christian name.

"As your commanding officer, I will stand again in a moment and tell you to take Miss Fortier and her father into custody and bring her to London. At which point I have no doubt you will tell me to go to hell." He held up a finger. "That would be a mistake. Another mistake would be to insist that the Fortiers escaped. Then you and I look incompetent, not that you will give a rotten fig because any idiot can see you're in love with the woman." He raised a hand. "Do not argue. Grantham told me you had your hands around Porter's throat. I could kill you for that, and if you didn't do it out of some excess of feeling for a woman, then I will."

"This isn't a very friendly conversation."

"That is because you are an idiot, Rafe Beaumont. If I wanted someone to fall in love with the daughter of France's most notorious assassin, I would have sent another man. I thought I could at least trust *you*, of all men, to remain impervious to female wiles."

Rafe's fist balled. Draven looked down at it. "Try it and you'll find yourself flat on your back. Your anger might land you a punch or two, but my experience will win in the end." He waited until Rafe's hand relaxed slightly. "Answer me this: Does she love you too?"

Rafe swallowed. "Yes."

"And are you willing to let her go to the Indies or Morocco or wherever the hell she is off to?" He waved. "Do not tell me where. I do not want to know, not even as your friend."

"Yes."

"Then take some advice from an old man who has stood where you are standing."

Rafe glanced at him. Draven was about fifteen years older than he, but he wasn't old. Rafe had no doubt the lieutenant colonel could easily best him in a fight.

"I let a woman go. It was years ago, but I haven't ever forgotten her. And there hasn't been a day when I haven't regretted my decision. Did I love her? Hell if I know. But I will spend the rest of my miserable life wondering what might have been."

Rafe stared hard at Draven. "Are you suggesting what I think you're suggesting?"

"Yes."

"Leave London? Leave my life, my family"—he gestured to the club—"my friends?"

"If you love her, yes. And perhaps if you wait a few years you could return. If, when I tell you to go and take the Fortiers into custody, you answer not 'go to hell' but 'yes, sir,' then I can only assume that if you disappear, you are still in pursuit of father and daughter. And if you return in a few years, when all of this has faded from memory, and tell me Miss Fortier and her father are no more, I will have no choice but to believe you did all you could to bring them to justice."

"And if they still live?"

Draven gestured to the coded letter. "He may be no threat, but he is never to step foot on British soil again. If I even *think* he is near to British soil, I will hunt him down and kill him myself."

"And Miss Fortier?"

"If she is married, then she is no longer Miss Fortier, is she?"

Rafe swallowed. Hard. *Married*. The word struck equal measures of hope and fear into his heart. She might refuse to marry him. And even if she did marry him, she might leave him.

But if he married her, he would have her by his side. She would be his, and he hers. He would wake to her beside him each morning and go to sleep with her in his arms each night. Even if she left him one day, he would have had that.

It was a risk. The pain of losing her now or the pain of losing her later. He looked at Draven and saw the man was regarding him with a bemused expression. "I almost feel sorry for you. Fidelity terrifies you, doesn't it?"

"It's not me I doubt."

Draven nodded. "It's always a risk when you put your heart in someone else's hands. And men such as you and I, Rafe, don't surrender easily." He sat forward in the chair. "And now our little chat is at an end. You either go or you stay, but if you stay, you sure as hell better be prepared to answer to the prime minister himself for your incompetence." He rose. "Beaumont, I order you to return to Wapping and take the Fortiers into custody."

Rafe rose. "Yes, sir," he said quietly.

Collette was awake to see the sun rise. She didn't know why she should be surprised to see it. It wasn't as though the whole world had changed—only her world. She could hear people laughing and talking on the street below. Hawkers were selling their wares and farmers driving carts to market. Life went on as it always had, and she was foolish to think that everything might be a little darker or a little sadder without Rafe in her world.

She still couldn't believe he'd left her. Was it wrong to hope that perhaps that night with Rafe had left her with child? Was it sinful to hope she carried some small part of him with her?

She lay on the bed, fully dressed, and stared at the window. How everything had changed in only a matter of hours. Two sunrises ago, she had a father and a lover. Now, she would leave that lover behind for an unknown place. She prayed her father was strong enough to survive the journey.

She'd never been so far from home. But she didn't have a home any longer. She didn't have anything save the few items she'd brought with her. She didn't know what she would do in the United States. Perhaps she could find work on a farm or as a teacher. She was not a bad seamstress, and she was not too proud to work as a servant. Really, it didn't matter what she did, as long as she was able to keep her father and herself fed. Perhaps one day she would feel something besides the numbness, besides the pain. Until that day, if it ever came, she would trudge through life, doing what she needed to survive.

A tap on the door caught her attention, and she sat. Her heart pounded, foolish hope flooding through her. It would not be Rafe. Why couldn't her heart accept what her brain already had?

"Miss Fortier?" It was Gaines. His voice held a note of concern. "Are you in there?"

How long had he been knocking?

"Yes!" She rose and walked to the door. She rose and walked to the door, her legs heavy as though trudging through mud. She opened the door, and Gaines gestured to a maid. It was the same maid who had helped her last night.

"Jenny brought you tea and toast. Would you like to dine in your father's room? He is sitting up and taking a little broth."

Collette stared at him. His words seemed too good to be true. She followed him to her father's room and could not suppress a smile when she saw him. She sat in the chair beside him, taking the food the maid offered. She couldn't recall when she'd last eaten, but the food held no appeal. "Thank you."

"That will be all, Jenny." Gaines gave her a nod and the maid bobbed and disappeared down the hallway. Gaines looked back at Collette and her father. "Don't let me stop you from eating. I've already broken my fast."

Obediently, Collette sat in front of the food. She considered lifting the teacup to her lips, but her hand refused to make the effort.

"Are you still wanting to sail to Pennsylvania?"

She looked at her father, but he was looking back at her. Collette nodded.

"The ship sails this evening. I'll escort you both on board and see you settled in a few hours. Is there anything else you need before you depart? Anything you want for the voyage?"

Collette shook her head.

"Come now," Gaines said, his voice soft. "A book? Some material to embroider? It's a long voyage. You'll want something to keep you occupied."

She looked up at him. "You've already done so much, Mr. Gaines."

"We cannot ever repay you," her father said, his voice hoarse.

"I want no payment, sir."

"Where is Beaumont?" her father asked. "I want to thank him."

Collette looked down, avoiding Gaines's gaze.

"What's wrong?" her father asked. "Did he betray us?"

"No!" Collette said quickly. She hoped he had not. "But he's gone."

"I see."

"It's for the best," she assured him.

Gaines snorted. Her gaze shot to his, and she was surprised to see anger in his face. "For the best? Do you want to know what I think?" he asked. "No, you probably don't, but I'll tell you anyway. I think Beaumont was a complete idiot. He was a fool to leave you."

"You don't know me. You don't know my father, Mr. Gaines. Rafe had his reasons."

"I know everything I need to know, and I realize you have your reasons for leaving England. But if you change your mind or ever come back, you can count me as a friend."

She smiled at him, her mouth cracking like dry ground in the midst of a drought. "You have been very kind."

He muttered something, which sounded something like *Not kind enough.* "Eat something, Miss Fortier, and rest. I'll return in a few hours to collect you. If you think of anything you need in the meantime, send for me."

"Now I know why you look like you did when Marie died," her father said.

Marie had been their cat. She'd been a sweet, old cat, who had lived a long life and died in her sleep. Still, Collette had been inconsolable for days. "I'm fine."

"You love him."

She rose. "I'll get over it."

Her father set the broth on the table. "Come here." He opened his arms wide. Collette hesitated, then rushed to her father, burying her head in his chest and wishing it were enough.

# Twenty

DAWN WAS VALIANTLY FIGHTING THROUGH THE FOG OF London when Rafe emerged from the reading room and into the adjacent parlor, where the heavy draperies had been pulled back. Standing in a loose circle, Jasper, Ewan, and Neil waited for him. He stopped. "This is quite the collection of rogues."

Jasper crossed his arms over his chest. "I think the word you're looking for is 'heroes.'"

"Ah. An easy mistake."

"Draven says you're leaving," Neil said.

"Draven is wrong."

"That would be a first." Neil looked at the others. Ewan scowled as though Rafe had just personally insulted him.

"You won't be rid of me so easily. I plan to go home, sleep for a few hours, and I'll return tonight to best all of you at billiards."

"Not likely," Jasper said.

Neil raised a brow. "We thought you might go chasing after that woman. Fortier's daughter."

Rafe straightened his shoulders. "I don't chase after women."

"You run from them," Ewan said, his words slow and deliberate.

Rafe rounded on him. He would have punched the man for the insult, except that doing so would have probably hurt Rafe's fist more than any part of Ewan's anatomy. The man was built like an ox. "I don't run from anything," Rafe said quietly.

"Then why haven't you found a woman and settled down?" Neil asked.

Rafe rolled his eyes. "Just because you and Ewan have married doesn't mean you have to drag the rest of us down with you."

"You didn't look dragged down when I saw you with her," Jasper observed.

"Stubble it."

"What are you afraid of?" Ewan asked.

"Besides your ham-sized fist rearranging my perfect face, Mostyn, nothing. I don't understand why you seem to think I should go after the woman. She's the daughter of a French assassin. I seem to remember we even had orders to terminate him at one point."

Jasper made a face. "That bastard."

Undoubtedly, Jasper was remembering his failure to track Fortier. Rafe imagined Jasper could count on one hand the number of men who'd eluded him and still have fingers left over.

"The war is over," Neil said. "How many times have you told me that? Go live your life, Rafe."

"I will." He strode past them to the door. "I'll see you at the billiards table in a few hours."

"Just in case, Rafe, you'd better put your dancing shoes on," Neil called after him, referring to their oft used farewell. He wasn't certain how it had started, something about dancing with the devil.

Rafe clenched his teeth as he stomped down the stairs and into the vestibule. Porter moved to open the door, and Rafe paused. "I apologize for my behavior earlier, Porter. I…wasn't myself."

"Think nothing of it, sir," Porter said with the same warmth he'd always had when he spoke to Rafe. "We all have bad days."

Rafe put on his hat and walked out the door. Once outside, he began to stroll. Was Porter correct? Was all of this simply a bad day? Would he wake tomorrow and find his chest didn't feel so tight, didn't feel as though a hand squeezed his heart? Rafe didn't think love worked that way. Infatuation, yes. But he knew Draven was right. He was in love with Collette Fortier.

He could ignore it and let her go. He could prove himself the coward his friends seemed to think he was. Or he could put on his dancing shoes and confront the devil that had been taunting him all these years. Rafe paused and looked about. He'd strolled into Mayfair and was not far from his father's house. Perhaps it was time he and the devil danced.

❧

Gaines led her aboard the *Egret*, and Collette could not help but look over her shoulder. The day was still young, but the captain was eager to be on his way. Collette was happy to board. Her father was being comfortably settled below. They had troubled Mr. Gaines enough. Once on the deck of the ship, Collette looked over the rail to the Wapping quay and warehouses. It was not a particularly pretty sight. She imagined she would see far lovelier views on the trip down the Thames and into the open ocean. But this was the last place she had seen Rafe. This was a place she did not want to forget.

She would never see England again. She couldn't risk coming back. She had no reason to ever come back. That was a blessing, even though it meant she would always be missing a piece of her heart. She had her father, and she would work hard to make sure he was not left with a shell of his daughter. In time, she would heal from this loss.

The captain approached, introduced himself as Mr. Booker, then led Collette and Gaines belowdecks, where they made certain Fortier was well-situated. When she was satisfied, Booker showed her to a small cabin with a berth and a porthole. Collette could practically touch either side of the cabin with her fingers when she stretched her arms wide, but she and her father had private places all to themselves, and she knew she owed that luxury to Mr. Gaines.

When the captain took his leave to oversee the rest of the preparations, Gaines held out a hand. "It was a pleasure, Miss Fortier."

Collette shook his hand, then held on for a moment longer. "Thank you again, Mr. Gaines. For everything."

"I hope you find happiness, miss," he said.

She gave him a sad smile and squeezed his hand. When he was gone, she stowed her belongings and tried out the berth. It was not nearly as uncomfortable as it looked. Above her, she could hear the sailors calling out, checking the ropes and the sails and rigging. She couldn't help but feel a little excited at the future that awaited her. She found her way back to the deck and asked where she might stand so that she would be out of the way. A sailor showed her to a little corner, and she stood on the deck and watched as cranes moved the last of the cargo aboard, the gangplank was pulled away, and the smaller tugboats pulled the larger ship into the currents of the Thames.

People stood on the dock and waved goodbye. Collette waved to them, even though she knew they weren't there to see her off. But she scanned the small crowd one last time, then turned away, berating herself for her stupidity.

He was not coming.

And with that thought, she gazed out on the bow and looked ahead.

❧

The Haddington butler opened the door. Abbot was a relatively young man, forty at most. He had a thick head of sandy-blond hair, ruthlessly combed into submission, and skeptical blue eyes. "Good morning, sir. We weren't expecting you."

"I'm aware of that. Is my father at home?"

"I'm afraid he is not, sir. He left early this morning—"

"I thought I heard your voice!" Rafe's stepmother, Lady Haddington, stepped out from the dining room, dabbing her lips with a napkin. "It is so good to see you, Rafe. Please, join me for breakfast."

Rafe kissed his stepmother on both cheeks. "I'm not hungry, Horatia. Thank you."

"Oh, but you can't leave. I'm here all by myself. You must join me."

Rafe didn't particularly want to join her, but perhaps his father would return shortly. Then he might get the answers he wanted.

He followed his stepmother into the dining room and took the cup of tea offered by the footman. His stepmother smiled at him over her own cup of tea. She was a pretty woman, petite and delicate, with wispy blond hair and green eyes. She looked nothing like the rest of the family, most of Rafe's siblings having coloring like his own. "How have you been, dear? I haven't seen you in ages."

"Good. Will my father be home soon?"

"I doubt it. He left early to ride out to one of the estates in Hampshire. Depending on how long it takes to deal with the issues there, he may not return until tomorrow. How is that young lady I read about? Miss Fournay, I believe is her name?"

By tomorrow, Collette would be well on her way to America. Not that anything his father said would make any difference. She would sail to the New World, and Rafe would stay here. In his Old World.

"Rafe?" his stepmother said.

"I'm sorry. Oh, you asked about Miss Fournay."

"Yes. I had heard the two of you were often seen together. Is she someone special? I would like to meet her."

"I'm afraid that's not possible, Horatia. Miss Fournay is leaving England."

"Oh, I see." She sighed, her green eyes looking troubled.

Rafe began to rise, to excuse himself, then he paused. "Horatia, may I ask you a question?"

"Of course, dear." She set her teacup down and smiled at him eagerly.

"Why are you so keen to see me married? All of my brothers and sisters are married and there are heirs aplenty. You never played matchmaker with any of my siblings, and I've never expressed any interest in matrimony. I'm quite content to remain a bachelor."

She blinked at him in surprise. "Oh, but that would be such a waste, dear. You would make such a wonderful husband."

Rafe raised a brow. "You do know my reputation?"

She waved a hand, dismissing the point. "And you would be an excellent father."

"I am an excellent uncle."

"You are." She sipped her tea again, her face clouding. When she looked up again, her expression was serious. "I know I am not your mother, Rafe. I never tried to take her place."

"But you have always been a very good mother to us." This was true. She was kind and caring. Some of his sisters had even taken to calling Horatia *Mama*.

"Thank you. But I want to say something and I fear I'll step out of place in saying it."

Rafe swallowed past the sudden lump in his throat. "Go on."

"I suppose another reason I took such an interest in you marrying is because of what happened with your mother."

"I don't know what you mean." But he did. He knew exactly what she meant, and his skin turned to ice at her words.

"You were the one who was home when she left. You were the one she left alone, and you were the youngest. I imagine her leaving was hardest on you. When I married your father, you were barely eight and just the most charming and handsome little man. But it often seemed to me that you had been forgotten, and that perhaps you bore the brunt of your mother's leaving on your shoulders. Did you ever feel that way? That her leaving was your fault?"

Rafe knew he should scoff and say no. He should make a witty remark to the effect that he couldn't imagine why anyone would want to leave him. But he couldn't seem to manage to do anything but nod his head.

His stepmother's face crumpled and she rose and moved to sit beside him. Rafe couldn't understand why he didn't move, why he'd allowed her to come to him, to put her hand on his arm, to embrace him. "Dear, dear, boy, listen to me, and listen well. I did not know your mother, but I know you. Whatever your mother's reasons for leaving, they had nothing to do with you."

Rafe shook his head. "She didn't want me." His voice was low and hoarse. "She didn't want another child."

"Then that is her loss. I wanted children and was never blessed with any of my own, and you and your brothers and sisters were nothing but a joy every day of your lives. Well, Cyril was not always a joy. He was something of a terror for several years. And Helen had a penchant for dipping her toes into scandal. But you, you always made us smile. Your father and I used to smile over all the darling things you said as a child. But we always suspected you hid much of the pain you felt from your mother's leaving."

Rafe looked away, not wanting her to see the truth of those words in his face.

"I don't know why your mother left. It's my opinion she was ill even before she left. Perhaps that had something to do with it, but you cannot let your mother be the model for all women. Not all women leave. Look at me. I would never leave your father. I love him, the aggravating man!"

Rafe felt a ghost of a smile tease his lips.

"And I certainly hope you won't spend the rest of your life leaving every woman you have feelings for just so she can't ever leave you."

Now Rafe did look at her. He'd never been close with his stepmother. He'd never been emotionally close to anyone except for a few of his brothers from Draven's troop. Now he wished he could change that. He wished he had spent more time with his stepmother, confided in her more. She had much more to give than he'd realized.

But all of that would have to wait because the *Egret*, bound for America, would not. Abruptly, he rose.

"Have I said something wrong, dear?" his stepmother asked, rising as well.

"No. You've said everything right. I love her."

"Love whom? The Frenchwoman?"

"Yes, and I have to go to America."

His stepmother's eyes widened. "But I thought I told you *not* to run away."

He waved a hand and strolled for the door. "No. She is bound for America. I have to catch her. I have to go with her."

His stepmother followed him into the vestibule. "But you can't go to America! You haven't even taken leave of your father."

"Do it for me, will you?" He took his coat and hat from Abbott. "And don't worry. I'll be back." He took a last look at the town house. "One day." Then to his surprise, he grabbed his stepmother and hugged her tightly. She squealed with astonishment and, if he wasn't mistaken, pleasure. "Goodbye, Mother," he said, then released her and ran for the street.

He hailed the first hackney he saw and climbed into the cab.

"Where to, gov'?" the jarvey asked, his tone bored.

"Wapping," Rafe said, head out the window.

The jarvey turned around. "Say again?"

"Wapping."

The jarvey shook his head. "I ain't licensed for Wapping. I stay in the city and—"

"I'll pay you five pounds."

The man's eyes widened. "Five pounds!"

"Six if you hurry."

"Six quid?" His eyes narrowed. "Let me see the blunt."

Rafe blew out a breath. It was almost noon. He could not afford to waste any more time going to the bank or finding another jarvey. "I don't have it with me."

The jarvey shook his head emphatically.

"But I'll write you an IOU, and my father will honor it." God knew he wouldn't be paying Rafe's allowance if he made it to America.

"And who's yer father?"

Rafe pointed to the earl's town house. "The Earl of Haddington. That is his residence."

The jarvey considered the town house, then looked back at Rafe.

Rafe clenched his fists in an effort to remain calm. "Look, what's your name?"

"Joshua Clarkit."

"Mr. Clarkit, I am in a dreadful hurry. I must reach Wapping before the ship carrying the woman I love sails for America. If we do not leave now, I may never see her again."

"And I may never see that six quid."

"I will give you my vowels right now. Do you have a slip of paper?"

The jarvey scowled. "You think I'm a printer or something?"

Panic at the delay making his heart pound, Rafe jumped out of the cab, ran for the nearest building covered with pamphlets, and tore one down. Then he searched the ground until he found a small piece of coal that had fallen from the cart of one of the deliverymen. He turned the pamphlet over and scrawled:

*I owe Joshua Clarkit 6 pounds for services rendered.*

He scrawled his name, pulled his handkerchief from his pocket to rub the coal dust from his hands, and then ran back to the hackney. He handed the paper to Clarkit. "Satisfied?"

Clarkit studied the paper. "How do I know this says what you say it does?"

Rafe wanted to slam his head on the yellowing sides of the conveyance. What had he ever done to deserve a distrusting, illiterate jarvey? "You can read numbers, can't you?" he asked, keeping his tone level.

The man nodded.

"You see I wrote 'six' there. The word after that is 'pounds.' And that is my name." He pointed to his signature. "Rafe Beaumont. I am a younger son of the Earl of Haddington."

The jarvey looked him over. Rafe had no idea how he looked, but he could guess. His eyes were shadowed, his jaw stubbled, and his clothing wrinkled. Fortunately, the jarvey seemed to be a man who noted details. His gaze traveled over the well-tailored coat Rafe wore and the muddy but expensive boots.

"Get in," the jarvey said, with a flick of his head.

Rafe jumped in and the jarvey turned toward Wapping.

A half hour later, Rafe banged his head on the back of the seat. The stuffing had been lost long ago and pieces of straw stuck out here and there. Banging his head against the hard, scratchy surface kept him from leaping out of the coach and banging the heads of the farmers together.

Of course, today had to be market day, and every farmer or country bumpkin from near and far was making his or her way into the city. The gates were clogged with carts, children chasing other children, and dogs chasing the livestock, which oinked or squawked or bleated and generally caused mayhem.

Rafe leaned his head out the window again. "What the devil is taking so long? Aren't the farmers supposed to arrive early?" It was nearly one.

Clarkit looked back. "From what I hear, there was an accident on the road this morning. A cart stuck in the mud and another didn't see it with all the fog. People stopped to help, and it blocked the road, so many had to wait until it was cleared."

Today, of all days, there had to be a collision. "Is there nothing you can do?"

The jarvey shook his head. "Naught but wait my turn. It won't be long. As soon as these pigs are rounded up."

Rafe allowed his head to fall into his hands.

When the hackney finally arrived in Wapping, Rafe didn't wait for it to stop before he jumped out. They'd stopped in front of the Wapping Inn and Coach House, Gaines's inn. "I know the proprietor here. I'll tell him to give you a meal and have the grooms see to your horses."

Clarkit raised his hat in thanks. Rafe sprinted into the common room of the inn. It was empty except for a man or two reading the paper, and Rafe skidded to a stop and looked about.

"Mr. Beaumont." A man Rafe recognized as the manager came out from behind a counter. "Good to have you back with us. Would you like a room?"

"No. I need Gaines."

The manager shook his head. "He is not here—"

"Where is he?"

"I'm not certain. I think he escorted the young miss and her father to the dock. To take them aboard *Egret*."

"Damn and blast!"

"Sir?"

Rafe turned to run for the docks, then paused. "There's a hackney from London in front. Will you see to him and his horses?"

"Mr. Gaines hasn't—"

"Put it on my account!" The pocket watch he'd had to give Gaines could have covered the cost of seeing to five hackneys.

"Yes, sir."

Once in the street, Rafe ran for the quay. He had to dart around some boys playing a game with sticks and rocks and somehow lost his hat, but he could have cried with joy when he finally spotted the muddy water of the Thames. He bent to catch his breath, scanning the docked ships for the one that might be the *Egret*.

There were far too many, and it would take hours for him to approach each and read the names. He had to find one of the customs officials who could direct him to the correct dock. Rafe began to push through the sailors and dockworkers, looking for someone in authority. He shouldered past one man, then felt a hand on his shoulder. The man spun him around.

Rafe recognized the sailor's yellow grin from the first night he and Collette had been on the river shore. This was the sailor who'd taken his purse.

"I've been looking for you," the sailor said.

"Look another time." Rafe struggled to free himself of the man's grip. But instead of releasing him, the sailor held on, ripping Rafe's coat. That was the last straw. The coat had been made by Weston, and how was Rafe to acquire another like it in bloody, savage America? *If* he even made it to America?

"I'm not done with you yet," the sailor said.

Rafe pulled his fist back and slammed the man in the face. His dirty hands released Rafe's coat and he fell backward onto the dock. "But I am done with you."

Rafe started away, only to come face-to-face with Thomas Gaines. Gaines nodded at the fallen man. "I was about to say you have a knack for finding trouble. But I take it back."

"Where is she?" Rafe asked, not caring that his voice was trembling. Not caring that sweat streaked his face, his throat was parched, and his head ached from hunger and the sun beating down on it.

He didn't care about anything but Collette.

"You're too late," Gaines said. "The ship has sailed."

Rafe felt his knees crumple. *Too late.* No two words had ever so crushed a man.

He reached out, his fist closing on Gaines's lapel. "I swear by all that is holy, if you don't take me to her, I will kill you with my bare hands."

Gaines raised a brow. "I don't think you can do it."

Rafe looked him in the eye. "Want to see me try?"

Gaines stared back at him, then shook his head. "Come with me. There's still a chance to catch her."

Rafe's heart leaped. Still a chance! "Show me."

Gaines's large form cut a swath through the people on the dock, and a moment later, they were in front of an empty berth. The ship that had docked there was being led into the center of the Thames by two tugs.

The tugs' work was almost done. In a matter of minutes, the ship would be under sail. Rafe would never catch it then. He might have swum to the ship—as disgusting as that idea was—but he would never have been able to swim fast enough. He turned to Gaines. "What do I do?"

Gaines pointed to an empty boat. "Can you row?"

Rafe had rowed when he'd been in school, but that had been years ago. Still, not wasting a moment, he jumped into the boat and lifted the oars as Gaines untied it and pushed him off.

"Hey!" a man yelled. Rafe assumed it was the owner of the boat. He didn't look back, sticking the oars in the water and beginning to row. Behind him, he heard Gaines speaking to the man. Rafe would have to send Gaines another pocket watch.

By the time he'd rowed halfway to the ship, his shoulders ached and his muscles burned. He was breathing fast, sweat dripping down his back. Not only was his coat ruined, but his boots were well on their way to ruination too. The boat had a leak—either that or it needed to be plugged—and it was taking on water. Rafe's feet sat two inches deep in muddy river water. But he continued to row, grunting with the effort of catching the larger, much faster ship. He would have no chance at all once the tugs released it. Another ship sailed toward him, and Rafe rowed faster, narrowly avoiding being clipped. The burst of speed had served him well. He had reached the *Egret,* and now he stopped rowing and looked up. Several unhappy sailors looked down.

"Move away from the ship!" one called.

"I need to come aboard!" Rafe called.

The sailor shook his head. "Any attempt to board will be treated as an act of aggression."

What the hell? Did the man think he was a pirate? He was in a row boat. A sinking row boat. "I just need to speak with one of your passengers."

"Write a letter!" the sailor answered. "This is your last warning." And he raised a large pistol and pointed it down at Rafe.

Rafe looked into the muzzle of the gun. At this point, he'd rather have been shot than row back to shore. "Collette!" he yelled. "Collette Fortier!"

"I will fire on three!" the sailor called.

"Collette!" Rafe called frantically. "Collette, I need to speak to you!"

"One!"

Hell's teeth. He had never imagined this was how he would die. "Collette!"

"Two."

Rafe heard the hammer cock.

"Collette!"

"Th—"

Rafe squeezed his eyes shut.

"Stop! I know this man."

Rafe opened his eyes. On the deck, beside the sailor with the gun, Collette's small white face looked down at him. "Rafe?"

He grinned at her. "Send down a ladder. I have to speak to you."

Another face appeared next to hers. "I am the captain, sir. You have not been given permission to come aboard."

"I need to speak with Miss Fortier."

"And I have a schedule to keep and paying passengers, not to mention valuable cargo, to transport to America."

"I'll pay for him," Collette said. The captain looked at her.

"Are you sure, miss?"

"Yes, she's sure. Drop the ladder," Rafe ordered.

"Not so fast," Collette said. "Let me hear what he has to say first."

Rafe scowled at her. "Drop the ladder."

"If you have something to say, Mr. Beaumont, say it."

Rafe looked at the ship's deck. It seemed every soldier and passenger on board peered over the railing or down from the rigging. He wasn't even sure what he wanted to say, much less say it in front of an audience. But then he looked at her again, and he knew he would do anything not to lose her.

"I came because—" His throat closed. He swallowed and tried to remember what his stepmother had told him. Not everyone woman left. And even if Collette did end up leaving him, even if she rejected him now, she was worth the risk. "Because I want to"—he felt light-headed—"I want to"—*just say the word, damn it!*—"I want to marry you."

Her eyes widened. "What?"

He gaped. Would she really force him to say it again? "I said, I want to m-marry you."

"But my father." She waved a hand, the gesture meant to encompass all that her father had been. "And I...I am not exactly welcome in London."

"We'll all go to America together. You and your father can start over there."

She shook her head. "But you belong in London. What about the balls and soirees—"

"Collette!" he cut her off. Hell's teeth, but this would have been easier if he hadn't had to yell up at her. Not to mention he had water past his ankles. "I want to marry you. None of that matters to me anymore."

"What are you saying?"

He let out a low growl. Couldn't she understand what he was saying? Did he have to say it in front of everyone?

"I'm saying lower the ladder!"

She stared down at him. "You're sinking, Mr. Beaumont. Your boat must have a leak."

"I know! Lower the ladder, goddamn it!"

"Because you want to marry me?"

"Yes!"

"You're certain?"

The boat lurched, and he felt the cold water on his knees. "Yes. I'm certain." He had to say it. She wouldn't lower the ladder until he said it. "Collette, I—" His heart thudded so hard he couldn't hear anything else. Blood rushed to his head, making it pound. These were words he'd never said, words he'd never thought he would ever say, ever mean. "I love you, Collette Fortier," he yelled. "I've loved you for…I don't know how long. I should have told you. I love how you blush when I get close to you. I love how your eyes squint when you're angry. I even love how you pontificate on hedgehogs when you're nervous.

I should have stayed with you. I'm standing here, on this sinking boat, because I cannot lose you."

She smiled, the expression making her face light up. "I love you too, Rafe Beaumont." She turned to the captain. "Lower the rope."

A moment later, a rope dangled down the side of the ship. Rafe looked up, not having realized how bloody high the ship was. He began to climb, holding on to the rope for all he was worth. And trying to ignore the jeers and kissing sounds of the ship's crew as he made his way to the top.

Finally, his arms shaking with fatigue, he crawled over the rail and collapsed. Collette knelt by his side. "Rafe?" She took his face in her hands. "You really came."

"You think I'd leave you?" he said between gulps of air.

"I did, yes."

"I was a fool."

"Yes." She hugged him.

"Your father?" he asked when he finally pulled back.

"He's below. He's not very happy with you."

"He'll have to get used to me." Reaching in his coat, he removed the lines Draven had decoded. "I took the coded letter from your bed and had it deciphered. You were right about him. The Foreign Office is willing to let him go free. As long as he never comes back."

"Oh, Rafe!" She embraced him again. "Thank you! Is this why you left?"

Her expression was hopeful that he wanted to say yes. But it was better if they began as they meant to go on. "Nothing so noble. I ran like a coward."

"You're no coward, Rafe, and you're here now." When he would have argued, she shushed him. "That's all that matters."

He would make this up to her, even if it took him the rest of his life. In America. "I'll never leave you again."

She helped him to his feet, and the captain stepped in front of him. "Welcome aboard. You have the fare for passage?"

"Would you take an IOU?" Rafe asked.

"Would you like to swim in the Thames?"

"As I said, I'll pay for his passage," Collette said. She looked at Rafe. "Gaines gave me a little money."

That was one more thing he owed Gaines.

"Thank you, madam." The captain bowed and left them.

Collette looked at Rafe. "So, America. With my father. The assassin."

"Don't remind me."

"I knew as soon as you said you would go to America with me you must love me."

Rafe narrowed his eyes. "And yet you made me say it. In front of the entire ship."

"I didn't know if I'd ever hear it otherwise."

He took her hand. "Madam, I hereby vow to tell you I love you every single day of the rest of our lives."

"And I'll do the same. I love you, Rafe."

He squeezed her hand. "I love you, Collette."

She took a quick breath. "Do you want to stay on deck and watch us set off? It might be the last you ever see of England."

He would be back. Rafe knew that as surely as

he knew he loved Collette. "Do you have a cabin?" he asked.

"I do."

"A private cabin?"

She nodded.

"Then England be damned. I have other business to attend to." He took her in his arms, but she pushed him back with one hand.

"We're not married yet."

Rafe froze, shock making him go rigid. "You want to wait? Of course you do. And we should. It's only what—three, four, six months until we arrive in America? I can wait."

She gave him a pitying look, and he straightened his shoulders.

"Really, I can."

She put her arms on his shoulders. "Oh, how I love you." She bent close and whispered in his ears. "Now, take me belowdecks and ravish me."

Rafe let out a breath. "Is that an order?"

"Yes."

"Gladly." And he pulled her into his arms and kissed her. All around them, the ship erupted with cheers.

# *Epilogue*

"FOR YOU, MY LORD," PORTER SAID AFTER TAKING Jasper's hat and coat. Jasper had his mask half-off, and he finished pulling the silk from his head before turning his attention to the slip of paper the Master of the House held out to him.

"Thank you, Porter." Jasper was used to receiving letters and correspondence at the Draven Club. He had enemies. Dangerous enemies, and he rather preferred they didn't know the location of his residence. Even his own father, the Marquess of Strathern, didn't know where Jasper laid his head at night.

"Dinner, my lord?" Porter asked.

"Yes." Jasper followed the man as he climbed the stairs. He'd finally stopped asking Porter to call him Grantham. Porter couldn't conceive of calling Jasper anything but *my lord*, even though Jasper hated the courtesy. He rolled his neck, enjoying the freedom that came whenever he removed the mask. The scar on his upper cheek and temple felt too warm and raw after being encased in the silk mask for so long.

In the dining room, Jasper sat at a table alone.

A few of the other members of Draven's troop were dining, but Porter knew Jasper preferred to eat alone. While he waited for Porter or one of the other staff to bring him wine and soup, Jasper opened what he now realized was a battered and abused letter. He moved the candle in the center of the table closer and peered at the writing. He read it once, then again. He looked up. Across the room, Ewan Mostyn sat with Neil Wraxall. Jasper rose and strode to their table.

"Grantham," Wraxall said with a nod. "Decided to be social tonight?"

"No." Jasper put the letter on the table. Neil frowned at it and pulled it closer, but Ewan just looked at Jasper.

"What does it say?" the blond asked, his eyes on Jasper.

"It's from Beaumont. Do you know why we haven't seen him in months?"

"Draven said he was on an assignment."

"He's not on any assignment. He's in America."

"And he's married." Neil pointed to the letter. "He says he met a woman in Philadelphia."

"Rafe?" Ewan asked.

"Where did you get this?" Neil asked.

"Porter said it arrived for me." He sat in one of the empty chairs. "Do you think this woman is Fortier's daughter?"

"No." Ewan shook his head.

Neil frowned. "You think Rafe chased the woman, the daughter of an assassin and a known spy, halfway across the world and married her?"

Jasper shrugged. "I saw them together. There was something between them."

"She's a woman, and he's Rafe Beaumont. Of course there was something between them." Neil handed the letter back to Jasper. "Still...America?"

"Stranger things have happened," Ewan said.

Jasper looked at the two men beside him, men he never thought would fall in love, much less marry. He had to admit stranger things had happened.

"Just as long as they don't happen to me," he said, rising to return to his own table. But if they could happen to Rafe Beaumont... Jasper shuddered. He wouldn't think about Rafe's fall now. He had more important business to attend to.

You love Shana Galen's sparkling Regency romances.
Have you read Jane Ashford's?
Read on for a look at

# *Brave New*
# EARL

Book one in Jane Ashford's witty,
poignant new series
THE WAY TO A LORD'S HEART

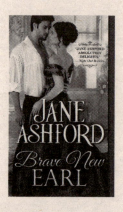

*"Charming... Ashford absolutely delights."*
—*Night Owl Reviews* **Top Pick
for** *Nothing Like a Duke*

# Prologue

As Benjamin Romilly, the fifth Earl of Furness, walked down Regent Street toward Pall Mall, tendrils of icy fog beaded on his greatcoat and brushed his face like ghostly fingertips. The rawness of the March evening matched his mood—cheerless and bleak. He couldn't wait to leave London and return to his Somerset home. He'd come up on business, annoyingly unavoidable, not for the supposed pleasures of society. His jaw tightened. Those who complained that town was empty at this time of year were idiots. Even though walkers were few in the bitter weather, he could feel the pressure of people in the buildings around him—chattering, laughing, as if there was anything funny about life. It grated like the scrape of fingernails across a child's slate.

Some invitations couldn't be refused, however, and tonight's dinner was one. His uncle Arthur was the head of his family and a greatly respected figure. Indeed, Benjamin felt a bit like an errant child being called on the carpet, though he could imagine no reason for the feeling. He didn't see his uncle often.

Well, lately he didn't see anyone unless he had to. He walked faster. He was running late. He'd had trouble dragging himself out of his hotel.

He turned onto Piccadilly and was instantly aware of several figures clustered in the recessed entry of a building on the right, as if the light from the tall windows could warm them. Ladybirds, not footpads, Benjamin recognized, even as a feminine voice called out, "Hello, dearie." One of them moved farther into the strip of illumination that stretched from the window, her appearance confirming his judgment.

Benjamin strode on. She hurried over to walk beside him. "A fine fella like you shouldn't be alone on a cold night," the woman said. "Look at the shoulders on him," she called to her colleagues. "And a leg like a regular Adonis."

"No, thank you," said Benjamin.

She ignored him. "Such a grim look for a handsome lad. Come along, and I'll put a smile on your face, dearie. You can believe I know how." She put one hand on his sleeve to slow him and gestured suggestively with the other.

"I'm not interested." Paint couldn't hide the fact that she was raddled and skinny. Gooseflesh mottled her nearly bare breasts, on display for her customers. She must be freezing, Benjamin thought. And desperate to be out on a night like this one. He pulled out all the coins he had in his pocket. Shaking off her hand, he pushed them into it. "Here. Take this."

She quickly fingered them. "Ooh, you can get whatever you want for this, dearie. Some things you haven't even dreamed of, mayhap."

"Nothing." Benjamin waved her off and moved on. Some plights could be eased by money, he thought. There was a crumb of satisfaction in the idea. When so much misery was intractable.

"Think you're so grand," the woman screeched after him. "Shoving your leavings at me like a lord to a peasant."

Benjamin didn't bother feeling aggrieved. It was just the way of the world. Things went wrong. Good intentions got you precisely nowhere. And he didn't blame her for resenting the position she'd found herself in. He pulled his woolen scarf tighter about his neck and trudged on.

Stepping into the warmth and conviviality of White's was like moving into a different world. The rich wood paneling and golden candlelight of the gentlemen's club replaced the icy fog. There was a buzz of conversation and a clink of glasses from both sides of the entryway. Savory smells rode the air, promising a first-rate meal.

Surrendering his coat and hat to a servitor, Benjamin was directed to a private corner of the dining room, where he found his uncle standing like a society hostess receiving visitors.

Arthur Shelton, Earl of Macklin, was nearly twenty years Benjamin's senior, but he hardly looked it. The dark hair they shared showed no gray. His tall figure remained muscular and upright. His square-jawed, broad-browed face—which Benjamin's was said to echo—showed few lines, and those seemed scored by good humor. Benjamin shook his mother's brother's hand and tried to appear glad to be in his company.

"Allow me to introduce my other guests," his uncle said, turning to the table behind him.

Benjamin hadn't realized there was to be a party. If he'd known, he wouldn't have come, he thought. And then he was merely bewildered as he surveyed the three other men who comprised it. He didn't know them, and he was surprised that his uncle did. They all appeared closer to his own age than his uncle's near half-century.

"This is Daniel Frith, Viscount Whitfield," his uncle continued, indicating the fellow on the left.

Only medium height, but he looked very strong, Benjamin observed. Brown hair and eyes and a snub nose that might have been commonplace but for the energy that seemed to crackle off him.

"Roger Berwick, Marquess of Chatton," said his uncle, nodding to the man in the center of the trio.

This one was more Benjamin's height. He was thinner, however, with reddish hair and choleric blue eyes.

"And Peter Rathbone, Duke of Compton," said their host.

Clearly the youngest of them, Benjamin thought. Not much past twenty, he'd wager, and nervous looking. Compton had black hair, hazel eyes, and long fingers that tapped uneasily on his flanks.

"Gentlemen, this is my nephew Benjamin Romilly, Earl of Furness, the last of our group. And now that the proprieties are satisfied, I hope we can be much less formal."

They stood gazing at one another. Everyone but his uncle looked mystified, Benjamin thought. *He* felt as if he'd strayed into one of those dreams where you show up for an examination all unprepared.

"Sit down," said his uncle, gesturing at their waiting table. As they obeyed, he signaled for wine to be poured. "They have a fine roast beef this evening. As when do they not at White's? We'll begin with soup though, on a raw night like this." The waiter returned his nod and went off to fetch it.

The hot broth was welcome, and the wine was good, of course. Conversation was another matter. Whitfield commented on the vile weather, and the rest of them agreed that it was a filthy night. Compton praised the claret and then looked uneasy, as if he'd been presumptuous. The rest merely nodded. After a bit, Chatton scowled. Benjamin thought he was going to ask what the deuce was going on—hoped someone would, and soon—but then Chatton took more wine instead. All their glasses were emptied and refilled more rapidly than usual.

It wasn't simply good manners or English reticence, Benjamin concluded. Uncle Arthur's innate authority and air of command were affecting these strangers just as they did his family. One simply didn't demand what the hell Uncle Arthur thought he was doing.

Steaming plates were put before them. Eating reduced the necessity of talking. Benjamin addressed his beef and roast potatoes with what might have appeared to be enthusiasm. The sooner he finished, the sooner he could excuse himself from this awkward occasion, he thought. He was about halfway through when his uncle spoke. "No doubt you're wondering why I've invited you—the four of you—this evening. When we aren't really acquainted."

Knives and forks went still. All eyes turned to the host, with varying degrees of curiosity and relief.

"You have something in common," he went on. "*We* do." He looked around the table. "Death."

Astonishment, rejection crossed the others' faces.

The older man nodded at Benjamin. "My nephew's wife died in childbirth several years ago. He mourns her still."

In one queasy instant Benjamin was flooded with rage and despair. The food roiled dangerously in his stomach. How dared his uncle speak of this before strangers? Or anyone? All Benjamin asked was that people let him be. Little enough, surely? His eyes burned into his uncle's quite similar blue-gray gaze. Benjamin saw sympathy there, and something more. Determination? He gritted his teeth and looked away. What did it matter? The pall of sadness that had enveloped him since Alice's death fell back into place. He made a dismissive gesture. No doubt his tablemates cared as little for his history as he did for theirs.

Uncle Arthur turned to the man on his left. "Frith's parents were killed in a shipwreck eight months ago on their way back from India," he continued.

The stocky viscount looked startled, then impatient. "Quite so. A dreadful accident. Storm drove them onto a reef." He looked around the table and shrugged. "What can one do? These things happen."

Benjamin dismissed him as an unfeeling clod, even as his attention was transfixed by his uncle's next bit of information.

"Chatton lost his wife to a virulent fever a year ago."

"I didn't *lose* her," this gentleman exclaimed, his

thin face reddening with anger. "She was dashed well *killed* by an incompetent physician and my neighbor who insisted they ride out into a downpour."

He looked furious. Benjamin searched for sadness in his expression and couldn't find it. Rather, he looked like a man who'd suffered an intolerable insult.

"And Compton's sister died while she was visiting a friend, just six months ago," his uncle finished.

The youngest man at the table flinched as if he'd taken a blow. "She was barely seventeen," he murmured. "My ward as well as my sister." He put his head in his hands. "I ought to have gone with her. I was invited. If only I'd gone. I wouldn't have allowed her to take that cliff path. I would have——"

"I've been widowed for ten years," interrupted their host gently. "I know what it's like to lose a beloved person quite suddenly. And I know there must be a period of adjustment afterward. People don't talk about the time it takes—different for everyone, I imagine—and how one copes." He looked around the table again. "I was aware of Benjamin's bereavement, naturally, since he is my nephew."

Benjamin cringed. He could simply rise and walk out, he thought. No one could stop him. Uncle Arthur might be offended, but he deserved it for arranging this…intolerable intrusion.

"Then, seemingly at random, I heard of your cases, and it occurred to me that I might be able to help."

Benjamin noted his companions' varying reactions— angry, puzzled, dismissive. No one, not even his formidable uncle, could make him speak if he didn't wish to, and he didn't.

"What help is there for death?" said the marquess. "And which of us asked for your aid? *I* certainly didn't." He glared around the table as if searching for someone to blame.

"Waste of time to dwell on such stuff," said Frith. "No point, eh?"

Compton sighed like a man who despaired of absolution.

"Grief is insidious, almost palpable, and as variable as humankind," said their host. "No one can understand who hasn't experienced a sudden loss. A black coat and a few platitudes are nothing."

"Are you accusing us of insincerity, sir?" demanded Chatton. He was flushed with anger, clearly a short-tempered fellow.

"Not at all. I'm offering you the fruits of experience and years of contemplation."

"Thrusting them on us, whether we will or no," replied Chatton. "Tantamount to an ambush, this so-called dinner."

"Nothing wrong with the food," said Frith, his tone placating. He earned a ferocious scowl from the choleric marquess, which he ignored. "Best claret I've had this year."

Benjamin grew conscious of a tiny, barely perceptible, desire to laugh. The impulse startled him.

"Well, well," said his uncle. "Who knows? If I've made a mistake, I'll gladly apologize. Indeed, I beg your pardon for springing my idea on you with no preparation. Will you, nonetheless, allow me to tell the story of my grieving, as I had hoped to do?"

Such was the power of his personality that none of

the younger men refused. Even Chatton merely glared at his half-eaten meal.

"And afterward, should you wish to do the same, I'll gladly hear it," said Benjamin's uncle. He smiled.

Uncle Arthur had always had the most engaging smile, Benjamin thought. He suddenly recalled a day twenty years past, when his young uncle had caught him slipping a frog between a bullying cousin's bed-sheets. That day, Uncle Arthur's grin had quirked with shared mischief. Tonight, his expression showed kindness and sympathy and the focus of a keen intellect. Impossible to resist, really.

In the end, Benjamin found the talk that evening surprisingly gripping. Grief had more guises than he'd realized, and there was a crumb of comfort in knowing that other men labored under its yoke. Not that it made the least difference after the goodbyes had been said and the reality of his solitary life descended upon him once more. Reality remained, as it had these last years, bleak.

# One

BENJAMIN RODE OVER THE LAST LOW RIDGE AND DREW rein to look down on his home. It was a vast relief to be back, far from the incessant noise of London. The mellow red brick of the house, twined with ivy, the pointed gables and ranks of leaded windows, were as familiar as his face in the mirror. Furness Hall had been the seat of his family for two hundred years, built when the first earl received his title from King James. The place was a pleasing balance of grand and comfortable, Benjamin thought. And Somerset's mild climate kept the lawn and shrubberies green all winter, though the trees were bare. Not one stray leaf marred the sweep of sod before the front door, he saw approvingly. The hedges were neat and square—a picture of tranquility. A man could be still with his thoughts here, and Benjamin longed for nothing else.

He left his horse at the stables and entered the house to a welcome hush. Everything was just as he wished it in his home, with no demands and no surprises. He'd heard a neighbor claim that Furness Hall had gone gloomy since its mistress died—when he thought

Benjamin couldn't hear. Benjamin could not have cared less about the fellow's opinion. What did he know of grief? Or anything else, for that matter? He was obviously a dolt.

A shrill shout broke the silence as Benjamin turned toward the library, followed by pounding footsteps. A small figure erupted from the back of the entry hall. "The lord's home," cried the small boy.

Benjamin cringed. Five-year-old Geoffrey was a whirlwind of disruptive energy. He never seemed to speak below a shout, and he was forever beating on pans or capering about waving sticks like a demented imp.

"The lord's home," shouted the boy again, skidding to a stop before Benjamin and staring up at him. His red-gold hair flopped over his brow. He shoved it back with a grubby hand.

Benjamin's jaw tightened. His small son's face was so like Alice's that it was uncannily painful. In a bloody terror of death and birth, he'd traded beloved female features for an erratic miniature copy. He could tell himself it wasn't Geoffrey's fault that his mother had died bringing him into the world. He *knew* it wasn't. But that didn't make it any easier to look at him.

A nursery maid came running, put her hands on Geoffrey's shoulders, and urged him away. Staring back over his shoulder, the boy went. His deep-blue eyes reproduced Alice's in color and shape, but she'd never gazed at Benjamin so pugnaciously. Of course she hadn't. She'd been all loving support and gentle approbation. But she was gone.

Benjamin headed for his library. If he had peace and

quiet, he could manage the blow that fate had dealt him. Was that so much to ask? He didn't think so.

Shutting the door behind him, he sat in his customary place before the fire. Alice's portrait looked down at him—her lush figure in a simple white gown, that glory of red-gold hair, great celestial-blue eyes, and parted lips as if she was just about to speak to him. He'd forgotten that he'd thought the portrait idealized when it was first finished. Now it was his image of paradise lost. He no longer imagined—as he had all through the first year after her death—that he heard her voice in the next room, a few tantalizing feet away, or that he would come upon her around a corner. She was gone. But he could gaze at her image and lose himself in memory. He asked for nothing more.

❧

Three days later, a post chaise pulled up before Furness Hall, uninvited and wholly unexpected. No one visited here now. One of the postilions jumped down and rapped on the front door while the other held the team. A young woman emerged from the carriage and marched up as the door opened. She slipped past the startled maid and planted herself by the stairs inside, grasping the newel post like a ship dropping anchor. "I am Jean Saunders," she said. "Alice's cousin. I'm here to see Geoffrey. At once, please."

"G-Geoffrey, miss?"

The visitor gave a sharp nod. "My…relative. Alice's son."

"He's just a little lad."

"I'm well aware. Please take me to him." When the

servant hesitated, she added, "Unless you prefer that I search the house."

Goggle-eyed, the maid shook her head. "I'll have to ask his lordship."

Miss Saunders sighed and began pulling off her gloves. "I suppose you will." She untied the strings of her bonnet. "Well? Do so."

The maid hurried away. Miss Saunders removed her hat, revealing a wild tumble of glossy brown curls. Then she bit her bottom lip, looking far less sure of herself than she'd sounded, and put her hat back on. When footsteps approached from the back of the hall, she stood straighter and composed her features.

"Who the deuce are you?" asked the tall, frowning gentleman who followed the housemaid into the entryway.

Unquestionably handsome, Jean thought. He had the sort of broad-browed, square-jawed face one saw on the tombs of Crusaders. Dark hair, blue-gray eyes with darker lashes that might have been attractive if they hadn't held a hard glitter. "I am Alice's cousin," Jean repeated.

"Cousin?" He said the word as if it had no obvious meaning.

"Well, second cousin, but that hardly matters. I'm here for Geoffrey."

"*For* him? He's five years old."

"I'm well aware. As I am also aware that he is being shamefully neglected."

"I beg your pardon?" Benjamin put ice into his tone. The accusation was outrageous, as was showing up at his home, without any warning, to make it.

"I don't think I can grant it to you," his unwanted visitor replied. "You might try asking your son for forgiveness."

She spoke with contempt. The idea was ridiculous, but there was no mistaking her tone. Benjamin examined the intruder with one raking glance. She looked a bit younger than his own age of thirty. Slender, of medium height, with untidy brown hair, dark eyes, and an aquiline nose, she didn't resemble Alice in the least.

"I've come to take Geoffrey to his grandparents," she added. "Alice's parents. He deserves a proper home."

"His home is here."

"Really? A house where his dead mother's portrait is kept as some sort of macabre shrine? Where he calls his father 'the lord'? Where he is shunted aside and ignored?"

Benjamin felt as if he'd missed a step in the dark. Put that way, Geoffrey's situation did sound dire. But that wasn't the whole truth! He'd made certain the boy received the best care. "How do you know anything—"

"People have sent reports to let his grandparents know how he's treated."

"What *people*?" There could be no such people. The house had lost a servant or two in recent years, but there'd been no visitors. He didn't want visitors, particularly the repellent one who stood before him.

"I notice you don't deny that Geoffrey is mistreated," she replied.

Rage ripped through Benjamin. "My son is *treated* splendidly. He is fed and clothed and…and being taught his letters." Of course he must be learning them. Perhaps he ought to know a bit more about the details of Geoffrey's existence, Benjamin thought, but that didn't mean the boy was *mistreated*.

Two postilions entered with a valise. "Leave that on the coach," Benjamin commanded. "Miss…won't be staying." He couldn't remember the dratted girl's name.

"It doesn't matter," she said. "Take it back. I'm only here to fetch Geoffrey."

"Never in a thousand years," said Benjamin.

"What do you care? You hardly speak to him. They say you can't bear to look at him."

"They. Who the devil are *they*?"

"Those with Geoffrey's best interests at heart. And no sympathy for a cold, neglectful father."

"*Get out of my house!*" he roared.

Instead, she came closer. "No. I won't stand by and see a child harmed."

"How…how dare you? No one lays a hand on him." Benjamin was certain of that much, at least. He'd given precise orders about the level of discipline allowed in the nursery.

"Precisely," replied his infuriating visitor. "He lives a life devoid of affection or approval. It's a disgrace."

Benjamin found he was too angry to speak.

"Please go and get Geoffrey," the intruder said to the hovering maid.

"No," Benjamin managed. He found his voice again. "On no account." His hand swept the air. "Go away," he added. The maid hurried out—someone who obeyed him, at least. Though Benjamin had no doubt that word was spreading through the house and the rest of his staff was rushing to listen at keyholes.

"Would you prefer that I report you to the local magistrate?" his outrageous visitor asked. "That would be Lord Hallerton, would it not? I inquired in advance."

She scowled at him, immobile, intolerably offensive. Benjamin clenched his fists at his sides to keep from shaking her. While he was certain that any magistrate in the country would side with him over the fate of his son, he didn't care to give the neighborhood a scandal. It seemed that spiteful tongues were already wagging. Who were the blasted gossips spreading lies about him to Alice's parents? The tittle-tattle over this female's insane accusations would be even worse.

The two of them stood toe to toe, glaring at each other. Her eyes were not simply brown, Benjamin observed. There was a coppery sparkle in their depths. The top of her head was scarcely above his shoulder. He could easily scoop her up and toss her back into the post chaise. The trouble was, he didn't think she'd stay there. Or, she'd drive off to Hallerton's place and spread her ludicrous dirt.

The air crackled with tension. Benjamin could hear his unwanted guest breathing. The postilion, who had put down the valise and was observing the confrontation, eyed him. Would he wade in if Benjamin ejected his unwelcome visitor? He had a vision of an escalating brawl raging through his peaceful home. Actually, it would be a relief to punch someone.

Into the charged silence came the sound of another carriage—hoofbeats nearing, slowing; the jingle of harness; the click of a vehicle's door opening and closing. What further hell could this be? Benjamin had long ago stopped exchanging visits with his neighbors. None would dare drop in on him.

When his uncle Arthur strolled through the still-open front door, Benjamin decided he must be dreaming. It was the only explanation. His life was a carefully orchestrated routine, hedged 'round with safeguards. This scattershot of inexplicable incidents was the stuff of nightmare. Now if he could just wake up.

His uncle stopped on the threshold and surveyed the scene with raised eyebrows. "Hello, Benjamin. And Miss…Saunders, is it not?"

"You *know* her?" Benjamin exclaimed.

"I believe we've met at the Phillipsons' house," Lord Macklin replied.

The intruder inclined her head in stiff acknowledgment.

Benjamin could believe it. His lost wife's parents were a fixture of the *haut ton*. Entertaining was their obsession. One met everyone in their lavish town house, a positive beehive of hospitality. Indeed, now he came to think of it, he was surprised they'd spared a thought for Geoffrey. Small, grubby boys had no place in their glittering lives. "And do you know why she's here?" he demanded, reminded of his grievance.

"How could I?" replied his uncle.

Too agitated to notice that this wasn't precisely an answer, Benjamin pointed at the intruder. "*She* wants to take Geoffrey away from me."

"Take him away?"

"To his grandparents," Miss Saunders said. "Where he will be loved and happy. Rather than shunted aside like an unwanted poor relation."

Benjamin choked on a surge of intense feelings too

jumbled to sort out. "I will not endure any more of these insults. Get out of my house!"

"No. *I* will not stand by and see a child hurt," she retorted.

"You have no idea what you're talking about."

"*You* have no idea—"

"Perhaps we should go into the parlor," the older man interrupted, gracefully indicating an adjoining room. "We could sit and discuss matters. Perhaps some refreshment?"

"No!" Benjamin wasn't going to offer food and drink to a harpy who accused him of neglecting his son. Nor to a seldom-seen relative who betrayed him by siding with the enemy, however illustrious he might be. "There's nothing to discuss, Uncle Arthur. I can't imagine why you suggest it. Or why you're here, in fact. I want both of you out of my home this—"

"*Yaah!*" With this bloodcurdling shriek, Geoffrey shot through the door at the back of the entry hall. Clad in only a tattered rag knotted at the waist, his small figure was smeared with red. For a horrified moment Benjamin thought the swirls were blood. Then he realized it was paint running down the length of his son's small arms and legs. Shrieking and brandishing a tomahawk, the boy ran at Miss Saunders. He grabbed her skirts with his free hand, leaving red streaks on the cloth, and made chopping motions with the weapon he held. Fending him off, she scooted backward.

# About the Author

Shana Galen is a three-time RITA nominee and the bestselling author of passionate Regency romps, including the RT Reviewers' Choice Award winner *The Making of a Gentleman*. *Kirkus Reviews* says of her books, "The road to happily ever after is intense, conflicted, suspenseful, and fun," and *RT Book Reviews* calls her books "lighthearted yet poignant, humorous yet touching." She taught English at the middle- and high-school level off and on for eleven years. Most of those years were spent working in Houston's inner city. Now she writes full-time. She's happily married and has a daughter who is most definitely a romance heroine in the making.

# The Duke Knows Best

Lord Randolph Gresham has come to London to find a suitable wife. Verity Sinclair may be intelligent, beautiful, and full of spirit, but her father knows a secret about Randolph that makes her entirely unsuitable as his bride. Not right for him at all. Never. Not a chance.

Verity knows that Lord Randolph lives in a country parish, and she wants nothing more than to escape to town. He may be fascinating, attractive, rich, and the son of a duke, but she'll never marry him, nor will she talk to him, flirt with him, walk with him, or dine with him. She'll sing a duet with him, but only this one time, and only because everyone insists. But one duet invariably leads to another...

*"Jane Ashford absolutely delights."*

—*Night Owl Reviews* **Top Pick for** *Nothing Like a Duke*

# Third Son's a Charm

# No Earls Allowed

### The Wars are over, but a battle of wills is upon them...

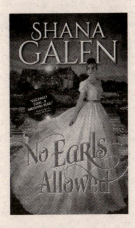

A veteran of the Napoleonic Wars, Major Neil Wraxall is as honor-bound as ever. So when tasked with helping the headstrong daughter of an eminent earl, he can't say no...

Lady Juliana will do whatever it takes to restore a boys' orphanage in her sister's memory. The last thing she needs is for a man to take over. But the orphanage and its charges need more help than she can give. And when Juliana pushes a local crime lord too far, she'll need a warrior. Good thing Neil never leaves anyone behind.

*"Bright, funny, poignant, and entertaining."*

**—*Kirkus Reviews***

For more Shana Galen, visit:
**sourcebooks.com**

# Also by Shana Galen